The
MX Book
of
New
Sherlock
Holmes
Stories

Part X – 2018 Annual
(1896-1916)

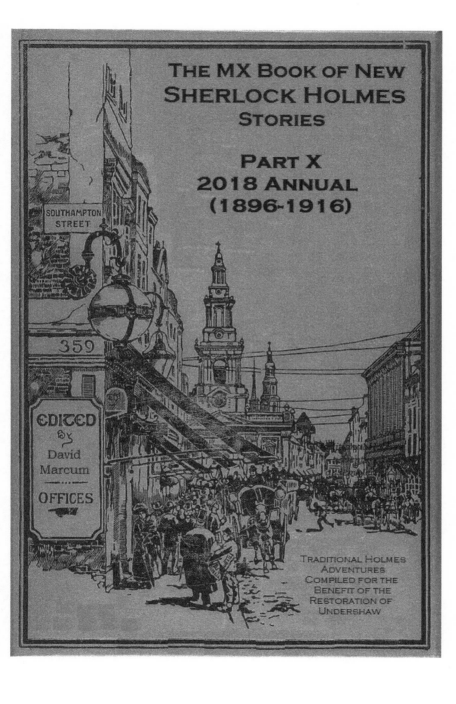

THE MX BOOK OF NEW SHERLOCK HOLMES STORIES

STORIES

PART X
2018 ANNUAL
(1896-1916)

SOUTHAMPTON
STREET

359

EDITED
By
David
Marcum

OFFICES

TRADITIONAL HOLMES
ADVENTURES
COMPILED FOR THE
BENEFIT OF THE
RESTORATION OF
UNDERSHAW

ISBN Hardback 978-1-78705-285-7
ISBN Paperback 978-1-78705-284-0
ePub ISBN 978-1-78705-286-4
PDF ISBN 978-1-78705-287-1

Published in the UK by
MX Publishing
335 Princess Park Manor, Royal Drive,
London, N11 3GX
www.mxpublishing.co.uk

David Marcum can be reached at:
thepapersofsherlockholmes@gmail.com

Cover design by Brian Belanger
www.belangerbooks.com and *www.redbubble.com/people/zhahadun*

CONTENTS

Introductions

Adventures

(Continued on the next page . . . .)

(Continued on the next page . . . .)

The following can be found in the companion volume
The MX Book of New Sherlock Holmes Stories
Part IX – 2018 Annual (1879-1895)

These additional Sherlock Holmes adventures
can be found in the previous volumes of
The MX Book of New Sherlock Holmes Stories

(Continued on the next page . . . .)

(Continued on the next page . . . .)

PART V – Christmas Adventures

(Continued on the next page . . . .)

PART VI – 2017 Annual

(Continued on the next page . . . .)

(Continued on the next page . . . .)

COPYRIGHT INFORMATION

*The following contributions appear
in the companion volume*
**The MX Book of New Sherlock Holmes Stories
Part IX – 2018 Annual (1879-1896)**

Pastiches: The Third Leg
of the Sherlockian Stool
by David Marcum

In his introduction to *The Return of Solar Pons* (1958), Edgar W. Smith, a legendary member of the Baker Street Irregulars, wrote:

> There is no Sherlockian worthy of his salt who has not, at least once in his life, taken Dr. Watson's pen in hand and given himself to the production of a veritable Adventure. I wrote my own first pastiche at the age of fourteen, about a stolen gem that turned up, by some unaccountable coincidence, in the innards of a fish which Sherlock Holmes was serving to his client in the privacy of his rooms; and I wrote my second when I was fifty-odd, about the definitive and never-more-to-be-seen-in-this-world disappearance of Mr. James Phillimore in a matrix of newly-poured cement.

I would love to read these stories, composed by this man whose undisputed efforts to promote the admiration of Sherlock Holmes helped to make the world's first consulting detective one of the most recognized figures on the planet. The essay "How I First Met Edgar W. Smith" by one of the BSI founders, William S. Hall, *(Baker Street Journal*, June 1961) describes an occasion in which Hall, Christopher Morley, and Smith met in 1939 for lunch. After a period of Morley asking several tough Canonical questions, *"[Smith] was accordingly dubbed, with the help of an additional whiskey-and-soda, a full-fledged member on the spot. Since then I have always rated the meeting of Morley and Smith second in importance only to that of Stanley and Livingstone. The rest we all know about. Almost from that moment on, Edgar was The Baker Street Irregulars, and that includes most of the Scion Societies as well."* Smith was a tireless advocate for the promotion of Holmes, and there are many who know much more about him than I who can provide specific examples. It's commonly known that he was the founder and first editor of *The Baker Street Journal*, and is still listed to this day on the title page of every issue. He edited the first "definitive" text of The Canon – if such a thing can actually exist – and that version, which was published in three amazingly handsome volumes in the early 1950's, is still being used today by the Easton Press for their beautiful leather-bound editions. He had an open-door policy that allowed and encouraged others to join the fun and take the spotlight, such as when he had noted Sherlockian Vincent Starrett write the foreword to the aforementioned definitive Canon, instead of doing so himself. He had the same inclusive spirit in his cornerstone volume *Profiles by Gaslight* (1944), an amazing collection of Holmesian essays. (An amusing side-note to those who have one of the 1944 hardcover editions: The page numbers proceed normally and sequentially, until one is in the middle of the Vincent Starrett contribution, "The Singular Adventures of Martha Hudson". This essay runs from pages 202 through 229. As one proceeds, the pages are numbered as one would expect: *218, 219, 220.* And then, where one would expect to simply see page *221*, Smith adds a letter, making it *221B.* Then the next page is *222.* That single added letter shows just how dedicated Mr. Smith was to the World of Holmes.)

Smith's contributions are innumerable. Yet, with all of his support of both The Canon and Sherlockian Scholarship, the first two legs of the Sherlockian stool, he didn't forget the third: *Pastiche.*

As shown above, when referring to *pastiche*, Smith says *"There is no Sherlockian worthy of his salt who has not, at least once in his life, taken Dr. Watson's pen in hand and given himself to the production of a veritable Adventure."* Strong words from the man who shaped the Baker Street Irregulars. And words that should not be forgotten or swept aside or spoke of, save with a gibe and a sneer, in the pursuit of the scholarly side of things.

In that same paragraph from that same introduction, Smith goes on to write:

> The point that does concern me – and it is a point that all of us who are tempted to emulation should bear in mind – is that the writing of a pastiche is compulsive and inevitable: it is, the psychologists would say, a wholesome manifestation of the urge that is in us all to return again to the times and places we have loved and lost; an evidence, specifically, of our happily unrepressed desire to make ourselves at one with the Master of Baker Street and all his works – and to do this not only receptively, but creatively as well.

There are several important points to be noted from these short passages. To be "worth one's salt" is historically assumed to refer to the practice of paying Roman soldiers enough wages that they could buy salt, necessary for both survival itself, as well as for tasks such as curing

2

meat. If a soldier wasn't effective in his job, he wasn't paid. The phrase has come down through the years to mean more generally that one must be competent, adept, and efficient to be "worth one's salt". And it was no accident that Smith began his essay in this way, for he understood, from those early days, the importance of pastiche. *"No Sherlockian worth his salt . . . ."*

Additionally, he wrote that this should be done *receptively*. For if one is truly a Sherlockian *worth his [or her] salt*, then there should be no resistance against this need to create or read additional adventures of Mr. Sherlock Holmes. It must be true. Edgar W. Smith said so.

I've long maintained, and written extensively in a number of forums, that pastiches are of supreme importance, and should receive as much credit as possible for promoting the continued and growing popularity of Sherlock Holmes. Sherlockian scholarship and speculation is a cornerstone of some people's interest in The Canon, but it can be somewhat esoteric. It is pastiche that fires the imagination of many people and serves to initially lure them to The Canon. Sherlock Holmes is recognized around the world, but how many people who admire and adore him read The Canon as their absolute first contact with him? Many, certainly, but not all. Instead, a sizeable number also encounter Holmes first in the form of pastiches – stories, films, radio and television episodes, comic books, fan-fiction – and then seek to know more about that actual Holmes Bible made up of the original (and pitifully few) sixty adventures, as brought to us by that first – but *not the only!* – Literary Agent, Sir Arthur Conan Doyle.

It's always been my contention that The Canon is the wire core of a rope, but pastiches are the strands that overlay it, giving it both thickness and strength. In other places, I've called the entire body of work, both Canon *and* pastiche, *The Great Holmes Tapestry.* It all weaves together to present a picture of the complete lives of Holmes and Watson, immensely complex and interesting. And that tapestry, with its threads of pastiches woven in and around and through the main supporting Canonical fibers, has been forming since nearly the same time when the first Canonical stories were being published.

In those earliest of days, the tendency was to parody Holmes, rather than produce true pastiches – possibly because Holmes was still new, and many of the tropes that have since become set in stone were then still in flux. However, some of those early parodies came very close indeed to having the feel of the real thing, and only a few changed words would be enough to nudge them into acceptable adventures.

In his introduction to *The Memoirs of Solar Pons* (1951), Ellery Queen presents an amazing comprehensive list that enumerates the various variations on Holmes from earlier decades, up to that time. (Richard Dannay, son of Frederic Dannay, who was half of the Literary Agent-team representing Ellery Queen, recently told me that his father's list "is truly a virtuoso, one that can't be duplicated or imitated.") It's amazing, from this distance of so many years since Queen's list was constructed, to realize just how widespread Holmes's influence was, even in those days.

I cannot say what the earliest Holmes parody or pastiche was — there is some debate on that point. It's clear from some that are on Queen's list, such as *Detective Stories Gone Wrong: The Adventures of Sherlaw Kombs* by Luke Sharp (1892), *The Adventure of the Table Foot* by "Zero" (Allan Ramsay, 1894, featuring Thinlock Bones), and the eight "Picklock Holes" stories which first appeared in *Punch* in 1893 and 1894, that the Master's influence appeared quite early.

There are numerous other Holmes-influenced stories from those early days, and more are being mined all the time. Many collections over the years have included these very valuable "lost" tales:

- *The Misadventures of Sherlock Holmes* (1944) – edited by Ellery Queen. (A most important book for any collection, with a publication history of its own that's as interesting as the contents of the book itself);
- *Sherlock Holmes in America* (1981) – edited by Bill Blackbeard. (A beautiful coffee table book of all sorts of obscure items);
- *The Game is Afoot* (1994) – edited by Marvin Kaye. (An incredible volume, with a great representation of both old and new stories);
- *As It Might Have Been* (1998) – edited by Robert C.S. Adey. (One of the first to be specifically devoted to rare old pastiches and parodies);
- *I Believe in Sherlock Holmes* (2015) – edited by Douglas O. Greene; (Truly a labor of love, with some great obscure ephemera.)
- *A Bedside Book of Early Sherlockian Parodies and Pastiches* (2015) – edited by Charles Press. (Definitely worth examining to find hidden treasures); *and*
- *The Missing Misadventures of Sherlock Holmes* (2016) – edited by Julie McKuras, Timothy Johnson, Ray Reithmeier, and Phillip Bergem. (This is a unique title,

4

which takes on the task of including the stories first mentioned – but not included – in Ellery Queen's *Misadventures*. I was honored to be able to bring this volume to Richard Dannay's attention, as he was previously unaware of it.)

Also, the Herculean efforts of Bill Peschel must be lauded. He has assembled six (as of this writing) massive (and very handsome) volumes of early Holmes parodies and pastiches – and I hope that he keeps going:

- *The Early* Punch *Parodies of Sherlock Holmes*
- *Sherlock Holmes Victorian Parodies and Pastiches: 1888-1899*
- *Sherlock Holmes Edwardian Parodies and Pastiches: 1900-1904*
- *Sherlock Holmes Edwardian Parodies and Pastiches: 1905-1909*
- *Sherlock Holmes Great War Parodies and Pastiches: 1910-1914*
- *Sherlock Holmes Great War Parodies and Pastiches: 1915-1919*

Initially, those early stories were created for simple amusement, with countless variations on Holmes and Watson's names that possibly seemed clever or funny in those long ago days – *Purlock Hone* and *Fetlock Bones*, *Dr. Poston* and *Whatsoname* – but now seem painfully like a first-grader's attempt at humor. Gradually, however, stories in the true traditional Canonical style began to appear. Vincent Starrett's "The Unique Hamlet" from 1920 is often referenced as a good early traditional pastiche. It certainly established that Holmes adventures did not have to be parodies, and that they could be presented to the public without first passing across the desk of the *first* Literary Agent, Sir Arthur Conan Doyle. In the late 1920's, a new kind of Sherlockian tale arrived, when August Derleth became Dr. Parker's Literary Agent, arranging for the publication of the first Solar Pons stories. While not actually about Holmes and Watson, these occur within Holmes's world, and are so precise in reproducing the style and substance of Holmes's adventures that they very much paved the way for additional stories using the correct format to follow.

In 1930, Edith Meiser advanced the cause of pastiche significantly. She was convinced that the Holmes adventures would be perfect for radio broadcasts. She worked out a deal with the contentious Conan

5

Doyle brothers, Adrian and Denis, and began to write scripts. Her efforts were rewarded when Holmes was first portrayed on NBC radio on October 20th, 1930, in a script adapted by Meiser from "The Speckled Band". In that first broadcast, Holmes was played by William Gillette, the legendary stage actor who had defined Holmes for Americans for a generation or more. The show continued after that with Richard Gordon as Holmes, and Meiser kept adapting the original stories throughout the early 1930's. Then she did a remarkable thing: She began to write pastiches of *new* cases, in the manner of the originals, and set in the original correct time period – and all of this with the approval of the Conan Doyle family. (At one point, she later sued the Conan Doyle heirs, asserting correctly that it was through her efforts that the entire perception of Holmes, by way of elevating Watson's role in the narrative, had been changed. But that's another essay for another time.) The first original story, "The Hindoo in the Wicker Basket", appeared on January 7th, 1932. Sadly, it's lost, but luckily a few of the pastiche broadcasts from that period still survive, either in their original form, or when they were re-done a few years later starring Basil Rathbone as Holmes.

Meiser deserves immense credit for setting these new stories in the correct time period, and not updating them to the 1930's. There had been several Holmes films made by that time, first silent pictures, and then with sound, such as *The Return of Sherlock Holmes* (1929) and *A Study in Scarlet* (1933). All of those were produced with contemporary settings as a matter of course – automobiles and modern clothing and all the rest. Sir Arthur would have been proud of Ms. Meiser for keeping things true. After all, he had written in his autobiography *Memories and Adventures* (1924) about his thoughts on modern aspects shown in the silent Eille Norwood films produced from 1921 to 1923, stating, "*My only criticism of the films is that they introduce telephones, motor cars, and other luxuries of which the Victorian Holmes never dreamed.*" (If Sir Arthur could see what's been to damage Holmes on screen in the present day, character assassination that goes far beyond simple modernization or the use of automobiles, he'd roll over in his grave. But perhaps, spiritualist that he was, he's already seen *and* observed it. I can hear him spinning now . . . .)

The run of the show under Edith Meier's guidance ended in 1936, but it resumed without her in 1939, due to the popularity of the Basil Rathbone film, *The Hound of the Baskervilles*. By that point, the radio show was being scripted by Leslie Charteris (under the sobriquet *Bruce Taylor*) and Denis Green. However, these two continued to use the exact same format created by Meiser during her run – something that still extends its influence even to the present day.

Traditional pastiches appeared through the years – books and short stories and films and broadcasts – all serving to bring new generations to 221b Baker Street. In 1954, *The Exploits of Sherlock Holmes*, containing twelve very traditional adventures, was published. Originally appearing in *Life* and *Collier's*, these stories were presented by agents Adrian Conan Doyle and John Dickson Carr. The creative process wasn't always smooth between the two authors, but the adventures themselves are excellent.

Traditional pastiches appeared sporadically throughout the following decades, often few and far between, and difficult to find. Radio continued to present original Holmes stories into the 1950's. The Holmes television show from 1954-1955, starring Ronald Howard, was made up of mostly original stories. The film *A Study in Terror* and the related book by Ellery Queen (1965) helped to represent Holmes in the 1960's – "*Here comes the original caped crusader!*" proclaimed the posters – but pickings were slim.

Then, in 1974, an amazing thing happened. Nicholas Meyer reminded us that Watson's manuscripts were still out there, waiting to be found. Meyer had discovered some of Watson's original notes, which were published as *The Seven-Per-Cent Solution*. A film quickly followed. An amazing Holmes Golden Age began that extends to this very day.

I was fortunate to jump on this Holmes Train around the time that it was leaving the station. I discovered Holmes in 1975, when I was ten years old, with an abridged copy of the Whitman edition of *The Adventures*. I was only prompted to start reading it after seeing a piece of *A Study in Terror* on television. (It's hard to believe that the film was only ten years old then, like me.) Before I'd even tracked down or read all of The Canon, I began to absorb pastiches as well. Very soon after reading my abridged copy of *The Adventures*, I received a paperback copy of *The Seven-Per-Cent Solution*. (This was through the Reading Is Fundamental [RIF] Program. I well remember being led into the school gymnasium, where one side was set up with countless long tables covered in books – a sight that thrilled me even then, as I was always a sensible lad. I was allowed to pick two books, and I chose *The Seven-Per-Cent Solution*, with Holmes on the cover, and another that looked like a boy's adventure, something called *Lord of the Flies*. I thought from the description on the back that it might be rather like one of my favorite series, The Hardy Boys. It wasn't. But I digress.)

I must admit that, even then, with my limited Canonical awareness, (and with apologies to Nicholas Meyer), I didn't agree with all that was proposed in *The Seven-Per-Cent Solution.* A benign mistreated Professor Moriarty? Hints that The Great Hiatus didn't actually occur? No, sir. I believed The Canon, wherein the Professor was the Napoleon of crime, and the organizer of half that was evil and of nearly all that was undetected in the great city of London. And I believed that Holmes had truly fought him at Reichenbach, as reported, instead of going off to recover from his cocaine addiction in the guise of Sigerson the violinist while in pursuit of a redheaded woman.

But that whole alternative set-up between the established Canon and this new adventure forced me to start thinking, even then, in a critical Sherlockian manner – though I didn't realize it at the time. *What did I believe? And why?* This was reinforced by other seemingly contradictory adventures that I also began to encounter. I discovered William S. Baring-Gould's amazing biography, *Sherlock Holmes of Baker Street* (1962), at nearly the same time I started reading about Holmes. I also read it before I'd even found all of the actual adventures, so many of Baring-Gould's theories are hard-wired into my brain right along with The Canon – such as certain aspects of Baring-Gould's chronology, and all about brother Sherrinford, and the *first* Mrs. Watson named Constance, and a love child (Nero Wolfe) with Irene Adler. Baring-Gould related a specific version of Holmes's defeat of Jack the Ripper. But Holmes also fought a *different* Ripper to a different conclusion in *A Study in Terror.* And then it happened again just a few years later in the amazing film and book *Murder by Decree* (1979) – which, by the way, is another incredible pastiche that helped to bring people to The Canon, and also personally showed to me the Holmes that Watson describes in "The Three Garridebs" as a man with both a great brain *and* a great heart.

I began to understand that these various accounts of Holmes versus The Ripper didn't contradict one another – rather, they were simply different threads of a larger story, with each pulled out and tied off so as to present a complete picture of this-or-that particular case (or piece of a case) without causing confusion by referencing other side issues. This became very useful later as I began to discover more and more versions of some of the famous "Untold Cases", such as the Giant Rat of Sumatra. Some readers might pick one or the other of these as the only "definitive" version of this case, but I believe that, as long as the different narratives are set within the correct time period, and don't stray into some Alternate Universe or modern or science-fiction or Lovecraftian or supernatural world, then each is true. Thus, there were lots of times – each of them unique – when Holmes and Watson

8

encountered Giant Rats. There were many Hurets that Holmes fought in 1894 – a whole nest of them, a regular *Al Qaeda* of Boulevard Assassins – instead of just one. There were a number of tobacco millionaires in London during 1895, and Holmes helped them all, while Watson lumped each of them into his notes under the protective pseudonym of "John Vincent Harden".

Back in the mid-1970's, however, before the Golden Age really began to bloom, it was still a bit hard to find good traditional Holmes stories. Nicholas Meyer's second Holmes discovery, *The West End Horror* (1976) is just about perfect – I thought so then, and still do. A few years later, I discovered *Enter the Lion* (1979) by Michael P. Hodel and Sean M. Wright, and realized that a view of Holmes's world didn't always have to be through Watson's perspective. This was reinforced when I found John Gardner's Moriarty books and Carole Nelson Douglas's histories of Irene Adler.

The 1980's and 1990's brought more and more new Holmes stories – although "more and more" is a relative term because, while there were certainly more than there used to be, they were still hard to find and hard to acquire. There were some great anthologies, including *The Further Adventures of Sherlock Holmes* (1985), *The New Adventures of Sherlock Holmes* (1987), and *The Mammoth Book of New Sherlock Holmes Stories* (1997). Master pasticheurs such as Barrie Roberts and June Thomson brought us multiple volumes of truly high quality narratives. Publishers like Ian Henry and Breese Books provided excellent stories which – with a little digging – were much more easily obtained than before. These books could now conveniently be ordered through chain bookstores and also Otto Penzler's remarkable Mysterious Bookshop. Then things became even easier with The Rise of the Internet. The world of pastiches changed forever.

I began to use the internet when I went back to school for a second degree in engineering in the mid-1990's. My tuition gave me access to the school's computer lab, where I spent a great deal of time between classes. More importantly, it allowed me to have free printing. I didn't feel any shame in printing whatever I could, literally thousands and thousands of pages, as I was being charged exorbitant fees for things like Intramural Sports, an activity in which I, as a grown-up part-time student, would never participate.

My time in the computer lab was spent searching for on-line Holmes pastiches – and there were many. I started by working my way through the links on Christopher Redmond's original mind-blowing

9

sherlockian.net website, and moved on from there, printing as I went. I'm glad that I archived these stories, because many of them have long since vanished, evaporated in an ephemeral e-puff of vapor. But I have them, along with all the others I've continued to collect since then, in over one-hundred-seventy-five big fat white binders lining the floor in front of the bookshelves containing of my Holmes collection.

As I progressed in my quest to acquire more traditional Holmes stories, I was able to refine my research techniques, aided by hints provided by my incredible wife, who is a research librarian – and very tolerant of my Holmes vice. These same techniques helped me to discover and track down a previously unknown myriad of additional traditional Holmes adventures, most of which I had never before encountered. I was already an addict, but this sudden tapping-in to the mother-lode of High-Grade Holmes only fed upon itself, and I began to collect more and more. I started reading and re-reading all of it, and along the way, making notes in a binder that I took with me everywhere, containing maps, useful information, and anything that would increase my understanding and pleasure in the stories. When I finished that first pass through everything I had at that point, I found that I had constructed a rough Holmes Chronology of both Canon *and* pastiche. Since then, it's been through multiple ongoing revisions, and now it's over seven-hundred-and-fifty densely printed pages, showing the *complete* lives of Holmes and Watson, and not just what is presented in those very few five-dozen stories funneled our way by the Literary Agent. And yet, even with all of that information about the lives of Our Heroes, *it isn't enough. More! Give me more!*

In the years since the mid-1990's, the opportunity to find, read, collect, and dive into more and more Holmes adventures has only increased. Holmes has been well represented on radio. Bert Coules, who first supervised and helped write one of the best adaptations of the entire Canon for radio ever, then continued with his own set of original pastiches. Jim French, along with his able right-hand Larry Albert as Watson and John Patrick Lowrie as Holmes, guided Imagination Theatre through one-hundred-thirty original adventures (so far), as well as the only version of the complete Canon featuring the same actors as Holmes and Watson, along with each script being by written by one person, Matthew Elliott.

Over the years, pastiches on screen have included *A Study in Scarlet* (1933) with Reginald Owen, the Arthur Wontner films of the 1930's, and the Basil Rathbone films from before, during, and after World War II. The 1959 version of *The Hound* with Peter Cushing had pastiche aspects.

It was followed by the previously mentioned *A Study in Terror* and *Murder by Decree*. A new generation of movie-goers encountered *Young Sherlock Holmes* (1985). After a long wait came *Sherlock Holmes* (2009) and *Sherlock Holmes: A Game of Shadows* (2011), each with a more action-packed Holmes, and then *Mr. Holmes* in 2014. (Some were unsettled at seeing Holmes in the aforementioned action-oriented films, showing such things as bare-knuckle boxing on screen, when those had previously only been presented off-stage. Likewise, others were uncomfortable viewing an elderly Holmes in his nineties – but if one has read about the *entire* lifespan of the man, then it's only natural to see him at any age.)

On television, the 1954-1955 series with Ronald Howard – mostly pastiches – was followed by a 1979-1980 series from the same production group, this time starring Geoffrey Whitehead. Douglas Wilmer starred as an amazingly Canonical Holmes on the BBC from 1964 to 1965, and Peter Cushing followed in his footsteps in 1968. *The Hound* was televised with Steward Granger as Holmes in 1972, and again with Tom Baker in 1982 and Richard Roxburgh in 2002. The early 1980's had *Young Sherlock* (1982), two Canonical films by Ian Richardson in 1983, and *The Baker Street Boys* (1983).

Holmes's popularity was greatly increased by way of the Granada films, which ran from 1984 to 1994, featuring Jeremy Brett as Holmes, and both David Burke and Edward Hardwicke as very sensible and intelligent Watsons. As the show progressed, some of these Granada versions tended to stray into most definite pastiche territory.

Holmes's other television appearances, both Canonical and stand-alone pastiche, have included *Sherlock Holmes in New York* (1976), *Sherlock Holmes and the Masks of Death* (1984), *Hands of a Murderer* (1991), *Sherlock Holmes and the Leading Lady* (1991), *Sherlock Holmes: Incident at Victoria Falls* (1992), *The Hound of London* (1993), four films starring Matt Frewer (2000-2002), *Sherlock Holmes and the Case of the Silk Stocking* (2004) and *Sherlock Holmes and the Baker Street Irregulars* (2007).

Except for these, there has sadly been nothing about Sherlock Holmes on television since, except for a couple of shows that shamelessly trade on the use of Holmes's name but only damage his reputation. A few others, such as *House, MD*, successfully incorporated Holmesian characteristics while forgoing any attempt to replace the originals with subversive and objectionable versions. (In this current bleak period when there has been nothing about Holmes and Watson on television for ever ten years, one would be well advised to contact master dramatist Bert Coules, who has a set of scripts – complete and ready for

11

filming – that depict Holmes and Watson in the early 1880's, the correct time period. I can't convince Bert to give me a peek, so someone is going to have to film them so I, and everyone else, will be able to know the stories!)

The discovery of new cases by Holmes and Watson only continues to increase – and that's a great thing. And it must be an indicator that people like me crave more and more adventures featuring Our Heroes. Still, I sometimes refer to myself as a missionary for The Church of Holmes, and my greatest task seems to be trying to make people respect these extra-Canonical Holmes adventures.

With ever-changing paradigms in communication and publishing, the discovery of new Holmes adventures seemingly accelerates every day. In addition to a few story collections or the rare novel presented by "mainstream" publishers, companies such as MX Publishing, Belanger Books, Wildside Press, Wessex Press, and others continue to make it possible for new "editors" of Watson's works to reach a public starving for additional narratives.

Sadly, there is sometimes an attitude from some quarters that pastiches are somehow less worthy than pure scholarly examinations of The Canon. Often pastiches are dismissed – except when a friend or celebrity has written one, in which case exceptions and are made and special dispensations granted. At other times, these new stories can only be considered "acceptable" if they are in a very pretty book from an approved list of publishers. In cases like this, where other adventures are rejected without a second glance simply because they don't have the right pedigree, the potential reader is left immensely cheated. There are some amazing Holmes tales out there – online as fan fiction, or appearing in print-on-demand books – that are as good as anything one can find *anywhere*, and with of them are better than the original Canonical stories!

In the Nero Wolfe book *The Mother Hunt* (1963), Wolfe's client asks, "But you're the best detective in the world, aren't you?"

"Probably not," he replies. "The best detective in the world may be some rude tribesman with a limited vocabulary."

Pastiches are the same way – some of the best aren't always to be found in a polished cleaned-up setting, like Wolfe in his Manhattan brownstone. Anyone who thinks so is limiting themselves and doesn't even realize it.

Thankfully, the opportunity to produce these volumes allows new adventures to be presented from all over the world, written *by* people who love the true Sherlock Holmes *for* people who love the true Sherlock Holmes. I'm incredibly thankful to be a part of it.

Pastiches are worth reading, and they're worth writing. Where do you and the Sherlockians with whom you're acquainted stand in regards to pastiches? Do you support them? Do you write them? Consider the question by way of foundational Sherlockian Edgar W. Smith's statement: As a Sherlockian, *are you worth your salt?*

As always, I want to thank with all my heart my patient and wonderful wife Rebecca, and our son, Dan. I love you both, and you are everything to me! I met my wife in 1986, when I was already settled into my habit of wearing a deerstalker everywhere as my only hat. She ended up being my friend anyway. By 1987 she was my girlfriend, and then she married me in 1988. She's put up with the deerstalker since then, and also my Holmes book collection, which has grown from a modest two or three linear feet when we met to around to around one-hundred-seventy linear feet, (based on the measurements I just made). She still goes places with me while I'm wearing the deerstalker, she keeps me company while I read and edit the stories for these books, and she's very tolerant as the Holmes books slowly devour our house, with only an occasional frantic eye-roll as the books creep ever closer . . . . My son was born into this – some kids enter a family of sports fanatics, but he joined a Holmesian Household. He's simply the best, and it turns out that he's amazing storyteller and writer. He watches and enjoys Holmes too, although with a bit less enthusiasm than his father.

I can never express enough gratitude for all of the contributors who have donated their time and royalties to this ongoing project. I'm so glad to have gotten to know all of you through this process. It's an undeniable fact that Sherlock Holmes authors are the *best* people!

The royalties for this project go to support the Stepping Stones School for special needs children, located at Undershaw, one of Sir Arthur Conan Doyle's former homes. These books are making a real difference to the school, having currently raised over $25,000, and the participation of both contributors and purchasers is most appreciated.

Next, I'd like to thank that impressive crew of people who offer support, encouragement, and friendship, sometimes patiently waiting on me to reply as my time is directed in many other directions. Many many thanks to (in alphabetical order): Bob Byrne, Mark Mower, Denis Smith, Tom Turley, Dan Victor, and Marcia Wilson.

Additionally, I'd also like to thank:

- Nicholas Meyer – As mentioned above, you started this Golden Age of Holmes. As if that wasn't enough, you also both saved *Star Trek* and nudged it in the right direction, allowing it to go – and keep going – correctly for many years to come. While it may seem as if I'm totally focused on Sherlock Holmes, I have many other interests, and one of them is *Star Trek*, which I first saw in approximately 1968, when I was three years old and a babysitter was watching an original series episode. *The Wrath of Khan* arrived in 1982, and I was blown away. I've seen it more than any other film in my life. What you brought to the *Trek* universe is reflected in every film, show, novel, and comic since then. I was thrilled to meet you at *From Gillette to Brett III* in 2011, and – even though there's no reason for you to remember it – you were very gracious when autographing all three of your Holmes books for me and answering my questions about when I could expect a fourth. Thank you very much for contributing to these volumes. Your importance to the World of Sherlockian Pastiche cannot be overstated.
- Roger Johnson – Thank you once again for showing incredible support for all of these books, and also all of the other projects. You are a scholar and a gentleman, and I'm very glad to know you. I'm looking forward to seeing you and Jean again, whenever I can arrange Holmes Pilgrimage No. 4.
- Steve Emecz – Many thanks for all that you do that helps so many people, and for the constant support for my various ideas designed to promote Mr. Holmes. It's amazing to see how far this has come in just a few years. (As of this writing, it was just about three years ago when I wrote to you about an idea that came to me in an early morning dream of editing a collection of Holmes stories. Wow.) It's always a pleasure, and I can't wait to see what we do next!
- Brian Belanger – Thanks once again for such wonderful work. I think these covers were the easiest we've assembled yet. I always enjoy when it's time for me to pick more Grimshaw paintings – luckily he painted a lot of them! – and to see how you prepare them. Excellent work, as usual!

- Derrick Belanger – I've enjoyed being your friend from the first time we ever "met" in this modern electronic sense. First came great Sherlockian discussions, and then great support as we both found our way into all of these projects. I've enjoyed every one of them, and I know that what we already have planned for the future will be wonderful as well. Many thanks!
- Ian Dickerson – In his introduction to "The Adventure of the Doomed Sextette" by Leslie Charteris and Denis Green, included in *Part IX (1879-1895),* Ian explains how he came to be responsible for this and other long-lost scripts from the 1944 season of the Holmes radio show. Ian, I'm very grateful to you for allowing this one to appear in these volumes before it's reprinted in one of your own upcoming volumes. When I first discovered Holmes, I quickly found a number of Rathbone and Bruce broadcasts on records at the public library, and that was where I first "heard" Holmes. I can't express the thrill of getting to read these rediscovered lost treasures, having been tantalized by their titles for so long. Thank you so much!
- Larry Albert – From the enjoyment you've given me playing Watson the RIGHT way, to the time we started corresponding about my first Holmes book, and on to the incredibly helpful advice you gave as I started writing scripts, and then the efforts you've made to gather materials for use in these books: Cheers to you, sir!
- Melissa Grigsby – Thank you for the incredible work that you do at the Stepping Stones School at Undershaw in Hindhead, which I was thrilled to visit in 2016. You are doing amazing things, and it's my honor, as well that of all the contributors to this project, to be able to help.
- Michael Rhoten – Although it's likely that he'll never know that he's being thanked here, I want to express appreciation to Michael, one of my co-workers. He's a true Renaissance man, and when one of the contributors of this book asked me about early twentieth century photography, I knew that Michael could help. I presented the question to him, and within minutes he provided a wealth of information, including illustrating

his points by producing an actual physical camera from that era that the keeps in his office. I passed on his comments to the author with great success, and I appreciate his time and enthusiasm.

Finally, last but certainly *not* least, **Sir Arthur Conan Doyle**: Author, doctor, adventurer, and the Founder of the Sherlockian Feast. Present in spirit, and honored by all of us here.

As always, this collection has been a labor of love by both the participants and myself. As I've explained before, once again everyone did their sincerest best to produce an anthology that truly represents why Holmes and Watson have been so popular for so long. These are just more tiny threads woven into the ongoing Great Holmes Tapestry, continuing to grow and grow, for there can *never* be enough stories about the man whom Watson described as *"the best and wisest . . . whom I have ever known."*

David Marcum
January 6th, 2018
The 164th Birthday of Mr. Sherlock Holmes

Questions, comments, and story submissions
may be addressed to David Marcum at
thepapersofsherlockholmes@gmail.com

Foreword
by Nicholas Meyer

There's a cartoon, known, I suspect, to all Sherlockians. It depicts a small boy in bed, staring with consternation and dismay at the last Sherlock Holmes story in the book he holds before him. *What now?* His expression seems to signify.

I was – and am – certainly not alone in identifying with the expression on the boy's face in the cartoon, as well as the feelings to be inferred behind it. When newcomers to the Holmes Canon reach the end of the sixtieth Doyle story, feelings of bereavement typically predominate. None of this is new. It is said that when Doyle killed off Holmes – (apparently!) – in "The Final Problem", young men in London went to work wearing black mourning armbands.

Just as surely, I am neither the first nor the last to have slid into the next phase of grief: Denial. The impulse to write my own Holmes story, to continue the adventures of that unique personage and of his Boswell. Fan fiction. Whether executed as straight-faced pastiche or broad parody, there are far more Holmes adventures penned by "divers hands" than the mere sixty penned by Arthur Conan Doyle, who remained oddly obtuse about the appeal of his creation and his own relations with The Great Detective.

Yet the unconscious plays strange tricks. Doyle, who kept trying to kill off Holmes, nonetheless seems to have expressed a knowing kinship with him. Holmes tells Watson he is descended from the sister of the French artist, Vernet. Being fictional, he is descended from no one. It is Doyle himself whose ancestor was Vernet's sister. One could thus term them cousins. Further, both Doyle and his alter ego bank at the same bank. Even more suggestively – as Holmes would observe – both are offered knighthoods in the same year. Doyle's impulse was to turn his down – he felt it would identify him as an establishment patsy. He relented at the insistence of his mother, under whose thumb he spent much time. By revealing contrast, Holmes disdains his knighthood without a second thought. And we never hear a word about Holmes's mother – only his skittish distrust of women in general.

Finally, and perhaps most tellingly, when Doyle did kill off Holmes, in the memorable struggle with his nemesis, Professor Moriarty, at the picturesque Reichenbach Falls, he conveniently failed to produce the detective's corpse, thus opening the floodgates for . . . the rest of us?

All of which leaves much from for speculation, embroidery, and additional Holmesiana.

In any event, even Doyle couldn't kill off Holmes, who, as we all know, rose from the dead, not on the third day, it may be, but still, there was a resurrection that has been going on ever since – first at Doyle's hands, but later, at ours.

Although cynical folk have argued that these "ripoffs" of Holmes and Watson are conceived with mercenary motives, speaking for myself, I don't think this is either fair or true. The small boy, despairing in his bed, doesn't dream of adding to The Canon as a way of enlarging his purse. Certainly I didn't. Writing my own Holmes story was simply an itch I had to scratch. Sixty stories are not enough! That my books went into profit surprised no one more than their author.

I hazard the guess that the stories that follow were all written out of affection and enthusiasm, not with any thought of piggy-backing on the genius of Doyle for pecuniary gratification. I could be wrong. You be the judge.

Nicholas Meyer
December 2017

We Can Make the World a Better Place
by Roger Johnson

Sherlock Holmes, as we all know, is the great English detective. Except that he was part French, his grandmother being "the sister of Vernet, the French artist". (But which Vernet? There were four generations of notable painters in the family: Antoine, Joseph, Carle and Horace. The last, born in 1789, was probably Holmes's great-uncle.)

It's little wonder, then, that the French have claimed the detective as their own, especially since his author, Sir Arthur Conan Doyle, freely admitted that an important influence on the creation of Sherlock Holmes was the great French amateur reasoner, the Chevalier C August Dupin – but Dupin was himself a fictional character, created by an American, Edgar Allan Poe. Holmes himself dismissed Dupin as "a very inferior fellow", but Conan Doyle made his position clear in "To an Undiscerning Critic":

> *As the creator I've praised to satiety*
> *Poe's Monsieur Dupin, his skill and variety,*
> *And have admitted that in my detective work,*
> *I owe to my model a deal of selective work.*
> *But is it not on the verge of inanity*
> *To put down to me my creation's crude vanity?*
> *He, the created, the puppet of fiction,*
> *Would not brook rivals nor stand contradiction,*
> *He, the created, would scoff and would sneer,*
> *Where I, the Creator, would bow and revere.*

And what of Arthur Conan Doyle himself? He seems always to have thought of himself as an Englishman, for all that he was born in Edinburgh, of an Irish mother and an Anglo-Irish father. Arthur's childhood was divided between his Scottish home town and his English boarding school, Stonyhurst College in Lancashire. He went back to Edinburgh to study medicine at the University, and after graduating in 1882, he moved to the south-west of England. He never lived in Scotland again, but, as you can hear in the interview filmed in 1927, he retained a distinct Scottish accent throughout his life. (The film is easily accessible on YouTube. The statement that it was made in 1930 is erroneous.)

Besides, he was happy to acknowledge another, even more important influence on Sherlock Holmes: Dr Joseph Bell, one-time President of the Royal College of Surgeons of Edinburgh and lecturer at the Medical School at Edinburgh University. In his memoirs, Conan Doyle wrote: *"I thought of my old teacher Joe Bell, of his eagle face, of his curious ways, of his eerie trick of spotting details. If he were a detective he would surely reduce this fascinating but unorganized business to something nearer an exact science."*

The Scots – and the Irish too – know that England has no exclusive ownership of the great detective, or of his creator.

The Americans have also asserted their right: *Elementary*, with its updated Holmes living and working in New York, is evidence of that. In fact, what Robert Keith Leavitt felicitously dubbed "221b Worship" has from the start been stronger in the United States than almost anywhere else. The first authorised dramatisation was the work of an American, William Gillette – there had been numerous unofficial adaptations and spoofs before Gillette's 1899 play *Sherlock Holmes* – and it was in America that the detective was first portrayed on film, on radio, and on television.

In 1944, President Franklin D. Roosevelt, not then widely known to have accepted honorary membership in the Baker Street Irregulars, rather dubiously declared that the detective was actually American, and that "his attributes were primarily American, not English".

Mostly, however, admirers around the world have been content with the idea that Sherlock Holmes is as English as, well, as most Englishmen – which is to say, not entirely. Nicholas Utechin, my predecessor as co-editor of *The Sherlock Holmes Journal*, has proud Russian ancestry; I, like Holmes, am part French. In all probability, there's no such thing as "pure English blood".

The authentic chronicles of Sherlock Holmes comprise sixty tales, long and short, nearly all narrated by the faithful Dr. John H. Watson. Only a few of those cases took the detective himself away from England, but in at least thirty-five of them, an essential part of the puzzle – not necessarily criminal – originated abroad. On occasion, Holmes acted as a spy or a counter-spy, as in the affair of "The Bruce-Partington Plans", which he investigated at the urgent request of his brother Mycroft – who sometimes, as Watson was astonished to learn, *was* the British government. The man behind the theft of the top-secret plans was one Hugo Oberstein, identified by Holmes as "the leading international agent".

We may mourn the days when hand-written letters were the norm, but Holmes himself, remember, preferred the telegram, and in later years had a telephone installed at 221b. He would surely approve of the amazing technology that helps strengthen the ties between the widely scattered groups of his devotees and enables us to keep in touch around the world almost instantaneously.

There are literally hundreds of such groups, large and small. Peter Blau, Secretary of the senior American society, *The Baker Street Irregulars*, maintains an invaluable list, accessible at *www.sherlocktron.com*, which shows that most of them are in the United States, though *The Sherlock Holmes Society of London* and the Japan *Sherlock Holmes Club* probably have the largest membership, with well over a thousand members each.

It isn't only clubs and societies. There are restaurants, bars, hotels, and shops throughout the world, all celebrating Sherlock Holmes, Dr. Watson, and their creator. Two of the finest screen adaptations of the stories are lavish television series made in Russia. The most important book on the Holmes phenomenon — certainly the most important of this century — is *Från Holmes till Sherlock* by the Swedish scholar Mattias Boström, published in the UK under the misleading title *The Life and Death of Sherlock Holmes*. (The American edition, printed from the same plates, is correctly entitled *From Holmes to Sherlock*.)

In these divisive times, with nationalism, racism, and xenophobia prominent in the news, the devotees of Sherlock Holmes form that elusive ideal, a genuine international community, and our divisions are guided by taste and informed opinion.

Never mind Hugo Oberstein! The *true* leading international agents are Sherlock Holmes and his creator, Sir Arthur Conan Doyle.

Roger Johnson, *BSI, ASH*
February 2018

Undershaw:
An Ongoing Legacy
for Sherlock Holmes
by Steve Emecz

Undershaw
Circa 1900

When the first three volumes of *The MX Book of New Sherlock Holmes Stories* came out less than three years ago, I could not have imagined that in May 2018 we would have reached volumes IX and X, and over two-hundred-and-thirty stories. It has been a fascinating journey, led by our editor David Marcum. We have raised over $25,000 to date for Stepping Stones School – the majority of which from the generous donation of the royalties from all the authors, but also from some interesting licensing deals in Japan and India.

MX Publishing is a social enterprise, and getting introduced to dozens of new authors has also helped our other major program – the Happy Life Children's Home in Kenya. My wife Sharon and I have spent the last five Christmases in Nairobi, and now lots of the Sherlock

Holmes authors are helping out with Kenya too. Long may the collection continue! It's brought us many new friends, and is something that all involved can be very proud of.

You can find out more information about the Stepping Stones School at *www.steppingstones.org.uk*

Steve Emecz
February 2018

A Word From the
Head Teacher of Stepping Stones
by Melissa Grigsby

Undershaw
September 9, 2016
Grand Opening of the Stepping Stones School
(Photograph courtesy of Roger Johnson)

Undershaw proudly grows with over eighty young people, with hidden disabilities and barriers to society flourishing and growing. Holmes states, "It may be that you are not yourself luminous, but you are a conductor of light." Whilst his comment is about dear Watson, I feel that my staff are also deserving of such comments: Calm and intelligent, they support and guide those under their watch to become the best they can be and embrace life ahead.

Undershaw offers us a home and place to support each of these young people to shine, with its beautiful demeanour providing the perfect place for the staff to ignite the light of learning in each young person's mind.

Melissa Grigsby
Executive Head Teacher, *Stepping Stones,* Undershaw
February 2018

Parts IX and X of The MX Book of New Sherlock Holmes Stories *are respectfully dedicated to* **Jim French**, *who passed away at the age of eighty-nine on December 20th, 2017, the same date that this script was being edited for these books. He was very supportive of this and other related projects from the first time that he was approached, and what he accomplished over his lifetime in the fields of radio and entertainment and imagination is immensely respected by all of those who knew him or were entertained by his efforts. He will be missed.*

Sherlock Holmes (1854-1957) was born in Yorkshire, England, on 6 January, 1854. In the mid-1870's, he moved to 24 Montague Street, London, where he established himself as the world's first Consulting Detective. After meeting Dr. John H. Watson in early 1881, he and Watson moved to rooms at 221b Baker Street, where his reputation as the world's greatest detective grew for several decades. He was presumed to have died battling noted criminal Professor James Moriarty on 4 May, 1891, but he returned to London on 5 April, 1894, resuming his consulting practice in Baker Street. Retiring to the Sussex coast near Beachy Head in October 1903, he continued to be involved in various private and government investigations while giving the impression of being a reclusive apiarist. He was very involved in the events encompassing World War I, and to a lesser degree those of World War II. He passed away peacefully upon the cliffs above his Sussex home on his 103rd birthday, 6 January, 1957.

Dr. John Hamish Watson (1852-1929) was born in Stranraer, Scotland on 7 August, 1852. In 1878, he took his Doctor of Medicine Degree from the University of London, and later joined the army as a surgeon. Wounded at the Battle of Maiwand in Afghanistan (27 July, 1880), he returned to London late that same year. On New Year's Day, 1881, he was introduced to Sherlock Holmes in the chemical laboratory at Barts. Agreeing to share rooms with Holmes in Baker Street, Watson became invaluable to Holmes's consulting detective practice. Watson was married and widowed three times, and from the late 1880's onward, in addition to his participation in Holmes's investigations and his medical practice, he chronicled Holmes's adventures, with the assistance of his literary agent, Sir Arthur Conan Doyle, in a series of popular narratives, most of which were first published in *The Strand* magazine. Watson's later years were spent preparing a vast number of his notes of Holmes's cases for future publication. Following a final important investigation with Holmes, Watson contracted pneumonia and passed away on 24 July, 1929.

Photos of Sherlock Holmes and Dr. John H. Watson courtesy of Roger Johnson

The MX Book
Of
New Sherlock Holmes Stories

PART X – 2018 Annual
(1896-1916)

A Man of Twice Exceptions
by Derrick Belanger

A man who sits with fingers steepled
A man for all to see
A man who is much more than a man
resides at 221b

A man who claims to have no friends
But he has one friend true
A man who is a thinking machine
But with emotions too

Some call this hawkish one detached
Without a care for fellow man
Solving crimes is quite enough
Consequence of actions not part of plan

But I argue
And you should see
There is much more to the man
Than pocketing a simple fee

Would a mere thinking machine
Ask his one friend, dear
To acknowledge his mistakes
With Norbury whispered in his ear?

Would a man consumed with thoughts
Of murder and of crime
Accept Miss Adler's photograph
As payment for his time?

Would an uncaring, emotionless man
Smile and proudly accept
Heaped upon statements of praise
from Scotland Yard's best?

Nay, I say
For I have assessed
That Holmes is a man

Twice exceptionally blessed

A man of exceptional mind
A man of exceptional heart
When a detective requires both love and logic
Then Sherlock Holmes should play the part

The Horned God
by Kelvin Jones

The year 1896 marked a turning point in the career of Sherlock Holmes. The Affair of the Zoroastrian Order and its devastating consequences had placed such pressure upon my companion that by the April of the New Year he had suffered a partial nervous breakdown. It left him listless and melancholic, and it became apparent that he required a complete rest and change of scenery or would have to face the consequence of a relapse. I was pleasantly surprised, therefore, to receive a letter from my old friend, Colonel Winget, asking us to spend a few days with him at his home near Ludlow, Shropshire.

Holmes's response to my suggestion was at first unenthusiastic, until I mentioned our destination.

"Linden? Why on earth did you not mention it before?"

"Because I did not consider it to be important."

"My dear Watson, it may not be of any importance to you, but to a student of ancient religions, it is a name steeped in mystery."

"You have me at a disadvantage."

He jumped up from the basket chair where he had been sitting, draped in his old mouse-coloured dressing gown, and began to pace the room, his lean face flushed and animated.

"You mean you have not read of Professor Goldman's discoveries there?"

"I confess I have not."

"Then you are not, like myself, a keen student of archaeology. On the hill overlooking Linden is a curious collection of blue stones. The resemblance to Stonehenge is most striking. They were put there by the Beaker people – at least that is what Professor Goldman believes – but the stones attracted other visitors. The Celts appear to have used the stone circle for ceremonial purposes."

"Religious sacrifices?"

"We have no proof – none scientifically verifiable, anyway. But among the finds from the later period were the bones of animals, buried entire. In addition, the body of a five-year-old boy was unearthed. It was unusual, for the cranium had been shattered by a sharp implement – probably a stone hurled from a sling. However, perhaps the most puzzling find was that of a huge collection of stag horns discovered in a

35

long barrow lying to the east of the circle. The results make fascinating reading."

He picked up a box of matches at this point and lit the oily briar that was his constant companion when confined indoors.

"Indeed, I cannot think of a more suitable location for the rejuvenation of the spirit than Linden."

I began to sense the danger signs when my friend said this, for his cheeks were flushed and his eyes bore that wild, excitable look which I had witnessed before at the height of his illness.

"If we do go, will you please make a promise to me?"

"That depends on what it might be, my dear fellow," he answered, his head cocked on one side like some strange bird.

"That you drop any work you have on hand. That you forget work all together."

He gave a theatrical bow and smiled as he lit his reeking pipe, tossing the spill into the fireplace.

"You have a most obedient and compliant patient at your disposal, Doctor."

And there, for the moment, the matter rested.

The next day dawned bright and sunny, and we arose early to a magnificent breakfast of eggs and bacon which my friend doggedly abjured, forsaking the plate for one of his oldest and most disgusting cherry-wood pipes. It was not long before we had caught a cab and were on our way Paddington Station to catch our train to the borderlands of England and Wales. Holmes sat back in the railway carriage for the greater part of the journey – his chin sunk upon his chest, saying nothing.

Outside, the wind and the rain beat mercilessly at the carriage windows. Inside, snug within the confines of our first class railway compartment, our legs swathed in travelling blankets, time seemed suspended. My companion and I are both inveterate pipe smokers and, by the conclusion of our journey hours later, the air inside the compartment had become stale and offensive in the extreme. At one point, I looked up from my volume of Tennyson's *Idylls of The Kings* to observe the hawk-like face of the detective, the lids of his eyes lowered and pipe smoke wreathing his face. At such times, I knew that he was not asleep, but wrapped in contemplation.

At last the reverie was broken by the arrival of the guard, a lean young man with an impatient gait. Whilst he clipped our tickets, I gazed out through the windows at an ancient landscape of deep-ridged valleys and hills bordered by twisted oaks and gnarled beech and ash. The sky had grown stormy during the course of our journey and a series of dark clouds gathered on the horizon, a single shaft of sunlight piercing the great masses of cloud above us. In a brief moment I saw, perched on the summit of a hill, the spire of a solitary church and beneath it fallen sarsen stones.

It was not until we were some three miles from our destination that Holmes suddenly sat up, put away his pipe, and pointed out of the window.

"See! We are entering the domain of the Celts!"

I followed his gaze and beheld on the side of a hill an enormous shape, cut out of the earth. It was a quadruped of some sort, but its shape seemed unfamiliar to me.

"Whatever is it?"

"It is almost certainly a horse. The horse had a magical significance for the Celts, Watson. They lived and breathed and traded with those magnificent beasts. You remember Pwyll in the Mabinogion?"

"Ah yes. And the White Horse of Uffington of course . . . ."

"And others. This carving is yet another memorial. But how closely it resembles the dragon of folklore! Look at that ferocious head and beak and those cruel eyes! I wonder if its function was purely symbolic, as archaeologists suggest.

Even as he spoke, the train rounded a bend and we entered a green valley, in the midst of which was a collection of low stone houses. The terrain was peculiar, having the rough, uneven quality of heath land, matched by patches of grass so violently green that it almost took my breath away. Here and there small fields lay separated by stone walls that looked as if they had survived for centuries, tinged with a melancholy beauty.

Time stood still here, it seemed, and the hand of Man was less in evidence than anywhere in the south.

We emerged from our first class carriage amid clouds of steam to see a solitary figure standing on the platform.

"Colonel Winget. This is Sherlock Holmes"

The colonel stepped forward briskly to shake Holmes's hand, a tall, stocky man with greying hair and keen blue eyes.

"I am most honoured. I have heard so much of your exploits through the pages of *The Strand*."

"Ah, then you must thank my friend Watson for those colourful accounts. I am merely the catalyst for the chronicles, not its chronicler!"

"The pleasure is mine, anyway."

"And I am pleased to be here. Excuse me for saying so, but that is a most interesting cranium, Colonel."

To my amazement, Holmes had leapt forward and with both hands grabbed the colonel by the back of the head.

"Really, Holmes!" I cried, anxious to apologise for my friend's extraordinary behaviour.

"A finer specimen of a Celtic head I have not seen," he concluded, releasing the colonel's head and ignoring my remonstrance. "You see, Doctor, there is no doubting the depth of the parietal fissure and that classical Indo-European nose."

Winget laughed at this last remark, for by now my face had coloured and I had opened my mouth ready to take further issue.

"Don't take umbrage, Doctor. He is quite right in his assessment of my origins."

"But your name!" I objected. "Surely it is Anglo-Saxon in origin?"

"No, my ancestors changed it at the beginning of the eighteenth century. The original family name was Gwynedd."

"An unfortunate decision on their part, if you don't mind me saying so," said Holmes. "I confess that I much prefer the sound of the original."

"So do I, but there is no allowing for one's antecedents' little quirks. Still, allow me to take your bags, won't you? It is a cold day, and I have a trap outside ready to take you to my home."

Holmes and I climbed into the back of the trap, the driver passing us two thick rugs to protect us from the cold. We left the station drive and passed into a series of narrow stone-walled lanes lined by ancient yews. The deep greens of the countryside were even more in evidence here, where the early spring flowers raised their meek heads.

Slowly the trap climbed a barren, stone-strewn hill, and we gazed out into the valley beneath us – a wild, desolate, and forbidding piece of countryside, the fields worked into a rugged patchwork where ancient lynchets protruded. On the summit of the hill shone a circle of white stones.

"Pwyll's Cavern," observed the colonel. "One of the highest spots from hereabouts, and once an Iron Age hill fort. Look over there!" he continued, pointing to another hill, set in an easterly direction. "A Celtic cemetery, no less. It yielded rich finds when we excavated some ten years ago."

"An ancient landscape, Colonel," Holmes observed, nodding.

It was indeed, as Holmes and the colonel had suggested, a place where the dead almost seemed to hold sway over the living. At each turn and twist of the road, one was confronted with signs and symbols of a race long since departed whose presence was still strongly felt.

Colonel Winget lived in a rambling mansion some distance from the town of Linden. It was a remarkable building, which originally had been built in the Middle Ages, but which had suffered much from the strife engendered by the Civil War and the further excesses of neo-Gothic architects. This had led to a bewildering confusion of styles and, on entering the driveway, we were confronted with a hybrid of arched windows and neo-classical pillars,

After we had revived ourselves with some of his excellent vintage brandy, the colonel began to expand on the subject of his ancestry.

"I found my family tree fascinating and easy to trace, for Linden is a small place and there is little movement of the population from one century to the next. My earliest ancestor appears to have been David ap Gwynedd, who was thought to have been the brother of Taliesin, the Welsh bard. At one time all the land hereabouts belonged to him. He was of course a Druid of a high order. Actually, it was Professor Rhys who supplied me with much of the information."

"Professor Rhys?" said Holmes. "Not *the* Professor Rhys, the expert on Welsh medieval literature?"

"The same."

"I found his work on the four branches of the Mabinogi most instructive and entertaining. I had no idea that he lived in Linden."

"Yes. After he retired from Bangor University, he purchased a small house on the edge of the town. In fact, he and his brother recently started to set up a small museum in the old Corn Exchange after Professor Goldman's discoveries were published. They are both keen amateur archaeologists."

"I should like to meet them," Holmes remarked, his eyes sparkling.

"I'm sure that can be arranged."

I cast a warning glance at Holmes, who averted his eyes and resumed his pipe, sending a plume of smoke to the ornate ceiling.

"Of course, Watson here thinks that I am a slave to Morpheus and one foot in the grave."

He gave me a mocking smile.

"Not at all."

"And while we are about it," added Holmes "why not a visit to the long barrow? *Mens sana in sanee corpore*, eh, Doctor?"

He grinned and helped himself to the tantalus.

The following day dawned clear and bright. The colonel had housed us in some of the smaller bedrooms, which lay in the upper storey of the east wing of the house, and from my bedroom window, I was able to gaze out over the surrounding countryside. In the far distance, I could make out the white outline of the curious hill figure we had seen from the train on our journey down. From this viewpoint, the horse seemed to be even more dragon-like, the head crooked at an angle in a posture that appeared menacing. In the foreground, the humped hill, with its strange, bluey white stones, stood out against a radiant sky, the seven oaks standing like sentinels around them. There was an air of secrecy about the hill which fascinated me.

The climb up the hill to the long barrow was no easy feat, since the burial mound itself lay some distance from the stone circle. However, when we reached our destination, we discovered that the view was everything we could wish for. From the barrow, the land sheered away in a breathtaking drop of some three-hundred feet to the barren plateau below. It was a bright, cold day in early April, and the sun gave to the stone circle a curious luminosity. Though many of the megaliths had tumbled or crashed to the ground, the majority were still standing. They stood like the frozen warriors of some bygone age.

At the top of the hill, beneath a mound of earth, the colonel turned to us and shouted above a bitter wind.

"Over here is the entrance. This is where the excavations were carried out."

He pointed to a small opening in the mound no more than waist high. One by one we climbed through the gap and emerged into a small chamber. Inside the atmosphere was dank and suffocating. There was a cloying smell of wet stones compounded with something indefinable. We stood in the darkness while the colonel fumbled for his matches.

"You were saying," said Holmes. His voice echoed strangely against the dry stone walling.

"A great deal of stuff has already been deposited in the museum," continued the colonel, lighting the lamp he had brought with him. Holmes held up his own dark lantern and the shadows began to abate, revealing a low chamber, supported by blocks of stone.

"This is most unusual." Holmes remarked, pointing to a marking on one of the foundation stones.

I knelt down and peered into the gloom at a primitive face etched into the rock. The features were animal-like, yet the eyes were distinctly human, watchful and cunning. The mouth was cruel and thin, and the general effect hideous in the extreme. Although the carving was crude and childlike in its execution, it was nevertheless eerily effective.

"Ah yes, the horned god," the colonel replied. "These figures are to be found all over the barrow. I forgot to mention that one of the principal finds was a bronze mask. Professor Rhys discovered it about a fortnight ago, whilst examining the inner chamber."

"Cernunnos, the Horned God. At least, that is what the Romans called him. The Celts had their own name. Interesting is it not, the resemblance to Pan, Watson?"

Holmes was examining the face on the stone intently at this point.

"Where exactly was the mask discovered?''

"At the entrance to the inner chamber. Look. Over here."

Holmes's voice took on a note of curiosity.

"Tell me, was the entrance to the chamber sealed before it was discovered, Colonel?"

"I really have no idea. You would have to ask the Professor."

Sherlock Holmes bent down again and began to examine the stone wall to the left of the entry. After a few seconds had elapsed, he suddenly stood up.

"Just a minute. What's this?"

His voice had an edge to it which I often associated with our moments of danger. We turned to him in the semi-darkness to find him kneeling before what appeared to be a bundle of old clothes.

"A more recent visitor I fear. Colonel, kindly lend me your lamp, will you?"

The colonel leant forward with the lamp, then uttered a low cry of surprise.

"Good God, it's Professor Rhys. Is he alright?"

Holmes examined the body thoroughly and then sighed.

"I am afraid that I have made the Professor's acquaintance, but in the way I least expected. He is quite dead, poor fellow."

The museum was a small, oblong building constructed of limestone, with the marks of Regency elegance about it. The front *fascia* bore a stuccoed porch, and the windows were slender and deep-set.

Inside, the effect was not nearly so pleasing. The rooms were dark and heavily veneered and had a smell of long disuse about them. Everywhere the dust lay thick upon the glass cabinets.

Rhys's brother was a tall, round-shouldered man who walked with the stoop of the academic. He peered at us from behind gold-rimmed pebble glasses in a somewhat unfriendly manner. As he advanced to greet us, I noticed that he had his eyes fixed on Holmes, the glasses making him resemble some strange bird of prey. After Holmes had explained the circumstances of his brother's death, Rhys sat for a while in silence, his head in his hands.

"I take it that you and your brother had not been working long on the museum?" Holmes asked him at length.

"No. Of course there is still a lot to be done before we can open to the public, but at least we had made a start."

We passed by a cabinet containing a collection of rusted swords and pendants.

"And your brother was largely responsible for this collection?"

"Correction. *We* were responsible. We both had an equal hand in the affair."

"You are something of an archaeologist, I believe?"

"Not by occupation, more by interest. I am an antiquarian bookseller by trade. However, I have assisted my brother on numerous digs around the country, the most important being here in Linden, of course."

"Ah, yes indeed. And the long barrow?"

"John did much of the exploratory work. I merely assisted with the labelling and cleaning of the finds."

"And this, I take it, is the Mask of Cernunnos?"

We had come to a halt at a tall, rosewood cabinet. Inside hung a magnificent bronze mask about three feet in length. I was at once struck by the similarity between this and the carving I had seen inside the barrow. There was the same mood of menace about the face, and somehow the bronze casting only served to heighten the overall effect of a living, sentient being trapped behind the glass. I began to feel myself tense as I stared at the thing, and I noticed that my companions had fallen silent.

Two gleaming eyes were set above the raised cheeks. The mouth was cruelly curved into a grin which gave to the face a brooding malevolence. But the most striking feature about the head were the horns. Twisted, blackened and gnarled, they sprang from the sides like ancient and unruly vines. Although many centuries old, the object had a living quality about it.

"A most magnificent object," said Holmes.

"Let me take it out for you," said Rhys, opening the glass door and removing the mask.

"The craftsmanship is indeed unique. Your brother was most fortunate in discovering this piece. Hallo, what's this on the back? It appears to be an inscription of some sort."

Holmes moved the mask over into the direct rays of the sun.

"I never noticed that before," said Rhys. "What does it say?"

"*Yfi ydwy cerne y ceidwadwr y lle yma,*
Mestillia y dyn a ddwyn fy ngwyneb."

"I confess my Welsh is rather rusty. Could you oblige me with a translation, Mr. Rhys?"

"It means – let me see . . . ." He adjusted his glasses. "*I am Cernunnos, the guardian of this place. May the man who steals my face be cursed.*"

A silence fell upon the room. After a while Holmes spoke.

"Tell me, did your brother never mention this inscription to you?"

"Not that I recall."

"Well, perhaps he did not think it important. Clearly the inscription must be of a later date. Would you not agree?"

Rhys nodded.

"Yes, it's couched in modern Welsh, not old Welsh. Your knowledge of Welsh is not so limited after all, Mr. Holmes."

My companion flashed him a glance.

"A curious thing, nevertheless."

"I must confess, I find the inscription a little disconcerting in the light of what has transpired," the colonel remarked.

"Tell me, Mr. Rhys, have you any idea as to why your brother wanted to visit the long barrow last night?"

"I'm afraid not."

"But you were on good terms?"

"Certainly."

"Well, no matter. Thank you for taking the trouble to show us round. Oh, incidentally, you don't happen to possess a pair of climbing boots that I could borrow? Dr. Watson and I are planning a walking expedition tomorrow, but I clean forgot to bring the appropriate footwear, and I observe that it is early closing in Linden."

"Yes, I think I have a pair back at the house, if you would care to call on me this evening."

"I should be most grateful to you."

As we made our way back to Colonel Winget's house, a light drizzle had started to stain the slate roofs of the distant town a dingy grey. Out among the mist, Cader Dyfed and its stone circle stood like grim giants, glowering at us.

"You are thinking about the long barrow," I ventured, trying to match his pace.

"No, Watson, I am thinking about the murder."

"Murder? Surely not?"

"There is a distinct possibility that Professor Rhys was murdered."

"What makes you so certain?"

"The condition of the skull makes me certain."

"But when we arrived at the museum you told Rhys that he had fallen. You said that he had hit his head on one of the foundation stones."

"What I *say* and what I *think* can be two entirely separate things. Come now, Doctor. Use your intelligence. Would a man falling a distance of five feet make an indentation that size in his cranium?"

"Possibly not," I answered, a little testily, "though I should say that it depended on the angle of the fall and the weight of the victim."

By now we had come into view of Colonel Winget's house.

"There is another thing I did not tell you. However, I must command you to keep this to yourself."

He dug into his pocket and brought out a fragment of paper.

"What is it?"

"I took it from the Professor's hand while you were outside."

I looked at the crumpled fragment. Across it, scrawled in untidy handwriting, were the words:

the thing has come at last.

I looked at my companion and an image of the bronze mask rose before me.

"What on earth does this mean?"

"It means that Professor Rhys went to the barrow for a specific reason that evening. Exactly what that reason was, I shall be endeavouring to find out. By the way, would you be so good as to collect those boots for me after supper? I only hope that they fit. Oh, and give this letter to Rhys."

We dined on grouse in the large dining room in the west wing of the house, surrounded by the memorabilia which Colonel Winget had collected from his numerous expeditions into the South American jungle. After supper had been concluded, I put on my sou'wester, for the rain which had begun on our return from the museum was still beating against the windows with a grim determination, and made my way up the driveway in the direction of Rhys's house.

Rhys ushered me into the hallway but did not offer me any hospitality, and I was left dripping by the cloak stand whilst he fetched the boots. A series of framed prints hung on the walls, and I stood staring at them while I waited. One particular piece caught my attention. Measuring only ten inches by eight, it was a mezzotint depicting the long barrow. By all accounts, it had been executed in the eighteenth century or early nineteenth century, for there seemed to be many more trees surrounding the summit of the hill and more of the stones were upright.

As I stared at the picture, I noticed a tiny detail which had escaped me on first glance. At the very centre of the circle, shrouded beneath the mightiest of the oaks, there appeared a horned figure. Because the figure was indistinct and, since it stood in profile, it was difficult to see more, but I noticed there was part of another figure present and only just in view, raised on a stone slab which lay in front of the first figure. This figure was prone and I could not see the head, but it appeared to be lifeless, and it occurred to me that it might possibly be the figure of a small child.

My examination of the two figures was interrupted by Rhys, bearing the boots I had requested. He said little to me, and when asked, seemed to know nothing about the origin of the picture, merely commenting that his brother had obtained it some years ago in an auction in Ludlow. I thanked him for the boots and, without further ado, made my way out into the lane.

Once outside, I was pleased to see that the wind and the rain had abated. I decided it might prove valuable to return to the long barrow, and subject it to a more detailed examination. I was sure that if I spent even a few minutes alone in the barrow, the mystery surrounding Professor Rhys's untimely end might well be lifted.

As I climbed the hill, the mist cleared away and I was confronted with the stones, etched against the darkening sky like hunched figures. I was reminded of the ancient character of the landscape and its curious timelessness.

By now I had reached the top of the winding path and, passing between two great oaks, I dropped down into the mouth of the barrow. Pausing to light my dark lantern, I crouched and went inside.

In daylight this subterranean cave had appeared to be small. Now, in the gathering darkness, the stone walls seemed even closer and the air even ranker. I closed my eyes, trying to attune my mind to the atmosphere of the place. Within seconds of so doing, found myself in the grip of a vision so real that I was forced to drop the lantern onto the earth, where it smashed and the light was extinguished, leaving me in utter darkness.

When I closed my eyes, I was confronted by a face – the very face that I had glimpsed carved upon the rock, the face I had later seen in the museum. But this time, the face was no man-made impression, no artist's carving. It was as real and as vibrant as my own. That face – how shall I describe it? – twisted and wizened with a skin as dark as tanned leather, yet mobile, full of guile and cunning. The eyes, seeming to laugh at me, the mouth revealing thin bloodless lips and a forked tongue. It was a face

I have seen painted on the murals at Pompeii or in the nightmare visions of Hieronymus Bosch, combining menace and trickery.

The horned head fixed its gaze upon me. What it conveyed to me were not words but *ideas* – foul, unspeakable ideas, murderous impulses from the deepest recesses of the mind, disgusting acts hewn from nightmare.

I knew immediately that it had been utter folly to come here. In so doing I had exposed myself to something ancient and nameless, and I realised that the fate which had befallen Professor Rhys would certainly befall me if I stayed longer. Forcing my eyes open, I plunged into the darkness. Half blind, I banged against one of the stone walls and felt a searing pain shoot across my forehead. Undaunted, I eventually found the opening, launching myself into the clean air.

I ran down the steep incline of the hillside, my feet and ankles tearing against the nettles and briars, for I saw that the presence in the cave was now close behind me and gaining ground. I knew because I could hear the clicking of its horned feet and rasping of its breath, making its way across the grass immediately to the left of me. When I glanced fearfully across I could see it against the shadows, a hunched figure moving with the rapidity of a stag in flight, its hideous head turned towards me.

How long that journey lasted I do not recall. But I do recall the painful relief of seeing the lighted windows of the colonel's mansion and noting, as I grew closer to the entrance, the figure to my left drawing back into the shadow, thinning into an insubstantial wisp as it came into the penumbra of the lamplight.

The colonel's butler admitted me. Observing me closely, he asked if I would care for a nightcap, to which I gratefully assented.

For the best part of an hour, I sat in the great leather armchair by the fire, my limbs shaking, staring at the embers, the table lamp to my left providing a comforting glow.

At length I fell into a fitful sleep, from which I later awoke, the nightmare vision still painfully vivid. Then to bed, where I slept lightly with the lamp on until at last the dawn brought me relief from the horrors of the night.

When I finally surfaced and made my way down to the breakfast room, I found a note waiting for me. It was written in my friend's usual laconic style:

Long barrow. 10 o'clock. Be there without fail. Bring Winget.

Fortunately, Colonel Winget was happy to fall in with Holmes's imperative and, after we had finished eating, I changed into my walking shoes and we left the house. As we approached the long barrow, I thought I could make out the outline of a figure pacing to and fro at the entrance.

"Well, well," said Winget. "That's Rhys, if I'm not mistaken."

We drew closer. Rhys, clad in tweeds and a peaked cloth cap, looked at us curiously.

"Colonel Winget. Doctor. I had no idea you also were coming. Have you seen Mr. Holmes this morning, by any chance?"

"No, I haven't. I was wondering . . . ." I began, but was interrupted by a familiar voice.

"I have kept my appointment, Mr. Rhys. Just as you kept yours."

Sherlock Holmes emerged from the barrow, his lean figure silhouetted against the early morning sun. In his right hand, he was clutching a pair of boots.

"Actually my foot is a shade smaller than your own. But I am grateful for the loan of these boots. They make a perfect fit with the prints left in the barrow."

I looked at Rhys, whose face had turned the colour of wax.

"So you know, then?"

"On the contrary. I am more perplexed now than ever before. This morning, I thought it was a simple case of murder. Now I am not so sure."

Rhys sank down onto a stone and held his head in his hands.

"Then if you think that, there is still some hope for me."

"I think that you owe us at least an explanation," said Holmes. Rhys looked up at us and clenched and unclenched his hands, expressing some inner torment.

"I did not murder him," he said at last. "Do you believe me, Mr. Holmes?"

"That depends on the circumstances. But you must tell me in detail what happened here the other night, and leave nothing out."

"Very well, then. I must explain that my brother had been acting peculiarly for some days. In fact, ever since the discovery of the mask, he was, I believe, a changed man."

"Changed? In what way?"

"At first, he kept the mask locked in his room and would not permit me to look at it. He told me he wished to examine it more closely. Then he began to tell me of bad dreams that he'd been having. They were always very much the same. In the dream, the mask would come to life and speak to him. The mask told him that since he had removed the guardian from the barrow, he was cursed. I laughed when first he told me. I failed to realise in the beginning how deeply it had disturbed him. Then, after a few days, there was a further development."

"What was that?"

"It was curious. He kept avoiding me and ignoring me. It was almost as if he had become afraid of me. God knows what effect that mask had begun to have on him by that time. Things became so bad that eventually he locked the door to his study and would not come out. I pleaded with him, but it made no difference. He was resolute. I decided then that I would get rid of the mask. I waited until he had left his room and then removed it. I took it to the museum. He came to me then in a state. He wanted to know what I'd done with it. The mask had to be returned, he said. When I asked him why, he said nothing. Anyway, we had an argument, and the upshot of it was that I flatly refused to give him the mask. It was shortly after that I received a message from him, asking me to meet him at the barrow."

Rhys handed Holmes a piece of torn notepaper.

"Ah. I thought as much. This is his writing."

"Oh, yes."

"That is a point in your favour, Mr. Rhys. In the beginning, I suspected that you had written the message, in which case you would have made yourself most suspect."

Holmes put together the two fragments. The message read:

Dear Arthur,

Meet me upon the hill by the Linden stones at twelve tonight. I have something of the greatest consequence to show. Don't be late. The discovery is something about which no one else has even dreamed. Make sure that you come alone. Please disregard all that has happened and be at the appointed place. Thank God the thing has come at last.

"What happened when you got there?" asked Holmes.

"At first I saw no one. Perhaps he had forgotten the appointment, I thought. Then I went inside the barrow. He sprang out at me from the dark and gripped me by the throat. Very little of what he said made sense. He seemed to think that I was in some way connected with Cernunnos, and that I had brought about 'the curse', as he called it. He said that he would sacrifice me to the god and procure his forgiveness. There was a struggle. However, my eyes are better than his, and in the blackness, I could see a stone in his hand. I rolled to one side and,

48

wrenching the stone from him, flung it at him. There was a groan, then silence. It took me some while to realise that I had killed him."

Rhys paused.

"Well," said Holmes, "there is little more to be said. It is a most tragic affair, and I am not surprised at your desire for secrecy."

"What made you suspect me?" asked Rhys.

"The odds were that, if you had seen the mask, you would not have failed to notice the inscription," Holmes replied. "Yet you seemed surprised when I showed it to you in the museum. The speed of your translation also made me suspicious, for the lettering was difficult to read. But I had formed an opinion about you from the start of our acquaintance. I observed that there were two sets of footprints in the barrow, and the fragment of paper I discovered in the Professor's hand was proof positive that whoever else had been there at the moment of his death did not wish to be known. What I could not understand was the motive."

"You know," said Holmes, when we had once more ensconced ourselves in our lodgings at Baker Street, "the law is a most inflexible animal at the best of times. But when the supernatural is mentioned, you would certainly see our learned friend's face wince with apprehension."

"Yet there is no question about the truth of Rhys's statement?"

"None whatsoever. How unfortunate it was that his brother seemed to have disturbed the sleep of centuries. There is often danger in store for the seeker after antiquities, although I for one discount such notions. I suspect that you yourself enjoyed a lucky escape, my dear Doctor."

"What on earth was the entity?" I asked, leaning towards the fire to restoke the embers.

"Pass me down that volume, will you," instructed my companion, pointing to the tall bookcase which stood to the left of the gas bracket.

"Yes, that's it. *The Mabinogion.*"

I gave him the crimson covered book and he began to leaf through its pages.

"Ah, here is what I was looking for. It is in 'The Lady of the Fountain', where Cynon, the son of Clydno, tells Arthur and his followers a tale of an adventure which had befallen him. A man from whom he has received certain hospitality tells him that he will meet him in a clearing and that:

> *A big black man shalt thou see on the middle of the mound who is not smaller than two men of this world. And one foot has he, and one eye on his forehead's core; and he has a*

49

club of iron, and thou canst be sure that there are not two
men who would not find their full load in the club . . . and he
is keeper of that forest.

"Then Cynon comes to the clearing. Listen to this, Doctor:

And when I came there, what wild animals I saw there were
thrice as remarkable as the man had said; and the black man
was sitting on top of the mound. Big the man told me he was;
bigger by far was he than that . . . . And I greeted the black
man. And I asked him what power he had over the animals.
"I will show thee, little man," he said. And he took the club
in his hand and with it struck a mighty blow till it gave out a
mighty belling, and in answer to its belling wild animals
came till they were as numerous as the stars in the
firmament, And he looked on them and bade them go graze.
And then they bowed down their heads and did him
obeisance.

"There you have him, Doctor. The lord of the wild beasts.
Cernunnos, the antlered one, the very spirit of the forest, a force to be
reckoned with. You will find his like in both India and Ancient Britain,
and he was worshipped by the Celts. To them he was a powerful entity, a
guardian figure. A primitive notion, but none of us is entirely rational,
after all . . . ."

"Do you think that there is any hope for Rhys?" I asked.

"I believe the court will find him guilty of manslaughter. After all, it
seems absurd to believe that the ancient Celtic gods still protect their
own kind in this sceptical age. But how the gods do play with us." And
so saying, he lit his cherry-wood and sat gazing into the flames of our
coal fire.

The Coughing Man
by Jim French

T*his script has never been published in text form, and was initially performed as a radio drama on February 27, 2011. The broadcast was Episode No. 95 of* The Further Adventures of Sherlock Holmes, *one of the recurring series featured on the nationally syndicated* Imagination Theatre. *Founded by Jim French, the company produced over 1,000 multi-series episodes, including one-hundred-twenty-eight Sherlock Holmes pastiches – along with later "bonus" episodes. In addition, Imagination Theatre also recorded the entire Holmes Canon, featured as* The Classic Adventures of Sherlock Holmes, *the only version with all episodes to have been written by the same writer, Matthew J. Elliott, and with the same two actors, John Patrick Lowrie and Lawrence Albert, portraying Holmes and Watson, respectively.*

Mr. French passed away at the age of eighty-nine on December 20th, 2017, the same date that this script was being edited for this volume.

CHARACTERS

- SHERLOCK HOLMES
- DR. JOHN WATSON
- INSPECTOR GREGSON
- WIXOM
- PENNELL
- FOX
- MRS. WIGGS
- CABBIE

SOUND EFFECT: OPENING SEQUENCE, BIG BEN

ANNOUNCER: *The Further Adventures of Sherlock Holmes*, featuring John Patrick Lowrie as Sherlock Holmes, and Lawrence Albert as Dr. Watson.

MUSIC: *DANSE MACABRE* (UP AND UNDER)

WATSON: (NARRATING) My name is Doctor John H Watson. In looking back at my long association with Sherlock Holmes, I can recall several cases that he declined to investigate for various reasons. Tonight, I've chosen to tell you about one that he considered to be "on a level more appropriate to the intellect of Scotland Yard, not Sherlock Holmes". However, since the case was brought to us by a man clearly in need of medical attention, I offered my own services, which the fellow gratefully accepted, and from that innocent beginning came the story I call "The Coughing Man". It began on a chilly Monday morning in early fall, and our visitor, wrapped in an ulster and scarf, sat tense and upright in the chair by the fire.

WIXOM: I don't like to take up your time, gentlemen, but I'm desperate! (COUGH) My name is Albert Wixom, and I was a clerk at Alderbright and Pennell, the pawnbrokers.

HOLMES: You use the past tense. Are you no longer working there?

WIXOM: No. (COUGHS BADLY)

WATSON: That's a bad-sounding cough, Mr. Wixom.

WIXOM: I'm sorry. No. You see, on Saturday I was sacked, most unfairly.

WATSON: Because of your cough?

WIXOM: No, no. I was accused of taking thirty pounds from the cash drawer. We have to keep quite a lot of cash on hand at all times, because customers want their money on the spot. (COUGHS) And speaking of money, gentlemen, I have almost no funds to pay you. (COUGH)

WATSON: Look here, Mr. Wixom. I'm a medical doctor and I don't like the sound of that cough. Be good enough to answer a few questions about your health before you continue. Do you have a fever?

WIXOM: I don't think – so.

WATSON: Let me feel your forehead. (PAUSE) You're warm. Possibly a low-grade temperature. Have you been spitting up blood at all?

WIXOM: No.

WATSON: Any pain in your lungs?

WIXOM: I'm a bit sore from coughing, that's all.

WATSON: Take a deep breath for me, please, and hold it in.

WIXOM: (HE DOES, WITH A WHEEZE)

WATSON: Now let it all out.

WIXOM: (HE EXHALES, WHEEZING)

WATSON: Again.

WIXOM: (INHALES AND HOLDS IT)

WATSON: All right, you may exhale.

WIXOM: (HE DOES, WHEEZING)

WATSON: When did this coughing begin?

WIXOM: Oh, a week or so ago. Perhaps ten days.

WATSON: Have you seen a doctor?

WIXOM: Uh . . . no. (COUGHS)

WATSON: You're quite thin. Have you been losing weight?

WIXOM: I don't think so. I'm naturally thin.

WATSON: You should let a physician examine you. Do you live alone?

WIXOM: I rent a room from a landlady. (COUGHS)

WATSON: Is she also coughing?

WIXOM: No, but she says my coughing keeps her awake at night.

WATSON: Well, I don't mean to alarm you, Mr. Wixom, but tuberculosis is rampant in London. It would be wise for you to see a doctor as soon as possible. In the meantime, although I am no longer in practice, I do have a preparation that should reduce the need to cough, although it won't address the cause. I'll be glad to give you some if you like.

WIXOM: I'd appreciate that very much, Doctor.

WATSON: But you must have a thorough examination as soon as you can.

WIXOM: I'll do it tomorrow. (COUGHS)

HOLMES: Fine. Now, if the medical consultation is finished, will you kindly tell us what other assistance you need from us, Mr. Wixom?

WIXOM: Well, as I was saying, (COUGH) large amounts of cash are kept in our office, and at close of business yesterday, when they tallied up the day's receipts, they said thirty pounds were missing.

HOLMES: And they think you took it?

WIXOM: (COUGH) Yes. Or so they say.

HOLMES: "Or so they say"?

WIXOM: Mr. Holmes, there are only the three of us working there, the two owners and myself. If I didn't steal the money, one of them must have done it.

HOLMES: You think the owners would steal from each other?

WIXOM: They, uh . . . they seem at odds with each other at times.

HOLMES: Hmm. Was there a great deal of trade yesterday?

WIXOM: Oh, yes. Sunday's trade is the best of the week.

HOLMES: Is your cash kept where anyone can come in off the street and see it?

WIXOM: Oh, no sir. (COUGH) We take a hundred pounds out of the vault every morning and put it in a drawer beneath the counter, but no one goes there except Mr. Alderbright or Mr. Pennell, or myself, to buy something being pawned or to make change. And now they think I'm a thief! (COUGH) So when I apply for a new position, I can't use them as a reference.

HOLMES: Did they notify the police?

WIXOM: No. They searched me and found nothing but the few shillings I'd brought to buy my lunch. Then they argued about (COUGH) whether the police should be called, and finally they decided to discharge me.

HOLMES: I see. As much as I sympathize with your plight, Mr. Wixom, I advise you to seek help elsewhere. I can give you the name of a detective at Scotland Yard who has studied my methods.

WIXOM: Oh. Well, of course. It was wrong of me to impose upon you.

HOLMES: You haven't imposed upon me in the slightest. But as it happens, I am about to leave for Manchester, and it would be unfair of me to take your case at a time when I couldn't devote my full energies to it.

WATSON: Holmes! When did –

HOLMES: I may have neglected to tell you, Doctor, about the telegram that came in the early hours this morning, summoning me to consult on a most critical matter. I'm grateful the bell didn't wake you.

WATSON: No, it certainly didn't.

HOLMES: But I have the utmost confidence in Inspector Hopkins at the Yard, Mr. Wixom, and if you should call on him, please say recommended him to you most highly. Now, if you will excuse me, I must get about my packing. (MOVING OFF) And don't fail to see a doctor!

SOUND EFFECT: (OFF) HOLMES CLOSES HIS BEDROOM DOOR

WATSON: Uh . . . Holmes is often in demand on very short notice.

WIXOM: I'm sure he is. (COUGH)

WATSON: If you'll wait another moment, I'll fetch that medicine for you.

WIXOM: I'm very grateful, doctor.

SOUND EFFECT: WATSON WALKS OFF, RUMMAGES AMONG BOTTLES, AND RETURNS

WATSON: (MOVING ON-MICROPHONE) Here we are. This is a tincture of benzoin. Put a spoonful in a pot of boiling water and inhale the steam. Do this repeatedly every hour and it should reduce your coughing, and as it does, you should reduce the dosage. It won't cure anything, but perhaps it will let you get a few more hours of sleep. Here, take the bottle.

WIXOM: And what do I owe you?

WATSON: Not a thing. It's yours.

WIXOM: Well, that's so kind of you. Thank you. (COUGH)

SOUND EFFECT: STEPS TO DOOR

WATSON: Don't forget to see a doctor!

SOUND EFFECT: DOOR OPENS

WIXOM: Oh, I won't. Good day, Dr. Watson, and a thousand thanks. And again, I apologize to Mr. Holmes. (COUGH)

SOUND EFFECT: DOOR CLOSES. A PAUSE, THEN HOLMES'S BEDROOM DOOR OPENS

HOLMES: (PAUSE) (OFF MICROPHONE) Is he gone?

WATSON: Yes, he's gone. I must say, I'm disappointed in you, Holmes. Making up that story about going to Manchester!

56

HOLMES: Your disappointment is duly noted.

WATSON: I'm sure it was a small matter to you, but to poor Wixom it must have been devastating, and I was embarrassed! Anyone could tell that you invented that telegram out of whole cloth! I'm sure it didn't fool him.

HOLMES: As ever, a shrewd observer, old friend. Now, if you'll excuse me, I'll continue packing.

WATSON: Packing for what?

HOLMES: Why, for my trip to Manchester, where else?

MUSIC: UNDERCURRENT

WATSON: (NARRATING) I was not convinced he was really leaving for a trip north until he emerged from his bedroom, dressed for travel with a suitcase and traveling bag.

SOUND EFFECT: DOOR OPENS

HOLMES: I don't know how long I'll be gone, Watson, but you may expect a wire from me if my plans require a lengthy stay. Be sure to tell Mrs. Hudson, and take care of yourself, old fellow. *Adieu.*

SOUND EFFECT: HE WALKS OUT, DOOR CLOSES

WATSON: (NARRATING) A cloud of apprehension hung over me as I sat pondering my next move. Then, after several minutes of thought, I decided what I must do. I called a cab and asked the driver if he knew the pawnshop in question, and he said he'd taken many people there.

MUSIC: FADE INTO . . . .

SOUND EFFECT: BUSY STREET. WATSON STRIDING ALONG, THEN STOPS

WATSON: Ah yes, here it is. "Alderbright and Pennell, Pawnbrokers".

PENNELL: (OFF, MOVING ON MICROPHONE) Good morning sir. Pawning, buying, or selling this morning?

WATSON: Actually, I'm looking for Mr. Alderbright or Mr. Pennell.

PENNELL: Mr. Alderbright's not in today. I'm Henry Pennell.

WATSON: How do you do. I'm here to inquire about your clerk, Mr. Wixom.

PENNELL: (ON MICROPHONE) Oh? And what about him?

WATSON: His state of health is my interest. I am Doctor John H. Watson.

PENNELL: Well, Mr. Wixom doesn't work here anymore, Doctor.

WATSON: Yes, I know. I'm concerned about his cough.

PENNELL: His . . . cough?

WATSON: You surely must have heard him coughing.

PENNELL: Maybe I did, but I didn't pay any attention to it. Everybody in London's got something this time of year. I suppose I'll be next.

SOUND EFFECT: (OFF) SHOP DOOR OPENS WITH BELL, CLOSES UNDER

PENNELL: Ah, excuse me for a moment. (UP) Good morning, sir. Interested in pawning something this morning?

FOX: (OFF, MOVING ON MICROPHONE) Not me, guv'nor. I'm the locksmith. R.L. Fox is my moniker.

PENNELL: I didn't order a locksmith.

FOX: No sir, a Mr. Alderbright did. Says he owns the store. He wanted the locks changed right away, but I had to do new locks at several

58

places Saturday and Sunday. I do a lot of lock-changin' at places where keys has fallen into the wrong hands. I understand one of your employees was let go, but he didn't give his key back.

PENNELL: I know nothing about that. Mr. Alderbright should have taken it back when he discharged him.

FOX: Then he's still got it, and could walk right in tonight and do the devil knows what! Lucky for you I'm here to keep that from happening!

PENNELL: Just a minute! What's it going to cost?

FOX: Depends on how many doors have the same locks.

WATSON: (CLEARS HIS THROAT TO REMIND PENNELL HE'S HERE)

PENNELL: Oh, I'm sorry, Doctor. Will there be anything else I can do for you?

WATSON: Well, there is one other thing: Do you have Mr. Wixom's address?

PENNELL: You're his doctor, but you don't know where he lives?

WATSON: I've only seen him at my surgery.

PENNELL: Well, it's written in my book . . . . (MOVES OFF) Give me a moment . . . . Ah, here it is. (MOVES ON) Number Seven, Loudon Mews, Southwark.

WATSON: Number Seven, Loudon Mews. (UP) Thank you Mr. Pennell.

MUSIC – UNDERCURRENT

WATSON: As I rode a cab to the Southwark district, I experienced a feeling of satisfaction; I was correcting a mistake in Holmes's judgment: I was assisting an unfortunate man who deserved better than what Holmes had given him, and I was putting my medical experience to use where lack of timely treatment could have serious health consequences.

59

CABBIE: (EXTERIOR, OFF MICROPHONE) London Mews, sir.

SOUND EFFECT: WATSON EXITS CAB AS HE SAYS:

WATSON: (EXTERIOR) Thank you, driver; and I would like you to
   wait for me no longer than ten minutes, and if I'm not back by then
   you're free to go. And here you are.

SOUND EFFECT: JINGLE OF COINS

CABBIE: Right, sir; thank you. I'll be right here.

SOUND EFFECT: WATSON WALKING ON PAVING

WATSON: (TO HIMSELF) Number five . . . Number six . . . ah,
   Number seven.

SOUND EFFECT: HE CLIMBS A WOODEN STAIR AND KNOCKS
   ON DOOR

MRS. WIGGS: (FROM INSIDE DOOR) Who is it?

WATSON: Doctor John H. Watson. To see Mr. Wixom.

SOUND EFFECT: (PAUSE) SHE OPENS THE DOOR

MRS. WIGGS: He's sick abed. You're a doctor you say?

WATSON: Yes. I was just coming round to see about his cough.

MRS. WIGGS: Well, it kept me awake half the night. Mind you, my
   room's in front and his is in the back, but I could hear him coughin'
   all the same.

WATSON: Right. And are you coughing as well?

MRS. WIGGS: Me? No, I can't afford to get sick. Too much to do, cleanin' other people's houses and shops besides keepin' house here.

WATSON: Oh, of course. Well, tell him I called, will you? And thank you for your help.

<u>SOUND EFFECT: DOOR CLOSES</u>

<u>MUSIC: UNDERCURRENT</u>

WATSON: (NARRATING) Feeling there was nothing more I could do for Wixom to remedy his dual problems of losing his job and his health at the same time, I had the cabbie drive me back to Baker Street, where I took some time sorting and rearranging the meager supply of pharmaceuticals I kept in a closet beside my bed. After that, I was so fatigued and the bed looked so inviting that I lay down, intending only to take a few minutes to soothe the old war wound that was acting up, but I soon drifted off to sleep and slept right through lunchtime. I was awakened when it was dark outside and Mrs. Hudson was at the door, asking about dinner. For once, I had no appetite. The circumstances just before Holmes's departure still weighed upon my mind. I seemed to have no energy, and I only asked for a pot of tea. The thought struck me that I might have picked up an infection from Albert Wixom. The only sensible thing was to take my own advice and go back to bed after I finished my tea, and before long I was fast asleep again, and quite unaware of the passage of time. And then . . . .

<u>SOUND EFFECT: (OFF) KNOCK ON DOOR</u>

WATSON: (NARRATING) I stumbled into the sitting room. It was just beginning to grow light outside. I'd slept the night.

<u>SOUND EFFECT: ADD CLOCK, DOOR OPENS</u>

WATSON: Inspector Gregson!

GREGSON: (FILTER) Is Mr. Holmes in?

WATSON: No, he's away. Oh, forgive me, step in.

GREGSON: Thank you, you're the one I need to talk to anyway. What do you know about a fellow named Wixom? Albert Wixom. He says he knows Mr. Holmes and yourself.

WATSON: Why, not very much. Why? Is he all right?

GREGSON: Well, I have him here at the Yard, and he tells me you know something about his whereabouts in the last several hours.

WATSON: Yes, that's correct. He came here to our rooms yesterday morning and told us he'd been falsely accused of stealing thirty pounds from the place he worked, and he wanted Holmes to help him.

GREGSON: I need to ask you some questions about him.

WATSON: All this over thirty pounds?

GREGSON: No, not any more, Doctor. This is now a case of murder.

MUSIC: STING

SOUND EFFECT: SCOTLAND YARD

GREGSON: Good morning, Doctor. I appreciate your coming here.

WATSON: Who was murdered, Inspector?

GREGSON: Man by the name of Alderbright. Owner of the pawnshop where Wixom had been working.

WATSON: Great heaven! I was in his shop yesterday!

GREGSON: Were you now? Well, his business partner, fellow named Pennell, thinks it was Wixom who did it, but Wixom swears he was at home in bed all night and his landlady confirms it. I have my doubts. Now what can you tell me about him?

WATSON: Very little more than you already know, I'm afraid. He said he'd been discharged for stealing thirty pounds, which he denies, and he came to ask Holmes to clear his name, but Holmes had other plans.

GREGSON: Small wonder he wasn't interested. Pretty small potatoes for a man with a reputation like Mr. Holmes. But now there's murder.

WATSON: I've talked to Wixom's landlady. She confirmed Wixom was sick all day with a very bad cough. I told him to consult a doctor for a thorough examination, and I gave him a small amount of medicine. I don't think he was in any condition to go out and do murder! Incidentally, where was Alderbright killed?

GREGSON: In the pawnshop. You see, Doctor, it all fits together. His motive was revenge and money, plain as porridge. There was no sign of forced entry, so whoever did it must have had a key. And there was a good deal of money missing, according to Pennell.

WATSON: Ah! You've just reminded me! While I was in the pawn brokerage, a locksmith came in to change the locks! He said Mr. Alderbright had ordered it! Apparently he'd forgotten to take Wixom's key when he sacked him.

GREGSON: This gets easier and easier. Wixom had the means to get into the shop, Alderbright lives above the shop, all Wixom had to do was wait until they were closed, let himself in, and take his revenge.

WATSON: So you've already decided he did it?

GREGSON: He had the motive and the opportunity.

WATSON: What about the weapon?

GREGSON: It was a very old dagger from a collection they had for sale.

WATSON: What irony! If the locksmith had come round to change the locks just one day earlier, this might not have happened.

GREGSON: Huh! If locks could prevent crime, I'd be out of a job!

MUSIC: UNDERCURRENT

WATSON: (NARRATING) Gregson left me with the feeling that, now that this had become a murder case, Holmes would have been intrigued enough to investigate it himself. I would have been glad to turn it over to him, for the fatigue and weakness I felt the night before returned, and I was more convinced than ever that I had picked up some kind of infection from Wixom. It reminded me of the sickness that claimed so many of us in the Battle of Maiwand sixteen years before. Thanks to the recent work of Pasteur in France and Koch in Germany, I was convinced that germs can live outside the body and be transmitted to another person by coughing and sneezing. I dreaded facing disease and the treatments, knowing all too well what they put a patient through. And that was what was on my mind when the door opened.

MUSIC: OUT

SOUND EFFECT: DOOR OPENS, CLOCK IN BACKGROUND. HOLMES WALKS IN. DOOR CLOSES

WATSON: Good grief! Holmes!

HOLMES: Ah, Watson. (Pause) Hmm. You've lost your ruddy complexion. Where's your customary military stance?

WATSON: I – I didn't expect you back so soon!

HOLMES: The affair in Manchester was disappointing, a waste of time, and the purse was far out of proportion to the minor efforts required. I should have given part of it back. For heaven's sake, Watson, sit down before you fall down! What's the matter with you, old fellow?

WATSON: I may have caught whatever Wixom has.

HOLMES: And what about Wixom? Anything new?

WATSON: He's in jail, and Gregson seems convinced that he murdered one of the pawnshop owners.

HOLMES: Really! Dear me, I leave town for hours and robbery turns into homicide.

WATSON: But I have every reason to believe he was at home in bed when the killing took place.

HOLMES: Can he prove it?

WATSON: His landlady says he was.

HOLMES: That may not be enough. Mrs. Hudson is bringing up a hot meal. Why don't you share it with me and tell me all the salient facts.

WATSON: I dare not, Holmes. The way I've been feeling these past few hours, I may be contagious.

HOLMES: See how you feel when you're outside a good slab of beef.

WATSON: That's generous of you, but if I am broadcasting germs, I should be isolated from contact with anyone until I feel better.

HOLMES: Then you would have no objection to my having a peek into this case of yours while you regain your energy?

WATSON: I'd be grateful if you would!

HOLMES: When it's done. Go to bed, old friend, and get well!

MUSIC: UNDERCURRENT

WATSON: (NARRATING) I gave him the few notes I had written, and went to bed with an easier mind, for I knew that the wisest course for me would be to give my body a chance to heal itself, and so I closed my eyes and allowed slumber to overtake me once more. In the meantime, as I would later learn, Holmes finished his meal and made straightaway for Scotland Yard, where he accomplished in mere minutes what I had failed to do: He was granted access to Albert Wixom.

SOUND EFFECT: BACKGROUND: ECHOING SOUNDS IN A JAIL

WIXOM: I'm flabbergasted, Mr. Holmes. I thought you wouldn't be available to me!

HOLMES: But I am, and so we need to make good use of this opportunity. According to Dr. Watson's notes, Monday after you came to Baker Street, Watson went to your home to check on your cough and you were sleeping, according to your landlady . . . .

WIXOM: Mrs. Wiggs. Right, she told me he'd been there.

HOLMES: And that night, Alderbright was found dead.

WIXOM: So they say, but I knew nothing of it!

HOLMES: Tell me, when did you get over your cough?

WIXOM: Why, it got much better after I took the medicine Dr. Watson gave me. (COUGH)

HOLMES: That would have been Monday? Afternoon or evening?

WIXOM: Why, uh . . . (COUGH) I really don't remember the time.

HOLMES: But by Monday night you were no longer coughing?

WIXOM: Well, not quite as much . . . (COUGH) He didn't give me very much.

HOLMES: I presume you turned in your key to the pawnshop when you were let go.

WIXOM: They never gave me a key.

HOLMES: I see. (GETS UP) I will have some more questions after I talk with Inspector Gregson. But meantime, my advice to you is to cooperate fully with the police and tell them everything they want to know, but nothing more than they ask. (UP) Guard!

WIXOM: Mr. Holmes! I didn't take the money, and I didn't kill Mr. Alderbright! (COUGH)

MUSIC: BRIDGE

SOUND EFFECT: STREET OUTSIDE THE MEWS. HOLMES RAPS ON A DOOR. DOOR OPENS

MRS. WIGGS: (EXTERIOR) Yes?

HOLMES: (EXTERIOR) Pardon the intrusion, madam, but are you Mrs. Wiggs?

MRS. WIGGS: Who's askin'?

HOLMES: My name is Sherlock Holmes.

MRS. WIGGS: If you're looking for a room. I've got none to rent.

HOLMES: I'm not looking for a room. I'm looking for a bit of information about your roomer, Albert Wixom. He's in trouble and I'm trying to help him.

MRS. WIGGS: He's not here, and you're the fourth bloke who's been snoopin' round.

HOLMES: The fourth? Is that so!

MRS. WIGGS: The doctor, the copper, the mechanic, and now you.

HOLMES: And do you know why they were interested in Mr. Wixom?

MRS. WIGGS: How should I know?

HOLMES: The papers have printed stories about him. Perhaps you've read them?

MRS. WIGGS: I don't read, but I'm not stupid. The doctor, he was worried about Albert's coughin', the copper asked me a ton o' questions about his comin' and goin', and the mechanic, he wanted to sell him somethin' I guess – he never said. I sent him packing. What do you want with Albert?

HOLMES: I should like to see his room for a few minutes, that's all.

MRS. WIGGS: Well, I can't let you do that. It's private.

HOLMES: I appreciate that, but he's in jail, and he needs my help. He's about to be charged with murder. Were you aware of that?

MRS. WIGGS: Murder? G'wan! He wouldn't harm a fly!

HOLMES: Then let me see his room and I may be able to help him. Here's a sovereign for your trouble.

MRS. WIGGS: (A LONG PAUSE, THEN GLUMLY) Awright. Come on. (FADE OUT)

WATSON: The woman led the way to a small room. Once inside, Holmes searched through the few belongings Wixom had left behind, then he returned to Baker Street and related his experience.

HOLMES: It is quite obvious that Wixom is something more to Mrs. Wiggs than merely her roomer, but there are at least two other characters in this little drama who've made an entrance. You've seen one of them and Mrs. Wiggs may have seen the other.

WATSON: Who are you talking about?

HOLMES: The locksmith. Alderbright wasted no time in contacting the locksmith after he fired Wixom, apparently because he forgot to retrieve the key from him.

WATSON: He was old, probably forgetful.

HOLMES: And then there's the "mechanic" who came to "sell something", according to Mrs. Wiggs. Who could that have been?

WATSON: I don't know. It could have been anyone.

HOLMES: I think it would be profitable to find out how he fits into this puzzle.

SOUND EFFECT: FADE IN: SAME STREET IN THE MEWS. FRONT DOOR OPENS

MRS. WIGGS: (EXTERIOR) You lot back again?

HOLMES: We're trying to save Albert Wixom from the gallows.

MRS. WIGGS: Mercy! Don't even mention such a thing!

WATSON: May we come in for a minute?

MRS. WIGGS: I suppose.

<u>SOUND EFFECT: THEY WALK IN, DOOR CLOSES. (STREET EFFECT OUT)</u>

HOLMES: When I was here earlier today, you mentioned that Mr. Wixom had had three other visitors: A policeman, Dr. Watson here, and a mechanic. I'm interested in the mechanic. What can you tell me about him? Can you describe him?

MRS. WIGGS: Well . . . . he was tall. Not much meat on 'im. Needed a shave.

HOLMES: And why do you think he was a mechanic?

MRS. WIGGS: He smelled of oil. He was spattered with it.

HOLMES: I see. And did you notice anything else?

MRS. WIGGS: Well . . . he had some little metal bars stickin' out of his pocket.

HOLMES: Metal bars . . . could they have been files?

MRS. WIGGS: Files?

HOLMES: A file is a tool with teeth cut into it for use in shaping material.

MRS. WIGGS: Well. You learn somfin every day.

HOLMES: Thank you, Mrs. Wiggs. We'll trouble you no more.

MRS. WIGGS: When are they going to let Albert go?

HOLMES: If he is innocent, we'll work to get him free immediately. But if he killed Mr. Alderbright –

MRS. WIGGS: He didn't do it! He couldn't have!

69

HOLMES: And why is that?

MRS. WIGGS: He was sick in bed, that's why! He never budged from this house all day and all night on Monday!

HOLMES: Now you know that isn't true, Mrs. Wiggs. On Monday, he came to my rooms in Baker Street to ask for my assistance.

MRS. WIGGS: Oh, well, I wouldn't know; I was at work scrubbin' floors. I work my fingers raw cleanin' other people's houses and shops, trying to put something by for my old age. But then along comes Albert. He's come to be like one of the family to me. He's very special to me.

HOLMES: The son you never had, perhaps?

SOUND EFFECT: FADE IN LIGHT OFFICE (BACKGROUND)

HOLMES: You seem to be ready to prefer charges, Inspector.

GREGSON: Any reason why I shouldn't?

HOLMES: I believe there are three others who could throw more light on the case and provide enough information to make an arrest. Perhaps if they could all be brought here to confront each other –

GREGSON: There'll be no need for that, Mr. Holmes. I have the right man under lock and key. Albert Wixom had the motive, he had the opportunity, and he had his choice of weapons right there in the pawnshop, so I won't need to convene any meetings! All that remains is to get his confession, and I won't need any help to do that.

HOLMES: It seems to me there are at least three more people we need to question more thoroughly before you extract any confessions, Inspector: The locksmith Fox, Mr. Pennell, and Mrs. Wiggs. How soon can you assemble these individuals?

GREGSON: A waste of time, Mr. Holmes.

HOLMES: Then why not prove me wrong, Inspector? Get them all together and have them hear each other's alibis. I'm confident that, with your training and experience, you will once again fit the evidence to the crime!

MUSIC: STING

SOUND EFFECT: STEPS TO DOOR. DOOR OPENS. STEPS IN. CLOSES

(AD LIB CONVERSATION CEASES AS DOOR OPENS)

GREGSON: (TO THE GROUP) All right. This inquiry is under my official direction, but I'll expect each of you to cooperate with Mr. Holmes in this interrogation. Who do you want first, Mr. Holmes?

HOLMES: Mr. Pennell, after your partner discovered the thirty pounds was missing, did you participate in the search for it?

PENNELL: Alderbright didn't need my help; he was very thorough. Now, gentlemen, I had to close the shop to come here, and I'm losing money every minute I'm gone, so may I be excused now?

HOLMES: Not quite yet. I may have some further questions for you.

PENNELL: (SIGH) Very well.

HOLMES: Now, Mr. Fox.

FOX: I don't see how I can help you gents. I just make keys and fix locks.

HOLMES: Were you at the pawnshop on Monday?

FOX: Yes I was. Mr. Alderbright ordered the locks changed. He said the man he sacked had a key to the place.

WIXOM: That's not true! They never gave me a key!

HOLMES: Mr. Pennell, this has become a recurring issue. Did Wixom have a key?

71

PENNELL: I thought he did. I thought Alderbright would have given him a key.

HOLMES: I see. Now Mr. Fox, did you pay a visit to Mr. Wixom on Tuesday?

MRS. WIGGS: Yes he did! I told him he wasn't home, but he wanted to come in anyway and I wouldn't let him!

GREGSON: Speak when you're spoken to, Mrs. Wiggs!

HOLMES: Mr. Fox, why did you want to see Mr. Wixom?

FOX: Just business, that's all.

HOLMES: What sort of business?

WATSON: Perhaps you wanted to sell him a copy of the new key you made.

FOX: You can't prove that!

HOLMES: One other thing: How did you know where Wixom lives? (SILENCE) Had you done business with him before?

FOX: No. I never saw him before in my life!

MRS. WIGGS: That's a lie!

FOX: That's the truth!

WATSON: Just a minute, Mr. Fox. How did you know where he lived?

FOX: I know how to track down customers. How else am I supposed to stay in business?

HOLMES: Then you thought of Wixom as a customer?

PENNELL: Now, wait a minute! We paid you to change our locks and make us new keys, and then you tried to sell copies to the thief who stole from us in the first place?

GREGSON: What about that, Mr. Fox?

FOX: Lies, total lies! I didn't go to see Wixom.

HOLMES: Then you went to see Mrs. Wiggs.

FOX: What's wrong with that? I knew she cleans the pawnshop every week and would need a new key to get in.

WATSON: You clean the pawnshop, Mrs. Wiggs?

MRS. WIGGS: 'Course I do. How do you think Alderbright and Pennell come to hire Albert in the first place? I knew they was lookin' for a clerk, so I told Albert, and he applied for the job, and he got it! If it hadn't been for me, they might still be lookin', and who knows what would've happened to poor Albert!

HOLMES: And at what hour did you clean the pawnshop this last time?

MRS. WIGGS: The usual time. Sometime after they closed on Monday night.

GREGSON: So you were in the shop the night Alderbright was murdered.

MRS. WIGGS: Well, he wasn't there when I was there!

GREGSON: Was Wixom with you?

MRS. WIGGS: At the pawn shop? No!

GREGSON: I'm sorry, Mr. Holmes, but I can't let this go on any longer! It's clear to me what happened: Wixom and Mrs. Wiggs were both in the shop when Mr. Alderbright appeared. There was a struggle, Wixom took the dagger and stabbed him, and as he lay dying, they both helped themselves to all the available cash. Then they locked the place and left.

MRS. WIGGS: (BREAKS INTO TEARS) No, that's a lie! You're makin' it up! (CONTINUES CRYING, LOUDLY)

WIXOM: Why are you doing this to the poor woman? She didn't have anything to do with it!

GREGSON: Oh? Then are you ready to confess, Wixom?

WIXOM: No, I didn't do anything either! Mr. Holmes. Help me! Please!

HOLMES: That has become difficult, for now I know you were not sick and your coughing was a sham . . . a very convincing one, for it deceived both Dr. Watson and myself.

WATSON: Wait a minute, Holmes! Why on earth would he pretend to be sick?

HOLMES: Unless I am very much mistaken, he intended to use his constant coughing as proof he wasn't well enough to leave his room the night of the murder. It was a novel plan, but he forgot one important detail. And – here it is!

WATSON: Wh – Let me see that!

HOLMES: Do you recognize it, Doctor?

WATSON: This is the bottle of tincture of benzoin that I gave him to take for his cough . . . *and it's still full*! It hasn't even been opened!

HOLMES: I found it in his wastebasket yesterday.

MUSIC: BRIDGE

SOUND EFFECT: IN HOLMES AND WATSON'S ROOMS

WATSON: Well! This is one investigation I won't bother to write up!

HOLMES: Is that so?

WATSON: It's the only one I know about where Gregson turned out to be right all along.

HOLMES: Meaning that if his conclusion was right, mine was wrong? I'm afraid not, Watson. Publish or not as you wish, but let us not forget that at no time did I declare Wixom to be innocent. My concern was to learn if he had an accomplice, which he did.

WATSON: Of course. Mrs. Wiggs.

HOLMES: I had barely met her when she lied about where he was on the Monday when he came asking for my help. She furnished a false alibi, which is a crime in itself.

WATSON: But if his pretended coughing fooled me, it certainly fooled Mrs. Wiggs. I prefer to think she was convinced he had a genuine illness.

HOLMES: No doubt. And now, I should like to close any association with this case, with only one regret.

WATSON: And that is?

HOLMES: I should have stayed in Manchester a few more days.

MUSIC: *DANSE MACABRE* (THEME UP AND UNDER)

WATSON: This is Dr. John H. Watson. I've had many more adventures with Sherlock Holmes, and I'll tell you another one . . . *when next we meet!*

MUSIC: (FADE OUT)

The Adventure of
Canal Reach
by Arthur Hall

In describing the extraordinary experiences that it has been my good fortune to share with my friend, Mr. Sherlock Holmes, I fear that I have been guilty of neglecting to mention that his brother, Mycroft, occasionally passed on to us cases that subsequently proved to be of great interest. In fact, I grew to consider a communication from him to be an almost certain prelude to some new and unexpected adventure.

When Holmes was beset with the lassitude that, if it were not interrupted, inclined him towards the cocaine bottle, such a brotherly intervention was particularly welcome to us both. At such times I found it impossible to rouse him from the onset of a deepening depression of the spirit, but the prospect of a new problem or a new client invariably acted as an instant restorative.

I recall one bright autumn morning when we were faced with such circumstances. Holmes was at the beginning of the perilous slope that led to his darkest moods, and as I finished my breakfast I searched my mind for a distraction. I saw that his meal was untouched.

"Holmes, these kippers are delicious."

He gave me a disinterested glance. "Are they, Watson? You can have mine if you are still hungry. As for me, I have no appetite."

"But you must eat something."

His eyes flashed with impatience and I readied myself for a bombardment of disparaging remarks when our landlady, Mrs. Hudson, entered to place a telegram before him. Knowing the signs she quickly withdrew, and silence descended upon us.

"Will you not open it, Holmes?" I prompted after a few moments.

He raised his head to look at me gloomily. "Doubtlessly you are hoping that this is some new affair to arrest my attention," said he. "There is nothing on the envelope to suggest that, so it may equally be a reminder of an unpaid bill."

"It would not be difficult to decide the matter," I remarked as I pushed my plate away.

With a shrug, he slit open the envelope with his unused knife. "Mycroft wishes me to see one of his employees."

He pushed the form across to me and I read:

My clerk, Marius Jackman, may prove of interest to you. I trust it will be convenient if he calls at ten o'clock.

Mycroft

"This could be something new." I was glad to see a slight change in his expression. "You must not despair, old fellow."

"Perhaps the man has lost his pen, or his cat."

"I recall that some of the cases that you have described as most satisfying have developed from small incidents."

Holmes nodded his head "That is true, I suppose. But wait. My pocket-watch tells me that the time is ten minutes to ten o'clock now. Be so good as to ring for Mrs. Hudson, so that the breakfast things can be cleared away by the time our visitor arrives."

This was quickly accomplished. At ten precisely, the door-bell rang and Mr. Marius Jackman was shown into our room. He was a tall young man of about twenty-five, clad in the sombre attire that clerks in government service invariably wear. He sat down with us, as we took the armchairs around the unlit fire.

"And now, sir," my friend began, "pray tell us how we can assist you."

I noticed that Mr. Jackman had no difficulty in distinguishing between Holmes and myself, as with new clients in the past, and concluded that Mycroft must have described his brother accurately. I saw also that, although our visitor had laid down his hat and stick, he had neglected to remove his gloves.

"My superior, Mr. Mycroft Holmes, has sent me to you, sir."

"My brother has notified me in advance. I assume you have a story to tell."

The young man shifted in his chair. "Indeed I do. But I see that you are scrutinizing me closely, Mr. Holmes. Have we, perhaps, met before?"

"I think not," my friend replied. "It is both my habit and a necessity of my profession to observe and draw conclusions from my clients. On occasion, the results can be helpful."

"May I ask what you have deduced from my appearance?"

"Certainly, but I fear that there is little to tell. I know already that you are a clerk in my brother's department at the Foreign Office, and I perceive that you write with your left hand, although you may not always have done so.

Mr. Jackman became very still. And eyes Holmes warily. "I am at a loss to understand your reasoning, sir."

His puzzled expression did not surprise me, for I had seen it on the faces of many before now. Sometimes I had been able to define the path of Holmes's thoughts, but this was not one of them.

"There is nothing mysterious about it," Holmes replied with a quick smile. "When I see that you remove your hat and hold your stick with your right hand, I naturally conclude that this is the hand you use most. However, when I observe that you do not remove your gloves, I ask myself for an explanation. As the index finger of your right hand glove is empty, it is apparent that you have somehow lost the finger. You could no longer wield a pen with such a damaged hand, yet you earn your living as a clerk. Therefore, you must now use your left hand for writing, at least."

"That is quite amazing," said our visitor. "Yet it is simple enough when you explain it."

"That observation has been made more times than I can count."

"My lost finger is the result of childhood foolishness. I picked up my father's shotgun when his back was turned. Until recently, I had a glove with a false finger fitted to it, but it seems to have been mislaid. My injury is rather upsetting in company."

"As much harm is done by accident as by deliberate intent," Holmes remarked. "A most regrettable misfortune, especially for a boy. But now sir, pray relate to us the story you mentioned."

"Since my experience, I have pondered over it constantly," Mr. Jackman began. "It seems to be harmless, and nothing but a silly practical joke. My preoccupation must have been noticeable, because on resuming my work, it was not long before Mr. Mycroft Holmes asked me the cause of it. I was surprised that he took the matter seriously, and immediately referred me to your good self."

"I cannot help you until you make me conversant with the facts," Holmes reminded him.

"Of course. A week ago, I took a few days holiday in Bath. I am an amateur historian in my spare time, and I wanted to look over the Roman remains there. I took a room at a small hotel and had been there a day when one of the other guests, a man who introduced himself as Mr. Peter Smith, struck up a conversation with me. We soon discovered that we had much in common and spent many hours together, touring the ruins and taking meals together. At his insistence, we shared a table for our meals in the hotel. Mr. Smith was extremely friendly and companionable, but I found it strange that he would allow me to pay for nothing. Our visits to coffee-shops, a theatre on one occasion, and even my hotel bill were paid for by him, to my utter astonishment. When I offered to pay my way he would have none of it, waving away my attempts."

"And what did this most generous fellow eventually ask in return?" Holmes asked with a knowing look.

Our visitor raised his hands in a confounded gesture. "Absolutely nothing. That is why this incident was so puzzling! In fact, what happened was the very opposite to what I had come to expect. When I made a final attempt to reimburse Mr. Smith for some of the expense, he merely laughed. 'I'll tell you what, Marius my friend,' he said just before we went our separate ways. 'You come to visit me this weekend. I'll show you some more historical places and you can buy me a meal if you've a mind to, although that doesn't matter. It's just your company I desire. Like you, I am unmarried, and loneliness sometimes overcomes me.'"

He paused, as if reflecting again on the situation.

"Did you agree?" I prompted.

"I did indeed," he replied. "for I felt obliged to. On Saturday morning, I caught the early train to West Byfleet and hired a trap at the station. Mr. Smith had told me that his residence is situated close to that section of the River Wey, which is a canal connecting West Byfleet to Basingstoke, and after asking directions several times, I was able to find the area. I left the trap and walked along the narrow towpath, and began to wonder if I had arrived at the wrong place. I found myself confronted by a waterway long disused, stagnant and thick with algae and weed. It was a silent place, without any sound, until I disturbed some birds that had nested in the clumps of vegetation at the edge of the thick brown water.

"I paused to look at my surroundings more carefully. There were houses spaced along both banks, but every one that I could see appeared derelict. I walked further, hoping to see Canal Reach, for that was the name of the house that Mr. Smith had used, to be an acceptable place of residence in the midst of all this decay. I passed a number of old barges, moored at the opposite bank and already half-surrendered to the elements, before there appeared a long plot of uncultivated land with a single house at its end. As I approached the house, I could already see that it was in a similar condition to the others, and that a faded sign hung awkwardly and proclaimed it to be the address I sought."

"You saw no one," asked Holmes, "for all this time?"

"The entire scene was deserted, up to then. I rapped upon the door with my stick, without any response, several times. When I realised that this was futile, I took the narrow path at the side of the house, in the hope that I could attract the attention of someone in the downstairs rooms or in the garden. At one point, I stopped to peer into the largest of the windows, and was appalled by what I saw. There was no furniture visible, no inhabitants, or anything else! The sun shone in, illuminating a room containing nothing but a broken chair, at such an angle that I could see through an open door that the next room was much the same. I confess that I was mystified for, if this were some sort of practical joke, then what purpose could it have? Mr. Smith had seemed such an agreeable sort, befriending me during our brief association, that I could not believe it of him.

"I could see that there was nothing else to be done, so I returned to the towpath and was about to retrace my steps when I realised that I was no longer alone. Almost opposite on the other bank stood a red-roofed house that looked as if it were about to fall down, and to my surprise a woman stood at the gate of the small garden watching me intently. She was of striking appearance, past her youth, but still dark-haired and handsome, and wearing a scarlet dress. I called to her but she did not reply, instead producing a spy-glass from a case and proceeding to watch me through it. I concluded that the unfortunate woman must be very short-sighted and raised a hand to show that I had seen her, whereupon she lowered the instrument and turned away abruptly to retreat into the house."

I saw that Holmes's face was alight with interest. His eyes glittered.

"Can you remember which hand you raised to wave?" he enquired.

Mr. Jackman paused thoughtfully, wearing a puzzled expression at such a question. "I believe . . . yes, I recall clearly," he said at last. "I held my travelling-case in my left hand, and waved with my right."

"You are certain?"

He hesitated. "Quite certain. Is that significant?"

"Perhaps. What action did you take then?"

"I could see that I would learn nothing at Canal Reach," our visitor resumed, "so I resolved to ask questions at the house where the woman had appeared. During my approach, I had seen no bridge to take me across to the opposite bank, so I knew that I would have to walk further. In fact, it was almost a mile before I was able to cross. Immediately upon reaching the house, I knocked upon the door. Then, having received no reply, I hammered upon it impatiently. This brought no result and so I encircled the place, only to find it as empty as Canal Reach, and with no sign of recent habitation. Finally, after peering through several windows, I retraced my steps. When I eventually came to the trap, I drove back to the station and returned to London."

"To return to work on Monday, where you eventually explained your confused demeanour to Mr. Mycroft Holmes," I finished.

"That was the conclusion of it."

There was a moment of silence, broken only by the traffic in the street below.

Holmes said to our visitor, "Pray describe Mr. Peter Smith to us, as accurately and precisely as you can."

"He is rather above average height. His hair is black, but greying at the temples. His moustache has a rather elaborate curl and his skin is dark or well-tanned. The style of his clothing is rather more flamboyant than is usual, and appears well-cut. I noticed a faint foreign accent creeping into his speech when he became excited, as he did several times in the course of our historical ventures and during conversation. He explained that he spent some time abroad in his youth."

"Excellent. A most concise appraisal," Holmes said approvingly. "Is there anything else unusual about him that comes to mind?"

Mr. Jackman considered, then recollected, "I distinctly remember overhearing an exchange between Mr. Smith and the receptionist at the booking-desk, shortly after I arrived. He was apparently desperate to secure a room, which he subsequently did, although he mentioned to me later that he had booked in advance. Probably I have misunderstood the situation, and my referring to it has no value."

"Much to the contrary, I consider the incident to have great significance."

"Indeed? Your ways are a mystery to me, sir."

"I will endeavour to clear up all that is strange from this affair before too long. Now, Mr. Jackman, is there anything more about this curious encounter and its aftermath that you wish to tell us?"

Our client sat very still, then shook his head. "I can think of nothing further."

"When you returned to your residence in London, was there anything amiss?"

"Nothing. All was as before."

Holmes rose from his chair. "Then we will wish you good day. Be so good as to convey my compliments to my brother, and to inform him that I expect to be able to throw some light on all this in a day or two."

Mr. Jackman left us then, looking more bemused than ever. When I returned from showing him to the door, Holmes stood at the window where I joined him.

"Can you make anything of this, Watson?" he asked as we looked down to see Mr. Jackman hail a hansom.

"It does seem as if Mr. Jackman's original conclusion that he has been the victim of a rather pointless practical joke could be correct. Certainly, this man Smith cannot have profited from it."

81

"Not financially, I agree. However, there are several points that require explanation."

"I can see none."

We turned from the window and resumed our seats.

"Consider," Holmes began, "the incident at the booking-desk. Why do you think Smith lied to Mr. Jackman about having made a booking in advance?"

"It appears to have been an oversight of some sort. It may have caused some embarrassment."

My friend smiled, perhaps at my lack of suspicion. "No, Watson, I consider it far more likely that Smith *followed* Mr. Jackman to the hotel, and could not have booked ahead because he did not know the destination beforehand."

"Good heavens! Was the whole thing arranged, and not a chance meeting?"

"Undoubtedly. Next, there is the woman on the canal. Why did she need the spy-glass to see our client?"

"The lady sounds regrettably short-sighted."

"And yet she saw him arrive, and only then went into the garden. She produced the spy-glass from a case, but not until she had drawn near."

"The significance of that eludes me," I confessed.

"It is simply that the spy-glass was necessary to confirm some detail. She could not approach Mr. Jackman because of the body of water that lay between them, so she obtained a closer view with the instrument. What small feature could have been so important, do you think? What is unusual about our client?"

I considered for a moment. As far as I could recall, Mr. Jackman had but one distinguishing mark. "His missing finger!"

Holmes beamed. "Excellent, Watson. I have said before that I never get your measure. His finger, indeed. If I have interpreted this situation correctly, the lack of that finger may have saved his life."

"You understand all of this?"

"At this stage I am still uncertain, although I have arrived at a partial explanation. Another point in question, and there are probably others, is that of Mr. Peter Smith himself. If I describe to you a rather dark-skinned man who speaks with a faintly foreign accent and wears clothes of an unusual cut or colour, what do you conclude?"

"That he is from outside these shores, surely. But Smith explained to Mr. Jackman that his speech was influenced by time spent abroad."

"I am inclined to believe that the truth is the exact reverse, that Smith is foreign and learned his English from time spent previously in this country. His skin colouring, mode of dress, and accent strongly suggest it. The final clue of course, is his choice of assumed name, that most English of surnames – 'Smith'."

"I suppose you may be right. But what is the meaning of it all? Why would an unknown foreigner befriend Mr. Jackman and then play such a purposeless trick?"

"The answer to that, I am hoping, lies in the vicinity of Canal Reach. If you are free, old fellow, you may like to accompany me there after lunch."

We caught the afternoon train as it was about to pull out of the station. This new problem had lightened Holmes's manner considerably, for he chattered uncharacteristically about varying subjects for almost the entire journey. On arrival at West Byfleet, we hired a trap, as Mr. Jackman has done before us, and obtained directions to the river. We turned off the road at a bridge that looked as if it had spanned the water for centuries and descended a gradual slope. Before long, the towpath grew narrow, and so Holmes tied the horse to an iron railing and we proceeded on foot.

Mr. Jackman had been accurate in his description, I thought, for the water was still and choked with weed. An evil smell arose from it that reminded me of marsh-gas, and the houses lining both sides of the canal were remote from each other and, under a dull autumn sky, appeared long since abandoned.

"This waterway was once the connection between West Byfleet and Basingstoke, as Mr. Jackman informed us," Holmes remarked. "It was used to great extent by the boatyards that flourished here. Since most of them have now ceased to trade, the area has fallen into disuse. I doubt if a single house within sight is still occupied."

"It certainly seems so. We have seen no one."

We walked on, passing the mouldering craft moored at intervals. Presently we came to the plot of rough land that our client had described, and then to the ruined structure that we sought.

Holmes's keen eyes swept over the place as we stood in silence before it. I saw nothing but a dilapidated house, but his enthusiasm was unaffected, as if it was exactly as he had expected.

"Wait here, Watson, while I make a short inspection."

With that, he proceeded to walk around the building, producing his lens to examine the doors and window-frames. When he emerged I asked him about his findings, but he had little to say.

"There has been no one, with the exception of Mr. Jackman, on the surrounding path for a considerable time. The doors and windows have not been opened for a good deal longer." He looked across the canal. "However, I am far more interested in the red-roofed house over there, so we will now make our way to it."

We continued on until we came to the bridge that Mr. Jackman had described to us. After crossing, we passed a good many abandoned houses, some far apart and some much closer, but all in various stages of ruination.

At last we approached the one we sought, and entered through the tiny garden. Holmes again examined every side of the house with the aid of his lens after rapping on the door without response.

"Here also, there are signs that Mr. Jackman was here before us," he observed. "However, this door at the side of the house has different footprints nearby. Also, it has been forced open recently."

"Then here we may learn something."

"We shall see." Holmes turned the door-handle and braced himself to shoulder his way in, but it proved unnecessary. The door opened with a groan from hinges that were in need of oil. "Stay where you are, Watson. Do not move!"

His sudden exclamation startled me, and I imagined for a moment that some hideous trap had been left to ensnare further entrants. As it was, my friend merely sought to ensure that we made no disturbance to the dust that lay thickly inside.

He stepped into the short corridor carefully. "Tread only where I do, with your back to the wall."

I complied, brushing away cobwebs as he walked slowly ahead with his eyes fixed upon the floor. When we reached the living-room, he was silent until he had studied the marks in the surrounding grime.

"It is quite clear what has taken place here," he said then. "Two people, a man and a woman from the shape of their footprints, entered by the side door as we did. They then came in here and the man dragged that heavy table from the centre of the room to a position near the window. He then brought over those two chairs that you see, and the lady sat at this side of the table." He gestured at the dust-laden surface. "Here is where she placed something, probably the spy-glass case, and that odd-shaped mark on the floor near the corner will be where the butt of a rifle rested when the weapon was propped against the wall."

"So their intent was murder?"

"At first, at least. At some point, the woman retraced her steps to the side door and walked to the garden gate, which would have been when Mr. Jackman saw her, and then returned. Afterwards, they both left the premises."

"You have deduced all this, from the patterns in the dust?"

"It is not difficult, if you form a hypothesis of what must have occurred and then check carefully that this is confirmed by the traces that have been left. As I have explained before, confusion arises when one attempts to bend the evidence to fit a supposition."

"What have you found?" I asked, as he took an envelope from his pocket and scraped something from the floor into it.

"A small pile of ash, from a cigarette or cigar. It may tell us something."

He spent a little more time looking around the room, then we returned to the corridor. The stairs received no more than a cursory glance, because the dust that lay thickly upon them remained in an undisturbed state.

"Back to Baker Street now, I think." Holmes said finally, and we began the walk to return to the trap.

We arrived back to find Mrs. Hudson poised to serve dinner. I ate my roast lamb with mint sauce heartily, since this afternoon's exertions had given me a healthy appetite. Holmes, as often when caught in the throes of a case, displayed little enthusiasm and hardly touched his food. The moment I laid down my knife and fork, he leaped to his feet.

"I have to analyse that tobacco, Watson. You can help me, if you will, by looking through the evening editions of the dailies and reporting to me anything, particularly of foreign activity in London, that strikes you as unusual."

"I am glad to assist," I replied to his retreating back, "as always."

I scoured the news sheets, all the while aware of my friend at his workbench mixing chemicals and holding up test tubes to examine the results. After half-an-hour I gave up in disgust. I could find nothing of any relevance.

At almost the same instant, Holmes turned to our sitting-room. "What have you discovered, Watson?"

"Apart from the arrival in London of a group of Hungarian jugglers and the departure of a French count whose proposal of marriage to a society beauty was rejected, I can find nothing involving foreigners."

"No matter. I would appreciate it if you would subject tomorrow's morning editions to a similar examination."

"Certainly. But have you made any progress?"

His eyes shone with satisfaction. "It is as I had begun to suspect. The tobacco was of an Italian mixture."

"The woman described by Mr. Jackman would have fitted that description well."

"And so the threads begin to untangle. There is but one missing piece to the puzzle, I think, for our case to be complete."

"I confess to being confused, Holmes."

"Not for long, old fellow, for I expect to be able to present the entire sequence of events to Lestrade shortly. For now, however, I suggest that we repair to our beds for a good night's sleep. I expect us to be busy in the morning. Good night, Watson."

With that, he turned abruptly and his bedroom door closed before I could reply. I realised then that weariness had settled upon me, and so followed his example.

Holmes was already halfway through his breakfast when I joined him. "The coffee is still warm in the pot," was his greeting.

I made trivial conversation throughout the meal, until I realised that he was irritated by it. It was clear to me that as soon as I mentioned the affair that we were engaged upon, he would either prove reticent or overwhelm me with his enthusiasm, and my enjoyment of my bacon and eggs would be ruined.

"At last!" he exclaimed as I finished my last slice of toast. I put down my empty coffee cup as Mrs. Hudson appeared to clear the table.

"I see that the papers have arrived," I remarked. "I will begin now, if you wish."

"Pray do so, while I consult my index."

I took the morning editions to my armchair, while he began to turn pages and select newspaper cuttings, only to discard them moments later.

I found something of significance soon after. "Holmes! I have it!"

He was beside me immediately, and we stared at the picture together.

"It is you, not I, who has solved this curious affair," he said then.

"The resemblance is very close, but Mr. Jackman and this man are not identical," I observed. "It is not difficult to see how one could be mistaken for the other, nevertheless. We can be sure that this is indeed someone different, since we can see clearly that he has no missing fingers."

"Watson, you excel yourself," Holmes beamed. "Not for the first time, I wonder which of us is the detective?"

I felt a keen embarrassment at such accolades of praise from my friend, especially twice in as many breaths. "I am always pleased to be of some little help."

"Stout fellow! I see that the photograph is of the recently-appointed Italian Minister of Justice, Signor Carlo Caruso, who is here on a state visit. This adds considerable weight to my theory, especially as I believe that I have discovered the true identity of Mr. Peter Smith from my index. The article states that Signor Caruso will visit the National Gallery this afternoon, to view the exhibition of Italian old masters."

"I fear that I am still a little at sea."

Holmes snatched up his hat and coat. "All will soon be made clear, Watson. For now, I must leave you for a short while. Pray inform Mrs. Hudson that we will be taking an early lunch."

With that he was gone, and from the window I saw him hail a passing hansom. I busied myself with a perusal of the remainder of the newspapers, and then with turning this affair over in my mind. I had just concluded that, while I understood some of the recent events that had surrounded us, I was unable to perceive the entire situation, when I heard the front door slam before Holmes bounded up the stairs.

"It is all arranged," he said at once. "I have sent telegrams to Mycroft and to Lestrade. We must be outside the National Gallery by one o'clock, to witness Signor Caruso's arrival."

By the time he sat down, I had many questions to ask, but he would not be drawn. Until our lunch was served, he talked of Ancient Greek architecture and the noticeable rise of Germany as a military power between long silences as we ate.

We finished our meal and left our rooms before Mrs. Hudson could clear away. For the second time that day, Holmes was quick to secure a hansom, and we found ourselves in Trafalgar Square soon after.

"There seems to be a surfeit of constables," I observed, "and the steps of the Gallery are quite crowded with onlookers."

"The exhibition has proved popular. Ah! I see that Lestrade is already in charge."

We joined the little detective at the base of the steps.

"Your telegram explained that this is a matter of some urgency, Mr. Holmes," he said after greeting us, "and before I know it, I have at my disposal thirty constables. Normally I would have trouble getting more than two or three. It is all most curious."

"Such is the influence of Mycroft," Holmes murmured to me.

"I have read that there are important talks in progress, between ourselves and the Italians," I said to Lestrade, "concerning some sort of alliance. Clearly, the government wishes to ensure that nothing occurs to threaten the outcome."

"That sort of thing is far above my head, Doctor," he replied.

Holmes's keen eyes swept the crowd, and I saw him grow suddenly tense.

"How many constables did you say, Lestrade?"

"I was allowed thirty, some of them from other divisions."

"So you are not familiar with all of them?"

The inspector looked at Holmes curiously. "Why do you ask?"

"Can you select three of their number, men that you already know, to join us here?"

"I can, but to what purpose?"

"The prevention of an assassination attempt on Signor Caruso. If you will instruct these men to obey my orders *absolutely*, I think I can promise that you will be arresting a criminal of some notoriety very soon."

Lestrade stared at Holmes for what seemed to me to be a long time. I had begun to fear that the old distrust of my friend's methods had resurfaced in the inspector's mind when he turned abruptly and walked across to the line of constables at the edge of the crowd. I heard him call three names and beckon, and the four made their way back to us.

"This is Mr. Sherlock Holmes," he explained to them. "I want you to obey his instructions in this business as you would mine." He turned to my friend. "Mr. Holmes, these are constables O'Rourke, Patterson, and Denley. I have known them since I was myself in uniform."

"Capital!" Holmes retorted. "Gentlemen, there is a dangerous criminal concealed here, but I believe I can expose him. I propose to search among the crowd lining the steps until I find the man I want. When I point him out I want you to restrain him immediately, one man to each arm and one to apply handcuffs. At my signal do not hesitate, *no matter who I indicate*. Is that understood?"

The three assented in unison.

While Lestrade and I looked on in a rather bewildered fashion, my friend and the three officers approached the crowd. Holmes at once produced his lens and, bending at the waist, appeared to be examining the steps, one by one, as they progressed upward along the line. They had not climbed further than the waiting constables when his arm shot out suddenly. "Good afternoon, Signor Atillio Parvetti."

To my surprise, it was one of the other uniformed officers that he indicated. Lestrade's three men instantly fell upon him, searched him, and led him away, struggling and cursing, to a waiting police wagon.

"You are sure of this, Mr. Holmes?" Lestrade said rather cautiously.

"If you need confirmation, Lestrade, you have only to look in your own files at Scotland Yard. You will discover that the murders of Mr. Howard Sangster, the industrialist, and Mr. Thomas Vernon, the newspaper magnate, have remained unsolved until now. Atillio Parvetti is a professional assassin who has visited these shores before."

"But how did you identify him?"

Holmes smiled. "It was not difficult when I realised that the number of constables in attendance was actually thirty-one, rather than the thirty that you stated. Probably Parvetti's intention was to dispose of one of them to maintain the expected number, had the opportunity presented itself. Having established that, it was simply a matter of deciding which constable was an imposter, and that was simplicity itself."

"I cannot see it," Lestrade admitted.

"Parvetti had made some attempt to alter his physical appearance, and there can be no doubt that he obtained his disguise from a costumier, but it occurred to me that he may not have considered his shoes. As I pretended to examine the steps I scrutinized carefully the footwear of each constable, until I saw a pair that were not only different from service issue, but of a foreign make. The design and pattern are quite unmistakable."

"Here is the coach containing Signor Caruso. You have undoubtedly saved his life today, Mr. Holmes."

"Not I, Lestrade, but Doctor Watson, who threw light on the true nature of the man's plight. You need not mention me in your report, but I would be grateful if you would permit me to be present when Parvetti is questioned."

"In the circumstances, I have no doubt that it will be in order."

"Thank you. Watson, I will see you back at Baker Street, presently."

With that we watched the dignified figure of Signor Caruso ascend the steps and enter the building without further incident. I returned to our rooms alone and settled myself in an armchair to read. I must have fallen asleep, and it was almost time for dinner when my friend returned in good spirits.

"Parvetti has confessed!" he announced. "I do not see that he could lose anything by it, however, since he is certain to face the hangman to pay for his previous crimes. I was able to point out his connection to at least two unsolved murders, and Lestrade agrees with my conclusions."

"Allow me to pour you a brandy before dinner," I offered as he sat down.

"Thank you, Watson. I confess to feeling the beginning of hunger pangs, stimulated no doubt by the aroma of the roast chicken that Mrs. Hudson is preparing."

He was very animated at the successful conclusion of the case, but spoke only of other things. When we sat down to smoke afterwards, I could contain myself no longer.

"Holmes, will you give me a full account of this affair?"

He gave me a knowing look. "So that you can exaggerate and over-dramatize it before committing it to your publisher? Well. Watson, you have been instrumental in bringing this case to its end, so I will tell you all. By listening to Parvetti's admissions at Scotland Yard, I was able to connect the entire chain of events."

"Kindly delay long enough for me to retrieve my notebook."

He nodded, drawing on his clay pipe. When I resumed my seat, he closed his eyes and began: "This case has its true beginnings some months ago, when Signor Caruso became the Italian Minister of Justice. He had long held an ambition to bring to trial Mario Conti, the head of one of the old crime families who had, until then, evaded all retribution for his considerable wrongdoings. This was a man who had lived a life of vicious crime, and of initiating it in others. He achieved his position through ruthlessness, and maintained it with threats and bribery. Signor Caruso was the first to refuse to capitulate, and Conti was imprisoned for twenty years. He did not serve much of his sentence, however.

"It so happened that a minor member of a rival family was also a prisoner, and the order went out to dispose of Conti. His wife, Signora Stefano Conti, swore revenge, on both the other family and Signor Caruso. The war between the families persists to this day, and Atillio Parvetti was commissioned to accompany Signora Conti on a journey to England, where they knew Signor Caruso was soon to visit."

"But they mistook Mr. Jackman for him," I ventured.

"Not at first. Parvetti watched government buildings in Whitehall and elsewhere systematically for weeks, and he may well have seen Signor Caruso from a distance, but when he set eyes on Mr. Jackman, as he would have done since Mycroft's office is close by, he became uncertain. I wondered at first why Parvetti did not murder Mr. Jackman regardless, as would be a routine precaution in his profession, but neither he nor Signora Conti wished to take the unnecessary risk of drawing attention to themselves. Parvetti, remember, was already wanted by Scotland Yard for at least two previous killings. So it was then that Parvetti became the shadow of Mr. Jackman, seeking confirmation of his identity on the Signora's instructions."

"Hence the 'accidental' meeting at the hotel in Bath, and Parvetti's pursuit of Mr. Jackman's friendship."

"Quite so. A rather inadequate photograph of Signor Caruso in their possession had proven to be of little use, and Parvetti was still undecided. Finally he devised the plan of luring Mr. Jackman to a lonely spot where Signora Conti could watch him closely, and then it would be decided if he should live or die. The confrontation occurred, of course, as he tried to gain entry to Canal Reach, and the spy-glass revealed that he had a missing finger. Knowing that this could not be Signor Caruso, despite the close resemblance, they then left the area at once. It occurred to me to wonder why Parvetti had not come to this conclusion earlier, but you will

90

recall that Mr. Jackman was reluctant to take off his gloves and that his disfigurement was a source of some embarrassment to him. Evidently he had lost the glove containing the false finger by the time the Signora saw him."

"The remainder of the story is not difficult to anticipate," I said. "Parvetti and Signora Conti must have seen the same picture and notification of Signor Caruso's visit to the National Gallery as ourselves, and the assassination attempt was arranged as a result."

"Indeed, Watson. The rest you know, since you were present. I do hope that Lestrade will see fit not to mention my trifling involvement in this affair in his report. To claim this as one of his successes will undoubtedly enhance his career somewhat."

A Simple Case of Abduction
by Mike Hogan

In the final two weeks of eighteen-ninety-six, after many years of mostly standing at Sherlock Holmes's right hand as an observer while he pitted his wits against the felonious fraternity, I found myself at the very centre of the web of a criminal mastermind whose exploits shook the foundations of the Bank of England. I was for a time incommunicado and unable to take notes as events unfolded, but I have assembled sufficient material from Holmes's recollections, and from interviews with the other participants (at least those unhanged) to put together a narrative of events, and I have been able to re-enact certain conversations from their memories. I hope the following will be accepted as an accurate reconstruction of a singular episode, and a counter to the highly-coloured accounts that appeared in the penny newspapers.

The affair started innocuously enough, as so many of my friend's cases did, in our sitting room at 221b Baker Street. I blotted the final sentence of my manuscript, sat back, and contemplated the short stack of foolscap on my desk with a certain amount of satisfaction. Despite Holmes's injunction that I publish no more of his case notes until after his retirement, I had persuaded him to allow an account of the quite extraordinary case of Wilson the canary trainer to appear in *The Strand Magazine*. The generous fee our agent had negotiated would go a long way to repairing our tattered finances, and I had hopes of adding more stories if my friend could be brought around. I flattered myself that I had compiled the facts of the case into a compact, yet thrilling, read, and I had done so exactly to my schedule. My slot in the next edition of *The Strand* depended on the manuscript being on the desk of the editor by noon of the following day, and for once, perhaps truth to tell for the first time, I was comfortably within my deadline without being chivvied nor yet scolded by the editor.

I slipped the sheaf of papers into an envelope and printed the address of the magazine in capitals on the front. Then I rummaged in my desk for a postage stamp, but found only empty stamp-books. I considered employing our local messenger to deliver the manuscript, but thought better of it when I recalled the low ebb to which my and my co-lodger's finances had fallen in the previous week or so. My attempts to impose fiscal restraint on Holmes during a quiet period of his detective practice had not prospered, and his insistence on dining at the Criterion the evening before to celebrate the successful conclusion of the matter of the veiled lodger had drained our resources to the dregs and a little beyond. I had been obliged to borrow from the house "float" to pay our cab fare home, and I had endured a supercilious smirk from the coal merchant's agent in the morning when I requested he return for payment in the New Year.

I swivelled my chair and regarded my friend with an indulgent smile. Holmes lay draped across our sofa in his dressing gown, dozing before a merry (and unpaid for) fire. One of his endearing characteristics (the fewer the more cherished) was his indifference to money. He was as happy championing a distressed waitress from a bar on the underground railway for a half-crown fee, or none as he was being consulted on an affair of state by a duke of the realm, with the reward of a cheque for thousands. I sniffed. In fact, he was more likely to receive timely payment from the girl than from His Grace, and unexplained delays in fee payment from several aristocratic and politically exalted clients was the immediate cause of the low ebb of our finances.

It was not yet three in the afternoon, but the shortest day of the year was almost upon us, and the room was already in twilight. I stood, lit the gas lights and set them to a low flame, a soft glow that illuminated the bright Christmas colours of Mrs. Hudson's holly boughs and the paper decorations that festooned our sitting room, but unfortunately disclosed the reproachful pile of unsigned Christmas cards that lay upon my desk, with their unstamped envelopes beside them. Holmes dozed on.

I picked up the manuscript in its envelope, took my hat and stick from the sideboard, slipped quietly out of the sitting room, and treaded softly down the stairs. As I put on my coat and scarf in the hall, I informed our page that I had decided to walk to the Strand to deliver a package and do a little shopping. The exercise, I suggested, would clear my head, fuddled by cigar smoke and fumes from Holmes's chemical experiments in our sitting room. Billy gave me an impudent, knowing look that I ignored.

In fact, the walk did clear my head, and I set myself a steady pace southeast across London, avoiding the main shopping thoroughfares until I passed Piccadilly Circus just as the street lamps were being lit. I crossed Trafalgar Square, slipped through heavy traffic to the south side of the Strand, and stopped at my usual tobacconist, hard by Charing Cross Station, where I stocked up with cigars and tobacco. I tucked my manuscript envelope under my arm as I bought a box of matches from a boy, and I paused under a lamppost, with a stream of pedestrians flowing past me on either side, shook a cigar from my new packet, and lit it, blowing a stream of smoke up into the cold, late-afternoon air. In the dying light I saw dark clouds massing above me, and I wished I had brought my umbrella.

Holmes added a few drops of clear liquid to the contents of a test tube, and he smiled in satisfaction as the mixture turned bright vermillion. He noted the result on a scrap of paper, placed a flask atop a Bunsen burner, and lit the flame. The doorbell rang downstairs, he heard heavy footsteps on the stairs and the sitting-room door opened.

"Watson," he cried, "you are just in time to – "

"Mr. Ballantyne," Billy said, and he ushered a stocky gentleman in an elegant frock coat into the room, then fled, coughing. The man frowned, took out his handkerchief, and put it over his mouth and nose.

Holmes turned off the Bunsen and flapped at the smoke and fumes from his experiments with the sleeve of his dressing gown. "I do apologise. A small matter of domestic poisoning. I will open the window."

"Don't mind me," the visitor spluttered.

Holmes dragged up the sash window and indicated the sofa with a wide gesture. The gentleman put his lucent silk hat, stick, and gloves on the sideboard and sat, breathing shallowly.

"Mr. Ballantyne, I have read of your exploits." Holmes said, turning up the gas lamps and giving the fire a sharp poke with one of the fire irons before slumping into his usual chair.

The visitor sighed. "You are thinking of my brother, Horace. He is the adventurer in the family. While he discovers new rivers, lakes, and waterfalls on the Dark Continent, his younger brothers pursue more sedentary careers in the law, or in my case, medicine. I am Doctor Henry Ballantyne." He passed Holmes his calling card.

"Of course," said Holmes. "I do apologise, Sir Henry. A doctor friend lent me your work on sucking chest wounds, and I read it with the very greatest interest. You are the country's leading authority on military trauma, particularly bullet wounds."

"I wish our generals and admirals shared your very flattering view of my authority on those medical matters, sir. They are feudal and reactionary to the core." Sir Henry settled himself back on the sofa. "Until recently, the Duke of Cambridge sat like the legendary immoveable object at the pinnacle of the Army command, and his notions of war were Crimean, or even Napoleonic – bright flags, befrogged hussars at the charge, and the thin red line in bearskin hats. He was not susceptible to any change, whether it be to the scarlet colour of our military uniforms or the deplorable state of our medical services, despite Miss Nightingale's noble efforts."

Sir Henry mopped his brow with his handkerchief as Billy edged through the sitting-room door with a tray of coffee. "I do apologise, Mr. Holmes," he said as he accepted a cup. "I grow a little warm on the subject."

Holmes waved away his visitor's apology, and Sir Henry took a moment to sip his coffee and compose himself before he continued. "I may be here on a wild goose chase. It is entirely possible that I have misunderstood a situation, seeing phantoms where none exist, and I am wasting your time and my own. In which case, I would be grateful if you would return this to Doctor John Watson, who I understand lodges here."

He held out a battered and grimy foolscap manila envelope. "The flap was unsealed, and I am afraid most of the papers inside blew away, and some were trodden under by horses or rolled across by carriage wheels before I could retrieve them. The title page remained, half out of the envelope, and under the circumstances I shall describe, I took it upon myself to read the address thereon, and do myself the honour of visiting you."

Holmes took the envelope and pulled out the half-dozen or so pages it contained. "This is Doctor Watson's manuscript of his notes on a recent case of mine. He prepared them for publication in *The Strand*." He looked up sharply. "Has there been an accident? Is Doctor Watson injured?"

"Let me tell you what I know," Sir Henry replied. He described his decision that afternoon to walk rather than take a cab from his house in Burlington Gardens to Charing Cross Hospital, where he was to inspect some new carbolic bandages for binding broken limbs. Nothing untoward had occurred as he strolled, although the sky grew ominously dark as he threaded through by-ways to avoid the crowded shopping arteries of the West End, and he wished he had brought his umbrella. Lamps were being lit as he dodged between omnibuses and carriages at Piccadilly Circus. As he reached the far side, Sir Henry heard a commotion behind him, and saw a four-wheeler cab crossing the circus against the flow of traffic and creating a jam. He had thought nothing of it until he reached Trafalgar Square, when again there was a disturbance as he crossed the street, and he turned to see the same cab, or so he thought, again pressing through the traffic towards him in defiance of the general direction of other vehicles, and causing a stir.

"I have seen enough drunken and obstructive behaviour by cab drivers not to be surprised when they ignore the rule of the road," Sir Henry said with a rueful smile, "but this driver seemed particularly intent on creating mayhem. His behaviour was not appreciated by other road users, even by his fellow cabbies, who shouted imprecations and abuse at him that would have put their licenses in peril, had a constable been present."

Sir Henry had passed on, turned into the Strand, and stopped in front of Charing Cross Station to buy a box of matches. Out of the corner of his eye, he saw a four-wheeler trundle past him and stop a few yards further on, by the Cross. He turned to pay the boy, then started, looked back, and saw that three men had jumped from the cab. One of them seemed to point towards him before they were swamped by a swarm of pedestrians surging from the station.

He lost sight of the men. Then, through a gap in the crowds, he saw them pounce on a gentleman in an overcoat and bowler under a streetlamp a few yards away and drag him to the cab. They bundled him aboard, and in the struggle the man dropped an envelope from which papers spilled. Sir Henry rushed to the gentleman's aid, but he could not force a way through the press of pedestrians before the cab doors slammed, and the cab took off at a furious rate.

Sir Henry picked up the envelope and what papers he could find, and immediately reported the incident to the policeman on fixed-point duty at Trafalgar Square. The constable escorted Sir Henry to the nearest police station, where he gave a statement.

Holmes had listened to Sir Henry's account with great attention. He now leapt from his chair and paced the room. "You were wearing a black overcoat and a bowler?"

"I was. And a red tartan scarf. It and my coat are on your coatrack downstairs."

Holmes strode to the door and called for Billy The boy confirmed that Doctor Watson had left the house that afternoon wearing a black overcoat, bowler, and red tartan scarf.

"You said you thought the same cab was behind you in Trafalgar Square and in Piccadilly." Holmes said, resuming his pacing. "What made you think so?"

Sir Henry frowned. "It was getting dark. I'm not sure – "

"Think!" Holmes stopped and shook his head. "I do apologise." He slipped into the chair opposite his visitor and leaned forward, his palms pressed together. "Was there anything about the horse, or perhaps the driver, that caught your attention? Let us start with the driver – was he wearing a hat? I imagine he was, in this weather."

Sir Henry closed his eyes as he tried to recall. "Yes, a battered stovepipe. The old-fashioned type, taller than the usual top hat, but bent, concertinaed, as it were."

"And his coat?"

"Nothing remarkable. A caped coat of some description. Perhaps an Ulster."

Holmes elicited nothing more from Sir Henry about the driver, and only the colour of the horse, difficult to determine in the poor light, but probably a bony chestnut, a typical cab horse. He had seen the three men who had jumped from the cab for a fleeting instance, through a dense crowd, and he could not swear to their clothing, although he thought one was dark-skinned and might have been an Indian.

Holmes considered for a long moment. "You say you started, Sir Henry. You paid the match boy, then you started and turned – Why? What surprised you?"

"I'm not sure – "

"A sound? A cry? A premonition of danger?"

"No, no. I am sorry, I cannot recall."

Holmes again seemed lost in thought for a few moments, his hands clasped before him, almost in an attitude of prayer, before he spoke again. "Can you think of anyone who might want to harm you, or kidnap you, perhaps to keep you from attending a vital meeting or event?"

"Enemies? No-one at all," Sir Henry answered. "I make no secret of my disdain for the War Office and all its works. The Duke of Cambridge, before he was ousted from office, was kind enough to refer to me as a 'meddling quack', but as for an attempt to silence me by violence, an attack or abduction – the idea is preposterous. Although it must be admitted that the incompetent execution of the kidnapping does suggest War Office staff work."

Holmes stood. "I must thank you for coming to me, Sir Henry."

"I was not a Jeremiah, then?" Sir Henry asked as he stood. "You really think there is cause for concern?"

"I do." Holmes held up his hand. "It appears that Doctor Watson has been abducted. I do not know why, but it is possible that this action is directed towards me. In my line of work, I have managed to accumulate a plethora of enemies, some of whom would stop at nothing to wound me, entrap me, or seek to bend me to their will. Let me see you out."

I awoke to find myself lying on a buttoned leather sofa, with a thick head and a foul taste in my mouth. The dingy room was brightly lit, illuminating a cracked ceiling and stained green paper peeling from the walls. I sat up, rubbing my eyes, and I blinked at a bald gentleman in evening clothes who sat opposite me on a matching sofa, regarding me benevolently over his half-moon spectacles and smoking a long cigar.

"Good afternoon, Doctor." The bald man said in a soft American accent. He turned to a thin, black-skinned, younger man in a frock coat who leaned against the mantel of an ornate fireplace. "Get the doctor a whisky."

I waved away the offer, my head still swimming. "Water, if you please."

I was offered a tumbler, and I gulped the water gratefully. "I seem to recall an accident – no." My recollection cleared, and I staggered to my feet and stood, very shaky on my legs. "I was *attacked*." I slumped back onto the sofa, breathing heavily. "This man and others attacked me with *Chloroform*." I waved a weak arm at the dark-skinned young man who had fetched my water. "I demand – "

"Professor Ballantyne – " the bald man overrode me.

I frowned. "My name is Watson."

"Come, come, Sir Henry, there is no need to be shy." The bald man blew a stream of cigar smoke across the room. "Your reputation puts you at the very pinnacle of your profession."

I shook my head to clear it. "I know of Sir Henry Ballantyne, of course, but I am not he." I rummaged in my coat pockets. "I am not Sir Henry. If I had remembered to carry my card case, I could have proved that fact to you."

"You try our patience, Doctor," the bald man said stiffly. "How likely is it that we should pluck the wrong doctor from a crowd of pedestrians in the Strand?"

My brows knitted furiously as I tried to recall what had happened to me. I had stopped outside Charing Cross Station to light my cigar – "You called for a doctor, and I turned to the cry." I patted my pockets again. "Where are my cigars, and where is my manuscript?"

Holmes directed Sir Henry to the cabstand beside the station. He closed the front door behind him and stood in the hall for a moment, head bowed, before he looked up and saw Billy and Mrs. Hudson peering out of the kitchen. "I do not have a clear picture yet, but I am afraid – "

The doorbell rang. Holmes opened the door and found Inspector Lestrade facing him, well-wrapped in an overcoat, scarf, and bowler. Holmes held up his hand. "I am sorry, Inspector, I am engaged in a most serious matter in which I must employ all my resources – "

"The London and Counties incident," Lestrade said, shaking his head. "A bad business, Mr. Holmes. Just passed to me from the C Division and the City Police. The bank guard lingered for a week, but died this morning."

"As I said, Inspector. I cannot – "

"But we have a lead on the gang, sir. The Negro who fired the fatal shot dropped this." Inspector Lestrade held up a black leather glove.

Holmes stiffened. He regarded the inspector with narrowed eyes for a moment, then he turned and led the way upstairs.

Inspector Lestrade accepted a glass of whisky and leaned forward in his seat on the sofa. "Just a week ago, on Friday morning, a man purporting to be an American businessman on a visit to this country with the intention of investing in a considerable building project, presented a promissory note from an American source at the counter of the London and Counties Bank in Oxford Street. He had successfully discounted a dozen or more large-denomination notes at various banks in the preceding days."

Lestrade gulped his whisky and continued. "What the gentleman did not know was that the Bank of England had issued a warning against such notes, several of which had been found to be forgeries. The work was brilliant, undetectable from the real thing, but a sharp-eyed clerk had noticed that a note drawn on a New York bank was dated next year, not this. The issuing bank was contacted by cable for clarification, and they repudiated the document."

Holmes refilled Lestrade's glass and he continued. "All London bank clerks were briefed on the suspicious notes, and when one was presented that morning by a gentleman in an astrakhan-trimmed coat, wide-awake hat, and with an American accent, the manager of the London and Counties requested the gentleman join him in his office. The man smelled a rat and bolted, and two other men followed him, racing for the door and a cab waiting outside."

"One of the gang was wounded," Holmes said.

"Shot by the guard. We have the hospitals closely watched, and a warning sheet was sent to doctors' surgeries and clinics."

The doorbell rang downstairs, and a moment later a thunder came on the stairs and Sir Henry Ballantyne was at the door, his face flushed with exertion. "It came to me just as I reached Baker Street Station, and I ran back to tell you. I started and turned from the match seller at Charing Cross because I heard a cry. Someone called for a doctor." He gasped for breath, his hands on his knees then looked up, frowning. "I heard a loud cry of 'Doctor!'"

Holmes passed Sir Henry a glass of whisky, and as the doctor gulped it and recovered his composure, he gave Lestrade a summary of the facts of the abduction. "If we accept the likely supposition that the gang called to you," Holmes said to Sir Henry, "then their intention may have been to single you out for attack or capture. I ask again, can you think of anyone who might wish you ill?"

"No-one."

"Have you written for the public press recently?"

"Only one article this year, for the American magazine, *Collier's Weekly*," Sir Henry answered. "I wrote on my experiences in the late War Between the States. As you may know, Mr. Holmes, my family is originally Canadian, with strong ties to the United States. After gaining a medical degree, I volunteered my services to the Union Army during the last two years of the War, and I saw a great deal of traumatic injury caused by shrapnel, rifle and musket bullets, and the bayonet. In recent years, I have attempted to convince the British Army that immediate treatment of wounds, at the battlefront, rather than in hospitals far behind the lines, saves soldiers' lives."

Holmes took down a copy of *Who's Who* from the bookshelf. He flicked to Sir Henry's entry and read it. "Your residence is noted as Burlington Gardens, and also detailed is your connection with Charing Cross Hospital." He closed the book. "You would not be a difficult person to track down, even for a visitor to this country." Holmes refilled the inspector's and Sir Henry's glasses and poured himself a whisky. "We may make certain reasonable suppositions. If Sir Henry was not targeted for personal reasons, then the abductors needed a doctor, specifically an expert on wounds. The evidence is inconclusive, but the presence of the Negro suggests that the abductors and the forgery gang are one and the same."

"What will they do when they discover they have the wrong doctor?" Sir Henry asked.

"Hopefully, attempt to persuade Doctor Watson to treat their wounded comrade."

Inspector Lestrade shook his head. "As I said, Mr. Holmes, the bank guard died this morning. That means they are for the gallows when we catch them. Even if Doctor Watson cooperates – "

"That fact must be kept from the evening newspapers," Holmes said, slamming his fist in his palm. "As far as the press are concerned, the guard is recovering."

Inspector Lestrade made to interrupt, but Holmes held up a restraining hand. "Only his immediate family may be told the truth. Once the fraudsters know they have murdered the guard, they will have no compunction in committing further murders – whether for one or a habit of homicides, the penalty is the same, death by hanging."

"I will certainly try, Mr. Holmes," Inspector Lestrade said doubtfully, "but the papers will have the story by now – they have their contacts within the Force, and not just desk sergeants – "

Holmes stood. "I am a resourceful man, Inspector," he said in a tone dripping with menace. "I will use all my cunning, and my connections to both the highest and lowest in the land, to blight the career of any reporter who jeopardises the life of my friend by reporting the guard's death. He will find all access to the inside information he needs to pursue his trade, whether from you gentlemen at Scotland Yard or the criminal fraternity, locked and barred against him."

Lestrade put down his glass and stood. "I appreciate your interest – your very intense interest – in this matter, Mr. Holmes, and you may count on me and on the cooperation at the Yard, but we will be hard put to see to it that every editor in London receives word before this evening, and tonight the morning papers go to press."

"Leave that to me, Inspector." Holmes turned to Sir Henry. "We must take precautions for your safety, Doctor. The possibility remains that our supposition that the gang aimed to abduct a physician is incorrect, and that you personally were the object of the attack."

"I will post a constable outside Sir Henry's residence," Lestrade said.

Holmes unlocked the drawer of his desk and took out his revolver. He checked the cylinder and pocketed a handful of cartridges. "As you say Lestrade, if the gang hear that the bank guard is dead, they will have reason to dispose of Watson, whether he treats their comrade or refuses to. We must find them, and capture or destroy them before that news reaches their ears."

Sir Henry stood. "If I would not be a burden, I would much prefer to join you in your pursuit of these miscreants. With the inspector at my side, I will be perfectly safe, and consider, gentlemen, you may have need of a doctor."

"What of the dropped glove, Mr. Holmes?" Lestrade asked, holding it out.

Holmes peered at it. "It is a perfectly commonplace leather glove, of no evidentiary interest at all."

"You have mistaken me for Sir Henry," I told the bald man, as I had several times, with increasing exasperation. "I believe he and I may be of an age, and from the *Spy* cartoon I saw in *Vanity Fair*, I know that he has a moustache of similar cut to my own. I have read Sir Henry's articles in the medical press, but I do not know the gentleman personally, and I have nothing like his experience of wounds, or his surgical expertise. I am a general practitioner, but I am not, at the moment, in practice."

I stood. "Kindly arrange for my immediate return to Baker Street." I wagged an admonishing finger at my captors. "You should be aware that my friend Mr. Sherlock – "

The bald man had also stood, and he and his young companion engaged in a whispered conference by the fireplace, ignoring me. I subsided onto the sofa, and I waited, with what patience I could muster, until their discussion ended.

The bald man turned to me. "Doctor Watson, I would be grateful if you would examine my friend. He has been the victim of an accident."

I stood again. "Certainly, but I do so without prejudice and with no obligation to treat him. You should apply to your own doctor or, if as I surmise from your accents, you are visitors from America, you will find that the American Exchange in the Strand publishes a list of gentlemen offering professional services to tourists. I am sure they could direct you to an able physician."

"This way, if you please, Doctor." I followed the bald man into a cramped hall where a pair of bruisers stood guard, and upstairs, along a gloomy corridor and into a small bedroom simply furnished with a narrow bed and a bright oil lamp on a table beside it. A young man lay in the bed with his arms on the counterpane, his right wrist wrapped in a bandage encrusted with dried blood. His face glistened with sweat, his eyes were shut, and he breathed irregularly through parched and cracked lips.

I examined him as well as I could without the instruments I usually carried in my medical bag. I unravelled the bandage and the smell of decay that had assailed me as I entered the room grew stronger. I elicited a low groan when I lifted the man's arm to examine a puffed and fiery-red bullet wound in his wrist, surrounded by black and yellow-stained skin. His lower right arm was severely bloated compared to his left. I put my arm around the man's shoulder, lifted him and gave him water from a cup on the bedside table.

"A bullet entered the wrist, ploughing up almost to the elbow," I informed the bald man. "I see no exit hole, therefore the ball is still in the wound, possibly with patches or threads of clothing. Judging by the powder burns on his skin, the gun was almost in contact when it was fired. If the ball had been extracted earlier, and the wound cleaned – " I shrugged. "But now, this man is very ill. The stink of putrefaction tells me that gangrene is setting in. I smelled enough of it in Afghanistan during my Army service to last a lifetime. Unless very decided and immediate measures are taken, this man will die."

The bald man held a handkerchief to his nose. "Can you not remove the bullet?"

"Matters have gone too far for that. Sepsis is marked by the colour and temperature of the skin. You can see its effects above the wound, past the elbow and halfway to the shoulder. It will continue to spread. There is but one course of action left, if he is to be saved."

"Amputation?"

"Above the elbow, where the flesh is yet untainted," I answered. "You need a surgeon. I strongly advise you to admit this man to a hospital immediately."

"The bank was expecting a delivery of bullion later that morning, and the commissionaire at the door had been reinforced with an armed guard," the manager of the London and Counties Bank, Oxford Street branch, informed his visitors in hushed, measured tones.

Holmes, Sir Henry, and Inspector Lestrade sat before his desk as he described the discovery of the forged note, and the gang's attempt to escape. Holmes listened, tense as a coiled spring, tapping his gloved fingers on his knee.

"According to witnesses," the bank manager continued, "the guard drew his pistol when he realised that the man at the counter was making for the door, chased by me and the cashier. He was shot by one of the companions of the fraudster, who witnesses aver was a person of African complexion. The guard managed to return fire before he fell, and several onlookers swear that the shorter of the three robbers, the lookout by the door, was wounded in the exchange, possibly in the arm or hand."

"Very well." Holmes took off his gloves, pulled an empty leather sack and his revolver from his pockets, and laid them on the counter. "I shall require money. Kindly furnish me with five-hundred guineas in gold, preferably half-sovereigns."

The manager gaped at Holmes, and Inspector Lestrade leaned forward in his seat and murmured in Holmes ear. "If you intend to rob the bank, Mr. Holmes, I would appreciate a few minutes' grace while I pull the coppers off guarding the front doors and make myself scarce."

"Eh? I intend nothing of the sort," Holmes replied stiffly. "I am requesting a deposit on my fee for collaring the forgers."

The bank manager wrung his hands. "I am sorry, gentlemen, I have no authority to – "

"But I do," said a commanding voice from behind them.

The bank manager shot to his feet and bowed to a stout, white-whiskered gentleman in a frock coat and top hat. "May I introduce Sir Solomon Hammond, the chairman of the London and Counties Bank?"

103

"There is not a moment to lose," Holmes said, turning to the chairman. "I am on the trail of the forgery gang who targeted your bank and several others in the City."

"I have just returned from a meeting with the Governor of the Bank of England," Sir Solomon said, heaving himself into the manager's seat. "This American devil's promissory notes are indistinguishable from genuine ones. He has defrauded British banks of enormous sums, and we have news of similar exactions in Chicago and Santiago." He lowered his voice almost to a whisper. "Between you and me, gentlemen, he has fleeced London banks of almost fifteen-thousand pounds, and if it weren't for his eccentric dating of a single page in one of the documents, and a sharp-eyed clerk spotting the mistake, he could have netted even more colossal sums. He has done significant damage to our liquidity as well as our reputation. The Governor was obliged to bring the matter before the Prime Minister, who suggested that Parliament might consider legislation requiring *external scrutiny* of our banking operations. It does not bear thinking about."

He snapped his fingers at the bank manager. "Chequebook." Sir Solomon filled in the details and handed the cashier's cheque to the manager. "In gold, I think you said, Mr. Holmes."

Sir Henry, Inspector Lestrade, and Holmes, carrying his heavy sack, pushed through the revolving door of the bank into Oxford Street. "Contrary to public opinion," Holmes said, "not more than a dozen or so cab drivers risk their badges by consorting with criminals. Those who do, know me, and I know them, or most of them." He followed his companions into their waiting four-wheeler. "We have plenty of witnesses: The cabbies at both Piccadilly Circus and Trafalgar Square who were cut off by the errant growler will be telling their tale in the cab shelters. If the driver of the cab into which Doctor Watson was dragged is a real cabbie, they will know him. Our problem is time." He called an address to the driver, and they set off at the trot.

I was escorted back to the sitting room. "Gangrene is ineluctable," I informed the bald man. "Unless that arm comes off within three or four hours, the gentleman upstairs will soon be past all human aid, and very likely dead before morning."

"His death would be a severe inconvenience to me, Doctor," the bald man said, frowning. "He is a genius. His hands are those of a great artist. He can take a slab of steel and tickle from it the printing block for a five-pound note that would fool the King of England." He poured himself a whisky and offered me a glass that I accepted. "We have worked together for several years on three continents, shoving the queer, as you have it in this country – "

He smiled a question, and I answered coldly. "Passing counterfeit money and notes."

The bald man's smile broadened, then he scowled. "But what good would he be to me without a right arm? Is there no hope it can be saved?"

"As I said, if he had been treated earlier, something might have been done, but it's been a week since the shooting. There are treatments, some involving the use of maggots to debride the necrotic skin, but I say again, this is not my area of expertise. I have no instruments, nor maggots for that matter, to hand."

The Negro man wrinkled his nose in distaste.

"You are very exact, Doctor," the bald man said in a musing tone. "You said our man was shot a week ago. I believe you know who we are."

"I read of the matter in the papers," I answered. "You are Augustus Lowe – at least, that is how you styled yourself at the London and Counties Bank. The police have issued a warrant in that name, and blank warrants for your associates."

Mr. Lowe glanced at his companion, who shrugged, then he turned back to me. "You were an Army Doctor, you say?"

"I was, years ago in Afghanistan."

"You must have dealt with bullet wounds. You amputated limbs."

"As I said, many years ago. Since then, when I have been in general practice, I have dealt with coughs and sneezes, varicose veins, stomach complaints, and pregnancy. No, no, you must let me take him to the nearest hospital. They will have the facilities and expertise he needs."

"We will pay you well."

I sniffed "Money is not the issue. I have taken an oath of care, and I would treat this man if I could. But he needs a competent surgeon."

"What's the point?" The Negro man accepted a whisky from Mr. Lowe. "Without an arm, Benny's useless to us."

"No names!" cried Mr. Lowe.

The young man smiled a cold smile. "It's time we got to know each other, Doctor. I'm Dark Harry." He pulled a revolver from his belt. "Benny's no use to us now – he's a liability. As are you, Doctor Watson."

Holmes emerged from under the tarpaulin of the cab shelter by Trafalgar Square, closing the drawstrings of the leather sack. "Harker, known as 'Bear Harker', is our man, and well known as a bad lot. He's not been seen all week. Likely on a binge, they say, as he came into money recently. I've had no dealings with Harker. Have you, Inspector?"

"No, Mr. Holmes. Not by that name at least. He's the driver?"

Holmes nodded. "His stand is by the American Exchange. Like any London jarvey, he knows every nook and alley in the city. I'd wager the forgery gang hired him last week to ferry them from bank to bank, and again for the abduction." He led his companions into Trafalgar Square. "Gentlemen, take care with your notecases, watches, and handkerchiefs. Some of the best dippers in the realm operate within a hundred yards of here."

Sir Henry frowned.

"If you ever have need of a pickpocket, Doctor," Holmes continued as he leapt onto the plinth of Nelson's Column, "here is your employment exchange." He clapped his hands, held up a gold half-sovereign that glittered in the lamp light, and soon had a circle of excited street Arabs gathered about him. "You know Harker, the jarvey?" Holmes asked. The boys yelled their answers and jumped for the coin, and Holmes smiled at the cacophony. He held the coin higher. "This to the boy who finds Harker or his growler."

One boy, a tousle-headed, malodorous young rascal with a squint, held back while his peers scampered away. He waited until the other boys had disappeared along the pavement or among the cabs and carriages, before he braced Holmes, bold as brass. "Which, Harker is in the Coal Hole, same as always when he's got a few bob. He leaves his cab at the mews in Savoy Row."

Holmes called the four-wheeler. "Come, time is short, and we have much to do."

Inspector Lestrade and Sir Henry piled into the cab, and Holmes joined them, pulling the tousle-haired street Arab in after him.

"To the Coal Hole?" Lestrade asked.

"First we have a more urgent task in Burleigh Street, off the Strand."

The cab was parked outside the offices of *The Strand Magazine* for no more than ten minutes before Holmes came out at the run. Lestrade had kept hold of the boy's collar, trying not to breathe in his foetid aroma. "The Coal Hole," Holmes called to the driver.

"Mr. Newnes was most helpful, as I expected," Holmes said as he settled himself opposite Lestrade. He smiled. "My name on the cover of *The Strand* is worth an extra hundred-thousand in circulation. He is in telephone communication with the offices of most major publications, and the rest he will reach by express messenger. My ultimatum will be on the desk of every editor in London within a half-hour. The news of

106

the guard's death will still get out, but we have gained a little valuable time." Holmes turned to Sir Henry. "If you were treating a gunshot wound, what medicines or other materials would you employ?"

"By now the wound may be severely infected," Sir Henry mused, "Amputation might be necessary. In which case I would require the following: A saw, preferably a surgical saw, forceps, tongs, sutures, bromide solution, or better carbolic spray, phenol, scalpels, bandages, needles, and thread. And anaesthetic, of course."

Holmes slammed his fist into his palm. "Watson knows my methods. If he is forced or cajoled into treating the wounded man, he will recognise an opportunity to compile a long list of items with few and specialised manufacturers and agents. He will use that as a flag to alert me. Where can these instruments be obtained?"

"A doctor could get them from Surgeon's Hall," Sir Henry replied. "And any member of the public may purchase them from the manufacturers – mostly, as you'd expect, in the Midlands, or through specialist shops in London."

"Such as?"

"I'm afraid there are a dozen, usually in the streets near major hospitals."

"Very well. We need to narrow down the location. Ah, here we are."

The cab wheels ground to a halt against the kerb before the entrance to the Coal Hole public house, a few doors from the entrance to the Savoy Hotel. They jumped down and Holmes addressed the boy. "Tell Harker there's a top-hole passenger for Paddington Station waiting outside, all of a quiver, willing to pay double fare, in gold." The boy pursed his lips, and Holmes signalled to Lestrade to open the leather bag. After a lingering look at the contents, the boy smiled and disappeared into the public house.

"Doctor," Holmes said, addressing Sir Henry, "let me have your scarf for a moment. I don't know Harker, but he may know me, and judging by his nickname, he may be a difficult customer." He wrapped the scarf around his neck, covering the lower part of his face. "You will act the top-hole fare, and the inspector and I will stand to one side."

A bedraggled, heavy-built man in a battered, concertinaed stovepipe hat staggered out of the doors of the Coal Hole followed by the street Arab. The man looked around, and addressed Sir Henry. "Paddington, is it then?" he leered. "A hurry, is it?"

Holmes grabbed the driver by the arm, and he and the inspector hurtled him across the pavement, forcing him into the cab. Sir Henry climbed in after them.

Holmes pushed Harker to the floor between Sir Henry and the inspector and pressed his knee into his back. "I know about the fare you took to the London and Counties, Harker. The same men grabbed the gent outside Charing Cross Station. Who were they?"

"How should I know?" Harker cried, his voice muffled by his position and thick from drink. "It was a pick-up."

"No, no, Harker, they did not come upon you by happenstance. They knew you, and knew that you were open for every kind of mischief." Holmes drew his revolver from his overcoat pocket and pressed the barrel into Harker's temple. "I have no time for finesse. I will offer you a simple proposition. If you give me the names and an accurate description of the men who hired you for the London and Counties job, and the exact location where you picked them up and dropped them, I will let you go. One or more of them may escape my net and exact retribution upon you: Yes, there is a chance of that. But if you do not oblige me, I will shoot you with this revolver, loaded with .44 Boxer cartridges. You must therefore weigh a chance against a certainty. It may be a clean kill, it may not – " Holmes cocked the action with a loud click. "Inspector, kindly turn your back. I intend to murder this man."

"Excuse me for a moment," Lestrade said, patting his pockets. "I'm out of matches." He opened the cab door.

"Foreigners," Harker gasped, "Americans."

Holmes pulled Harker up and slammed him onto the bench beside him, and Lestrade softly closed the cab door and sat back in his seat.

"No need for violence, gents," Harker said, brushing at his clothes. "I met them in the Duke of Sussex in Lambeth, through a mate. They give me twenty pound to take 'em round the City, then another ten to dog a top-hole gent." He frowned at Sir Henry.

"Where did you drop them after the London and Counties last Friday?" Holmes asked.

"St. George's Circus. One of 'em was took poorly, and I had blood all over the seat." He described the leader of a gang of five, a bald man with half-moon glasses, and his companions, a young dark-skinned man with a fiery temper, a quiet, short man who had been wounded at the bank, and two or more local thugs.

A knock came at the window, and the street urchin pressed his face against the glass. At a nod from Holmes, Lestrade opened the door and threw the boy a couple of coins from the sack. Harker watched with a glint in his eyes. "They left a Gladstone bag in the cab when they went into the last bank." He smiled and gave the sack a meaningful look. "I had a quick gander while they was mucking about in there, and I saw some letters. From America, they was."

Holmes grabbed a handful of gold coins from the sack, and threw them to the floor.

"Addressed to *Nordstrom*, initials *J* and *N*." Harker scrabbled for the coins.

"Get out." Holmes opened the cab door, pushed the cabbie onto the pavement, and kicked out the remaining coins. "I hope you are a praying man, Harker, for I would advise you to petition Divine Providence that I find Doctor Watson well and hearty. If not, you shall hear from me."

He banged his fist on the cab roof. "The American Exchange."

"Have you watched your forger at work?" I asked Dark Harry.

"What's your point?" he answered. He tipped out the cylinder of his revolver and replaced a spent cartridge. "One bullet gone," he said with a grin, "and one copper down."

"Have you?" I sipped my whisky and tried to control my breathing and my racing heart.

"No."

"Then you don't know that your artist is left-handed, or perhaps double-handed."

Dark Harry narrowed his eyes. "How do you know? You're making it up to save your skin."

"Come and see." I put down my glass and led the way back to the bedroom.

Dark Harry stood by the bed, his handkerchief over his mouth, as I held up Benny's uninjured left arm and indicated his spatulate thumb, characteristic of the print compositor or, in this case, the forger. Ink was ingrained in his calloused finger ends, and ink stains extended up to and beyond his wrist. His right hand was soft, its bloated fingers unmarked. "Your engraving artist is left-handed."

"Will you amputate, Doctor?" Mr. Lowe asked from the doorway.

"If you will make no other effort to save the wretch's life, I will." I took a pencil and pad of notepaper from the sideboard and sat on the side of the bed, by the lamp. "I need some surgical equipment."

"We have Chloroform," Dark Harry said with another dangerous grin.

"I am very much aware of that. I will make a list of the other items I require."

"Where's your medical bag?" he asked.

"I did not have it with me when you attacked me. I was carrying my contribution to *The Strand Magazine*, the product of a week's creative endeavour, which I very much hope was not lost."

I handed the list to Mr. Lowe, and he frowned at it. "Where can we get this stuff?"

"The address of a medical instrument and supplies merchant is on the back. I strongly advise you to move with alacrity. Time is very short, and this man's life hangs in the balance."

Holmes leapt from the cab and pushed though the door of the American Exchange, one of the principal money exchanges and advice and service centres for tourists in London. A queue that looked to be mostly composed of foreign tourists wound from the doors to a long counter manned by clerks.

Holmes marched past the line, followed by Inspector Lestrade and Sir Henry, and he summoned a clerk to an empty place at the counter. "*Nordstrom*, initials *J. N.*, letters to be picked up." Holmes laid his pistol on the counter top. "Fetch."

The clerk frowned, his gaze flicking from the pistol to Holmes. "Are you Mr. Nordstrom, sir? I will need some identification – a passport, letter of recommendation or business card – " He tailed off as Holmes slammed his fist on the counter.

"I am interested in this man Nordstrom in one particular, and one only," Holmes said in a menacing tone. "If he knows where my friend is being held, then his life is worth that much and no more to me. Do not you *dare* to obstruct me." The clerk gaped wide-eyed at Holmes, who glared back at him, breathing deeply for a tense moment, before he smiled a jaguar smile and held out his hand to Lestrade. He received a handful of gold coins which he slid across the counter. The clerk's jaw dropped.

Lestrade pursed his lips. "I think I might take a little stroll."

He and Sir Henry were waiting by the cab when Holmes strode from the Exchange holding two letters. "Awaiting pick up."

Lestrade winced as Holmes tore open the first envelope and held the letter to the light of a street lamp. "Rubbish, from a purported wife." He ripped open the second. "From a business partner, more rubbish." He threw the letters onto the pavement. "We have no time for such nonsense." He held up the envelopes. "But here is something. His forwarding address is Conway's Hotel, in Lambeth, south of the river. That corresponds with what Harker admitted."

Sir Henry took the envelopes, picked up the letters, and peered at them. "This letter might be in code."

Lestrade scribbled on a telegram form. "I'll have the hotel checked."

"The gang will have flown the coop," Holmes said, looking up and down the Strand. The street was lit by a double line of streetlamps, bright shop windows, and the lamps of the carriages, omnibuses, and cabs that thronged the carriageway. "They cannot stay at an hotel, encumbered by the wounded man. No, they have rented alternative premises. Perhaps they already had a house where they'd set up their printing press." His eyes narrowed. "We need to focus – "

Holmes struck his forehead with his hand. "Of course. Watson spoke to me of the Army Surgeons' training centre at Netley, where he completed his military surgeon's qualification. He was provided with an instrument set before he set sail for India, which was lost in Afghanistan when he was wounded. The Army required reimbursement for the loss until I let a Queen's Counsel loose on them. Watson called the set a – let me think – a Davies' set. No, a *Down's* set."

"Down Brothers," said Sir Henry, "of St. Thomas's Street, London S.E. I know them well."

Holmes rubbed his hands together. "Watson will bait our trap." He glared at our four-wheeler cab. "We must make haste to be in our hide before the gang visit the shop." He scrutinised the line of cabs waiting outside the Exchange. "These cabs are all pulled by old nags. We need a fast carriage." He scanned the traffic passing along the Strand. "That one looks fresh."

Holmes darted into the road and grabbed the traces of a closed, four-wheel carriage with a coat of arms emblazoned on the door pulled by a magnificent pair of greys. The coachman wrenched at the reins and raised his whip. Holmes brandished his pistol. "This is a national emergency, and you and your equipage are requisitioned. I require you to drive to St Thomas's Street in the Borough, just by the hospital." He indicated Lestrade and then Sir Henry. "This person is a veteran officer of the law, and the other gentleman is a famous doctor." He looked up at the driver. "And I am a vexed man with a hair-trigger pistol."

He, Sir Henry, and Inspector Lestrade jumped aboard the coach, and it turned across the traffic and picked up speed.

Holmes settled on the Morocco leather bench on the left, and Sir Henry and Lestrade slumped down opposite him. An empty game bag and a monogrammed leather gun case lay on the bench beside them.

Holmes opened the gun case, handed one finely chased shotgun to Lestrade, and hefted the other. "Purdey hammerless .410's, the monogrammed property of the Duke of Holderness." He handed the other shotgun to Sir Henry with a bandolier of cartridges. "I shall stay with my pistol."

"I am no stranger to firearms or to stalking," Sir Henry said as he took the second gun and bandolier from Holmes. "I shot a poacher on my Highland estates two years ago at two-hundred yards, on the run and in flitting moonlight." He blinked at the inspector's set expression. "Using bird shot, naturally."

"What is your intention, Mr. Holmes?" Inspector Lestrade asked in a stiff tone.

"I will enter the surgical instruments shop and bribe the shopkeepers to hide me in a place where I can see the counter. When our man comes with his list, I shall emerge from my hide and – "

Inspector Lestrade and Sir Henry exchanged pitying glances and shook their heads. "No, no, Mr. Holmes," said Inspector Lestrade. "That will never do. What if the miscreants are watching the premises. Your face and your general demeanour are far too well-known – "

"What then?" Holmes cried. "We must have someone inside to spot the man with Watson's list of instruments and give us the signal to strike." He frowned. "You are known to them, Doctor, and the inspector is no stranger to the penny papers."

The carriage stopped, and the coachman called down that they were in St Thomas's Street. Sir Henry borrowed Inspector Lestrade's coat and grey scarf and Holmes's top hat, and Holmes handed him the leather bag of gold coins.

Sir Henry hefted the bag. "Good Lord, whom do you intend to bribe, the Lord Chancellor?" He opened the bag, took out two half-sovereigns and tossed the bag back. "That will be ample. We are south of the river, after all."

Less than a fifteen minutes later, Sir Henry had marked their quarry, a short man in a heavy, astrakhan-trimmed overcoat and wide-awake hat, and he sauntered behind him as he carried a heavy package from the surgical instrument shop. The man turned into a narrow street, then looked back for a moment, and Sir Henry had the sense to cross the road away from him and stroll towards the carriage, whistling a music hall tune.

The man stopped at a newsagent's for a moment, and looked carefully up and down the street before he set off again, crossing the road and hailing a hansom. Sir Henry instructed the driver to follow at a discreet distance and climbed into the carriage.

The journey was a short one. The hansom pulled up at the mouth of an alley halfway down the New Cut in Lambeth and the carriage stopped a few yards farther along, shielded by a furniture van. Inspector Lestrade jumped down and took up the surveillance, his face wrapped in Sir Henry's scarf. He slipped into the alley, and a moment later he reappeared and waved for the carriage to join him. "Third house on the right, with the scraggy garden in front and netted windows."

Holmes checked his pistol. "Sir Henry, you will join me in a frontal assault. Inspector, I suggest you work your way behind the premises and enter from the rear."

Sir Henry held his shotgun at half-port. "I will gladly take post with you, Mr. Holmes. I sniped a Rebel colonel at Appomattox Station in the American War. The Union Army advanced, and he was brought to my surgery tent where, unfortunately, he died under my knife."

Lestrade crooked his shotgun over his arm and addressed Holmes. "Is that pistol loaded, sir?"

"With .44 Boxer cartridges."

"Might I strongly represent to you that you release the action? We don't want anything going off at half- or even full-cock, now do we, Mr. Holmes?" Inspector Lestrade mopped his brow with his handkerchief, turned, and slipped along the fence beside the house.

I inspected the instruments and the bottles of chemicals brought by Mr. Lowe, then I rolled up my sleeves and addressed Dark Harry. "Fetch hot water, clean towels, and the Chloroform."

I laid out my scalpel, saw, and forceps on a disinfectant soaked towel on the pillow next to my patient, together with ligatures, needles and thread, and Chloroform. I mixed a strong disinfectant solution, filled the glass barrel of a spray device, and handed Dark Harry a rubber bulb of phenol solution. "Soak my hands and the wound, then the patient's skin up to the shoulder," I ordered. I took a smaller syringe and injected the solution directly into the wound. Dark Harry seemed to blanch to a grey colour, and he dropped the spray on the bed and retreated to the door of the bedroom.

"Middleton Goldsmith, a surgeon in the Union Army during the American Civil War, meticulously studied gangrene," I mused as I stropped my scalpel on a patch of chamois. "He developed a revolutionary treatment using debridement and topical and injected bromide solutions to reduce the incidence and virulence of what he called 'poisoned miasma'. That is the method I learned at the British Army training centre at Netley and used in the field before Lister revolutionised our understanding of disease agents."

I dipped the scalpel in phenol solution. "Come here and make yourself useful," I said to Dark Harry. "Keep the patient down and immobilise his good arm."

Dark Harry eyed my scalpel warily. "Don't try no funny business with the toothpick, eh?"

"The only comedian in the room is you," I replied.

He fingered his pistol. "Don't push me – there are other doctors."

113

"Not immediately to hand."

Dark Harry laid his arm across Benny's chest and glared at me.

"Take it easy," Mr. Lowe told him from the doorway. "Let's not do anything stupid. You were lucky with the bank guard. The papers say he's recovering. Don't risk your neck."

"Keep a firm hold," I instructed Dark Harry. "If he jerks at the wrong moment, I might sever an artery."

Dark Harry smiled a cold smile. "That would be a pity, Doctor, both for us and for you."

I paused, my scalpel raised. "I should say before we start that if you gentlemen do intend to remunerate me for my work, my fee is one hundred guineas. You will understand that in the circumstances, I would prefer gold to a printed cheque."

I made the first incision in the flesh above the elbow, ligating the limb, transecting the flesh and tying the blood vessels with ligatures. When the bone was clear, I picked up the saw and cut through the humerus, the grind of bone under my saw provoking a flood of unhappy recollections of my days with the Berkshire Regiment in Afghanistan. I removed the arm and placed it on the bed out of the way as I filed the rough edges of bone smooth and folded the first two flaps of upper-arm skin together. "Pass me the needle and thread."

Dark Harry's face glistened with sweat, and his eyes were closed. I reached for the needle and paused as gunshots echoed from downstairs. I turned to Dark Harry. "Drop your weapon. Those shots herald the arrival of Mr. Sherlock Holmes, who will not hesitate to shoot you down if you defy him."

He hesitated, backing from the bed and raising his pistol.

"Do you want to be in the dock for forgery, or kidnapping and murder? The choice is yours."

Dark Harry blinked down at the severed arm on the coverlet and dry-retched. He wiped his face with his sleeve and lowered his gun as the door opened.

"There you are at last," I said, "and with Inspector Lestrade, I see. Holmes, would you mind pressing your thumb on this skin flap while I rethread my needle? And Inspector, you might relieve this gentleman of his pistol."

Ten minutes later, I patted the stump and leaned back, pleased with my efforts. I smiled at Holmes. "What a cacophony of gunshots. I thought we were under attack by the Brigade of Guards."

"The Canary Trainer papers?" I asked as I dried my hands with a towel and I helped myself to a whisky in the sitting room downstairs.

114

Holmes smiled. "Mostly lost, I'm afraid. We might put that down to benign providence, and leave Wilson and his canaries for our sere and yellow years."

"You may be right." I slumped onto a sofa and returned Holmes's smile. "Amputation is not quite like riding a bicycle, but it is a simple enough procedure, not easily forgotten, and I am owed a hundred guineas. Not bad for an afternoon's work. We can pay our arrears, wipe the eye of the coal agent, and treat ourselves to Amati's for supper tonight."

Inspector Lestrade and a gentleman with a shotgun crooked over his arm joined us, prodding the forgers and the two buckshot-peppered bruisers before them. I recognised Sir Henry Ballantyne. "The amputation went quite smoothly," I said, after the introductions. "I have hopes that my patient will do very well."

Sir Henry smiled. "Unlike some of my more conservative colleagues, Doctor, I always consider the survival of the patient one of the hallmarks of a successful surgical procedure, but I'm afraid in this case, the patient's existence on this earth may not be prolonged."

"The guard died," I murmured to myself. I frowned at Mr. Lowe and Dark Harry. My captors faced The Rope.

"All clear," said Inspector Lestrade, "there's just the four of them, plus the invalid. I sent the carriage driver to fetch a police van. Their printing press is in the basement."

"How did you find me?" I asked as Holmes and I led our party outside, preceded by our prisoners carrying the wounded forger on a door.

"Oh, it was a perfectly straightforward case," Holmes answered, "solved by strict adherence to the tenets of deduction and logical synthesis." He sniffed. "Your abduction was a simple, secondary element." He smiled and took my arm. "I am so glad you are safe, old friend. Mrs. Hudson and Billy were becoming a little anxious."

Holmes weighed in his hand a heavy leather bag that clinked agreeably. "We might think of the roast at Simpson's." He turned to our companions. "A table for four, if you gentlemen are free?"

A Case of Embezzlement
by Steven Ehrman

Chapter I

It was a cool autumn morning. I was reading one of the many daily newspapers to which Holmes subscribes. He was languidly smoking in his chair, seemingly lost in thought. Suddenly, there was a sharp knock at the door to our digs, followed by the entrance of our page-boy. He handed a note to Holmes and stood by, apparently waiting for an answer. Holmes quickly scanned the message. He then scrawled a return and gave it to the lad who left with a bow. I set my paper to one side and turned to Holmes.

"It would seem, Doctor, that we can expect a visit from Inspector Hopkins tomorrow morning," said Holmes in answer to my unspoken question.

"Does the Good Inspector say what it is he wishes of you?"

"He does. We are about to meet Mr. Gordon Whitworth. Are you familiar with the case, Watson?"

"It would be difficult to remain ignorant of it," I replied. "There is the matter of a missing twenty-thousand pounds."

"I see that you have indeed followed the publicity that Mr. Whitworth has generated. Will you tell me the particulars as you understand them?"

"Holmes, surely you have followed the events as closely as I."

"True, but hearing the facts of the case through the words of another can be quite illuminating at times."

"Very well," said I, concentrating my mind and attempting to recall all that I had read. "It would seem that Gordon Whitworth, late of the Capital and Counties Bank, was caught executing a plot to embezzle a large sum of money from his employers. When arrested, he held himself mute, admitting nothing. No money was found, and Scotland Yard is apparently at a loss to explain what happened to the stolen sum.

"Several of the papers have been somewhat sympathetic to Mr. Whitworth. He had a splendid career in the army and has fought gallantly for the Crown across several continents. I must admit, Holmes, that I do not understand how a man with a record such as this could be guilty of such a foul crime as embezzlement. Could he be innocent?"

"That hardly seems likely, Doctor. The papers outlining the scheme were found on his desk and written in his hand. It would seem that the bank became aware of the incident by mere happenstance. Some important papers were to have been forwarded by Whitworth to the branch president that morning. When they did not arrive by the deadline, an assistant was sent to retrieve them. As Whitworth was at lunch during that time, the assistant looked for them. The papers were on top of the man's desk, but the assistant was startled to find the plans for the crime under them, and that the crime had been perpetrated that very morning. The authorities were notified, and Mr. Whitworth was put under watch by Scotland Yard."

"That is one thing I have failed to understand. Why was the man not arrested at once?"

"The plot was apparently a very clever and involved one. It consisted, as I understand it, of creating false accounts and shifting monies to them. Whitworth, of course, came into possession of the money while it appeared all the while to still be under the bank's control. It would seem that the bank officials were not entirely convinced that the money was gone at all. Only after two days of auditing the books was the crime, and the amount of money, confirmed. At that point, Mr. Whitworth became acquainted with our law enforcement. It would seem to have been a very clever plan."

"And yet he was exposed and caught, Holmes," I observed.

"That has not escaped my attention," said he. He pondered for a few moments with his chin in his hand. "Have you read whether Gordon Whitworth has any issue?"

"One daughter. I saw mention of her in an early article about the crime. She is married to a minor French Count and has not answered any questions posed to her by reporters."

"And Whitworth was arrested at a Channel port with baggage," said Holmes.

"True, but he had not purchased nor inquired about a ticket. He claimed to be on a weekend holiday."

At that we both lapsed into silence for some time. Holmes presently sprang from his chair and began pacing. He was soon out the door, saying only that he had affairs to attend to. This behavior was so typical of the man that I had long since stopped being surprised by his disappearances. This one lasted for the entirety of the day, and I retired without him returning home.

When morning came, Holmes arrived at our dining table as usual. I asked if yesterday's jaunt had proven productive, but he merely shrugged in answer. I made no further attempt to press him on matters he clearly did not wish to share with me.

Inspector Hopkins arrived at eleven o'clock, accompanied by two sergeants, a man in handcuffs that I took to be Gordon Whitworth, and an officious looking man introduced as Charles Leeds, who was a representative of Capital and Counties Bank. Gordon Whitworth's face was devoid of emotion. After all were seated, Inspector Hopkins began proceedings.

"Mr. Holmes," he began, "we have arrived at an impasse in this matter and I have come to seek your counsel. Shall I tell you what we know at present?"

"Has Mr. Whitworth made a statement as of yet?" asked Holmes.

"He has not, sir," said Hopkins.

"Then a brief summation, Inspector," said Holmes. "It is possible that the newspapers have missed something of importance."

Hopkins cleared his throat and gave a very straightforward account of the case to date. There was little in it that we had not read before and the evidence seemed damning. As he finished, Hopkins looked to Holmes, waiting for the great detective to speak.

"Why have you come here?" asked Holmes finally.

"Why, as I – as I said, sir," he stammered. "I wished your counsel."

"It is obvious to a child that there is ample evidence to convict," said Holmes. "Put it before twelve Englishmen and be done with it."

Inspector Hopkins seemed a bit crestfallen and said nothing. However, the bank official sprang to his feet.

"But what of our money?" he demanded in a shrill voice. "We have been defrauded!"

"And we have a court system that punishes wrongdoers," said Holmes mildly. "The fact that Mr. Whitworth has concealed his ill-gotten gains will engender a heavy sentence, I am sure."

Charles Leeds turned to Inspector Hopkins with disdain.

"I thought you said this man could help us!"

"Calm yourself, sir," said the inspector. He turned to Holmes. "Surely, you know we came for your help in finding the money."

"I do realize that, Inspector," said Holmes with a bit of a smile. "I merely wished it baldly stated. I therefore propose a solution. Mr. Whitworth must have had several hours from the time the police were called in and before he was put under surveillance to secrete the cash somewhere. I propose that he will tell you where he has hidden the money and the bank will promise not to prosecute."

To my great surprise, Mr. Whitworth and Mr. Leeds both shouted, "Never!" in unison.

Gordon Whitworth added nothing else and returned to his stoic demeanor. Mr. Leeds, however, had more to say.

"Speaking for the bank, we categorically reject such an offer. It would set a terrible precedent. Our employees would know that they could steal at will and if caught, simply return the money to avoid a jail sentence."

"I must say that I understand the bank's position, Mr. Leeds," said Holmes. "It is entirely logical. What I am curious about is why you rejected such a proposition so vehemently, Mr. Whitworth?"

"I have my reasons," said the prisoner.

"Of that I am certain," said Holmes. "I call upon you to unburden yourself. I can assure you that I will listen with an open mind. I can tell you that I have looked into your background as a soldier and I have been impressed with your service to the country. My friend, Dr. Watson, is a former soldier himself, and we both find this crime completely out of character for a man such as yourself."

Gordon studied Holmes for some minutes and I also came under his gaze.

"Very well, Mr. Holmes," he said. "You have convinced me. I will tell you my tale."

Chapter II

I must admit that I was surprised that Gordon Whitworth had chosen to speak to us after Holmes's rather mild cajoling, but my friend could be quite persuasive. In any case, I leaned forward, eager to hear his story.

"It is a tale long in the making," he began. "This incident – "

"Crime!" cried Mr. Leeds in interruption.

"Really, Mr. Leeds, we will make no progress with such dramatics."

Leeds glowered, but said no more for the time being.

"Proceed, sir," said Holmes.

"Thank you, Mr. Holmes. Thirty years ago, when I was ten, my family was a member of the landed gentry. My father, never a good man of business, squandered much of his inheritance, but we needed nothing more than we had. I dreamed of Eton, followed by Oxford. My father came to worry that we would need greater sums in the future and he brooded on his losses.

"One day, he was approached by agents of the bank Mr. Leeds represents and offered the opportunity to invest in timber land in Canada. The promised returns were robust, and the bank assured my father that they were investing as well. Father invested through them. Twenty-thousand pounds was needed, and that was borrowed against the estate.

The stock was purchased, but the returns never arrived. As the months slipped away, Father became frantic. Word finally arrived that the company in which he had invested through Capital and Counties was a fraud. Clear title to the lands had never been purchased. The bank must have known that investment was shaky."

"Why is that, Mr. Whitworth?" asked Holmes.

"Because they sold their shares before the fraud became public knowledge."

"A mere coincidence," said Mr. Leeds. "A concern as large as ours is constantly adjusting our capital."

"You sued of course," said Holmes.

"We did, sir, but our foes were too slippery, and too well versed in covering their tracks."

I saw Leeds tense, but he remained silent.

"Their crime knocked my father from society to that of a workman. These monsters stole my birth right. Now, my good father never uttered a word of shame at his new station. He simply went about to attempt to rebuild our fortune through his labor and force of will, but the backbreaking work caused him to die years before his time.

"Any chance of Eton and Oxford was now forever gone. With those dreams shattered, I resolved to serve in the army when I came of age and perhaps rise through the ranks. Those were happy but dangerous years. I fought for the Crown on three continents, until I mustered out two years ago. My wife had passed away while I was away, but I have a fine daughter and she is well."

"I know that," said Holmes in a detached tone. "She seems to be of more than moderate means. I have looked into her finances. She recently made an investment in a steel mill in the United States and is, by all accounts, a lady of intelligence."

"You had no right to bring my daughter into this affair," said Whitworth with controlled anger.

"I apologize for your distress," said Holmes. "I merely wish to make plain that your daughter could have provided you with funds if you needed them."

"I did not want her money!" said Gordon Whitworth at a near shout. "I wanted the money that was stolen from me. I hated those bankers."

"I see," Holmes said. "However, in spite of your hatred of bankers, you became one yourself."

"A simple clerk, sir, but it gave me the opportunity to slake my vengeance."

"But you were caught, and the outrage you describe is unredressed as a consequence."

120

"Such are the fortunes of war, Mr. Holmes."

"*C'est la guerre,* sir?"

"If you wish," replied the prisoner.

"Please complete your tale from after you left the army," said Holmes.

"Very well. Once I was a civilian again, I applied for a position at the Capital and Counties Bank. I used my real name, but the crime they committed against my family was so long in the past that they never gave a thought to who I actually was. I took my time and let an entire year pass. I finally carried my plan to fruition, but was brought down by mistake on my part, of which I am certain you are aware. I left some incriminating papers on my desk and they were discovered. I could tell right away that the atmosphere at the bank had changed, and I became aware that I was under watch by the police. I made a dash out of London and was arrested before I could make my way out of the country."

"Where were you going to go?" I asked.

"I am not certain, Doctor. South America perhaps, but I honestly had no set destination in mind."

"I'll tell you where you are going. You'll go to prison for a long term, and when you are released, we will be waiting," said Mr. Leeds. "You'll spend not a farthing of the stolen funds. We will hound you until your death!"

"That is quite theatrical, but I doubt it will come to that," said Holmes. "Now, Mr. Whitworth, you say that you were attempting to leave the country when you were arrested."

"That is so, Mr. Holmes," replied the man. "I could feel the police closing in on me, and had hoped to make a dash for it."

"Then you must have had the money on your person."

"What do you mean, Holmes?" asked I.

"Simply this, Doctor. If Mr. Whitworth was planning his exit from England, then surely he would take the money with him. His mail has been watched, so he would have to have it with him if he were to enjoy his plunder."

"Those were my thoughts as well, Mr. Holmes," said Inspector Hopkins, "but he and his baggage have been thoroughly searched. It is impossible that he has concealed it."

"You surprise me, Hopkins. You know well my axiom that, when all other possibilities are eliminated, that which remains, however improbable, must be the truth."

"I do know that, sir. That is why I have sought your expertise."

Holmes was not above enjoying flattery, though he would likely deny it, and I saw that the words Hopkins spoke had their intended impact.

"I take it that you have had the foresight to bring along all the effects that Mr. Whitworth was carrying with him."

Hopkins nodded to one of the sergeants and he brought over two bags. I brought a small table and sat it before Holmes. The items in them were removed and put before him.

"I have made a list, sir," said Inspector Hopkins.

Holmes examined the list and then handed it to me. It contained the following:

> *A stamped envelope*
> *One box of brass buttons*
> *Matches*
> *One jewelry box with key*
> *Large Bible*
> *Wallet with eleven pounds*
> *Playing cards*
> *Fishing reel with no rod*

Holmes examined the list and the items for some minutes before he spoke. The items seemed very ordinary to me, if a bit eclectic. He sent for our page-boy and dashed off a quick message for him to carry.

"I see that the envelope has been torn open," said Holmes finally, turning his attention back to the matter at hand.

"Yes, sir," Hopkins said. "I was obliged to open it. There was only a simple poem. It is not in the prisoner's hand. He, of course, has given us no clue as to who wrote it!"

Holmes barely glanced at the letter before handing it to me. It was mere piece of doggerel and I saw no connection to the case.

"How did this come into your possession, Mr. Whitworth?" asked Holmes holding the envelope in his hand. "It is neither addressed to you, nor apparently written by you."

Gordon Whitworth gave no answer.

"It is addressed to a James Smith at the Harrington Hotel in Liverpool, Holmes," said I. "Perhaps he can shed some light on this matter. I suggest we make inquiries there."

"We have already done so, Doctor," said Inspector Hopkins. "The Harrington Hotel has no such resident. The manager of the establishment tells us he often receives mail for people not actually at the hotel at the

122

moment. It is their policy to hold letters for several weeks in case the addressee checks in."

"The letter has not even been postmarked," observed Holmes.

"Is that important?" I asked.

"If the letter was never postmarked, then it was never sent, and since it is not in Mr. Whitworth's hand, someone else wrote it," said Holmes. "The question becomes where *did* the letter come from, and who wrote the poem. Read it aloud please, Watson."

I cleared my throat and began:

> *My uncle was almost a tramp.*
> *His cellar was always quite damp.*
> *He once had a horse,*
> *that was well-loved, of course.*
> *Of his bit he would thoroughly clamp.*

"Inspector, must we continue to listen to this?" asked Charles Leeds. "We are making no progress. I say we lock this thief up until he tells us what he knows!"

"Patience, sir," said Holmes mildly. "I believe we can come to a satisfactory conclusion."

"I am still against any amnesty in return for the stolen money," said Mr. Leeds.

"Of course," said Holmes with a slight smile. "I have realized the logic of the bank's position from the beginning. Any fool would. No, I mean I believe that with simple reasoning, we can solve this little mystery."

"Do you really mean it, Mr. Holmes?" asked the inspector. "I knew you were the man to consult."

"Holmes, do you mean to say that one or more of these items on the table is worth twenty-thousand pounds?" I asked with skepticism.

Holmes did not reply and began to make a thorough examination of each item. He employed his magnifying lens on most of them. This went on for a full twenty minutes. I could see that the patience of Charles Leeds was growing thin, and even Inspector Hopkins glanced more than once at his pocket watch. At one point, Holmes carried the envelope and the letter over to his desk. He rummaged about the drawers until he found what he was seeking. It was a jeweler's glass, and he closely examined the two pieces of evidence. This went on for a short while. Finally he put both items in his jacket pocket and returned to his seat, bringing a candle back with him.

"Gentlemen, I believe that I have made a discovery," he said.

"I hope it is one you are willing to share with us," said I.

"I have no reticence in doing so, Doctor. I'm convinced that both the letter with the poem and the envelope contain a message written in invisible ink."

"What?" exclaimed Gordon Whitworth.

He looked around the room in embarrassment and lapsed back into silence.

"Is there something you wish to share with us, sir?" asked Holmes.

The man shook his head no, but he kept his eyes locked onto Holmes. For the first time, he seemed a bit uncertain, even apprehensive.

"Very well then. We will proceed," said Holmes.

"Mr. Holmes, if there is some type of invisible writing on these items, how will we read the message?" asked Hopkins.

"It is quite easily done, Inspector. I merely need to apply a flame to the surface of the paper. The heat will react with the fluid and it will become visible."

"Fascinating," murmured Charles Leeds as he leaned forward to watch Holmes more closely.

My friend brought the letter forth, lit the candle, and began to slowly apply the heat from the flame to it. He first began holding the paper well above the candle and then gradually lowering it. I began to faintly smell burning parchment and a wisp of smoke appeared.

"Take care, Holmes," I said. "You are on the verge of setting it afire."

"Have no fear, Doctor. I am well aware of what I am doing," said he as he ran the letter back and forth across the flame."

I saw no hidden writing appear, and with a grim shrug Holmes withdrew the letter from the flame.

"Nothing to see here, but we are not yet defeated.

He next took hold of the envelope and proceeded in the same manner. It too began to smoke lightly and suddenly, before I could cry out a warning, it exploded in flames and fell to ashes in Holmes's hand.

Chapter III

There was a moment of stunned silence and then the prisoner made an anguished cry. "You ignorant fool!" shrieked Gordon Whitworth. "You've ruined everything!"

He lunged at Holmes, but was held back by the sergeants.

"Holmes, any message, if there was one, is now destroyed," said I. "What will you do?"

"Why, drink Mrs. Hudson's tea, of course," he replied.

At just that moment, the door opened and the lady herself came in, carrying a tray with a steaming pot and a single cup.

"Thank you, Mrs. Hudson," said Holmes. "I will pour for myself."

With a nod she quickly left the room.

"It is a bit early for tea, isn't it?" I asked.

"I asked for it to be brought up at exactly this moment, Doctor. That was what I wrote in the note that I gave to Billy."

Hopkins and Leeds exchanged a glance, and I saw doubt cross the face of the inspector.

"Now," began Holmes, speaking as though from a rostrum, "I call your attention the reaction of Mr. Whitworth when the envelope was destroyed. What did his emotional outburst convey?"

I was fogged, but Inspector Hopkins broke into a broad smile.

"Of course, Mr. Holmes," he said. "The envelope was obviously very important to him. It was a clue to the location of the money."

"Not quite, Inspector," said Holmes. "That it was important to Mr. Whitworth is indeed obvious, but it was not a map to locate the missing funds."

"Then what, Holmes?" I asked.

"We will never know now because you have foolishly burned it," said Charles Leeds.

"Have you heard of Mr. George Alfred Cooke?" Holmes asked.

"The famous illusionist, Holmes?"

"The very one, Doctor. I handled a trifling matter for him some years ago. In addition to a handsome fee, he repaid me by teaching me several tricks of his trade that I have found very handy in my work. Among those small illusions that he demonstrated to me was the ability to palm items. The envelope is quite undamaged."

As he spoke, he drew the original envelope from his sleeve.

"Holmes, that was a magnificent performance!" I exclaimed. "You fooled us all completely."

"You speak for me, Dr. Watson," Inspector Hopkins.

Even Mr. Leeds seemed to have become totally dumbfounded. What Gordon Whitworth felt I could not see, as his face had become an emotionless blank.

"But what does the envelope contain that makes it so valuable?" I asked. "Is it an invisible message after all?"

"Not quite," said he. "Ah, but I must not let my tea get cold."

At those words, Holmes moved the still steaming pot in front of him, but instead of pouring, he placed the corner of the envelope over the spout. Inside of fifteen seconds, he laid the envelope on the table and gently removed the stamp – followed by another underneath it.

"There you are, gentlemen. This is where the twenty-thousand pounds has been hidden."

We were all taken aback at this new development.

"My goodness, Holmes. Is that the King George Stamp?" I asked in wonderment. I knew it to be quite valuable.

"I've lost everything," said Gordon Whitworth in anguish.

"Can a single stamp actually be of such value, Mr. Holmes?" asked Charles Leeds.

"Indeed so, sir. I have written a slight monograph on the subject. The King George Stamp was produced, but never distributed. Most were destroyed. The few remaining are were worth thousands. Where did you obtain this, Mr. Whitworth? Only a complete confession can be of any good to you now."

For a moment, I thought the man might remain mute and take his secrets to prison with him, but he let out a long breath and began to speak.

"Very well, Mr. Holmes. You have found me out, and you may as well have the entire tale. The day that my plans were discovered, I had already taken the money. I was carrying it on my person when I realized that I might be arrested at any moment. I had grown increasingly anxious over the previous weeks. I imagined that eyes were upon me at all times. It was then that I thought to convert the money into something else. An old friend from my army days had once told me about a gin shop in Swan Lane called The Black Stag Tavern."

"That is a notorious criminal den," said Holmes.

"That it is, sir, but that is just what I needed. I quickly made my way there in search of I knew not what. I made myself known to the proprietor and he set me down in a quiet booth. Within minutes, a man sat across from me. It was very dark and I could barely make out his features. He was a tall, bearded man with a hat drawn down low to cover his eyes. We parried a bit, and I eventually told him I was looking to trade a large amount of money for something small of equal value. He left the table, went through a side door, and returned with the stamp you see before you."

"And you never learned the man's name," said Holmes.

"That's right, sir. The Black Stag is not the sort of place where names are exchanged. I know something of stamps. My father was a collector, and in my travels during my army days, I made it a point to seek out rare stamps among the locals. I made some money in a small way. As soon as I saw the King George Stamp, I knew that I had found a way to carry the money on my person without it being detected. At least until now," he said with a rueful smile.

"But how did you know, Holmes?" I asked. "It is obvious that you were already certain that the envelope held the treasure."

"It was the poem, Doctor."

"That piece of doggerel?" asked Inspector Hopkins. "It makes no mention of any stamp."

"That is true, but three lines from a five line poem rhyme with stamp."

"That is rather thin gruel, Holmes," said I.

"I will not argue that, Doctor. That is why I conducted my small illusion. It certainly told any observant person," he shot a glance at the inspector, "that there was something of value contained by the envelope. What else but a rare stamp carefully covered by a common stamp? As you can see it, had the desired effect."

"But Holmes? Who was this James Smith, and who wrote the poem?" I asked "Remember, the poem is not in Mr. Whitworth's hand."

"There was no James Smith, Watson. That is an invention of Mr. Whitworth. He never intended to post the letter. And the gentleman is certainly intelligent enough to disguise his writing by using his left hand. Is that correct, sir?"

"You are too clever by half, Mr. Holmes," said Gordon Whitworth. "It happened just as you say."

"But why the odd collection in your baggage, and why was the poem written at all?" I asked.

"It was simply to create confusion, Doctor. I thought my ruse would hold up to any search. Of course I hadn't counted on Sherlock Holmes. I thought it just possible that I could brazen my way through if I was arrested. Without the money, I had hoped the case against me might collapse."

"I can assure you that was a false hope," said Holmes.

"In any case, it is another triumph for you, Mr. Holmes," said Hopkins. "I knew coming to you was the correct course. Wouldn't you say so, Mr. Leeds?"

"Without reservation," said the bank official. "Mr. Holmes, I withdraw my intemperate words from earlier and apologize."

"No apology is necessary, sir," replied Holmes in a distracted tone. He was scrutinizing the stamp with his magnifying glass. "And perhaps you should prepare yourself for a jolt. The stamp is a fake."

There was a moment of stillness, and then the room erupted with everyone speaking at once. Holmes held up a hand to halt the cacophony of angry voices. However, Gordon Whitworth would not be denied.

"I do not know why you are expounding this lie, but I told you I know something of stamps. This one is genuine."

"It is a cunning reproduction, but I have already noted several discrepancies in the background," said Holmes. "I am certain that Mr. Leeds and the bank will wish it to be examined by experts of their choosing, but it is a forgery. I am afraid that the money is gone for good."

"Not quite, Mr. Holmes," said Hopkins. "We still have a description of the man, and we know where the transaction took place."

"I believe you will find the denizens of The Black Stag to be most unhelpful in any Scotland Yard investigation, Inspector," said Holmes. "In addition, the description of the seller is so vague as to be useless.

"I suppose you are right, sir, but we will make the effort nevertheless."

"I, for one, applaud your devotion to duty, Inspector," said Holmes.

Charles Leeds had an expression of utter desolation on his face.

"Twenty-thousand pounds gone," he muttered. "The directors will never understand."

"I am certain that you will be able to make them understand, Mr. Leeds," said Holmes with little charity. He turned to Whitworth. "Have you anything to say for yourself, sir?"

"Only that it seems that I am as unschooled in the arts of finance as my father to be swindled as I have been," he said. "My only happiness is in knowing that the bank has lost the money as well. I consider myself satisfied."

"But you will still be tried and likely convicted for embezzlement," said Holmes. "In fact, your own account this day will make that conviction a near certainty."

"That's correct, Mr. Whitworth," said Hopkins. "You were warned that your statements will be given as evidence."

"I am prepared for what is to come," said Gordon Whitworth firmly.

He squared his shoulders and came to parade ground attention. Once again, I felt a kinship to this former soldier. To my surprise Holmes rose and shook the man's hand.

"Good luck to, sir. I remember the scandal that felled your family and, as I recall, many other good English families. It is a shame that the guilty parties were not called to account."

At this speech, I saw a grimace cross the face of Charles Leeds. There was little else to be said, and our visitors departed leaving Holmes and myself alone.

Chapter IV

128

"I do not believe that there has ever been a sadder ending to case before this," said I. "Tell me, Holmes. What is your personal opinion of Gordon Whitworth?"

Holmes was in his chair and lit a pipe before answering.

"He is a very clever man, Doctor."

"How can you say that? He was caught embezzling, and then was fleeced out of his booty by a counterfeit stamp. I should say that a clever man would have done much better."

"He was not fleeced, Watson."

"How can you say that?" I asked. "Then where is the money?"

"The daughter has it, of course."

"The daughter? I don't understand this at all."

"You will recall that I mentioned to Mr. Whitworth that I had discovered that his daughter had recently made an investment in an American steel mill. The investment came to twenty-thousand pounds exactly."

"How would the daughter have received the money? Gordon Whitworth's mail has been watched?"

"He has been watched since the discovery of the theft. He is an intelligent man. He actually stole the money much earlier and sent it out of the country. As I said, the man arranged it all quite cleverly."

My head was spinning at this point.

"Half-a-moment, Holmes. If he took the money earlier, then why did he wait until the theft was discovered to make his way out of the country? He was caught so easily."

"Being caught was always part of the plan. He will now be tried, but he will be a sympathetic defendant. The bank broke his family, now he is penniless again, and he has served the empire with gallantry as a soldier. He will do little prison time, I judge less than a year, and the authorities will not look to recover the money because they believe it to be lost."

"Couldn't he have accomplished the same outcome if he had simply buried the money and refused to tell where it was? He still could have recovered it after his release from prison."

"There are two reasons he did not do as you describe. Firstly, he would not have been a sympathetic defendant. He would be simply one more unrepentant criminal. Secondly, you heard Mr. Leeds. If Whitworth had gone to prison with the sum still missing, they would have hounded him upon his release. Whitworth could never have enjoyed his money. This way, everyone believes the money to be gone. Once he wins freedom, I expect he will travel to the United States and live a very comfortable, obscure life."

"But how did he manage to find a counterfeit stamp on such short notice? It is a miracle that he happened upon one."

"You forget again, Doctor, that he had years to put this plot into operation. At some point, he acquired the stamp. Overseas most likely, during his time as a soldier. Oftentimes, a man telling an elaborate lie will tell some parts of the truth. Remember, Mr. Whitworth said that he dabbled in rare stamps during his time abroad. When he came across the fake King George Stamp, he shrewdly realized he could use it in his plan to avenge his family tragedy."

"When did you first suspect that the money had already been spirited out of the country?" I asked.

"As soon as I my inquiries into the daughter found that large, recent investment, I knew the money was gone, but I was not certain of the entire scheme until I saw his response to the envelope seemingly being burned. His reaction was not at all of a man who had lost twenty-thousand pounds. Rather, it was what one might expect from a man whose elaborate plan has gone awry. Indeed, he quite realized that he might have given himself away because after that outburst, he relapsed into silence to attempt to think of the best way forward. He was greatly relieved, of course, when I produced the actual envelope."

"Holmes, if all this true, are you saying that you actually approve of this crime?"

"*Approve* is perhaps too strong a word, Doctor," he said, "but my sympathies are decidedly *not* with the bank. I had no client, and therefore was free to follow my conscience, which I have done."

"So you will have nothing further to do with the case."

"On the contrary, Doctor. I believe I will contact one or two newspapermen and allow an interview on this matter."

"To what possible end?" I asked.

"Why, to emphasize that Gordon Whitworth was a man merely attempting to return to his family that which was stolen from them."

"What you are saying is you wish to generate sympathetic coverage of the case."

"Precisely, Watson," said Holmes. "Several of the newspapers already seem inclined to highlight that aspect. I believe young Webster of *The Times* would be just the man for the job."

"I still wonder at the eclectic collection Whitworth was carrying on his person."

"He simply did not want the unearthing of the fake stamp to be so simple as to arouse suspicion. He designed his plot to be difficult to solve."

"In other words, since it required the great mind of Sherlock Holmes to crack the mystery, no further questions would be asked."

"Please, Doctor. My modesty."

The Adventure of the
Vanishing Diplomat
by Greg Hatcher

"**M**r. Holmes, you are my last and only hope."

The slender young man that had just uttered those words had identified himself as Horatio Bellwether, an undersecretary in the Foreign Office. Visitors to our Baker Street lodgings had uttered that phrase innumerable times during my years sharing rooms with Sherlock Holmes, and I occasionally thought that, though he would be averse to admitting such out loud, my friend rather relished hearing his name invoked as a last hope, for that was invariably the overture to a new case that would challenge his faculties to the utmost. Holmes was fond of pointing out that he had invented his profession, that of consulting detective, and as such his clientele presented him with problems that were by their very nature too abstruse, or upon occasion too sensitive, for the London police to handle with traditional methods. More often than not, their cases possessed both qualities. I would have wagered that young Bellwether had brought Holmes one of those.

Bellwether's agitation had been apparent from the moment that Mrs. Hudson had ushered him in to our sitting-room in Baker Street, and her offer of tea and biscuits went unheeded. Holmes smiled at the trembling figure sitting bolt-upright on the divan. "Please do take some tea, Mr. Bellwether, and compose yourself. Then you can better explain the difficulty that has befallen you, and how it involves my brother Mycroft."

I would not have thought it possible, but the spindly figure managed to straighten even further, his expression one of shock. "But I have said nothing yet! How – "

"Tut! Your mouth may not have spoken, but your clothing and attitude speak volumes. You have not slept in the last twenty-four hours, for your collar is stained with perspiration and your tie is somewhat askew, and your fatigue is obvious. That, along with your card proclaiming your employment in government service, and the note you are holding in my brother's handwriting, make it easily apparent." Holmes waved it away. "It is no great feat to connect your current state of crisis to your professional associations in the diplomatic corps, particularly if it concerns Mycroft. We are well aware of the sensitive nature of the political matters he handles for the Crown." Holmes was alluding to his brother's unofficial position as the chief analyst and *de facto* administrative head for the various intelligence services reporting to the Foreign Office. "I assume you are here on his behalf. You may speak freely before us both." Holmes nodded at me, adding, "Were he here, Mycroft would assure you that you may trust Dr. Watson completely. His honor and discretion are beyond reproach. What does my brother require? Is it a criminal matter?"

"Indeed it is, Mr. Holmes. A kidnaping. Your brother has been taken hostage, along with another foreign national. They were taken last night, as Mr. Mycroft was escorting Teodoro to his lodgings. This note came this morning." He handed Holmes the sheet of paper he had been clutching.

Now it was Holmes that sat up straight in his armchair. He inspected the missive closely, reading it through and then holding it up to the light for a moment before handing it to me. "What do you make of it, Watson?"

I read:

> *First, I implore you, Bellwether, to tell no one of this. You must follow these instructions to the letter; I fear our captor's patience will not last. I need you to procure for me the Treaty of Montenegro and its various subsidiary contracts, discreetly, without letting anyone in the office see you. None must suspect. Teodoro must not be endangered; his life and mine depend upon your discretion. We have been given eighteen hours, and after that our fate will be in question. His constitution is more fragile than mine, though both of us are bearing up. There is nothing for it but to give them what they ask, there is no other aid. Seek no outside help. Further instructions will be coming by wire, but for the sake of authentication this is the only message they are permitting me to get out. Waterfront rendezvous likely forthcoming. We have no option but to submit if we wish to preserve the Montenegrin alliance we have been building.*
>
> *Yours,*
>
> *Mycroft Holmes*

"But this is terrible!" I stared at Holmes in shock, then turned to Bellwether. "You were specifically instructed to seek no help. You have risked their lives by coming here, have you not?"

133

"I could think of nothing else." Bellwether's expression was equal parts misery and desperation. "I took care not to be followed, though I think the Whitehall office is being watched."

"From the beginning, Bellwether. Who is this Teodoro? Why would he be included as a hostage?" Holmes voice was clipped and tight. I knew he was deeply concerned about his brother's welfare, though a casual observer would not have noticed. Both he and Mycroft kept their emotions tightly in check, and it was only because of our long association that I was aware of how Holmes' mouth had tightened as he read the ransom demand.

"Teodoro is the representative of a small eastern European nation, the name of which I cannot disclose. He is here to negotiate the possibility of British military aid against a larger power threatening its borders – forgive me, Mr. Holmes, but I cannot say more, even to you. The situation is fraught with tension, and could possibly erupt into a bloody and costly war. We have considerable interests in the area and British lives are at risk, though as yet nothing has been disclosed to the public. In view of these tensions, Her Majesty requested that Mycroft take over the negotiations. Only an intellect as brilliant as his, she feels, can thread the way through the delicate balance of diplomacy and threat that is required."

"And this document? The Montenegro Treaty?"

"That is the problem, Mr. Holmes!" Bellwether burst out. "There is no treaty! The document he names – it does not *exist*! I have searched for it everywhere!"

Holmes brows knitted. "You are certain of this?"

"I am Mr. Mycroft's closest aide. If this document existed, I would know of it. And the alliance he refers to – there is none! There is no possible matter currently before the F.O. which would require a treaty with Montenegro in the first place – there is simply nothing of any import that occurs there." Bellwether flushed, realizing the callousness of the remark, and added, "That is, nothing of import on the scale with which we are used to – "

Holmes held up a hand. "Enough. I understand your meaning. So what was my brother trying to accomplish, then? If there is no treaty, then the entire ransom demand is fatally flawed – but the kidnaping is real enough. So then the ransom these kidnappers require must be some sort of sensitive document. But clearly Mycroft seeks to prevent the criminals from obtaining whatever secret papers they would genuinely be able to use. It is obviously a diversion."

"But what kind of diversion?" I interjected. "Holmes, surely your brother would know Bellwether would be baffled by the reference."

134

"And thus forced to seek aid, despite the specific injunction against it." Holmes smiled thinly. "I have no doubt that my brother intended Bellwether to come here. He dared not suggest it openly. The kidnappers were doubtless standing over him as he composed this message, so he inserted an insoluble conundrum. Naturally Bellwether would turn to a specialist in such things, and as it happens I am the only such expert in London, to say nothing of my personal familial interest. It was a worthy gamble, especially given that Mycroft's specialty is predictive analysis. He knows Bellwether, he knows me, he knows the kidnappers and their agenda. This mention of a phantom treaty was the only way he could engage my services without alerting his captors." He turned to Bellwether. "Very well, then, let us not waste any time. We must assume the deadline of eighteen hours, at least, is real. How long has it been since you received this note?"

"A messenger delivered it at nine this morning. Just a lad. We questioned him closely, but he knew nothing. A man on the street gave him a crown to bring it to the office."

"And it is now noon. So we have fifteen hours of the allotted time left." Holmes nodded. "How were they taken?"

"From the coach taking Teodoro to the lodgings provided, apparently." Bellwether looked grim. "Mr. Mycroft had arranged rooms at the Diogenes Club, since its various prohibitions against members socializing provided an excellent umbrella of secrecy."

"It has the added advantage of allowing my brother to conduct business without varying his routine," Holmes put in. "Heaven forbid Mycroft should alter his orbit, even for an international crisis. So you are certain they were taken *en route*? Not at the station?

"We would have known sooner if they had," Bellwether explained. "But the Diogenes Club's doctrine of silence and discretion worked against us. No one on the staff thought to let us know that the expected guest never arrived – we had no inkling anything had gone awry until late last night. Naturally, once we did, we instantly dispatched agents to investigate. The coach was left near the Diogenes and the driver was found inside, shot dead. No sign of struggle – the driver must have been taken unawares, though I cannot think how. We were alerted to the possibility of attack, and we took the matter very seriously. It was Mr. Mycroft himself who insisted we use an agent as the coachman. I cannot think how the kidnappers even learned of Teodoro's visit, let alone the time of arrival and the route of the coach. This meeting was utterly clandestine, and all was carried out under the strictest conditions of secrecy." Abruptly he leaned forward, his head in his hands. "If we cannot find Mr. Mycroft, then Her Majesty loses an invaluable asset . . .

135

and should Teodoro die, then we will face an international incident that might well result in a worse military conflict than the one he was striving to prevent. Gentlemen, I cannot . . . ."

"Steady on, Bellwether," I said. "There is still hope. I have seen Holmes unravel more tangled matters than this."

Holmes raised an eyebrow. "Watson, you are ever the optimist," he said. "But your confidence is appreciated. Let us apply ourselves to the problem. Assume for the moment that the route was known to the kidnappers. Never mind how they learned of it; that is a matter that can wait. But perhaps if we examine the route itself, we can extrapolate their actions. Watson, the map of Metropolitan London is rolled up on the floor, under the desk to your left. If you would be so kind – "

I retrieved the map and Holmes unceremoniously shoved the tea setting to one side as he spread it out on the dining table. "Show us, Bellwether. From the train station onward."

Bellwether seemed to revive somewhat from his previous despair upon seeing Holmes's decisive manner. He stood opposite Holmes, scowling in concentration. "It was arranged for Mr. Mycroft to meet the carriage at Victoria," he said. "Then he – "

"Hold on," Holmes said. "Private carriage? Teodoro had engaged a special?"

"Of course." Bellwether blinked. "But . . . ."

"Such a train would of necessity be routed to a different platform." Holmes was clearly holding his impatience in check. "As such, it renders all your secrecy precautions useless. The kidnappers, knowing his arrival was imminent, merely had to position themselves – but no. There would still be the problem of the driver. You say he was an agent as well? Armed?"

"Yes. A good man, Trumbull. One of Mr. Mycroft's most trusted. We had arranged a circuitous route from the station to the club, with the idea that Trumbull would more easily spot any possible attempt to waylay the coach. Mr. Mycroft was concerned there might be some sort of attack made on the ambassador."

"And yet, despite all your precautions, the attack *was* made – successfully. With sign of a struggle," Holmes mused. "Somehow they contrived an approach that did not arouse suspicion. How? What would be a reason to stop mid-route? If the driver was an agent assigned to protect his passengers above all else . . . ." He leaned forward over the map. "Victoria is here – the Diogenes is here. No additional agents stationed along the way? No one standing watch along this circuitous route to which you refer?"

"None were thought necessary," Bellwether said. "It was assumed the secrecy of the proceeding and the cunning nature of the route Mr. Mycroft had planned was protection enough."

"So there were no other operatives assigned to the protection of the ambassador? Just this man Trumbull?"

"It was thought best to keep the circle as small as possible."

"Did Ambassador Teodoro have any staff of his own?" I asked.

"An additional diplomatic aide dispatched to London arrived this morning. Naturally he is demanding swift action."

"Then Teodoro's people know of the kidnaping. That is bound to muddy the waters. It makes the need for haste that much more acute." My friend shook his head once and returned his attention to the map. "It must have been something along the route itself that prompted them to stop." Holmes scowled at the route Bellwether had indicated with his finger. "Vincent Square . . . cross at Lambeth Bridge . . . past Waterloo to Blackfriars . . . hmm." He straightened. "Let me see that note again, Bellwether."

The young undersecretary proffered it to Holmes.

"Ha!" Suddenly Holmes' eyes were alight. "Look here – Mycroft managed to impart some information to us after all. '*Waterfront rendezvous likely forthcoming.*'"

"I hardly see how that helps us, Holmes," I objected. "The waterfront extends for miles."

"But the *route* does not, Watson. There is only a brief stretch of the Thames between Lambeth and Blackfriars, and that narrows our search considerably." Holmes rubbed his hands together and smiled. "Remember, my brother's corpulent physique would make him exceedingly difficult to transport if he were rendered unconscious. So he was awake when he was taken, as Teodoro must have been. So we must postulate either his transfer to a different coach – something I think unlikely, given the circumstances – or the two passengers were taken somewhere on foot after Trumbull was disposed of."

Bellwether looked helplessly at me, then at Holmes. "Even so, how does this help us? I still cannot fathom . . . ."

Holmes' impatience was becoming more apparent. "Think, man! Trumbull was a loyal soldier, a trained operative, yes? An overt attempt to waylay them, even from some seemingly innocent citizen, would have aroused his suspicions. An open attack would be met instantly with deadly force. Those were his orders?"

Bellwether nodded.

"Then, perforce, the only way to stop the coach would have been to place an obstacle in its path, a physical impediment. Anything would do.

A toppled fruit-cart, something of that sort. Something to turn them to a side-street or an alley." Holmes was speaking more to himself than to either one of us. "Let us examine the requirements of the kidnappers. They would have to divert the coach to a place away from witnesses, cut off a retreat, and give themselves adequate time to dispose of Trumbull before he could react . . . . Traffic on the streets would also be a determining factor." Abruptly Holmes looked up and addressed Bellwether. "What was the scheduled time of arrival? Teodoro's train?"

"Seven in the evening," the undersecretary replied. "But I cannot see – "

"Think it through." Holmes whirled away from the table to stare out the windows at the street below. "Traffic from Victoria at seven in the evening. Lambeth to Blackfriars. At least forty minutes to Lambeth . . . a few more minutes added to allow for greetings, arrangements for luggage – the luggage was still with the coach?" Bellwether nodded and Holmes went on. "Then my presumption holds that the criminals' primary requirements were speed and avoiding witnesses. Given that, the attack on the coach must have taken place sometime between eight and nine p.m., then." He returned to scowl at the map. "Let us narrow that margin further. The coach could not have been taken before they passed Waterloo. You found it abandoned close to the Diogenes. How close?"

"A side street, just around the corner. Not far."

"But nevertheless, out of sight of the entrance?" Bellwether nodded and Holmes muttered, "Suggestive, but not definite . . . given the times required . . . and Mycroft specified the waterfront, so he must have seen. Ha!" His finger stabbed at the map. "There! This section of the waterfront is where we must begin our search." He glanced up at me. "And we have little time. Watson, I think you had better arm yourself."

Bellwether looked startled. "Should we not summon the authorities? If you have already guessed – "

"I *never* guess." Holmes looked severely at the young man, who withered under my friend's gaze. "I have a working hypothesis, but that is all. We must investigate further, and I should prefer not to inadvertently alarm our foes into taking some precipitate action that might result in harm to my brother or the Ambassador. For now, we shall keep this to ourselves."

"Where shall we begin?" I asked Holmes.

"This corner here." Holmes tapped the map. "Laurelhurst Mews. Close to the waterfront, a small distance from the street to where the coach was found, and any number of stables and alleys wherein our kidnappers could have secreted my brother and the ambassador. We can progress no further until we discover additional clues at the scene. Even in our narrowed search area, a standard door-to-door police approach would accomplish nothing save to alert our quarry. Come, gentlemen! The clock is ticking!"

Bellwether had retained his hansom, so we were soon at the place Holmes had indicated on the map. Laurelhurst Mews was a crowded and squalid district, with a number of abandoned stablehouses and bricked-over doorways to what must have once been coachmen's quarters. The cobblestone street where we stood was crowded with wagons and vendor's carts.

My heart sank as I beheld the tableau before us. "Holmes, this is impossible. How can we possibly single out . . . ?"

"Ah, Watson, have some faith in my methods." Holmes was not the least bit discouraged. He fairly leapt from the coach and whirled about, looking carefully at each building before us in turn, resembling nothing so much as a great tweed-coated hunting dog casting about for a scent. It was just after one in the afternoon, and the street was busy with cart-vendors, as well as a few idlers in threadbare clothing and a cluster of dirty-faced children that regarded us with interest.

Holmes in his turn looked at this last group with speculation, then took out a shilling and spun the coin on his hand. "Who'd like a shilling? I have need of some information."

At once he was swarmed by the entire band of youths, each pleading to be heard. "Here, here, we must be orderly," Holmes told them. "Now! Yesterday evening, sometime between eight and nine, there was a cart accident blocking the street. Who can show me where it happened?"

"I can, guv." A redheaded lad with a spray of freckles across his nose shouldered forward. "That was my Uncle Hiram's rig, what my da' drives for him, picking up from the docks. Me and Jake here saw it. But it weren't no accident, see. These two toffs tipped over the whole wagon and then ran. My da' was in a rage, he was. Cost him almost an hour to get it righted and get his horses settled down. No one lifted a hand to help him neither. The swells what done it just cut down the side street and was on their way. Whole street was a mess and my da' lost half his load."

"Like Rusty says, sir." Another boy stepped forward to join the first, this one slightly younger with an untidy mop of dark hair escaping out from a cap perched precariously on the top of his head. He pointed. "Right that way."

Holmes's eyes glittered with triumph. "A shilling for each of you, then, if you take us there now." At once the boys were in motion and we hastened to follow.

"Holmes, how did you know?" I asked him as we ran after the two lads.

"I did not actually know. Merely testing a theory. A very long shot," Holmes admitted. "But there had to have been something of the sort, for otherwise the kidnapping would have been seen. Since there has been nothing in the morning newspapers, not even talk of a mysterious wagon crash in this area, it follows that the diversion worked." He smiled. "But you will recall from our experiences with the Irregulars that, though these street urchins are largely invisible to adults, they miss nothing. Even something as trivial as a tipped wagonload of goods was bound to have attracted their notice, especially since they spend most of their day scavenging."

By this point, we had caught up to Rusty and his companion. "Right here is where it happened, guv'nor." The redheaded boy pointed. "Scattered fish every which way."

Holmes thanked them, gave each the promised shilling, and sent them on their way. Then he turned to examine the street and surrounding buildings where we stood. "The street narrows here," Holmes mused. "The bridge is that way, behind us. So they must have been approaching from the south end of the street and forced to turn – Ha!" He straightened and smiled in triumph. "That alley, gentlemen."

Bellwether and I followed Holmes to the alley's entrance. The buildings on either side of us were set closely enough together that hardly any light penetrated to the cobbles, despite the early afternoon sun. "The darkness will aid us as much as it would our quarry," Holmes said quietly. "Here, now, stay close to the wall, out of sight of the row of windows above."

Bellwether looked ahead of us. "But look, the alley extends all the way to the docks. How can we be certain they did not meet a boat, or – "

"We cannot be certain." Holmes shook his head. "But I think it unlikely. Why add to the complexities of the plan? The further they transport the hostages, the greater the risk of discovery. As it was, they took a dangerous chance moving the empty coach from here to the Diogenes. No, I think they must be very close by."

"Even so, I cannot see how you hope to trace them further, Holmes," I said. "The afternoon is warm and dry, there is no way to follow their footsteps on these cobblestones. Were we in the country, there would at least be the possibility that they left tracks. But here in the city – "

Holmes shook his head again, dismissing the objection. "There are other methods. For example, there are seven different gates along this row, but only one of them has a newly-installed Saunders and Haddon padlock." He strode to the gate and knelt before it, taking a small set of tools out of his pocket.

I was surprised. "You brought your lock-picks?"

"I generally do. As you can see, they proved necessary." I could not dispute it, and Holmes went on, "I believe this model can be sprung without too much difficulty. Watson, have your revolver at the ready. Bellwether, now would be the time to summon the authorities. I assume you have men at the Diogenes Club still?" The young man nodded. Holmes said, "Off with you, then."

The young attaché ran back the way we had come. Holmes let out a small grunt of satisfaction and bent to his work again. "Watson, if you would be so kind as to move to your left, so that I may use what little light we have – Ah! There it is." The lock sprung open and I followed him in.

The interior of the building was musty and damp, despite the sunny afternoon outside. "Step carefully on these old boards, Watson," Holmes murmured. "Keep close to the wall. Any creaks will lose us the advantage of surprise." I nodded and gripped my revolver, determined to be ready for anything.

We ascended a short flight of steps and rounded a corner, and there we beheld Mycroft Holmes, bound and gagged. His eyes widened and he ducked his head toward us. I could not grasp his meaning, but Holmes grasped my shoulder and yanked me bodily to one side as a gunshot exploded from behind us. I whirled and beheld a dusky-skinned man with a black beard raising his pistol to fire again, but my own revolver spoke first. I got him in the shoulder and his gun went flying. He moved to retrieve it and I fired again, barely missing his head. Realizing the futility of further resistance, he slowly sagged against the wall, clutching his wounded shoulder. He glared at us, his eyes glittering with hatred.

Behind me, Holmes had succeeded in freeing his brother, who looked wan and tired but otherwise unharmed. He regarded us with a thin smile. "I trust the authorities are on their way?"

Holmes nodded. I asked, "But where is Teodoro?"

"He was never here," Mycroft Holmes said. He gestured at the wounded man on the floor. "Or, rather, this ruffian was playing the role." he added. "His accomplice – "

"At the Diogenes," Holmes interrupted. "Posing as a concerned aide. He has probably fled, but he will not get far. We shall have him as well, when young Bellwether gets here with reinforcements."

A few hours later, we had settled in the Stranger's Room at the Diogenes Club, where Mycroft was looking much improved after a late-afternoon supper. He offered cigars along with brandy, and though Holmes declined, preferring his pipe, I permitted myself to indulge.

"It was what we call a 'false flag' operation," Mycroft explained. "A ruse designed to penetrate my department and collect the sensitive documents of which I am the custodian. It was deemed necessary for its success to take me off the board, so to speak." He shook his head. "I had my doubts from the beginning about the ambassador's authenticity but there was the chance it was a legitimate back-channel overture. The region he claimed to represent is a troubled one. I have conducted such negotiations before. I did not consider that the actual objective was the theft of my personal papers, and thought having Trumbull along was sufficient precaution. Certainly I did not expect the attack to come from the Ambassador himself – when the wagon-crash occurred, he demanded Trumbull steer us into the alley and then shot him dead without warning."

"I wonder that he did not shoot you as well," I said.

Mycroft smiled with wry humor. "I was still of use to them. No doubt they intended to sell me along with my papers. Fortunately, you read my cypher and . . . ."

"What?" Holmes said, baffled. "There was no cypher."

Now it was Mycroft that looked baffled in his turn. "But you said it was the note – "

"Your allusion to the nonexistent treaty and the mention of the waterfront were sufficient clues," Holmes said. "The rest was timetables, maps, and deduction. But – "

"No, no!" Mycroft looked rather put out. "The cypher in the ransom note! *First*, then *last*! Do you mean to tell me that you did not see it? Do you still have the note?"

Looking chagrined, Holmes fished it from his waistcoat pocket and handed it to his brother. Mycroft took the stub of a pencil from a nearby cribbage set and quickly underlined a few passages. Then he handed it back to Holmes. My friend flushed in embarrassment and then handed it to me. "I am as blind as a beetle, apparently, Watson," he said.

I looked at the note, seeing the words Mycroft had underlined.

> First, *I implore you, Bellwether, to tell no one of this. You must follow these instructions to the letter; I fear our captor's patience will not* last. *I need you to procure for me the Treaty of Montenegro and its various subsidiary contracts, discreetly, without letting anyone in the office see you. None must* suspect. *Teodoro must not be endangered; his life and mine depend upon your discretion. We have been*

given eighteen hours, and after that our fate will be in <u>*question. His*</u> *constitution is more fragile than mine, though both of us are bearing up. There is nothing for it but to give them what they ask, there is no other* <u>*aid. Seek*</u> *no outside help. Further instructions will be coming by wire, but for the sake of authentication this is the only message they are permitting me to get* <u>*out. Waterfront*</u> *rendezvous likely forthcoming. We have no option but to submit if we wish to preserve the Montenegrin alliance we have been* <u>*building*</u>.

Yours,

Mycroft Holmes

"'*First, last,*'" I read aloud. "'*I suspect Teodoro. Question his aid*' — meaning the accomplice?" Mycroft nodded. I went on, "'*Seek out waterfront building.*' Well, I must admit that message would have saved us some time. But it all ended well anyway, did it not?"

Mycroft merely shook his head. "Honestly, Sherlock," he said. "We used that first-and-last cypher when we were boys. And to think I was worried about it being too transparent."

Holmes had turned beet-red. "Well . . . ."

I held up a hand. "Gentlemen!"

They both turned to look at me.

"Only a Mycroft Holmes could have conceived such a clever coded message under the very noses of his captors," I said. "And only a Sherlock Holmes could have divined the whereabouts of the criminals without reading it. Can we not concede that you are both brilliant and then leave it at that?"

For a moment the Holmes brothers were silent, and then both of them dissolved into helpless laughter.

The Adventure of the
Perfidious Partner
by Jayantika Ganguly

It was a pleasant evening in the summer of '97 that my friend Sherlock Holmes and I found ourselves in the company of several of my acquaintances at a rundown private club near the Tower Bridge, being subjected to an endless litany of complaints about the hardships of setting up one's own business. Holmes shot me an accusing look, for I had begged him to accompany me and lured him out with the promise of a superb steak. The club was small and ill-kept, but their steaks were good enough to rival the Langham's. The promised meal had yet to arrive, however, and I could see my friend's growing annoyance with the company.

I offered Holmes a weak smile and the club's best tobacco. Slightly appeased, he glanced longingly at the door. I looked at the wall-clock and decided that if our steaks were not served in the next ten minutes, we would depart. I had persuaded Holmes to leave the flat for the evening because he had been in a post-case slump, and I had thought that a good meal would cheer him up. My plan, however, did not seem to be working. Quite the contrary, in fact.

"You would not understand our dilemma, Mr. Holmes," young Roberts whined. His nasal voice grated even on my nerves; I could imagine exactly how irritated Holmes must be. I willed Roberts to stop speaking, but it was futile. The young businessman had imbibed a glass too many, and continued without pausing for breath. "You are quite famous. You do not need to go out on the streets to find work. I would bet that you get cases by the dozen, and you can afford to refuse the ones you detest. You never have to step out of the house to grab a client for yourself, do you?"

I was incensed. I knew, better than anyone, how hard Holmes had worked over the years. His fame had been won through talent and diligence. I opened my mouth to speak, but Holmes stood up abruptly and winked at me. His keen grey eyes sparkled with amusement.

"Let us see if I can still 'grab a client', Watson," he declared and dashed out of the club, without collecting his coat or walking stick. I ran after him, vaguely aware of some of our dinner companions following us.

Holmes had reached the edge of the Tower Bridge. He grabbed a young man who was dangerously close to the railing and pulled him back.

"Let me go, damn you!" the young man screamed, but Holmes had locked his arms securely around the boy.

"What happened?" I asked Holmes, finally catching up with him.

Holmes did not reply. The young man thrashed about, spewing forth a string of colourful invective directed at my friend, but Holmes did not let go.

"Please . . . please let me die. I deserve it. Please," the young man begged, his slight frame trembling with sobs. Tears spilled down his face, and he finally stopped struggling.

I stepped closer, and noted the comely face and expensive clothes of the young man. He was hardly more than a child – perhaps eighteen or twenty years of age, with wide green eyes and floppy blond hair. He was as underdressed as Holmes – clearly he had run out of somewhere without pausing to wear his coat or hat.

"Have you calmed down?" I asked gently. "Would you like a drink?"

The young man nodded and then shook his head. I glanced at Holmes, who had not yet relinquished his grip on the boy.

The others reached us.

"Why, that is The Duke of Mannington's youngest, is it not?" Roberts exclaimed, his nasal voice louder than ever before. "Why is Mr. Holmes . . . ?" Several passers-by stopped and stared at us.

"Do not cause a scene," I warned Roberts.

"Holmes?" the young boy cried. "Sherlock Holmes? The detective?"

"Consulting detective," Holmes corrected.

The boy sighed. "So this is how it ends," he muttered. "Well then, if you would not let me die, you may as well turn me over to the police. I have killed my fiancée, Mr. Holmes."

Holmes loosened his grip, but did not let the boy go. "How?" he asked quietly.

The boy stared at him, confusion written on his tear-stained face.

"How did you kill her?"

The young aristocrat blinked. "I . . . there was blood . . . Oh, God, so much blood! Lisa was on the floor . . . I . . . I must have stabbed her?" he babbled incoherently, ending with a question.

"Do you not remember?" Holmes asked sharply.

The boy shook his head, tears pouring down his face. That a young man old enough to be engaged could weep in such a heart-rending

145

manner was a revelation to me. He must have truly adored his fiancée. Could he have killed her?

Holmes's eyes gleamed. He was excited. He must have sensed a mystery. He released the boy, but kept a hold of his wrist.

"You could not have stabbed anyone. There is no blood on you except the bottom of your shoes," Holmes told him firmly. "Therefore, unless you washed up and changed your clothes prior to fleeing the scene of the crime – which is unlikely, given your state of undress – you could not have committed the murder you think you did."

"But . . . ."

Holmes peered into the boy's face. "You have been drugged," he declared. He turned to me and released the boy. "My dear Doctor, would you kindly confirm?"

"Certainly, Holmes," I replied, and checked the boy quickly. "You are correct, as usual."

"But I only had one glass of wine!" the young man protested. "And I didn't eat anything either!"

"In that case, we can only surmise that something was slipped into your drink," I told him. "Did it taste strange?"

The boy shrugged. "I don't know. It was a vintage I had never sampled before. Lisa said her friend brought it from South Africa." His emerald eyes welled up with tears again and he wobbled unsteadily. "Lisa . . . ."

Holmes caught him swiftly as he fainted. We carried the boy back to the club, and I administered some brandy. Holmes wrapped his own coat around the boy.

"How did you know?" Roberts asked Holmes as soon as the detective sat down.

Holmes smiled slightly. "I saw him through the window."

"But how did you know he was going to commit suicide?" Roberts pressed.

"That is a trick of my trade I would rather not disclose," Holmes replied. I looked at him, surprised, for he usually explained his observations whenever asked. I glanced at the unconscious boy and realised why Holmes had deflected the question. The boy was stirring, and almost as soon as my gaze shifted to him, he opened his eyes.

The young man blinked at us, confused, and sat up slowly. Then comprehension dawned and his eyes filled with tears again.

"I would be happy to look into what happened with your fiancée," Holmes said gently. "If you are feeling up to it, Lord Alistair, could you lead us to the scene?"

146

"I am not titled anymore," the boy whispered despondently. "My father disinherited me when I announced my engagement to Lisa yesterday."

"Why?" Roberts asked rudely.

Holmes stepped in, uncharacteristically. "We will determine if that is relevant to our investigation later. For now, how would you like to be addressed?"

"Just Alistair," the boy said, his voice quavering. "I doubt if I will be permitted to retain the 'Drake' surname, either."

"Well, then, Alistair, shall we?" Holmes asked, springing from his seat, grabbing his hat and stick, and holding out his hand. Alistair took his hand and stood up gingerly. I followed them to the door.

"Wait! Should we not call the police first?" Roberts cried, just as we were about to step out of the door.

"If you would be so kind, Mr. Roberts," Holmes said, without turning back, and strode out of the door, pulling Alistair and me with him. We hailed a hansom cab quickly and were already on our way by the time Roberts appeared on the street, looking bewildered. Holmes waved merrily at him and even as we rode away, I could see the young businessman's cheeks redden with anger.

To diffuse the situation, I turned to our "grabbed" client. "Could you tell us whatever you remember?" I asked gently. "Could you talk about your fiancée?"

Alistair blinked. "I met her in the West End last month. She was a lady of the night. We met every day for a fortnight, and I knew then that I loved her. She felt the same, and she left her establishment immediately when I asked her to. She found modest but decent quarters, and I helped her with the payment. Yesterday, I asked her to marry me, and she agreed. We visited my family, but my father . . . my father . . . ." The young nobleman dissolved into a fit of tears.

"Your father was suspicious of her intentions, I surmise?" I asked softly.

Alistair nodded miserably. "He insulted her with reprehensible words I cannot repeat. He called me a brainless idiot overcome with lust and commanded me to leave her side. When I refused, he promptly disinherited me and we were shown the door. Lisa and I returned to her rooms, and she suggested opening the wine her friend had given her."

"*In vino veritas*," Holmes murmured absently.

"Did you know this friend of hers?" I asked.

The boy shook his head. "She said it was someone she had known as a child, and that he had recently returned from South Africa. She was going to call him to join us for a meal soon."

147

"What happened next?"

"We toasted to our future and drank," Alistair replied. "The next thing I remember is Lisa lying in a pool of blood. There was so much blood and she would not move, no matter how I called for her . . . ." He choked a sob. "I cannot live without her, Dr. Watson! And if I have killed her, then I . . . ." He trembled violently, unable to speak.

I reached out a lay a reassuring hand on the young man's shoulder. "If Holmes says you have not killed her, it must be true," I said firmly. "Believe in that."

The boy nodded tearfully and clung to me for support.

"Are you certain that both of you consumed the same wine?" Holmes asked.

Alistair frowned. "Lisa poured two glasses and she took a sip, I think. I drained my glass quickly. I was . . . upset." He buried his head in my shoulder and wept again. I was reminded of small hysterical children I have attended as a doctor, and suppressing a sigh, I rubbed his back gently. It often calmed them.

I glanced at my friend ruefully and found him gazing at me with a strange expression on his stoic face. I looked away and asked Alistair how old he was.

"Eighteen," he said, looking up at me with tear-filled eyes. "Father wanted me to study law, and I, too, was looking forward to Oxford."

The cab came to a stop in front of a run-down building. Alistair led us to the first floor, to an unlocked door. Holmes looked around, his raptor gaze sharp and assessing.

"Did you leave the door open when you left?" Holmes asked.

The boy nodded. Holmes examined the floor carefully. "Freshly cleaned," he remarked.

Alistair frowned and shook his head.

Holmes stepped in without a word. There was nothing inside. No corpse, no furniture, no signs of anyone living in these rooms.

Alistair fell to his knees, the very picture of despair. "How . . . ?" he wailed. "How is this possible?"

I attempted to placate the distressed boy. Holmes, meanwhile, examined every nook and cranny of the abandoned apartment. Several times he knelt on the floor and picked up some items, wrapping them carefully in sheets torn from his notebook.

"You have had a narrow escape, I daresay," Holmes muttered finally, looking at Alistair with gentle eyes. "No blood was spilt in this room."

Alistair stared at my friend with wide eyes. "Lisa . . . do you mean Lisa is alive?"

148

"In all probability. She was certainly not murdered here in the manner you think."

I looked up at Holmes curiously. "Did you find evidence of her living here?"

Holmes nodded. "If she has long, curly, red hair, then yes."

"She does," Alistair exclaimed happily. "It is a most beautiful shade. It matches her eyes in the sunlight . . . ."

I stifled a chuckle, amused at the sight of Holmes making a tremendous effort not to roll his eyes, while our young noble waxed eloquent about the love of his life.

When Alistair finally stopped speaking, he frowned. "If Lisa is not dead, what happened here? Why would she pretend to be dead and then leave?"

"Perhaps you were no longer useful," Holmes said flatly.

To my horror, Alistair burst into tears again. "No," he moaned. "Lisa loved me. She would not leave me in such a cruel manner because I was disinherited. We were going to be married."

Holmes opened his mouth to speak, but I glared at him and he nodded. I patted the boy's back and spoke softly, attempting to calm him down.

"It is possible he was given a potent hallucinogen?" I asked Holmes.

The detective shook his head. "No, Watson. There are traces of red dye in the room. I do not believe it was a figment of his imagination."

"I do not understand, Holmes. What was the purpose behind such a farce? What could she hope to gain?"

"Perhaps the intention was to drive him away for good," he replied.

Alistair whimpered. "But . . . ."

"You have to admit it looks suspicious," I said gently. "The lady disappeared with a most horrific pretence upon your loss of inheritance."

"She knew I cannot live without her!" he cried. "She would not – "

Holmes and I exchanged a look. That may have been her aim, but we were reluctant to point it out to the poor chap. He had already attempted suicide at the imagined loss of his duplicitous fiancée.

"Do not treat your own life so lightly!" Holmes said sternly.

"But – "

"What do you intend to do? Do you wish to let yourself waste away in the memory of a false love?" Holmes's tone was clipped and his eyes shone with the hard glitter of diamonds. I had rarely seen him so enraged.

Alistair stammered in the wake of the detective's fury. "I . . . I do not know."

I could see that Holmes's patience was at its last tether, and I could also see that the boy would be reduced to a whimpering mess again if Holmes uttered another angry word. So I spoke up. "Perhaps we should visit your father, Alistair, and let him know what transpired," I suggested gently.

Alistair nodded tearfully.

I turned to Holmes, who had a faint smile on his lips. He nodded and left, while I helped the boy up and took him down the stairs. By the time we reached the gate, Holmes had already flagged down a cab. We rode in silence until the cab pulled up in front of the familiar Diogenes Club.

"Is the Duke a member of your brother's club?" I asked Holmes.

The detective shrugged. "I recall Mycroft saying that he had arranged for late-night dinner with the Duke here tonight in the telegram he sent this afternoon requesting my presence."

I stared at him in surprise. The telegram must have arrived just before we left Baker Street. What a coincidence! Could it be that the Duke wished to consult Holmes about his son's unsuitable affair? And why on earth had Holmes agreed to accompany me when he already had plans to meet with his brother later?

I turned to Holmes with a silent enquiry. He shook his head gave me a small smile.

"Let us not keep my brother waiting," he said and strode in, and we followed him into the Stranger's Room. Mycroft and a distinguished looking elderly gentleman were already seated.

Alistair, who had worn a befuddled look so far, suddenly wailed, "Papa!"

Mycroft's companion, presumably the Duke, turned to look at us and stood up abruptly. He rushed to us and embraced his son.

"Alistair," he cried, relief evident in his face and voice. "My child! Thank the Lord you are safe!"

"Safe?" I asked, confused.

Mycroft spoke up from his seat. "The Duke received a ransom note for his youngest son this morning. I had invited Sherlock to dinner to discuss the matter." He smiled beatifically at Holmes. "You have outdone yourself this time, brother mine. You have solved the case before it came to you." He held out two pieces of paper.

Holmes took them. He read the first one without any expression, but frowned at the second one. He passed it to me, and I stifled a cry of shock. The first note demanded a thousand pounds in exchange for Alistair's life and contained the usual threat of avoiding the police or the hostage would be killed. The second one listed the time for the exchange as midnight, and the address we had just visited as the venue.

Alistair came over and studied the notes. His face lost all colour. "That . . . that is Lisa's handwriting!" he whispered, and burst into tears. "Papa was right after all . . . ."

"Are you certain?" I asked.

He nodded and withdrew a letter from his trouser pocket. He handed it to us. It was a rather embarrassingly overt epistle of an *inamorata* to her *paramour*, but the boy was right – the handwriting was the same.

"How were you able to rescue Lord Alistair from his abductors, Sherlock? The second note arrived later in the evening, and I did not have time to apprise you of the address."

"The boy was not abducted, Mycroft. He was attempting suicide when I saw him," Holmes replied bluntly. "It was mere coincidence."

"What?" The Duke exclaimed. His eyes, the same as Alistair's, brimmed with tears and he pulled his son closer. "Why?"

Alistair flushed and stared at the carpet. "I thought I had killed Lisa. Mr. Holmes saved me, though, and we went back, and there was nothing in the apartment, Papa! Everything was gone!"

Mycroft frowned at us. "Apartment?" he asked.

Alistair nodded. "The one Lisa shifted to because I did not want her to continue living at the brothel. It is this address." He waved the second note.

Mycroft looked at Holmes and me, arching an eyebrow.

Holmes smiled. "Go on, Watson," he said. "Storytelling is your forte."

Repressing a sigh, I took the seat Mycroft indicated. He introduced everyone, though it was unnecessary at this point – but then, the older Holmes was a man of routine and etiquette.

I summarised the events of the evening as precisely as I could. The Duke made sounds of distress occasionally, and held on to his son's hand tightly. When I finished narrating, he left his seat, walked to Holmes, grabbed his hands and thanked him tearfully. It was apparent from where Alistair had inherited his emotional disposition. Holmes shifted uncomfortably, and Mycroft and I shared a grin.

"How can I ever thank you for saving my child, Mr. Holmes?" he cried.

"The work is its own reward," Holmes muttered, clearly wanting the elderly nobleman to release his hands.

"Oh, how noble!" he exclaimed. "The House of Drake shall forever be in your debt, Mr. Holmes! And should you ever require our assistance, please do not hesitate to call upon us."

Holmes thanked him and extricated himself. He turned to his brother. "Should I continue?" he asked.

Mycroft smiled faintly. "Would you not, even if I asked you to refrain?" he challenged.

Holmes chuckled. "Probably not."

The Duke and I stared at the Holmes brothers, unable to understand. Alistair, however, did.

"Are you going to look for Lisa?" he asked Holmes.

My friend nodded.

"What will you do when you find her?" he demanded. "You would not send her to gaol, would you? Will you let me speak to her, even if it is just once?"

The Duke bristled. "I do not want you anywhere near that scarlet woman ever again, Alistair. She nearly caused your death," he commanded.

"But Papa . . . ."

"Listen to me for once, son. Have you not learnt your lesson yet? Could you even imagine what it would do to your poor mother and me if you were to be taken from us?" His eyes shimmered again. "Have you any idea how worried we were?"

Alistair hung his head. "I am sorry, Papa. I was a fool."

"Sometimes, love makes fools of us all, my dear boy," his father said kindly. "I am glad you are unharmed. You can start afresh, and someday, you shall have a woman truly worthy of you, who will cherish you with all her good heart."

Alistair nodded.

The Duke and his son took their leave soon after. Mycroft, quite generously, offered us board for the night in his rooms across the street, which Holmes took up reluctantly. I understood why as soon as we entered Mycroft's abode, for barely had the door closed behind us that he whirled on Holmes and demanded, "What are you hiding from me, Sherlock? This does not make any sense at all! Even the most amateur abductor would have secured their captive appropriately before sending out a ransom note, and staging of a false murder of the girl is ridiculous! If she desired the money, she would have kept the boy sedated until midnight and made the exchange with his father. Why would she stage her own death in such a clumsy manner, and for what purpose?"

Holmes shrugged. "I do not know, brother."

Mycroft, still breathing heavily from his tirade, sank upon the couch, and waved his arm at the chairs in front of him. Holmes and I took a seat silently. I looked around the living room curiously. The ornate furnishings, the perfect symmetry, the immaculate maintenance –

Mycroft's rooms were quite different from the messy, eccentric décor of our Baker Street apartment. If Holmes believed dust to be eloquent, his brother certainly deemed it to be his mortal enemy – for there wasn't a single speck of dust nor a single thread out of place in Mycroft's home. Even the pens and paperweights on the desk were lined up according to their size. Everything was neatly organised and perfectly aligned. In fact, the only imperfect items in the room were the three humans.

"Remarkable," I muttered.

"Mycroft's house is as orderly as his brain," Holmes commented dryly.

The older Holmes appeared pleased. "Indeed," he said.

"We are tired, Mycroft. Can we speak in the morning instead?" Holmes asked.

The bewildered look on Mycroft's face was almost comical. "How can you possibly be tired, Sherlock?" he questioned, disbelief dripping from his voice. "You have always had more energy than the rest of our family put together." He narrowed his eyes. "Something has disturbed you. What is it, Sherlock? What did you see?"

Holmes laughed mirthlessly. "Your precious Duke and his son are safe, brother. For what else could you wish?"

"The truth," Mycroft replied promptly. "And my brother's well-being."

Holmes sighed. "I cannot win against you, Mycroft," he conceded. "There was another man at that apartment. From the tobacco ash I collected, it is apparent that it was her South African friend. The girl was not alone, and I do not believe she was acting for her own benefit. The man, however, is likely to have borne our young aristocrat ill-will."

I frowned. "Could it be . . . was she being blackmailed? Was she threatened into compliance?"

"I do not know."

"Is she in danger?"

"I do not know."

"Will you be able to find her?"

"Perhaps." Holmes sighed again, closed his eyes and leaned back in the luxurious wingback chair. Mycroft really did have good taste.

I looked at Mycroft and found him regarding his younger brother with concern etched into his large face. His piercing grey eyes, the same as his brother's, turned to me. I shook my head, for I knew no more than what Holmes had said. I did understand Mycroft's anxiety, though. It was uncharacteristic of Holmes to be so upset about a case. The older Holmes made a silent entreaty to me to keep him updated about his brother's activities, and I nodded my agreement. However impersonal

153

Mycroft might appear to be, I knew for certain the depths of his affection and his protectiveness for his younger brother.

Holmes was unusually quiet the next morning. Mycroft served us an excellent breakfast and sent us on our way. We returned the short distance to Baker Street, but Holmes left within the hour, promising to be back by the evening. He came home fairly late at night, and did not speak except to tell me that he would be out again the next day. This went on for several days, until, one morning, I found him seated at the breakfast table.

"Not going out today?" I asked tartly.

"Apologies, Watson," he replied, amused at my annoyance. "I did not realise my investigations were causing you grief."

"Your brother and I have been worried about you," I retorted. "Do not tell me that the most observant man in the world failed to observe such a blatantly obvious fact."

Holmes threw his head back and laughed. "*Touché*, my dear doctor."

Still miffed, I took my seat and rang for breakfast.

"I met Roberts yesterday," Holmes said.

"The rude young chap from the club the other night?" I asked.

Holmes laughed again. "You really are an excellent judge of character, my friend. Young Roberts did, however, provided invaluable assistance to me, albeit inadvertently."

I frowned. "How?"

Holmes simply smiled in response.

The answer came in the form of an anxious young woman who burst into our rooms, Mrs. Hudson at her heels.

"Mr. Holmes!" she cried. "You are Mr. Holmes, are you not?"

"I am, indeed, young lady," Holmes replied, springing from his seat and leading her to a chair.

Mrs. Hudson huffed. "Are you certain it is all right to let her be here, Mr. Holmes?" she demanded. "Two gentlemen of your caliber – "

"The young lady is as welcome to my rooms as any other client, Mrs. Hudson," Holmes said curtly.

Mrs. Hudson left reluctantly. She was usually a rather sweet-tempered lady. I turned to look at the young girl who had incurred her wrath, and immediately realised why. The girl was beautiful, certainly, but her ensemble was provocative to the point of vulgarity, and her profession was as clear as day. However, she was also quite distressed, and her lovely red hair was wild and uncombed. Her red-rimmed brown eyes were brimming with tears.

Epiphany struck. "Lisa?"

The girl nodded. "You must be Dr. Watson." Her eyes returned to Holmes. "Is it true, Mr. Holmes? Did Alistair try to kill himself because he thought I was dead?"

"Yes," Holmes said, and the girl slumped with a cry of agony.

I was surprised. "Did you not know?"

She wept inconsolably. "Oh, Alistair! I thought he would return to his father and his rich life if he believed that I had betrayed him. I drugged the wine and sent a ransom note to his father. I knew Alistair would not be able to live in poverty. He has always had a privileged life – he does not understand how much effort it takes to simply survive. I intended to send another note later and clear out before his father arrived to retrieve him. I may have even taken the money."

"I take it that your friend did not approve of your sacrifice?" Holmes said.

The girl nodded, fresh tears spilling from her eyes. "I did not know what had happened. When I came to, William told me that I had fallen unconscious and he had carried out my plan, and Alistair was back with his father. He also asked me to marry him and move to South Africa with him. I refused, at first, but I have been considering it. Yesterday, I overheard that brash man speaking to you about how you saved Alistair. I confronted William, and he told me what he had done."

"What did he do?" I asked, morbidly curious. What a tragic, dramatic tale this was!

"He himself can tell us," Holmes said. "If I am not mistaken, I hear his footsteps on the stairs."

A well-built young man marched in, once again followed by a harried Mrs. Hudson. Before she could speak, however, Holmes reassured her of the credibility of the newcomer, and she left, muttering to herself. Our landlady was a long-suffering woman, indeed.

"You!" he spat at Holmes. "You are Holmes! You deceived me!"

The detective chuckled. "And how exactly did I do that, Mr. Hart, if I may ask?"

William Hart bellowed and launched himself at my friend, but the girl sprang from her chair to stop him. He paled as soon as he saw her.

"Lisa?" he said faintly. "Why are you here, my darling?" He eyed her clothes with distaste. "Why are you wearing that again?"

Lisa stamped her foot defiantly. "This is who I am," she snapped. "I am no longer the girl you knew, Will. Go back to South Africa."

Hart shed his cloak silently and draped it over the girl's shoulders. He smiled slightly. "You are every bit the girl I knew . . . as fiery as her flaming hair. Come with me, dear Lisa."

"No, Will," she said sadly. "You nearly killed Alistair. I cannot forgive you for that."

"I told you I would not have let him die! One of my mates followed him all the way to the Tower Bridge, and if Mr. Holmes hadn't saved him, Jimmy would have!" His face crumpled. "I had to see if he did love you after all, Lisa. I couldn't bear to let him go without a scratch when you were giving up your entire life for him. A proper man would never let you sacrifice yourself like that! I never would!"

Lisa glared at him. "Are you satisfied now? You staged my murder and made him think I was dead – no, even worse, you made him think he had killed me! It made him try to kill himself! Does that make you happy?"

"No," William said softly, falling to his knees. "When you look at me like that, it makes me the most miserable wretch in the world. What do you want me to do, Lisa? Should I go and apologise to this Lord of yours? If that is your wish, I will confess to my wrongdoings and beg at his feet until he takes you back as his fiancée."

Lisa knelt next to him. "No, Will," she said gently. "I am not suited to be the wife of a nobleman. It was an insane, impossible dream from the start. I am glad Alistair has returned to his family. I, too, shall return to my work."

"Come with me, my love. Be my wife. There is no man on this earth who loves you as I do. You used to care for me. Do you detest me now?"

Holmes and I stared at each other. The dismay on Holmes's face at the emotional drama playing out in our living room was almost comical.

"Will . . . you are a wealthy and respectable businessman now. A wife like me would only be a liability and an embarrassment for you," Lisa said, tears pouring down her face.

Hart cupped her lovely face with a big, gentle hand. "Then I will leave my wealth behind. Let us go to a new place and start all over. I have worked my way up with my own hands, and I can do so again. With you by my side, I would be the happiest man alive, whether we live in a hut or a castle."

"A man does not get sincerer than that, young lady," Holmes declared. "You may as well marry him and put us all out of our misery."

The young couple looked up at us in shock. They had clearly forgotten our presence until Holmes's rude interruption. They flushed, mumbled incoherently, and left in a haste. Holmes groaned and dropped into a chair, while I burst out laughing.

"That was a good conclusion," I told him.

He moaned piteously. "Agony, Watson! Sheer agony! I would rather have dealt with a real criminal than these young fools in love."

"You were concerned enough to go looking for them," I reminded him. "I am certain nothing they said today was new to you. Admit is, Holmes. You were happy just now."

"*Et tu*, Watson?"

I laughed again. "Perhaps we should visit your brother and let him hear the tale in full detail."

Holmes smiled. "Ah, but you are diabolical, Watson."

Mycroft was as horrified as we had expected. He did give us an update on Alistair, though. The boy would be attending Oxford as planned. He went on to become one of the best barristers in the country.

Nearly a year later, Holmes received a letter from South Africa. Lisa and William Hart had married almost immediately after their departure from our rooms, and were now happily settled in Johannesburg and expecting their first child. Holmes scoffed at their words of gratitude, but he placed the letter carefully in a drawer.

A Revenge Served Cold
by Maurice Barkley

There are times when a surprise is neither pleasant nor unpleasant, but worthy of note. One such example was the situation presented to us on a day in 1898. The surprise was that we left Baker Street before mid-day, and were back and enjoying a cigar and a brandy before the dinner hour – case solved. At least it was solved to our satisfaction and that of Inspector Gregson, who is now safely retired and immune from censure. The adventure began one fine summer morning, just after breakfast.

"I say, Holmes." I lowered my newspaper to look at my companion, who was slumped on the sofa reading the agony columns. "Do you remember that episode last year when you almost came to blows with Lord Garrod?"

"Not with any degree of fondness," Holmes replied. "I only regret that I did not bash him a good one. The nerve of the man, asking – no, *demanding* – that I do anything, even fabricate evidence, to keep him out of jail. I was sorely tempted to throw him bodily down the stairs."

"Yes," said I. "The man was a thorough swine. The way he treated his tenants was criminal. And, Emma Brunnel – that poor girl, he kept her locked in that dreadful room. She passed away in hospital. I try not to think about it. "

Holmes laid his paper aside. "I do recall that he managed to escape prison, but in the process, he lost over half of his estate, though unfortunately not his peerage – it was hereditary. Justice was not served by that turn of events. At minimum, the man should have gone to jail. I hope he has not returned to his unlawful behavior."

"Perhaps he has," I replied. "It says here the man is dead – murdered yesterday morning."

"Really," said Holmes. "The details, please."

I went back to the article. "Very little, I'm afraid. He was served breakfast as usual in his room at about eight o'clock. The servant girl, one Ada Jade, then went to the basement to join the butler, Mr. Darwin Langdale, to have her own meal. I note that the writer of the article emphasized the fact that the two servants were in the basement at the time of the murder, and there were no other people on the premises.

"While still eating, they were surprised by the ringing chimes of the mechanical call device. Almost simultaneous with the bells, they heard what proved to be a gunshot from above. They both ran upstairs, but they were unable to enter the master's room. The police were summoned and broke through the door, which was secured from the inside by two sturdy dead bolts. Once inside, they discovered Lord Garrod shot precisely between his eyes. No gun was found. He was alone." I paused to refill my coffee cup. "That is the essence of the news writer's story. There was some additional information attributed to Inspector Tobias Gregson."

"He is a good man, Watson. I would like to hear his comments."

"Mostly details," said I. "For the past year, Lord Garrod used as his bedroom the room in which he imprisoned poor Emma. There is only the one entrance, and the windows are soldered shut. There are no secret panels. It is assumed that the man moved into that room in order to feel safe. The inspector only added that the investigation had just begun.

"Of course, this did not satisfy the reporter, who went on to speculate about ghostly apparitions and the possibility that the dead girl came back to gain her revenge."

Holmes tapped his pipe on the iron ball of a fireplace andiron. "I wonder, Watson. Was the fact that ghosts as a rule do not use firearms of no concern to the man?"

"Apparently not," said I, while putting a match to my morning pipe. "The Garrod estate is just across town. We could be there within the hour."

"It does interest me, my friend," said Holmes, a thoughtful look on his face. "However, knowing Gregson, I think it would be wise to let him come to us if he cannot puzzle this out."

I set down my cup. "I will wager that the inspector will be at our door before this day ends."

"Today, you say?" Holmes looked at me with raised eyebrows. "That strikes me as being overly optimistic. I will wager half-a-crown that he will arrive tomorrow."

I did not hesitate to say, "Done."

The wager was set. Holmes went back to the agony columns while I read more of my share of the paper. Later, Holmes went into the lumber room and returned with a folder labeled "Garrod". We both spent a half-hour reading the old accounts.

"A swine indeed," said Holmes. "That poor girl was kept in that room for just over one year until one of the servants had the courage to summon the police. To think that he went on a two-week holiday and left her there without food or water. She was rescued after six days, but she was so dehydrated that she could not recover. An immigrant from Australia, she had siblings there – a sister and a brother – but no relatives here."

159

"Well," I commented, "I can't say he didn't deserve a bullet in the head. I wonder what happened to the servants?"

"Oh," he replied, "I am sure they are long gone and the house has new staff. If they stayed, the beast would have had his revenge."

By then, the morning had passed and we rang Mrs. Hudson for lunch. As was our warm weather preference, the good lady served us cold sandwiches and some fruit. We had only to wait a few minutes for her to bring the tea water to a boil.

I answered her soft tap on our door and stood aside. "My dear Mrs. Hudson, I see three cups on your beautiful Benares tray. Will you be joining us for lunch?"

"Oh, no, Dr. Watson, I will not, but the gentleman behind me will."

She continued on to the table, and the welcome figure of Inspector Gregson took her place in the doorway. Mrs. Hudson arranged our plates, poured the tea, and left with her precious tray.

"I must say, Inspector," said Holmes, as we sat down, "after having read this morning's paper, your visit is most welcome."

Gregson took a large bite out of his sandwich. "I was sure," he wiped a crumb from his moustache, "you and Dr. Watson would find this a dandy puzzle – I know I did."

I handed him the cream cruet. "You are correct, Inspector, and you have our undivided attention."

At that point, I picked up my sandwich and discovered half-a-crown hidden under the bread. I swear, to this day I do not know how he did it.

The inspector had a healthy appetite and quickly finished a second portion and spoke to us between sips of tea. "I know there must be an answer, but blessed if I can see any light. We did a right proper search – only one way to enter the room. When the girl was there, the locks were such that she could not get out. Now they have been changed so that a person on the inside can seal the room. We had to smash through two inside deadbolts. Ruined the door, we did."

Holmes interrupted the inspector. "Were the dead bolts the type that can be engaged from the inside before the door is shut?"

"No, sir," said Gregson, "If you twist the knob, the bolt springs out, and it's not tapered or spring-loaded. In that position, the door can't be shut."

"Did you locate a key?" Holmes asked.

"That type has no key on the outside, only a solid metal plate. The window is soldered shut. I measured the room inside and out. There is no space unaccounted for. My boys moved what furniture there was – probed walls, the floor, the ceiling – and came up empty." He sat back and looked at both of us. "That's it, then. The trail ends there, unless you can make some sense of it."

"Most interesting," said Holmes, his half-eaten sandwich forgotten. "I suggest we go immediately to the Garrod estate."

"Very good," said Gregson, "I have a wagon waiting." As he stood, he reached and took a third sandwich. He nodded toward the object. "If you please – for my driver. The lad's had naught to eat today."

"Of course," said Holmes, "Very thoughtful of you. Take some of the fruit. Let me fetch my cigar case and we shall be on our way."

"Back to Sevenoaks, Alfie," said Gregson, while handing the driver his lunch.

The approach to the Garrod estate showed signs of neglect due to, I supposed, the disgraced Lord's reduced circumstances. The main house was an unremarkable pile of stone – two stories topped by an elaborate garret. Inside, the rooms through which we passed also showed considerable inattention and a good amount of dust. Holmes did not bother with the visible footprints on the dirty floor. Any of potential importance were obliterated by the back-and-forth of official traffic.

Walking past the shattered door, I saw that the deceased owner had since done considerable redecorating and the former prison room was much more elegant. It was the only room I had seen that was in good order. A large but rumpled carpet covered the floor. It had been pulled back in the search. The master's writing desk stood in front of the leaded glass window and a large canopied bed rested against the opposite wall. A screen in one corner hid a common chamber pot. No pictures decorated the papered walls.

Holmes went directly to the servant's call device. It was a box fixed to the wall, much like those used for a ship's communications. A speaking tube was mounted to the centre of the box and a small handle protruded from the left side. A metal rod sticking out above the speaking tube supported a curved metal spring that held the three bells. "You tested both ends of this device?" he asked Gregson.

"I did, myself," the inspector replied. "The one in the basement is larger because it has several terminals for the other rooms in the house."

Holmes bent over and leaned close to flick one of the bells and poke the call wire that ran to the basement. "This speaking tube is somewhat low, but I recall that Lord Garrod was rather short."

"I saw the corpse," said Gregson, "and he was below average in height."

Holmes then made a show of examining the rest of the room. I am sure Gregson did not realise that my friend was no longer investigating, but I knew the signs. I looked again at the call device, but saw nothing out of the ordinary. Eventually the inspector began to get restless. It was not his nature to stand idly by and watch others at work. I could see that Holmes sensed this and was waiting for this moment.

"Inspector," said he, "I can see why you have had difficulty here. This may take more time than I had anticipated. Rather than have you wait while I work, perhaps you would like to carry on with your other duties while Watson and I familiarize ourselves with the house and the servants."

"Good idea, Mr. Holmes," said Gregson, with a degree of relief. "I will just go round and check with my men. Give a call if you need me."

After he left, Holmes and I stood silently in the middle of the room, gazing out of the leaded glass window. I knew he was waiting for me to say something, so I remained silent.

"You are not curious?" said he.

"About what?" I asked.

"You did not notice my behavior?"

"Oh, that. Was it indigestion – ? Perhaps Mrs. Hudson's sandwich?"

"Then you saw what I saw."

"Of course I did."

"And your conclusion?"

"Magic. Black magic."

"How can you say that the barrel of a gun is magic?"

"A gun you say? I request a demonstration."

Holmes walked over to the call device. "Lean close and smell the gun powder."

I didn't need to inhale much. "Yes, the odor is quite distinctive, but where is the gun?"

"Look at the metal rod that supports the bell spring."

I looked and saw the hole in the middle. "Good heavens! How diabolical."

"Indeed it is," said Holmes. "There is a pistol mounted inside the box." He pulled at the cover and the right side swung out and away, showing the revolver and the wire connecting the trigger to the call wire pull rod. "Once the trigger is cocked, the first person to pull the call lever will cause it to fire. The pistol can only be fired once, but the speaking tube guarantees that the unfortunate user is standing close to and directly in front of the weapon."

As soon as Holmes closed the box face, we were startled by a vigorous ringing of the chimes. He again bent over and said, "Ahoy, who is calling?"

"Is that you, Mr. Holmes?" Inspector Gregson's voice was easy to recognize.

"Yes, it is me. Are you testing this device?"

"No, sir. The chimes rang down here in the basement. You must have pulled the handle."

Holmes looked at me with raised eyebrows. "Perhaps we did, Inspector. If so, it was accidental. We are finished up here. Are the servants available for questioning?"

"Yes, they are here in the kitchen."

Stepping away from the call device, he said, "When I opened the front, it stretched the wire going down to the basement. That is what caused those bells to ring,"

We looked at each other, knowing that the mystery was essentially solved.

"Any questions?" asked Holmes.

I shook my head. "When will you tell Gregson?"

Holmes smiled. "Watson, your head told me no, but your voice asked a question."

My companion, fresh from solving a riddle, was in a good mood and having some fun at my small expense.

"You remind me," said I, "of my old commanding officer, Major Smyth. He once told me to stand up straight and keep my head down. I had no response then or now."

As we walked from the depressing chamber, Holmes had more to say. "We know the *how* of the crime, and most likely one of the perpetrators, but who installed the device and why? It was probably put in place when the room was redecorated. We still need to learn more details and the motive. I am a bit selfish in that I would like us to present the inspector with a complete explanation. If this is related to the girl who was confined here . . . ." Holmes's voice trailed off and he paused for a moment. I knew he was considering the possibilities. "Watson, the motive must be revenge. Lord Garrod had many enemies for many reasons, but his treatment of Emma Brunnel must be at the top of our list. Whoever planned his death was not satisfied with such punishment as was given to him at the time, and we shall proceed with that assumption." Holmes and I were now in Lord Garrod's former bedroom. "Look there, Watson. Another servant's call device, but this one looks to be older and of a different design." There was no box – simply a pull chain. The bells were higher up on the wall and the speaking tube was hung by a hook.

"Before we go to the basement," said Holmes, "I would like to see if I can formulate a rough chain of events." We walked over to a large window that looked down on an unkempt garden. "I speculate that this crime was a year in the making – beginning with the redecoration of that room. At least one of the contractors was somehow connected to Emma Brunnel. He designed and installed the device, leaving the pistol loaded, but uncocked."

"Why would he not leave it armed when the job was finished?" I asked.

"I can think of two reasons," Holmes replied. "Perhaps the man finished while other workers had not. He could not leave it armed and risk one of them using the device. In addition he might have wanted some time to pass to separate his involvement from the crime."

I picked at the loose window leading. "It seems to me that the man had skills as a carpenter and a metal worker."

"True," said Holmes, "but the workmanship I saw was only adequate for the task. I think the average homeowner could fabricate such a device. We will not seek him out among the upper classes. It looks as though there is more than one person involved, but we must not be too quick to speculate. We need more information, and perhaps it is waiting for us in the basement."

The two servants, a woman and a man – quite young – were huddled around a small table. Due to the narrow windows, the lighting was barely adequate. It was a dismal work place. We sat opposite them while reading the statements given to the inspector, who excused himself and left on an errand.

According to the notes, there were seven tenant farmers that stayed on through the whole ordeal, but they never had reason to visit the house other than a daily delivery of milk, eggs, and various garden produce. None were interviewed. The two house servants were employed shortly after the now-deceased Lord had settled his legal and financial problems. They agreed that he was cold and aloof, but was otherwise an adequate master. Both assumed that he lived in fear of the authorities and would do nothing to bring them around. Neither had any previous connection to Lord Garrod or any of the tenants – so they stated.

Holmes set aside the papers. "The two of you are key witnesses to the tragedy – the only witnesses." He turned his attention to the small dark-haired girl. "Now, Miss Jade, I know you have told the story to the police, but I need to hear it directly from you. You are the cook, and you took the breakfast tray to Lord Garrod's chamber yesterday morning."

"I did, sir," said she, with a squeaky voice.

"Did he summon you?"

"No, sir. I delivers it at eight sharp. I does it every day, always the same time."

"What food did you deliver?"

This seemed to startle the girl. I thought it might be a question she had not been asked.

"Ah, 'twas porridge and some tea, if I remember proper."

"When you approached the locked door, what did you do?"

"I knocks and stands in front of the door. He has a peep hole, he does. He opens the door, I take the tray in, and leave it on the great desk. Then I leave."

"What was Lord Garrod doing while you were in the room?"

"I know naught, sir. I keeps me eyes down."

"You saw nothing out of the ordinary?"

"No, sir. Same as every day."

"You came directly down to the kitchen?"

"I did, sir."

"Mr. Langdale was here?"

"For certain he was, sir."

"What did you do then?"

"I served up the porridge to me and Darwin – Mr. Langdale."

"And then?"

"We sat at this table and ate until we heard the chimes and the shot."

Holmes turned to the man. "Mr. Langdale, do you have anything to add to what Miss Jade has told me?"

"No, sir, except when we heard the chimes and the shot, we both ran up to the master's chamber, but it was locked solid. We came back here and used the telephone to call the police. We waited at the front door until they arrived."

"Miss Jade," said Holmes, "do you agree with Mr. Langdale's statement?"

She nodded. "I do, sir. The master dead and all had me in pieces."

Holmes tapped the index finger of his left hand on the table. I knew he was considering his next move. He looked at me for a moment and then stood up. "Please wait here with Dr. Watson. I shall return soon."

I had no idea what my companion had in mind. I reviewed the recent testimony, but I could shed no light on our mystery. I suspected I was probably in a room with the guilty party – a girl who was now making tea for us.

It was a good pot and Holmes returned before I had finished my cup. Miss Jade poured a cup for him as he joined the three of us. After a few sips, he addressed the two servants. "I know this has been a trying time for both of you, and unfortunately the next few days will be no easier. Dr. Watson and I will be leaving shortly, as will the police, but we will return in the morning. Since we have no answers, we must investigate in depth. We will require a complete history from both of you

– place of birth, relatives, former employers, and your travels in general. It will be very intrusive, but I am sure you can see the necessity."

I was as bewildered as the maid and butler, but I tried not to show it as we left them huddled in the kitchen. Gregson was waiting for us in his wagon. He had nothing to say for the whole return drive until he let us off at our door.

"Mr. Holmes, I am a bit nervous just now, but I think we made the right decision – to let them worry overnight. We will know tomorrow."

Mrs. Hudson met us at the door and informed us that our dinner would arrive in thirty minutes. This was welcome news because I was hungry, but I was also curious. Holmes was silent until he stoked the fire and retrieved his oily clay pipe. He picked up the carton that held the papers that we were studying earlier and shuffled through the pile.

"So, my friend," said he, as he looked at the clippings, "do you know where this is going?"

"I think I do."

"Excellent," said Holmes. "Let me relax here with my pipe while you tell the tale."

I had my own briar in one hand and a small glass of sherry in the other. I took an appreciative sip and began: "From the first, I believed that the maid, Ada Jade, had to be the person who set the trigger. That particular day was unimportant. She delivered food under the watchful eye of Lord Garrod, so she had to wait until such time as he was distracted. Perhaps on the fateful day he went behind the screen. No matter. She saw her opportunity and took it.

"At the table in the kitchen, Darwin Langdale's story was lacking. When you opened the call device, it rang the chimes in the basement kitchen. If Ada did the same then Darwin, who said he waited at the table, had to have heard the ringing, but he said nothing. That was when I was sure of the events. The two of them were in league in some manner.

"What I do not know is why you decided to leave more questioning until tomorrow, and why you left the kitchen for a time. Based upon what I heard when Inspector Gregson departed, I assume it was to make the two worry. You must have made a plan, but I will hazard no guess at this point."

All the while, Holmes was sorting through the papers on his lap. As I finished, he picked up a clipping, smiled, and turned his attention back to me. "You have my congratulations, Watson. You have described the events accurately. As I talked to the two, I was also considering the entire chain of events, beginning with the death of Emma Brunnel. I thought about his abominable treatment of her and his treatment of others. At the time, I was also angered to learn that he suffered only a financial penalty.

"Near the end of my session with them, I suddenly remembered an article that I had read earlier this morning when we went through the clippings." He handed the slip of paper to me. "It is about the deceased girl's family in Australia. Read down to where they give the names of her brother and sister."

I scanned the brief story and quickly found the names. "Great Scott," I exclaimed, "her sister's name is Adaline Brunnel and her brother is Dawson Brunell." I set the paper aside and retrieved my glass of sherry. "Incredible, the two of them came from Australia and devoted a year to extract their revenge."

"Quite so," said Holmes. "They retained versions of their first names to make the transition easier. The article also notes that Dawson was an apprentice clockmaker, which gives him the skill to fabricate the call device."

I jumped up from my chair. "Obviously you decided to give them the opportunity to flee, but damn it, man, they'll be fleeing back to Australia as we speak. You all but told them they were done. They can't be fool enough to think the truth won't out during the 'intrusive' investigations you described."

"Indeed," said Holmes, puffing on his pipe, "Justice, Watson . . . it's a funny thing. What moral obligation does one have if such terrible and awful abominations as were suffered by Emily Brunell go unpunished? Should one simply accept it and move on? This, I think, was the quandary that faced the two siblings, and indeed the quandary faced by myself in these past hours."

I sat down again. "Is it justice or revenge we're talking about here, Holmes?"

Holmes looked at the fire. "I have oft thought of asking the hangman the same." He was silent for a moment. "The inspector will join us once again for lunch. I have asked Mrs. Hudson to make enough for four. After we have eaten, we will travel to Sevenoaks and, if I am correct, we shall show considerable surprise to find them gone. I am sure they have long had passage secured. And if they are not, well then, you shall have your justice, such as it is."

Conversation over lunch the next day was very amiable. Inspector Gregson sampled one of Holmes fine cigars over coffee, and Alfie the driver received a full share. The trip was uneventful and, as expected, the two servants were absent. Gregson made a show of questioning the tenants, but Holmes and I declined to participate. The disposition of Lord Garrod's estate was of no concern to us.

167

As we were leaving, the inspector said to Holmes, "If I didn't know better, I'd say you deliberately gave them warning, Holmes."

My friend did not reply and nothing more was said on the matter.

Back at 221b, we relaxed before a small fire where we spent some time discussing the adventure. Holmes summed it up very well. "I feel rather good about all of this. Come. Pick up your cane and hat. I will treat you to a celebratory dinner at Wagner's."

I got up from my chair, but somewhat slower this time. "Do you know, Holmes, I feel quite good about it myself. Quite good indeed."

The afternoon sun gave us elongated shadows that we followed up the street. Somehow, even they reflected our good mood. Everything was satisfactory.

A Brush With Death
by Dick Gillman

Chapter 1 – A Corpse in Surrey

It was late in the afternoon, one day in late August 1898, that Holmes and I were to begin the case that I have here recorded as that of "A Brush with Death".

I had spent the morning in my former practice and, upon the completion of my surgery, I had endeavoured to carry out a small, but supremely important, errand. Before returning to Baker Street, I had ventured towards Carlin's, the tobacconist's. There I hoped to discover something that might provide, at least, some small distraction for Holmes.

For the past week, I had endured the growing impatience of a man whose mind desperately craved stimulation. Finding nothing to intrigue him, Holmes had begun that descent towards darkness which might again lead to his use of the syringe. For several months he had resisted, but I now feared that he might see it as his only means of escape.

At the entrance to Carlin's, the wonderful tobacco emporium, I was almost overwhelmed by the aroma released by a multitude of tobaccos. These, I knew, had been gathered from as far afield as the Americas, the Ottoman Empire and even Africa.

Looking about me, I was drawn to the vast, glass-fronted display cabinet that seemed to fill one complete side of the shop. Upon its surface were small china bowls filled with, perhaps, an ounce or so of different tobaccos. Each was labelled, in fine copperplate script, with its name, price per ounce, and its origin. As I moved from bowl to bowl, dipping my head towards each like some inquisitive heron, I marvelled at how the pungency, colour, and texture varied between each one.

I must confess that I was entranced. Several minutes passed before I determined to buy an ounce of three quite different tobaccos. These I judged to be the most obscure and, therefore, difficult to identify. Paying for my purchases and gathering up the small, brown-paper packages, I joyfully hurried back to our rooms, hopeful that I might lift Holmes's spirits with this intriguing challenge.

Upon entering our sitting room, I could see from the wildly torn and tossed newspapers that his mind had continued to turn inwards upon itself. Holmes was slumped in his leather armchair, his old dressing gown draped roughly around his shoulders, his head bowed and his chiselled chin resting firmly upon his chest.

I was dismayed when he made no effort to greet me on my return. It was as I walked past this sorry figure that I sought to engage him by asking, brightly, "I have made a small purchase on my way back to Baker Street, Holmes. I was hoping that you might indulge me by helping to identify . . . ."

Without looking up or raising his head, Holmes interrupted me, saying "Your visit to Carlin's was not a single purchase, Watson, for you have clearly bought two . . . no, *three* different tobaccos. I presume that this is some pale attempt, on your part, to stir me from my lethargy." Holmes paused before adding, "I am sorry, but at present, I am not in the mood."

On hearing this, I was immediately crestfallen and sank down heavily into my chair. I sat in silence for some minutes before taking the bundles from my jacket pocket and arranging them on the arm of my chair.

It was just as I opened the third package that our doorbell in the hallway below rang loudly. Looking up, I observed that Holmes had stirred slightly, his eyes, I thought, brightening as he strained to hear even a snippet of the conversation at our front door.

A few moments later, the door closed and the familiar footsteps of Mrs. Hudson could then be heard upon the stairs to our rooms. Holmes, I saw, had slipped his dressing gown from his shoulders and moved a little way forwards in his chair. The gentle knock on our sitting room door announced our landlady and, as she entered, I saw that she was holding before her a buff-coloured envelope.

Holmes had taken all this in with a single glance and had risen, striding towards her, asking, "I hope the government messenger bringing mail from my brother did not greatly disturb you, Mrs. Hudson?"

Mrs. Hudson smiled as she passed the envelope to him. "Oh, no, Mr. Holmes. I was only just beginning to crochet some small jam-pot covers for your breakfast tray,"

Holmes smiled in return, announcing, "As always, Mrs. Hudson, I look forward to seeing the fruits of your labour."

Mrs. Hudson beamed, closing the door behind her. I frowned and strained to observe the envelope in Holmes's hand. "As the afternoon post has already been delivered, I appreciate that any further post would be brought by messenger . . . but knowing it to be from Mycroft? It is beyond me, Holmes."

Holmes smiled thinly. "The envelope is clearly one from Her Majesty's Stationery Office, given its distinctive colour and size." I pursed my lips and let Holmes continue. "I had the advantage, Watson, as from my chair I was able to discern not one, but two, wax seals upon its reverse."

At this, I raised my eyebrows. Holmes paused for a moment and, as I watched, a look of concern troubled his face. "This is a rare, yet not unknown occurrence, Watson. Why might this have happened? A simple case of Mycroft becoming distracted? Unlikely, or is there something – "

Holmes fell silent, deep in thought. Filling his pipe, he then proposed, "Perhaps, on this occasion, it may simply be a subconscious nod to his own paranoia, brought upon him by that labyrinth of Whitehall secrecy within which he moves." Lighting his pipe, Holmes drew upon it before continuing, "Let us see if the importance of the contents will enlighten us as to the need for such security."

Taking up his fine Italian stiletto, an elegant memento from the Cagliari affair, Holmes carefully slit the envelope. Sitting once more, he removed from it a single sheet of paper and began to read. As I watched, his increasing interest began to animate his features. Sitting back, Holmes was silent for a few moments before leaping from his chair. His angular figure now raced towards his bedroom whilst over his shoulder he cried out, "Pack a weekend Gladstone, Watson, for we have an appointment with a singularly important corpse in Surrey."

I stood and blinked for a moment before quickly gathering up my purchases of tobacco and stuffing them into my jacket pocket. Seeing Holmes's haste, I too hurried to my bedroom to fling the necessary items into my bag.

Barely two minutes had elapsed before I was then being chastened by Holmes as a laggard and hurried down the stairs and out into Baker Street. Once at the kerb, Holmes held up his cane and furiously flagged down an approaching hansom. With a cry of, "Waterloo Station, as quick as you like, cabbie!" and a florin tossed up to the driver, we clambered inside and were soon off at a fearsome pace.

As we travelled towards Waterloo, Holmes, I saw, was once more his old self. His countenance had lost its pallor and his eyes were bright, like some wary, garden bird, ever watchful and alert. Seeing his eagerness, I took the opportunity to ask him of the contents of the letter from Mycroft. "Tell me, Holmes. Whose corpse are we to examine in Surrey?"

Holmes turned towards me, saying, "We are to travel to Guildford and, for both privacy and, I believe, some element of secrecy, we are to examine the body of Sir Charles Cavendish Short, at the Watts Cemetery Chapel." Holmes paused for a moment, his brow now furrowed and his lips pressed firmly together. "Her Majesty's Government, it seems, requires us to confirm that his death was due to natural causes and that his life was not prematurely curtailed."

I considered this for a moment before replying, "Would not a local pathologist be able to determine this, or . . . or if not, surely they would be able to transfer the body to London for examination?"

Holmes nodded. "Normally so, but it is the supreme importance to the government of this late gentleman, and the rather disturbing international aspect to this matter, that precludes them from acting openly."

I was, I admit, a little mystified by this remark and sat back in the cab for a moment to consider it. The name of the deceased was not unknown to me, but it took me half-a-minute or so to recollect where I had heard it. I sat and muttered to myself, "Short . . . Short . . . Ah! I have him! I have seen his name mentioned in *The Times* as . . . as an advisor to the government upon . . . upon affairs in Africa!"

Holmes smiled and nodded before tapping me sharply on the knee with his cane, saying, "Bravo, Watson . . . but there is more!" At that, the cab lurched to a stop and Holmes leapt from it. With his Gladstone grasped tightly in one hand and cane held aloft as though wielding a sabre, he half turned and cried, "This way, Watson! I believe there is an express passing through Guildford that leaves shortly."

Gathering my own bag, I stepped down gingerly from the cab and hurried after the rapidly retreating figure. Cursing my old war wound and the excesses of my somewhat sedentary life, I was only able to catch up with Holmes as he turned away from the ticket office window. With an impish grin, he pushed two first class tickets into my jacket breast pocket. With a cry of "Platform Four!" he raced away, leaving me to follow, panting, in his wake.

After some fifty yards or so, Holmes paused for a moment and looked up briefly to consult some station signage. With a cry of triumph, he continued onward, only stopping on reaching a first class carriage of the London and South Western Railway. Reaching out, he grasped the exterior brass handle of the compartment door before turning on his heel and beckoning me, rather too energetically, to approach with a little more haste.

Chapter 2 – Game Pie and Spotted Dick

Once ensconced in the compartment and with my Gladstone carefully stowed away, I found it necessary to rest for a moment to catch my breath. Holmes, however, seemed quite unaffected by his exertions and was, indeed, most eager for the train to depart. He looked out, impatiently, onto the platform, glancing one way and then the other. At one point, he took it upon himself to slide down the compartment window to see if, by leaning out, he might catch sight of the guard and his green flag.

After suffering this in silence for some minutes and as he began to rise once more, I caught hold of the corner of Holmes's jacket and gave it a sharp tug. In exasperation, I cried out, "For pity's sake, Holmes! Calm yourself! The man we are to see is already dead and, therefore most unlikely to run away!"

Holmes looked down sharply at me and, for a moment, I thought he was going to rebuke me. However, his features softened and he smiled before retaking his seat. Nodding, he replied, "Of course, you are quite correct, Watson."

Barely two minutes passed before there was the sound of the guard's whistle close by our carriage, followed by the shrill response from the engine. Moments later, we were jolted in our seats as the carriages were pulled raggedly away from Waterloo. With Holmes now at ease, I took this opportunity to ask him for further details of Mycroft's request for our assistance. "Does Mycroft explain what has happened to this fellow, Short?"

Holmes took from his pocket the buff-coloured envelope and briefly scanned its contents before replying, "Little enough. He says that Sir Charles had taken a few days' leave and had secured a room at The Bull's Head, an inn in Guildford. This, apparently, was so that he could pursue his hobby of watercolour painting. Whilst there, he fell gravely ill one evening with severe abdominal pains. These were followed, within a few hours, by coma and death." Holmes turned over the letter, adding, "Mycroft advises that he has reserved rooms for us at The Bull's Head, and that a Doctor Weaver will meet us at Watts Cemetery Chapel at ten o'clock in the morning."

Holmes paused for a moment and reached for his pipe before continuing. "It would appear that a discreet *post mortem* was carried out yesterday at Guildford mortuary, the results of which will be waiting for us tomorrow at the chapel." Holmes filled and lit his pipe and drew strongly upon it before taking it from between his lips and then wagging the stem towards me. "However, what intrigues me is that Mycroft states that a Dutch fellow, who was staying at the same inn, has been questioned regarding the death. The Dutch government have been informed and are taking a very dim view of the affair. Unfortunately, and which I find most vexing, Mycroft does not supply any further details in this matter."

173

I sat back and considered what Holmes had said and then suddenly jolted upright as a thought struck me, blurting out, "A Dutchman . . . a *Boer*!"

Holmes looked across at me and was nodding slowly. Tilting back his head, he blew out a ribbon of blue smoke towards the carriage ceiling, before saying, "Yes, that thought had crossed my mind, Watson. Mycroft mentions, briefly, that Sir Charles had been a close confidant of the Prime Minister for some time, and was the draftsman of much of Britain's future plans for Southern Africa. This included, specifically, our relations with the Boers, upon which Sir Charles took a particularly hard line."

On hearing this, my mind was now racing, and I began to speak my thoughts aloud: "Then this so called Dutchman could well be a Boer assassin, sent to . . . ."

I looked towards Holmes whose face looked most stern. He held up his hand with its palm facing me . . . cautioning me. "Facts, Watson! Facts! You know my methods. We will have to wait until the morning and our examination of Sir Charles before we can move forward."

At this, Holmes closed his eyes and would say no more. He simply continued to draw steadily upon his pipe and seemed to withdraw into his own private temple of contemplation. For my part, I sat back and watched as the last remnants of the houses that made up the ever expanding city of London fell away to reveal the leafy countryside of Surrey.

The train sped onwards and seemed eager to consume the thirty-odd miles to Guildford, thanks partly to the new railway line that served Leatherhead and the Epsom Downs. Before long, Guildford Station came into view and, upon leaving the station, a cab from the rank on Station View was engaged to convey us to The Bull's Head.

I had visited Guildford before and, as we rode along the High Street, I again marvelled at the fine array of shops that were present, many with black and white Tudor facades. The cab slowed as we passed beneath a huge, ornate, double-sided clock which protruded outwards over the High Street on an iron beam. Looking about me, I was indeed pleased when the cab came to rest beside an inn with a rather fine, mock-Tudor facade. This grand building, with its overhanging upper storey, proudly proclaimed itself to be The Bull's Head. From its signage, it offered both accommodation and a profusion of ales, beers, and spirits.

Holmes, on tossing the cabbie a shilling, stepped down with some enthusiasm, eager to venture inside. As I struggled to alight a little more cautiously, Holmes smiled cheerily, taunting me with the remark, "Come along, Watson. I would imagine that you to be in considerable need of

174

sustenance after your exertions!" In return, I forced the best smile that I could muster before following him, wearily, inside.

Stepping into the porch of the inn, I peered manfully through the stained glass of the door in the direction of the bar. Here could be seen the familiar figure of my friend, already in deep conversation with the landlord. As I entered, I dropped my Gladstone, whereupon he patted me soundly on the shoulder, exclaiming, "Ah, Watson! Come along old fellow. We are still in time for dinner!"

With the thought of nourishment, all tiredness seemed to fall from me. Looking behind the bar, I noticed a large blackboard lodged between the shelves of spirits. This I regarded most closely as upon it was chalked the menu of the day. Some popular items already had a line drawn through them to show that they were no longer on offer. However, my eye now fell upon the game pie. A rare treat, so early in the grouse season!

Seeing my considerable interest in this dish, Holmes decided to join me in opting for it. Once ordered, we found a table and were soon enjoying a pint of Carter and Stone's best bitter, whilst waiting for our meal.

As we sat, sipping our beer, I asked Holmes if he had any further thoughts regarding the Dutchman. Holmes was now sitting back with a somewhat distant look in his eyes, as he answered, "I am at something of a loss to comprehend the situation, Watson. We are told that a man has been questioned, presumably, for some suspected involvement in the death of Sir Charles. However, as Sir Charles was seriously ill for some hours prior to his death, why would a guilty man remain at the scene? To allay suspicion? A possibility . . . but unlikely." Holmes paused for a moment and briefly shook his head. "I find it unbelievable that the Boers would leave their agent *in-situ* after an assassination. No, Watson. It simply won't do."

As I pursed my lips and considered this, the landlord appeared with a tray containing our dinner. The two steaming plates were placed before us and, on seeing the fare, I rubbed my hands together gleefully in anticipation. Without delay, we tucked in with relish. I have to admit, the game pie served with wonderful, rich gravy was a delight! We sat back, replete, for a few minutes and it was as the landlord returned, to ask us what we would like to follow, that Holmes engaged him further in conversation.

"Tell me, landlord. I understand there was an unexpected death at the inn a little earlier in the week?" asked Holmes, quite innocently.

The landlord was about to gather together our well cleaned plates but stopped and looked a little taken aback. "Why, yes sir! I'm surprised

175

you heard of that in London. It was a gentleman that was staying here. He had been out, painting, I believe, and then fell ill and died within hours. Out of the blue, it was. He was fine one day and then gone the next!"

The landlord then lowered his voice before continuing, "They questioned a Dutchman who had been with him and then, bless me, they let him go!" On saying this, the landlord turned slightly and pointed a stubby finger towards a middle-aged gentleman sitting some small distance away, in the corner of the room.

Holmes nodded slowly before looking over his shoulder to consider, once more, the blackboard bearing the day's menu. "Knowing my colleague's sweet tooth, I think we both might have a little of the 'Spotted Dick' and custard, if you please." I smiled in agreement at my friend's choice, for Holmes was well aware of my penchant for steamed puddings.

As Holmes reached for his beer, I took the opportunity to look past him and regard the gentleman that the landlord had pointed out. The fellow appeared to be well dressed, although in clothes of an unfamiliar cut. He was of medium build, having a round face topped by unfashionably long, grey, hair swept back from his temples. He sat, drawing upon a clay pipe, with a solitary drink in front of him. He seemed to me to be a figure that was far removed from my vision of a Boer assassin.

Once the pudding had been enjoyably dispatched, I suggested to Holmes that, from my observations, the Dutch gentleman appeared to be quite harmless. Holmes took his pipe from his lips. "As you are well aware, Watson, looks can sometimes be deceptive. I am sure that I need not remind you of Julia Moriarty! However, on this occasion, I believe that you are correct." With that, Holmes rose, adding, quietly, "Let us introduce ourselves."

Chapter 3 – A Dutchman and a Challenge

As Holmes reached the Dutchman's table, I saw him draw from his waistcoat pocket one of his cards. This he then proffered to the gentleman, saying, "Excuse the intrusion, sir. My name is Sherlock Holmes, and this is my good friend, Dr. John Watson. May we join you, briefly?"

The Dutchman looked up, rather shocked, and then took Holmes's card. He looked at it for a moment and then, in excellent English and with a fine accent, replied, "Why, yes, Mr. Holmes." The man offered his hand, saying, "I am Jacob De Witt . . . from Rotterdam."

Sitting down, Holmes continued by asking, "Tell me, Mr. De Witt, what do you know of Sir Charles Short, the gentleman who died earlier this week?"

Jacob De Witt puffed out his cheeks before saying, "Well, Mr. Holmes, I must say, very little. I had met him twice on the banks of the River Wey. I had taken my paints and easel and, on meeting a fellow artist, we had sat together as we painted. I paint in oils, whilst Sir Charles painted in watercolours." Holmes nodded and waited for De Witt to say more. "He painted the most exquisite flowers and, to do this, he used the finest of brushes." De Witt paused as though recalling his meeting. "Yes, to obtain the intricate detail, he had the most curious habit of drawing out the hairs of his brush with his lips."

At this, Holmes raised an eyebrow. De Witt continued, "As we spoke together, I discovered that we were, indeed, staying at the same inn and, on the day of his death, we had taken tea together." De Witt paused for a moment. "Perhaps that is why I came under suspicion. The police have retained my passport and I have been told not to leave Guildford. I believe that it is only after the intervention of the Dutch Embassy that I was released from questioning."

I shot Holmes a glance, with my eyebrows raised. Holmes pulled his chair a little closer to the table, asking, "Are you here on business, Mr. De Witt?"

De Witt nodded. "Why, yes. I am a representative of the Amersfoort Tobacco Company, one the oldest in Holland. I have been coming to England for many years now, selling cigars and pipe tobacco."

Upon hearing this, Holmes's eyes lit up, crying, "Ah, splendid! You may, then, be of some assistance, Mr. De Witt. My friend here, Dr. Watson, purchased three types of tobacco this morning and, unfortunately, omitted to label what he bought. Do you have them with you, Watson?"

I was confused for a moment and then delved into my jacket pocket and retrieved the three small parcels. These I carefully placed on the table in front of De Witt. I watched eagerly as he unwrapped a parcel, examining the contents before holding it to his nose and then rubbing the tobacco between his fingers. He then proceeded to the next parcel.

Sitting back, he beamed at us, saying, "You have made some interesting choices, Dr. Watson. The first is Latakia, a fire-cured tobacco used in Balkan blends. It has a smoky aroma and is probably from the island of Cyprus. The second is an American blend of Perique, originally from Louisiana. I think you will find that it is often combined with a more delicate, lighter leaf from Virginia."

177

Holmes was seen to nod in appreciation and he held out his hand in an invitation to proceed to the third parcel. De Witt ran a little of the tobacco through his fingers before he raised it again to his nose and sniffed, saying, "This is another interesting tobacco, Doctor. I believe this to be a North American Burley, air dried and quite mild . . . but there is an addition . . . a little Kentucky, I think, to add some spice."

Holmes clapped his hands, saying, "Bravo, Mr. De Witt . . . although I might argue that the first one may, perhaps, come from a little further east, although still within the Ottoman Empire." De Witt smiled, in appreciation of Holmes's knowledge, and nodded in return.

It was as I began to gather the packages together that Holmes stood up, saying, "There you are, Watson. I think that they will all be a good smoke . . . *Stem jy saam?*"

On hearing this, I was indeed baffled! I looked towards Holmes and then to De Witt. The Dutchman's face looked firstly confused and then his expression hardened. "Ah, I see what you are saying, Mr. Holmes. So that is why I was questioned."

Holmes nodded, sombrely. "Yes, I believe it was, Mr. De Witt, I will do all in my power to have your passport returned so that you might be on your way." With that, Holmes gave a polite nod and strode off towards the bar to seek out our rooms.

Holmes would say no more of our meeting with De Witt, and I slept fitfully that night. As we were to have an early start, I had asked the landlord to awaken us at eight a.m. After his knock on my door and my call of thanks in return, I rose straight away. However, I was still in my nightshirt when Holmes rapped loudly upon my door, barely some ten minutes later, summoning me to breakfast. Dressing as quickly as I could, I made my way downstairs to what, I hoped, would be a good, country meal.

Finding the breakfast room, I saw that Holmes was already tucking into sausages, bacon, and eggs, accompanied by thick slices of black pudding and fried bread. I ordered the same and, upon finishing, I enjoyed buttered toast, heaped with a generous helping of some delicious Seville marmalade. It was as I relished my cup of Darjeeling that I had a mind to ask Holmes the meaning of his curious question to De Witt. "Tell me, what did you ask in Dutch last night?"

In reply, Holmes raised his hand and wagged his finger at me, saying, mischievously, "Ah! I asked him, '*Do you agree?*' but it was not Dutch . . . it was *Afrikaans!*"

He answered just as I was taking a further swallow of tea. In truth, I almost choked upon it, causing me to quickly grasp a napkin to cover my mouth. I spluttered for some moments before being able to ask, "Afrikaans? Do you believe that he is a Boer?"

Holmes chuckled. "No, Watson. He is as he appears, I have little doubt of that. The small challenge regarding the tobacco that I set him last night was proof enough . . . but I wanted him to be aware of the reason why he had been questioned."

Chapter 4 – The Late Sir Charles Cavendish Short

Now breakfasted, we rose from the table with Holmes leading the way towards the High Street. Once outside, it was but a simple task to flag down a passing cab, Holmes tossing the cabbie a shilling and shouting out our destination of Watts Cemetery Chapel.

Our ride to the chapel was short, a mere three miles from the centre of Guildford. Climbing down from the cab, Holmes asked the cabbie to wait for us and tossed him a further sixpence. On arriving at the chapel, I was immediately impressed by the new, Romanesque edifice with almost-pink brick that stood before us. I had read of its recent completion in *The Times*, and this grand, circular-shaped chapel now towered above the countryside around it.

As we made our way around the outside of the building towards the entrance, one could not fail to be impressed by its grandeur. The fine terracotta reliefs were splendid and, to me at least, had a strong, Egyptian influence. Standing before the ornate, arched doorway was a tall figure whom I took to be Dr. Weaver. He was a thin-faced man of, I would estimate, forty years, dressed in an overcoat. I noticed a head of greying hair crowned by a dark hat. At our approach he smiled and extended his hand, asking, "Mr. Holmes? I am Dr. Weaver. Shall we go inside?"

With the door now closed behind us, I was immediately impressed by the vast circular space before me. The immensely high, domed roof was vaulted, supported by eight painted columns. These rose majestically, being embossed and gilded. The decoration reminded me of intricate, Celtic knot-work.

At the very centre of the building, there had been erected a trestle table, upon which the corpse of Sir Charles Short had been placed, covered from the neck down by a single mortuary sheet. Alongside this was a smaller table, where Sir Charles' personal possessions had been set out, including, it seemed, all the items from his room at The Bull's Head.

Dr. Weaver reached into his overcoat pocket and withdrew a large Manila envelope. This he offered to Holmes, saying, cryptically, "This is the *post mortem* and toxicology report, Mr. Holmes . . . . I believe that you'll find that it makes interesting reading."

Holmes gave Weaver a questioning look as he took the envelope from his grasp. For several minutes he stood, brows furrowed, reading the report. With his forefinger now held against his lips, he passed the report to me before turning and asking, "May I examine the body, Dr. Weaver?"

At this, Weaver pulled down the sheet, exposing the dead man for Holmes's inspection. Rough, exposed stitching indicated where the incisions for the *post mortem* examination of the internal organs had been carried out. Holmes stood back for a moment, as though observing the posture of the corpse, before moving forward to examine it more closely. I noticed that he seemed to be looking particularly at the limbs and extremities of this sorry figure. As I watched, he inclined his head briefly, a clear signal for me to join him at his side.

I stood close to Holmes and he turned slightly towards me, asking, "Do you notice anything particular about the fingers and the toes, Watson?"

I moved a little closer and examined the wrists, fingers, and toes of the deceased. I also took it upon myself to flex the elbows and the knees, which appeared to me to be unusually stiff, given the time that had passed since death.

With the body having been examined in some detail, our task was now complete. Holmes pulled up the mortuary sheet and moved to consider the personal effects laid out upon the side table. He spent several minutes closely examining these items, showing particular interest in Sir Charles' pocket watch.

The watch, I noticed was a gold, stem-wound half-hunter. Holmes, his glass in his hand, again beckoned me to come to his side. On the shield-shaped cartouche decorating the back of the watch, I saw the inscription of two sets of intertwined initials, *CCS* and *MK*. The open, back cover comprised a glazed frame which contained a circular photograph of a man who was clearly Sir Charles, and a slim, unknown, woman, together with a girl of, perhaps, fourteen or fifteen years. All three were dressed formally in what I presumed to be their best attire and jewellery.

Replacing the watch on the table, Holmes now busied himself with his examination of Sir Charles' painting regalia. I was intrigued as he picked up both the heavily-used paint palette and the blocks of colour, proceeding to offer each one up to his nose. Satisfied, he carefully replaced these items into their case . . . but his quizzical expression piqued my interest.

With his examination completed, Holmes turned back to Dr. Weaver, asking, "Might we be able to retain the *post mortem* report for a little while? I would like to consider it further with my colleague, Dr. Watson." Weaver nodded in agreement and, on touching his hat, Holmes bade him farewell and we returned to our waiting cab.

Once more at The Bull's Head, we sought out a quiet corner of the bar and laid out before us the report. Holmes took out his pipe, as did I, and we settled in to further consider the findings. Blowing out a gentle plume of smoke, Holmes asked, "What do you infer from the report, Watson?"

I was silent for a moment whilst I gathered together my thoughts. "Well, I was indeed concerned by the contents of the toxicology report. The dangerously high levels of poisonous metals that were found, particularly cadmium, arsenic, and white lead, was initially puzzling." Holmes nodded and briefly waved his hand as a sign for me to go on. Gaining confidence, I continued, "However, I then recalled our conversation with De Witt and how he had observed Sir Charles being in the habit of placing his brush tip between his moistened lips to obtain a fine point. The metallic pigments in the paint would then account for their presence."

Holmes nodded again, but then asked, ". . . and the concentrations? Fatal, would you say?"

My brow furrowed as I considered this. "I presume, after seeing his well-used paint box and paint-bespattered easel, that Sir Charles was an experienced painter. As such, he had been exposed to the toxicity of these paints for some considerable time and had built up some tolerance to them. That being the case, I would say probably not."

Holmes clapped his hand down upon the arm of his chair, crying out, "Bravo, Watson! My thoughts entirely . . . although the summary of the *post mortem* findings leans heavily towards poisoning from the imbibed paint as being the cause of death. In light of this, I would expect a coroner to pronounce a verdict of 'death by misadventure'."

Holmes sat back and then asked another question. "When we examined the body, I was taken by its awkward posture, for I could not imagine an undertaker arranging it so. What was your impression?"

Again I took my time to answer, thinking back to the alignment of the limbs and, particularly, the stiffness of the joints and the curvature of the hands and feet. "This aspect troubles me, Holmes, for I have seen something similar before, but cannot quite put my finger upon it."

Holmes held his right forefinger to his lips before replying, "It is not something that is commonplace, but if I were to say to you . . . prussic acid?"

"Cyanide!" I cried out. "Yes, of course. I recall being required to provide a death certificate for a careless photographer who had ingested

181

a small, but fatal, quantity whilst in his dark room. His limbs were twisted in the extreme due to the severe muscle contractions that it invoked." Only after saying this did the full import of what was being suggested strike me. I sat, open mouthed, for a moment before asking, "You are proposing that Sir Charles may have been poisoned by cyanide? Surely that would have been evident in the *post mortem* report?"

Holmes's face was grim. He drew strongly upon his pipe and then held the stem aloft, saying, "Not necessarily. The body showed no physical evidence of gross cyanide poisoning. The pathologist, on having found high levels of the presumed culprits, might have failed to observe a small dose of cyanide. However, even a small dose, to a man whose system was already heavily impaired by the paint's toxicity, might well have been fatal."

I sat back, thinking through the implications of this revelation. "Is it possible that the cyanide was ingested accidentally, as happened with the paint?"

Holmes shook his head. "With my suspicions raised, you will recall that I examined Sir Charles' belongings most carefully at the chapel, including his artist's equipment. There was nothing amongst his effects to suggest that he had ever been exposed to cyanide. Indeed, I smelt his paints and palette to see if they were contaminated, but they clearly were not."

My mind was now in turmoil. "If cyanide had been administered deliberately, then this is murder and . . . and the murderer must have known that a small dose would probably be sufficient to end Sir Charles' life." The consequences of my words now overwhelmed me! "But . . . but there is only one person here who knew of Sir Charles' habit of sucking his brushes. De Witt!"

Holmes pursed his lips. "This is indeed most puzzling, Watson, for I am certain that he is not our man. There must be another who had observed Sir Charles' behaviour and sought to profit from it. We must talk again with De Witt."

Chapter 5 – Tea and a Slice of Cake

It was some little time after luncheon before we were to have that opportunity. We were taking afternoon tea in the bar as Jacob De Witt entered, carrying his paints and easel. On seeing us, he gave a cheery wave. At this, Holmes called out to him and beckoned him towards our table, asking, "Mr. De Witt, won't you have a cup of tea?

De Witt nodded in thanks, put down his equipment, and was happy to join us. I sought to catch the eye of the landlord to bring another cup and, having done so, we were soon at our ease, each with a delightful cup of Darjeeling. As we sipped, Holmes asked, "Tell me, Mr. De Witt, did you and Sir Charles have to travel far to find a suitable location from which to paint?"

De Witt laughed. "No, Mr. Holmes. We barely had to travel at all for, it seems, we had both independently found the ideal viewpoint. It was a small patch of grass alongside a tea-shop which stands on the tow path beside the river. Over the years in England, I have acquired a taste for tea, to match that of Sir Charles. It would seem that he had taken tea there before, as he told me that he had seen me the previous day from the bay window of the shop, sitting close by with my easel."

De Witt paused to take a further sip. "We had sat together painting on the day of his death. Sir Charles used his watercolours, concentrating on the flowers of the riverbank, whilst I tried to capture some of the essence of the flow of the river with my oils. At around five o'clock in the afternoon, he paused for tea and invited me to join him in the tea-shop. We shared a pot together, and the young lady who served us seemed pleased that Sir Charles had brought her a new customer, offering him a piece of fruit cake with his tea in thanks."

At this, I saw Holmes edge forward slightly on his chair, asking, "Ah, and was it delicious?"

De Witt again laughed. "I do not know, Mr. Holmes, for I did not taste it. It looked wonderful: Lots of fruit, and with the top decorated with almonds. I asked if I could have some too, but I was told that, unfortunately, Sir Charles had been served the last piece."

I saw Holmes stiffen, asking, "Did the proprietor say 'Sir Charles' as she answered your question?"

De Witt's brows furrowed for a moment before he answered. "Why . . . yes, yes, I believe she did. How strange! I expect that he was an old customer of hers."

Holmes nodded and smiled, but it was clear to me that something was amiss. Having finished his tea, De Witt was about to leave when Holmes turned to him, asking, "I wonder, Mr. De Witt, if I might have sight of your paints? I have been known to dabble in oils, but that was quite some time ago . . . ."

Jacob De Witt beamed and moved to an empty table, upon which he placed his paint box before opening it. The box itself was of an ingenious cantilever design, and had sections for brushes, paints, cleaning rags, and various jars of oil and turpentine. Holmes moved in closer and peered at the contents most carefully. Finally, he passed his nose across the whole box, exclaiming, "Ah, how I miss the vivid colours and the smell of oils. You have a fine paint box, Mr. De Witt. I am most grateful for your indulgence." De Witt gave a mock bow and, once all was packed away, he left us to our thoughts.

Holmes now looked deeply concerned. He had sat back in his chair, fingers steepled against his lips and eyes fixed, staring at some point in the distance. "It appears, Watson, that we are in need of a little more tea and, perhaps, a slice of cake!"

I looked quizzically at my friend and then suddenly realised what his intentions were. After an innocent inquiry of our landlord and some brief directions, we were soon on our way to seek out further refreshments.

Setting off from The Bull's Head, our destination was but a brief walk from the town, along the banks of the River Wey, abutting the towpath. At first glance, it appeared to be a small cottage with a fine, lawned, flower garden in front and a fruit orchard to the rear. The cottage, it seemed, had once been a simple dwelling. However, on looking through its bow windows, one either side of the door, there could be seen several small tables, covered with checked tablecloths and decorated with small bunches of flowers. Around the tables sat a mixed clientele made up of couples, young families, and some fashionable ladies, all of whom were taking tea.

Holmes and I stood for a few moments observing not only the customers, but also who was serving them. The staff was comprised of a single waitress, a young, fresh-faced girl, aged less than twenty years, and also a young woman of, I would say, twenty-five years, whom I took to be the proprietor. As we watched the pair moving between the tables, it was clear that each had her own area to serve. Holmes looked quite stern and, with a tug at my sleeve, he moved with some determination towards the doorway of the tea-shop.

Once inside, I noticed that he deliberately chose to sit in the area served by the young woman. Although Holmes now appeared to be completely at his ease, I knew that, as he casually looked around, he was taking in every single detail.

After perhaps only a minute or so, the young lady approached. She was a tall attractive figure with honey-coloured hair. She moved with an elegance that appeared to be a little out of place in this setting. She was dressed in a long, ankle-length, grey skirt above which she wore a soft, white, pleated blouse. This was open at the collar to reveal an elegant gold-and-sapphire pendant. Standing beside our table, she turned over to a fresh page in the small notepad she carried and greeted us by saying, "Good afternoon, gentlemen. What may I get for you?"

Holmes smiled in return, asking, "I think we might have a pot of tea for two and, perhaps, we might choose a slice of cake? I have it on good authority that it is most excellent."

The young lady nodded appreciatively. "It is all homemade, sir. I try, wherever I can, to use our own fruit and produce. Perhaps you may like to choose something from the display?"

Turning to me, Holmes inclined his head slightly, saying, "Watson, would you be a good fellow and allow me to peruse the cakes and make a choice for both of us?" I raised my eyebrows at this but, on seeing the determination on his face, I nodded in agreement.

Holmes smiled and gave me a brief nod before walking the few paces to the back of the shop. It was here that a large glass-fronted cabinet displayed a mouth-watering selection of scones, fruit tarts, and cakes. In truth, I was a little dismayed that I was being denied the opportunity to make a choice of my own.

Straining to obtain a better view of the wares on display, I could see that Holmes had attracted the attention of the young waitress and was now deep in conversation with her. After a minute or so of deliberation and discussion, he smiled and then pointed towards what appeared to be a dark, rich fruit cake. Whilst I judged it to be an acceptable choice, I was disappointed, as I had a particular craving for a piece of ginger cake.

It was on his return that he lowered his voice, saying, "This is most interesting, Watson. It appears that this establishment is owned by a Miss Annie Knight, and it has been open barely a matter of weeks." Holmes raised an eyebrow before continuing, "Hardly time, wouldn't you say, for a customer, who might only be an occasional visitor from London, to be addressed as 'Sir Charles'?"

I pondered this for a few moments as I observed that, given the hour, the tea-shop's customers had now begun to drift away, homeward.

Within a few minutes of our order being taken, the pot of tea arrived, together with two rather impressive slices of plain, dark, rich fruit cake. Holmes examined the cake and then shot me a questioning look.

It was as Miss Knight placed the final item of our order upon the table that Holmes presented her with his card. "My name is Sherlock Holmes and this is my companion Dr. John Watson. I wonder if you might spare us a moment of your time?" The young lady looked about her and, on seeing that no new customers had entered and needed her attention, she pulled out a chair from the table and joined us.

Holmes was immediately direct and began, "My companion and I are investigating the death of Sir Charles Short, a visitor from London who, from what I can gather, died from poisoning. He was, it seems, something of an amateur artist who enjoyed painting the flora and fauna of our waterways. I am trying to determine his movements over the last two days and was wondering if you might have seen anyone along the riverbank with an easel?"

The young lady pressed her lips together and frowned, before replying, "Why no, Mr. Holmes. I have seen no one. But he may, of course, have been further up the river, towards the mill? Many artists, it seems, use the mill as a subject for their paintings."

Holmes nodded and smiled before he tapped his forefinger against his lips, saying brightly, "Ah, a pity, but nothing is lost, for I have an appointment tomorrow morning with his painting companion, a Mr. De Witt. Apparently, he had been constantly at Sir Charles' side for the last day or so as they painted together."

As I watched, all colour seemed to drain from the young lady's face. To this, Holmes appeared to be oblivious as he continued, "Whilst I was choosing my cake, I asked the waitress about your splendid garden and orchard. She told me you had only recently moved here from London, but you do, indeed, seem to have 'green fingers'."

Miss Knight forced a weak smile, saying, "Thank you. It is because, for the several years that my mother was ill, I tended our lawn and flower garden. Upon her death, I left my employment in London and came here to begin a new life."

Upon hearing this, a subtle change came over Holmes and he appeared to observe Miss Knight most carefully as he asked, "I'm so sorry. Did your father accompany you to Guildford?"

At this, the young lady rose, saying, in a voice that was ice-cold, "No, Mr. Holmes. My father left us years ago, under particularly harsh circumstances. Now, if you'll excuse me . . . ." Holmes nodded and we both rose as Annie Knight left us in some haste.

Holmes sat impassive for a minute or so and, although the cake was delicious, Holmes frowned and asked, "A little different in appearance from the description of that offered to Sir Charles, do you not think, Watson?" I looked at my cake and, on seeing nothing amiss, I made no reply and continued to devour it with some gusto.

We finished our tea and cake in silence, for I could see that Holmes was most troubled. On paying the bill, he hurried from the tea-shop, stopping only briefly to send a telegram before we returned to The Bull's Head.

Chapter 6 – Flushing Out the Quarry

Finding once again a quiet corner, Holmes filled his pipe and proceeded to smoke incessantly for perhaps twenty minutes without uttering a single word. At last, he broke his silence by asking, most bluntly, "What might drive a young woman to poison her own father, Watson?"

On hearing this, my pipe almost fell from my mouth as I spluttered, "You believe Annie Knight to be a poisoner and that she disposed of her own father in this way? Are you suggesting that there is a connection between her father and Sir Charles?"

Holmes tilted back his head and slowly breathed out a ribbon of smoke. "I believe that her father and Sir Charles are one and the same. It is her motive that I wish to discover. I am hopeful that my telegram to Mycroft might enlighten me before further damage is done."

I looked at Holmes in some horror. "Do you mean that she intends to strike again?"

Holmes shot me a glance and, in an angry tone, rebuked me, saying. "She is not some common poisoner, Watson! I believe her to be a woman who has been severely wronged and, whether for revenge or in self-defence, has acted against a single individual."

I sat back, feeling somewhat scolded, but I was eager to hear Holmes's reasoning. Seeing my disquiet, he drew steadily upon his pipe before proceeding thus. "I was unsettled by this case from the outset, Watson. Mycroft's letter, you will recall, bore a double seal, which was, indeed, unusual. I believe that it was a measure of both his own discontent and the need for complete discretion in this matter."

Nodding, I urged him to continue. Steepling his fingers against his lips, Holmes frowned, saying, "Let us consider what we know of the case. Sir Charles was seen as an invaluable asset to the government and, upon his death, it was feared that he may have been assassinated by the Boers. In light of which, a secretive *post mortem* was carried out to discover if that had been the case. Mycroft requested that we confirm the findings and also to ascertain any part played in Sir Charles' death by the Dutchman, De Witt."

I nodded in agreement, but it was the actions of Annie Knight and her relationship to Sir Charles Short that I found perplexing. "What, then, have you discovered that might link Annie Knight to his death?" I asked.

Holmes was quiet for a moment before answering, "If you recall our examination of Sir Charles' effects at the chapel, Watson, the cartouche on his watch bore his initials . . . but also the initials, *MK*. Those, I suspect, relate to the maiden name of his wife." Thinking aloud, he added, "Yes . . . perhaps the watch was an engagement present?"

187

I pursed my lips and frowned, before saying, "But the photograph within showed Sir Charles and, presumably, his wife and their child!"

Holmes wagged his pipe stem in my direction, saying, "Quite so, but the Leopard hallmark and date letter 'n' revealed that the watch was assayed in London in 1868. The family photograph is, I believe, a later addition."

With something of a twinkle in his eye, Holmes now asked, "Did you observe anything in common between the figures in the photograph and Annie Knight?" On saying this, he smiled, whilst seeming to be adjusting his necktie, an action which I considered to be unnecessary.

For a moment, I wondered if I had failed to observe a family resemblance within the photograph when, suddenly, Holmes's actions triggered a memory. "The . . . the necklace! Annie Knight was wearing a necklace identical to the one in the watch worn by . . . ." My voice trailed away, as the full import of what I was saying became crystal clear.

Holmes was nodding slowly. "Yes, no doubt a family piece. However, Watson, I made a serious error in my subsequent deduction regarding Sir Charles' curious habit."

I frowned, asking "How so?"

Holmes face was blank as he recalled, "After we had talked to De Witt, I presumed, wrongly, that whoever had administered the cyanide must have seen Sir Charles refining his brush tip whilst he was painting by the towpath. That was incorrect. Fortunately, for us, circumstances led us to his daughter, Annie Knight, who, undoubtedly, would already be aware of her father's habit."

On hearing this, I thought back to the toxicology report and I was disquieted by it. "Tell me, Holmes. How would Annie Knight have the knowledge to administer the precise dose of poison for it to be effective, and yet not to be detected at a *post mortem*? From where did she obtain it and . . . and how was it administered?"

Holmes tapped his forefinger against his lip and looked thoughtful. "It is something, in part, that I hope that Mycroft may well be able to confirm, in response to my telegram."

Almost on cue, a uniformed telegram boy opened the door to the Saloon bar, calling out, "Telegram for Mr. Holmes?" Holmes leapt from his chair and then, after pressing a sixpence into the lad's hand, took the telegram from him.

Upon reading its contents, Holmes was silent for perhaps a minute, standing quite immobile. Consulting his watch, he then suddenly lunged for his hat, coat, and cane, and ran full tilt from the bar. For a moment, I was stunned by his actions, but followed him as quickly as I could.

By the time I reached the High Street, Holmes had already obtained a cab and was waving frantically to hurry my approach. Breathless, I clambered aboard, hearing Holmes call out, "Guildford Station, as quickly as you can, cabbie!"

The jolt from the cab as it sped away flung me backwards against the seat. Exhausted as I was after my enforced exercise, I barely managed to gasp, "What is afoot, Holmes?"

Holmes's eyes burned. "We must stop Annie Knight from leaving Guildford. It is I who have caused this! I have flushed her out, and must now make amends!"

I thought this statement to be most curious, but had no time to ask Holmes to explain himself before Guildford Station came into view. Leaping from the cab, Holmes raced up the station approach, heading directly towards the platform that served the trains travelling towards London.

Looking around him wildly, Holmes started to pace, scouring the platform until he suddenly froze and then walked calmly towards a tall, slender figure in the shadows.

Touching his hat, Holmes spoke in a gentle but firm voice. "You must not leave Guildford, Miss Knight. I know what you have done and the terrible reason why. I give you my solemn word that I will not reveal this to the authorities . . . unless you force my hand by leaving."

Annie Knight's frightened face, part covered by a veiled hat, peered back at Holmes. "You . . . you know . . . ? And the reason?" Holmes nodded slowly and then offered her his arm. With a questioning look, she hesitantly took it.

In the forecourt of the station, Holmes spotted a four-wheeler that had just brought a party to the station. With a wave of his cane and a loud cry of "Hold!" he was able to secure it for our return to The Bull's Head.

Chapter 7 – Kew and Greengages

Seeking out a secluded area in the corner of the bar, Holmes ordered tea. Nothing was said until we were all served, and I was gratified to observe that Annie Knight looked a little more at ease in our company. However, it was evident that there was still tension present in her body. Her hands shook as she cradled her tea cup.

Holmes now leant forwards slightly, asking, "When did you first recognise your father, Miss Knight?"

Annie Knight took a sip before replying, "I recognised him as soon as he walked into my tea-shop. He was alone and, on seeing him, I

189

instantly chose not to serve him. However, as he sat at one of the tables, he called me over to him. He must have recognised me also as he greeted me by name."

She paused. Her voice faltered slightly as she then said, "Mr. Holmes, I . . . I despised this man and had wished never to set eyes upon him again. He all but killed my mother with his bare hands." Her voice trembled as she continued. "Apart from the grievous harm from the beatings, her mental health suffered. She was never the same again, Mr. Holmes. I was overjoyed when he finally left us, some eight years ago."

Tears now flowed down her cheeks in rivulets. Holmes's face was set like stone as he nodded, grimly, saying, "So I understand."

With a sob, her voice was now little more than a whisper. "He told me that as my mother was dead and my duties of nursing and caring for her were at an end, he expected me to return to London to live with him. I . . . I told him that I could not, Mr. Holmes, for I knew that it would be the same for me. I did not want to be dominated, beaten, and, perhaps, pushed headlong down the stairs, as she had been. He . . . he had said, in the past, that it was his right and, indeed, his duty, to instill absolute obedience."

As I watched, Holmes's hands became as white as marble from his ever tightening grip upon the arms of his chair. I sat aghast at hearing this tale of brutality and was barely able to ask, "When your mother was assaulted, did not the authorities hold your father to account? Surely, since . . . since 1891, it has been the law that husbands do not have the right to beat their wives?"

Before Miss Knight could reply, Holmes's steel-like voice answered, "You forget, Watson, that whilst that is the law, violence in the home towards women and children is quite often overlooked. Indeed, it is deemed not even to occur amongst the upper classes. An immensely powerful man, such as Sir Charles, a most valuable asset to the Crown, would most likely be immune from any such charges."

Holmes paused, seemingly reluctant to ask, "Can you recall what happened on the following day, when your father returned to your tea-shop with his painting companion?"

Annie Knight nodded. "Yes, Mr. Holmes. I had observed them sitting together, with their easels, a little earlier. My father appeared quite jolly, no doubt confident that I would finally bend to his will."

Holmes became more serious, asking, "Was it then that you determined to . . . to accelerate his demise?"

Annie Knight looked directly at Holmes and, with a strengthening voice, replied, "You choose your words with considerable skill, Mr. Holmes. I had decided, the previous evening, that I could never return to the brutality of his household." She paused and took a further sip of tea. "The day before I had baked a dark, rich fruit cake, and I had also gathered some greengages from the orchard to make fruit tarts. It was an easy enough task to take the stone from inside the fruit and then crack it with a rolling pin. This revealed a very almond-like seed and, taking five, I put them safely to one side."

Holmes nodded. "Your time in the classification department and specimen rooms of Kew Gardens would, no doubt, have given you an insight into the toxicity of a variety of seeds."

I do not know who was more shocked by Holmes's revelation. I looked, wide eyed, towards Miss Knight, who now sat open-mouthed, barely managing to stammer, "You . . . you could not know . . . ."

Holmes looked grim as he held up his hand, wagging his forefinger, whilst saying, "There is very little that the state does not know about those in its highest echelon . . . their activities . . . their weaknesses, misdemeanours, and also information relating to their family members. A simple telegram to my brother in Whitehall produced all the information I required."

Annie Knight gave a thoughtful nod. "Then, perhaps, you will know of the hospital admissions of my mother for both her injuries and mental health. It will be of no surprise to you, Mr. Holmes, that I felt no guilt as I arranged the five greengage seeds on the top of a piece of fruit cake and then served it to my father."

Holmes face was impassive as he sat forward slightly. "Then your motive was revenge?"

Miss Knight looked directly into Holmes's eyes and shook her head. "No, Mr. Holmes. It was self-preservation. Self-defence, if you will."

Holmes sat back and was silent for almost a minute before he announced, in a very business-like tone, "Dr. Watson and I will return to London on tomorrow morning's express. It is my intention to leave unchallenged the results of the *post mortem*, which indicate the probable cause of death as being the ingestion of poisonous substances from the victim's own paints. This will, no doubt, lead to a coroner's verdict of 'death by misadventure'."

With that, Holmes rose, and on saying, "Good evening," to Miss Knight, he gathered his coat, hat, and cane, and disappeared towards our rooms. Feeling a degree of responsibility for Miss Knight's safety, I made ready to accompany her back to her lodgings. However, she declined and would only accept my offer of summoning a cab.

At breakfast the following morning, nothing was said of the case. Indeed, hardly a word was spoken between Guildford and Baker Street.

It was only when we were at our ease in our rooms that I ventured to raise the question of the actions of Miss Knight.

Holmes was drawing steadily upon one of his favourite briars when I asked, "What do you intend to say to Mycroft, Holmes?"

He remained silent for a minute before replying. "I shall send him a note to inform him that De Witt is no more a Boer than you or I, and that his passport and freedom of movement should be restored forthwith. Mycroft, no doubt, will have the *post mortem* and toxicology reports, and I will suggest that he should take note of the findings, bearing in mind Sir Charles' curious brush habit."

Holmes was, of course, being deliberately obtuse and, therefore, I determined to take a more direct approach. "And of Miss Knight?"

Holmes added to the layer of blue smoke that hung around us like some pungent scarf before answering, sharply. "If you are nurturing some notion of injustice, Watson, then, perhaps, Sir Charles Short should have been placed out of harm's way in Pentonville."

Holmes now paused and then pointed the stem of his pipe directly towards me, saying, "It was certain what fate would have befallen Annie Knight had she returned to her father's brutal regime. No, Watson! I will not denounce her, for there is scant evidence save that of inference and supposition."

I was about to say more when he resumed, in a most strident tone, "Her 'confession' was made to you and me . . . in private. I feel no dishonour in remaining silent and neither, I hope, do you!"

Following this outburst, nothing more was said about the case. However, I did detect an underlying disquiet and tension in Baker Street that continued for some days afterwards.

It was, perhaps, a little over a week later that I read in *The Times* that a coroner's court had, indeed, been convened and had delivered, as expected, a verdict of 'death by misadventure'. For my part, I was content as I saw this to be a judgement that I could honourably accept.

As for Mycroft, I was greatly relieved when he did not press his brother for further details of the actions of Miss Knight. Even now, as I recall the case, I am still unsettled by it. It is my hope and belief that there will come a time, in the future, when the law of the land will be applied, with an even hand, to all our citizens.

The Case of the
Anonymous Client
by Paul A. Freeman

One cold morning in early spring, I was awakened by a sulphurous odour hanging in the air of the apartments I shared with Sherlock Holmes. The smell was somewhat more nauseating than that which accompanies London's notorious pea-soup fogs – fogs that had much plagued the metropolis in recent months. Unable to sleep further, I put on my dressing gown and descended to the sitting room. To my surprise, Holmes was up and about, working on some elaborate question of practical chemistry.

"Ah, Watson!" he said. Still dressed in his previous evening's attire, he peered at me from above a maze of test tubes, retorts, and glass vessels. "It appears my experiment has disturbed you."

"How can you possibly breathe this infernal atmosphere?" said I, resentful at being awoken at such an unaccustomed hour. "Are you trying to poison us?"

Chuckling, Holmes threw open a window. The conditions of asphyxiation hardly improved, however, for Baker Street was once again enshrouded in a choking fog. Across the way, the Georgian façade was nothing more than a grey phantom, the lit streetlamps no more than ruddy smears. Holmes's good humour immediately deserted him at the sight of the pea-souper. "It seems my effort has been compromised," he said, and filled the clay pipe he always smoked when in thoughtful mood.

My curiosity had been pricked, and I could not but inspect the experiment which had so absorbed my friend's interest through much of the night. What I saw surprised me. "But you're burning a lump of household coal!" I ejaculated.

"This humble fossil fuel may well be responsible for keeping you so busy of late."

It was indeed true that several elderly private patients had recently called me out, suffering from palpitations and exertions of the heart. Examining the glowing coal more closely, I said, "My dear Holmes, I fail to see that common or garden coal can lead to the recent upsurge in cardiac and pulmonary complaints."

Holmes shook his head at my evident doltishness. "The one may not seem related to the other, but if we follow the three separate branches of

193

this experiment, you will see a connection. Here," he explained, indicating a white filter stained almost black with soot, "are the particulates captured after burning a mere six ounces of coal." He then traced out the route taken by the gaseous materials emitted from the burning coal. The resulting gas was bubbling through discoloured liquids held in two separate beakers. "The white liquid is a measure of carbon monoxide and carbon dioxide, the only gasses in my experiment that place you and Mrs. Hudson in any immediate danger."

"Very reassuring," I said. "And what of the yellowish-brown liquid in the other beaker?"

"A weak solution of sulphuric acid, such as is caused when coal smoke mingles with our London fog." Holmes pointed a long finger accusingly towards the open window. Beyond it, brown wreathes of pollution floated in the air. "Imagine if you will, Watson, the effect on the lungs of this acidic mist, laced as it is with soot particles and higher-than-normal concentrations of carbons monoxide and dioxide. With the lungs starved of oxygen, what stresses and strains these toxins and irritants must place on the heart. No wonder your elderly patients are suffering so much from cardiac problems. The truth of the matter is academic, however, since the results of my experiment have been contaminated by yet another filthy fog descending on the city." And with this, Holmes began dismantling his apparatus.

I was unconvinced by Holmes's conclusions. "I'm sure the human lung is a more efficient filter, and the heart a more resilient pump, than what you credit."

Holmes drew meditatively on his pipe. "This industrial age of ours has produced telephonic sound and promises televisual pictures. Yet for all this century's wondrous inventions, what a price we are paying in our filthy cities."

Further debate on the pros and cons of industrialization was curtailed by a ringing at the front door.

"It appears your elderly patient, Mr. Farrow, is in need of your ministration," said Holmes. To my quizzical expression, he explained, "Firstly, the hour is extremely early, so we can infer a medical emergency. Secondly, a fog has formed over the city. Therefore, it is likely the patient is suffering a stressed heart caused by the smoke trapped in the air. Thirdly, we have heard no clattering of hooves. The person ringing the doorbell has thought it quicker to come to you on foot than to flag down a hansom or ready a landau." With a twinkle in his eye, Holmes asked, "Mr. Farrow lives in the mews behind Baker Street, does he not?"

Just then, Mrs. Hudson, flustered and ill-tempered at being woken up at such an ungodly hour, rapped on the door to our rooms. "Mr. Farrow's manservant is here. Can Doctor Watson go to his master immediately?" Our landlady's words elicited a not entirely modest grin from Holmes, until she added, "What's that awful smell coming from your sitting room?"

With the hour still early, and the noxious London fog thicker than ever, I was returning home on foot from Mr. Farrow's when a hansom cab rattled past me. Moments later I heard the cab come to a stop. "This is it," the cabdriver shouted down. "221b Baker Street."

I was wondering whether I was being called out to a second patient when a tall figure sprang out of the shop doorway next to me, pushed past, and hurried off along the road until he was lost from sight in the fog. He had been wearing a brown, wide-brimmed hat made from cowhide, and a black greatcoat with a sheepskin collar and lapels. I thought little of this oddly attired apparition until a cry and the sound of a fight reached my ears from up ahead.

The hansom cab loomed out of the fog as I ran towards the source of the commotion, and beside the cab two men were embroiled in a life-or-death struggle. From up on the driver's box, the cabbie was shouting, "Help! Police! Murder!"

A metal object flashed in the lamplight, a second cry filled the night, and one of the men went down. The second man, the fellow in the greatcoat, took to his heels. His footfalls echoed along the pavement, while the clang of metal informed me he had discarded his weapon.

"Help! Police! Murder!" the cabbie repeated, jumping down to soothe his skittish horses.

Within seconds, the street was in pandemonium. Police whistles sounded, guiding constables to the scene of the brutal attack, while those habitually awake at such an early hour came rushing from all quarters.

Holmes's voice suddenly cut through the confusion. From above, his gaunt, energetic frame was silhouetted against the open sitting room window. He pointed to the gathering constables toward the direction the assailant had taken. "Your man wears a wide-brimmed hat and a greatcoat!" Holmes shouted after the departing policemen, and to me he said, "See to the victim, Watson. He's a client, if I'm not much mistaken. I'll be with you momentarily."

I needed no second urging to render assistance to the injured man, though my presence was of little consequence. The young man on the ground – dressed as he was in a frock jacket, beige cotton trousers, and a flat cap – was fatally wounded.

"Your name, sir?" I asked, but perhaps because of the trauma of the attack, the man could not answer my question.

In spite of two gaping wounds in his side, the dying man struggled in a determined attempt to pick up his fallen wallet. Evidently the assailant had surprised him in the process of paying the cabdriver and the object dropped from his grasp.

As the pale-faced young man fumbled with the catch to the wallet, I became aware of Holmes crouching beside me, his features as stern as cold granite.

"Your prognosis?" Holmes asked, to which I gave a brisk shake of the head. Gently, he prised the wallet from the young man's fingers and opened it wide. Then we watched as the man picked out two coins before succumbing to his wounds and expiring in front of us.

"One-and-a-quarter pennies!" said the cabbie, for the young man had selected a single penny and a single farthing from amongst coins that were mostly of a higher denomination. "My fare was more than that," he whined.

"I believe our deceased friend had more on his mind than paying your cab fare when he chose these two coins," said Holmes, dryly. "And the cab fare is from . . . ?"

"From Waterloo, guv'na."

The cabbie's answer seemed to surprise Holmes, yet did not distract him from his single-minded task of assessing what evidence was at the murder scene. Having apparently seen enough, he said, "We have sufficient data to trace and identify this man, Watson, so let's hunt down the weapon which the murderer so ill-advisedly threw away."

Hampered though we were by poor visibility, the dull gleam of metal soon caught Holmes's eye, and once the weapon, a common agricultural baling hook, was secured, we returned to the scene of the heinous killing.

By now a fair-sized crowd had gathered, including Mrs. Hudson, who stood at the door to 221b, somewhat distressed that a murder had occurred on her doorstep.

"You said this man was your client," I said as we forced our way through the gawping onlookers, Holmes holding the baling hook aloft. "How can you be so sure?"

"Our dead friend arrived in the type of hansom commonly seen touting for custom at the city's train termini. None of your patients' lives near a train terminus, so he can hardly be the manservant of a patient. Also, since Mrs. Hudson is unlikely to have young men visiting her at so improper an hour, we must surmise that the visitor's purpose in coming to 221b Baker Street was to consult with me."

The logic behind Holmes's deduction was undeniable.

We reached the police cordon, which consisted of several burly constables with linked arms. A Scotland Yard detective was already at work searching the body. To Holmes's disappointment, the detective proved to be Inspector Lestrade.

"The murder weapon," said Holmes, and with a magnanimous gesture handed the baling hook to the detective.

Lestrade passed the object to a constable, then looked Holmes up and down with those ferret-like eyes of his. "Don't think that finding the murder weapon gives you special privileges in this case, Mr. Holmes. You're merely a member of the public doing his duty."

"And if I can be of any further assistance . . . ." Holmes offered, with a slight bow.

Lestrade gave a dismissive wave. "The cabman has already described the assailant to us. Is there anything you can add to his statement?"

"Not a thing," said Holmes. "I'm sure you have everything under control."

"Exactly, Mr. Holmes. Leave this one to the professionals." And with that, Lestrade ordered the attendants of the waiting mortuary van to load up our anonymous client.

Once the crowd had dispersed and Mrs. Hudson had gone inside to lie down with a glass of brandy, Holmes sat on the step leading to our front door. Leaving him to meditate on the tragic events that had so unexpectedly come our way, I went upstairs to freshen up. I could not rest, however, and eventually went back downstairs and sat on the front step beside Holmes.

The light of the rising sun cut through the pea-soup gloom and began to burn off the foul air that had been trapped by the fog. Ignoring the strange glances we were getting from passing pedestrians, Holmes remained deep in thought until, all at once, he pointed a long bony finger at where the pavement met the road. "There on the curb. Our client has left us that sample of chalky soil. It must have dislodged from his shoe when he alighted from the hansom. I've been meditating on its significance ever since."

Holmes rose, collected the soil sample, and placed it in his palm.

To my layman's eye, the lump of grey soil looked like marl or chalk. Holmes, however, would offer no opinion on the subject, but instead took the soil up to our apartments, where he began reassembling that part of his previous experiment which had tested for carbon compounds.

197

"You seemed surprised that the cabbie picked up your client at Waterloo Station," I noted.

"*Our* client!" Holmes corrected. "*Our* client! And yes, Waterloo has somehow flummoxed me." He placed some clear lime water in a beaker, set it above a Bunsen burner, and proceeded to crumble the soil into the heated liquid. "This soil, which looks undoubtedly chalky and which was also on the dead man's shoes, is not consistent with a soil of the Surrey area. Since Waterloo Station deals exclusively with Surrey trains, what business did our client have being there?"

Holmes took out his pocket watch and began timing the chemical reaction of the soil and the lime water. Gradually the clear liquid became milky, and then more and more opaque until one couldn't see through to the other side of the beaker. At this point, Holmes checked his watch.

"The carbon content is too high for marl," Holmes concluded, "and the consistency is too dense to be conventional chalk."

"Then what is it?" I asked.

"It's *clunch*, Watson, a compressed variety of chalk." He reached for Volume One of his *Encyclopaedia of the British Isles*, handed it to me, and instructed me to look up the village of Elmswell.

It transpired that Elmswell, a once prosperous market town, was the location of England's largest church constructed principally from clunch, and that there were several clunch quarries in the area. Close to the village was a small country train station situated on the Great Northern Line.

"Our client must have disembarked from his train at King's Cross," I noted.

"And what can we deduce from him making his way to Waterloo before backtracking to Baker Street?"

"Perhaps he was concerned about being followed and wished to throw off his tail."

"It would certainly account for the facts," said Holmes, his eyes shining in anticipation of this new and intriguing case. "Are you up for a countryside jaunt?" he asked.

Indeed, I was.

Only after we had left King's Cross Railway Station, and were wiping the city grime from our hands and faces, did I realise how far from certain of success our task of identifying the victim of the Baker Street attack was. However, Holmes had instructed me to pack only for a single night, so I guessed he knew more about our dead client than he had thus far divulged.

As for Holmes, on the journey to Elmswell he retreated into that introspective mood of his that was so characteristic when a case was taxing his faculties. With his elbows on his knees and his hands clasped before him as if in prayer, he sat in the corner of our carriage, away from the window.

Knowing that even the most prosaic observations would invite a sharp rebuke from my friend, I contented myself to watching the newly-ploughed fields of Hertfordshire pass by. The undulating farmland and the budding trees spread beneath a sky free from pollution were certainly a welcome change from the dirt and crowds of "The Big Smoke", as London had become known. Yet try as I might, I could not turn my thoughts entirely away from the events of earlier that day at Baker Street.

It was only when the train reached Blinxworth, our penultimate stop, that Holmes spoke. "Did you notice anything unusual about our client's attire?" he asked.

I confessed that beyond a general observation of his clothing, I had noticed very little.

"Although his clothes were not those of a farm labourer," said Holmes, "his flat cap and frock jacket were equally not the garments of a gentleman farmer."

"Then you believe our client was employed in agriculture?"

"His rough hands may have suggested a rural tradesman if they weren't so deeply sun-tanned. I'm of a mind he was a farm foreman."

"And was anything else suggestive?" I urged.

Holmes eyed me as a school master might view an underachieving pupil. "Our client travelled wearing a pair of those beige cotton trousers so beloved by young, outdoor sportsmen these days."

"Then perhaps he rode a horse to the train station," I hazarded. "I gathered from your encyclopaedia that the station is some distance outside the village."

"But Elmswell is a small place, hardly big enough to warrant stabling facilities at its train station. The clue, Watson, was in two indentations encircling the cotton material near ends of his trouser legs."

"Bicycle clips!"

"Precisely! We'll make a detective of you yet. It does appear that our client cycled to the station before boarding the early train to London. Which tells me his bicycle should still be at the station."

Which indeed proved to be the case. When we disembarked at Elmswell, we handed the ticket stubs for the forward half of our journey to the station master, passed a tramp who sat begging at the station entrance, and found a single bicycle sheltered beneath the corrugated iron of the bicycle shed.

Holmes stood thoughtfully for a moment. Then we retraced our steps, once more passing the gentleman of the road at the front of the station, to talk with the station master.

John Harrison was a genial old railwayman, close to retirement judging by his age, whose tasks at the rural train station included the sale of tickets, collection of tickets, platform maintenance, as well as being the porter.

When Sherlock Holmes introduced himself, Harrison was all too eager to entertain the "Great London Sleuth" to tea and biscuits in his humble office.

Having refused Harrison's offer of telegraphing for a dogcart to transport us to the village, Holmes got down to business. "The bicycle in the rack outside. To whom does it belong?"

"Is this part of a case you're investigating?" asked Harrison, his eyes positively gleaming as he poured the tea. "I don't see what Charlie Dayton's bicycle could have to do with a Sherlock Holmes case, though."

Using our client's name for the first time, Holmes said matter-of-factly, "Charles Dayton has been murdered."

The railwayman paused in mid-pour, then lay down the teapot on the crude wooden table. "Murdered?" he ejaculated. His shock was momentary, however, for in the next instant he was bustling about, almost beside himself with joy that such an illustrious person as Sherlock Holmes was investigating Elmswell's very own murder.

"We were wondering," said I, rather put out by Harrison's jubilant demeanour, "what you can tell us about Mr. Dayton."

"Charlie Dayton is the foreman at Sebastian Merridew's farm. Only yesterday, I sold two train tickets to Charlie and Mr. Merridew – return tickets for today's early train to King's Cross."

"Did both men take that early train?" asked Holmes.

Harrison shrugged. "What with the railway company's cutbacks and all, I'm only on duty from nine to nine, Monday to Friday. Mind you, we're not as undermanned here as they are at Blinxworth. There the station's only manned three days in a week."

"Would anyone have seen Mr. Dayton arriving at the station at such an early hour?"

"It's possible that Randolph saw him."

"Randolph?"

The station master's mood became suddenly less genial. "Randolph Gatts," he spat, "is the filthy beggar sitting outside the train station, whose presence makes the place an eyesore."

"You mean the gentleman of the road we saw sitting in the entranceway?" I ventured.

"That's him," said the railwayman. "And he's no gentleman. Gatts is little more than a London rough. Came up from the city, did Gatts, and chased poor Thaddeus Chad away."

"And Thaddeus Chad is . . . ?" Holmes enquired.

"An old timer. A genuine gentleman of the road. This train station was Thaddeus's patch for donkeys' years. Then, along comes Randolph Gatts, who bullies Thaddeus until he ups and leaves. Went to Blinxworth Station, Thaddeus did, though the pickings are leaner there. The Blinxworth folk seldom travel down to London."

I could see by the swiftness with which he drank down his tea that Holmes had gleaned all the information he needed from the station master. So taking my friend's lead, I gulped down my own beverage and thanked Mr. Harrison for his time. Picking up our overnight bags, we made to set off on the mile-long walk to the nearby village.

We didn't get far, however.

"Before we take our leisurely perambulation through the English countryside," said Holmes, "I suggest we consult with Mr. Randolph Gatts, who has so recently adopted Elmswell railway station as his favoured begging spot."

It must have been a lucrative patch of begging turf, for on closer inspection I noticed that Gatts was the least grimy tramp I had ever encountered. Clean-shaven, his newly-cut hair glistening with lemon-scented cream, he sat with an air of superiority in front of the station's decorative flower boxes, his nose angled arrogantly skywards. Gatts's clothes were not at all unstylish, either, as well as being crisply ironed and redolent of washing detergent.

"A singular chap, indeed," said Holmes before introducing himself to the imperious tramp.

Gatts looked at us along his upturned nose. "Yes, I've 'eard of you, Mister Sherlock 'Olmes. Or is it 'Olmes the Meddler?" he sneered, his accent purely Cockney.

"Quite," said Holmes, not in the least put out by Gatts' insolent tone. "We were wondering if you might answer one or two questions for us."

In reply, the tramp smiled unpleasantly, presenting us with a set of stumpy black teeth. Rubbing his thumb and forefinger meaningfully together, he said, "Information don't come for nuffin', guv'na."

When Holmes produced a florin from his wallet, Gatt's looked upon the coin with undisguised disgust. In the end, nothing short of a crown would do.

"This morning," asked Holmes, "did anyone come to the station and board the early London train?"

"Aye! They did at that. Charlie Dayton parked his bicycle in the shed over there. Then 'e went onto the platform. Didn't give me nuffin', neither."

"And was Mr. Dayton the only passenger?"

"He might've been."

Taking the hint, Holmes fished out a half-crown from his wallet.

"Mr. Merridew came storming up on foot, his face all angry and red."

"By Mr. Merridew, you mean Sebastian Merridew, Charles Dayton's employer."

Gatts rolled his eyes as though he were dealing with a dunce. "Sebastian Merridew's as meek and mild a man as God ever made. He wouldn't say 'boo' to a goose. No, I mean his brother, Bartholomew. Chalk and cheese, those two are. The one is as quiet as a mouse, the other's a raging devil."

"So, when Bartholomew Merridew arrived on the platform," said Holmes, "did he and Mr. Dayton talk?"

"Talk? They had one of them verbal altercations, so I steered well clear. Even when Bartholomew Merridew's temper isn't 'ot, 'e's more likely to give me a taste of 'is riding crop than a miserly farthing."

Holmes readied a further half-crown. "One last question, Mr. Gatts. What was Bartholomew Merridew wearing when he boarded the London train this morning?"

"A black greatcoat wiv a woollen collar and a brown 'at wiv a brim that covered 'is eyes."

"You've been most helpful," said Holmes, tossing the tramp the half-crown.

We strode along an arrow-straight lane, hemmed in by wayside hedgerows. The road was speckled with pieces of clunch, the chalk-like rock which had set us on the trail of Bartholomew Merridew, the man apparently implicated in Charles Dayton's murder.

"What did you think of our friend, Mr. Gatts?" Holmes asked.

"I must admit," I said, puffing as I attempted to keep up with Holmes's enthusiastic pace, "the man seems as pampered and perfumed as any London dandy."

"Which makes me wonder how such an unlikable beggar could be so apparently successful at his profession. And what did you make of his testimony?"

"If Bartholomew Merridew did indeed follow Charles Dayton to London, that would explain why Dayton tried to shake him off and come to us via Waterloo."

"So it would appear. All we need do now is make the acquaintance of this Bartholomew chap, and I do believe our sojourn in the countryside will come to a successful end. But we must hurry, for even if Lestrade doesn't discover identification documents on Charles Dayton's body, he can't fail to find the stub of a return ticket to Elmswell on the dead man's person."

Strangely enough, our meeting with Bartholomew Merridew occurred sooner than expected. The lane to Elmswell took a sharp dog-leg, and there ahead of us was a fine village church dating from Elmswell's pre-eminent era as a market town. While I admired the architecture of the medieval church, Holmes was eying a gang of men digging out a drainage ditch at the side of the road. The excavation disappeared under a field entrance that ended at a farm gate. Evidently the drainage pipe running under the entranceway was blocked. Yet what had really gained Holmes's attention was the greatcoat lying over the top bar of the gate and the floppy brown hat hanging from the gatepost.

Leaving his overnight bag in the middle of the road, Holmes jumped the drainage ditch, much to the bemusement of the labourers. He was examining the hat when its owner – munching on a sandwich and disturbed in the midst of his lunch – suddenly stood up on the other side of the hedgerow.

"What the devil's this?" cried a man with the most villainous features I had ever seen. His hair was jet black, his eyebrows long pointed triangles, and his moustache was a pencil-thin affair, twisted upwards at either end.

As amiably as could be, Holmes said, "Bartholomew Merridew, I presume."

"You seem to have the drop on me, sir," the man snarled back. His response was made all the more threatening when he slapped a riding crop across the top of the hedgerow.

"The name's Holmes. Sherlock Holmes. And this is my associate, Dr. Watson."

"Really? Then I *do* know you two – but only by reputation. You're a couple of London toffs, busy-bodies, probably sent for by my spineless brother Sebastian to accuse me as the vandaliser of his property."

I was about to inform Bartholomew Merridew that the case was far more serious than one of simple vandalism, but Holmes stayed me with an all but imperceptible shake of the head.

Turning his attention to the greatcoat lying across the farm gate, Holmes said, "I perceive this is a garment of quality," and he ran his fingers down the material of the coat.

Bartholomew Merridew rushed to the gate, his riding crop held high. "I don't know what jackanapes trick you're playing, but touch my greatcoat again and I'll thrash both of you within an inch of your lives."

With a disarming gesture Holmes backed away, picked up his overnight bag, and we continued our brisk walk to the village. Behind us, Bartholomew Merridew was cursing the ditch diggers, threatening them with his riding crop if they didn't put their backs into the work.

"The man's an absolute brute," I said, but Holmes was not listening. Introspection had once again overtaken him as he examined the fingers with which he had touched Bartholomew Merridew's greatcoat.

"What have you discovered?" I enquired, and Holmes showed me a set of clean, but otherwise unremarkable, fingertips.

"This case is a curious one," said Holmes, then added: "I think we should find somewhere to stay for the night."

After our frankly bizarre meeting with Bartholomew Merridew, a further surprise was in store. On the outskirts of Elmswell, set amidst a row of labourers' tenements, we came across the Penny-Farthing public house. The sign hanging above the doorway bore a painted likeness of the obsolete conveyance of the same name.

Holmes tugged at my sleeve, pointed to the pub sign, but the import of Holmes's gesture took some time to register.

"This seedy looking establishment explains why Charles Dayton, with his dying strength, extracted a penny and a farthing from his wallet," said Holmes. "He was guiding us here. It's too dilapidated a public house to cater for board and lodgers. However, let's enter under the pretext of asking for directions to an inn which does offer such accommodation."

The Penny-Farthing turned out to be as rough on the inside as it looked from outside. Dressed in our city clothes and weighed down by our luggage, Holmes and I were much out of place as we crossed the sawdust-strewn floor. In spite of the sudden hush, we gave our hearty hellos to the rustic labourers who sat huddled around the pub's roughly-hewn tables.

At the bar, Holmes ordered two glasses of beer from a pretty-faced barmaid, then pushed a half-sovereign coin across the counter.

The girl looked down at what must have seemed to her a small fortune. "We have no change for that, sir."

204

"For a little information," said Holmes. "I shall need no change." And in hushed tones, having gained the young woman's attention, Holmes proceeded to conduct his interrogation.

As we drank our beer, the barmaid informed us that the Penny-Farthing was owned by Bartholomew Merridew. This was a fact I reckoned to be of the utmost significance, since our dead client had led us here. Under Holmes's further questioning, she told us that the influence of the Merridew brothers had divided Elmswell. For it transpired that Bartholomew was somewhat of a Luddite, averse to the machinery that was revolutionising England's agricultural landscape. In the village, he drew his support from the rural poor who feared being replaced by machines. His brother Sebastian, on the other hand, was more forward thinking and had recently streamlined his workforce through the acquisition of a mechanised seed planter and a baling machine. He drew his support from the budding population of gentleman farmers in Elmswell, men who were usually to be found ensconced in the Wheat Sheaf Inn, a public house owned by Sebastian Merridew. This public house was situated on the High Street, and was apparently a place where two weary travellers could rest up for the night.

We finished off our beers, wished good health and prosperity to our hostess and the pub's raggedy patrons, and made our way to the High Street, a street that boasted a great variety of architectural designs, including everything from timber-framed Tudor to Victorian Gothic.

The Wheat Sheaf Inn was housed in a red-brick building of Queen Anne style. Inside, the structure had the air of a museum about it, for the interior walls were adorned with nostalgic photographs from Elmswell's historic past. The clientele of the Wheat Sheaf Inn, however, were dressed in the most modern gentleman farmer's attire and spoke in refined accents.

Holmes soon got into friendly repartee with the men at the bar. He explained away our presence in Elmswell by saying that we were writing a guidebook on the Hertfordshire countryside and that we wished to speak to Mr. Sebastian Merridew, the owner of the Wheat Sheaf Inn, with a view to including his establishment in our book.

When asked how he liked Elmswell so far, Holmes was in his element, using the opportunity to subtly elicit from those around him the information he deemed pertinent to the case of our deceased client.

"My first impression of your village," said Holmes, "has been somewhat coloured by the unique though surly gentleman of the road who demands charity from his pitch outside your train station."

There was an angry murmur, then one gentleman farmer said, "Randolph Gatts is a poor mascot for our village. Anything short of

205

sixpence he throws back in the giver's face. Yet surely someone's spoiling him, for he boasts a veritable wardrobe of nearly new clothes."

"Not to mention his twice-weekly bath and shave at the Penny-Farthing," a second farmer added.

"Rumour has it," said a third, "that Gatts has discovered a horde of Roman treasure, turned up by a ploughshare. I hear he could give up begging any time if he wanted."

"And how we wish he would be off," the first farmer said. "Oh, that we could have old Thaddeus Chad back again."

"Thaddeus is now panhandling at Blinxworth Station, I hear," said Holmes.

"Aye! And Thaddeus is a gentleman of the road who deserves that appellation of 'gentleman'."

Holmes ordered a round of drinks for everyone in the public house, and in the ensuing atmosphere of bonhomie, continued fishing for information. "We met up with Bartholomew Merridew on our way over from the train station. He was not very welcoming."

Our drinking companions found this last comment most amusing. "You've been unlucky," said the second gentleman farmer, "in having run into the two least desirable denizens of Elmswell since your arrival."

"Is that so? And what makes Mr. Bartholomew Merridew so undesirable a character?"

The first farmer explained. "Bartholomew is in constant conflict with his brother, Sebastian. Between them, the Merridew brothers own more than half of the land and property around Elmswell, and the conflict comes about over how to manage it. Bartholomew enjoys nothing more than exerting power over his fellow man. He treats his labourers like slaves, and has nothing to do with the new agricultural devices that can make agriculture less labour intensive."

"And Sebastian Merridew?" asked Holmes.

"Sebastian, meek and mild though he is, does stand up to his brother's bullying ways when he steels himself. A very progressive man is Sebastian, a man who puts efficiency and profit first – as he should. But he's seen his plans of agricultural advancement dashed time and again by his stubborn brother."

"There's been some vandalism, perhaps?" Holmes prompted.

"That's so, indeed," said the third farmer. "There've been threats from Bartholomew, agricultural machinery sabotaged, even cows poisoned. Only yesterday, we heard Sebastian suggesting to Charlie Dayton, his foreman, that he should call in a London detective to consult on the matter."

At that moment, the door to the Wheat Sheaf Inn swung open and in staggered a tall gentleman in a cream suit and a panama hat. He looked about himself in some agitation, spotted Holmes and myself at the bar, and lurched towards us on legs so wobbly that I thought he might collapse on the floor.

"Is it true, Mr. Holmes?" he cried. "Is it true that Bartholomew has murdered my foreman? The station master says it is so, and that Charles was killed on his mission to engage you."

The man whom we rightly assumed to be Sebastian Merridew sat heavily in a vacant chair. Holmes immediately ordered the hysterical man a glass of brandy. Such was the shocking effect of the news of Charles Dayton's murder that none of the patrons in the Wheat Sheaf Inn seemed to notice the subterfuge Holmes had played on them in claiming to be writing a guidebook to Hertfordshire.

"We were so careful in our plans," cried Sebastian Merridew, wringing his hands in desperation. "We were to have travelled to London together. We had even bought the tickets, but at the last minute decided I should stay behind and protect my property from Bartholomew. Charles was to shake off Bartholomew if he had the slightest suspicion the villain was following him."

As I administered brandy to the nerve-stricken man, Holmes said, "It appears, Watson, that Mr. Dayton was acting on behalf of Mr. Merridew as his agent."

"'Twas futile!" Sebastian Merridew wailed. "'Twas futile!" And with that he burst into tears.

Once more the door to the Wheat Sheaf Inn suddenly burst open, and the dirty face of a village idler peered around the jamb. "It's Scotland Yard," he shouted over the hubbub caused by the revelations of Dayton's murder. "They're arresting Bartholomew Merridew at the Penny-Farthing."

A roar of approval erupted, and was followed by a mass exodus from the public house. A reinvigorated Sebastian Merridew, emboldened by this fresh news, led the way out onto the street, while Holmes and I, leaving our overnight bags in the saloon bar, joined the rear of the excited mob.

By the time we got back at the Penny-Farthing, Lestrade was manhandling Bartholomew Merridew out of the public house with the aid of two burly constables. For his part, Bartholomew, dressed in the greatcoat and floppy hat that were such damning circumstantial evidence against him, was swinging a tankard at the agents of the law and letting forth a stream of the basest oaths.

"Apparently Randolph Gatts' identification of Bartholomew Merridew as the man who followed Charles Dayton to London has proven crucial," said Holmes.

A gauntlet of gawkers had formed all the way to the waiting B-Wagon – the enclosed, horse-drawn carriage that was to transport the prisoner to the nearby town of Royston.

"Get your filthy hands off me!" cried Bartholomew. "I've done nothing wrong."

Sebastian suddenly rushed out of the crowd and pointed accusingly at his brother. "This is the murderer of Charles Dayton!" he cried. "Slap the handcuffs on him, officer! The next time we see this scoundrel, we want his carcass to be swinging from the end of a rope!"

Obligingly, Lestrade clapped his handcuffs on Bartholomew's wrists and was rewarded by a further string of curses. I glanced at Holmes and, to my surprise, his lips were pursed in the slightest of smiles, a habitual expression that told me the case was utterly clear to him now.

Taking a fresh handkerchief from his pocket, Holmes said, "Let me conduct that little experiment again. The one I performed earlier. Just for Lestrade's benefit."

Holmes pushed his way into a crowd that was alternately cheering, then howling in consternation – such was the division of opinion at Bartholomew's arrest. While the constables struggled to force the man into the back of the B-Wagon, Holmes stepped forward and gave his greatcoat two vigorous rubs with his handkerchief.

"You again!" he roared. "Do you mock me, sir?"

"I seek only the truth," Holmes assured, as the doors of the B-Wagon closed behind the prisoner and the two constables guarding him.

Lestrade was eyeing Holmes suspiciously. "And what was the purpose of that little stunt?" he asked.

Holmes held out the handkerchief for Lestrade's inspection. It was perfectly clean and white."

The Scotland Yard detective shook his head, chuckled, then opined that as an unofficial agent of law-and-order, Holmes had queer ways. Then, smug in the knowledge that he had his man, Lestrade climbed up onto the driver's box of the B-Wagon. The driver whipped the horses into a gallop and, once the police van disappeared from view, the crowds began dispersing.

"Well," said Sebastian Merridew, coming up to us and shaking Holmes's hand enthusiastically. "It seems that you and your associate are no longer required. Good day, sirs." And at that he turned on his heels, adjusted his panama hat and strode away.

208

I was flabbergasted by the abruptness and the rudeness of the man's behaviour, and said so to Holmes.

"Yes," he agreed. "Abrupt and rude, indeed. A man plans to engage our help, yet dismisses us like servants once our help is no longer needed. However, more extraordinary still is Mr. Sebastian Merridew's transformation from a quivering wreck to the bold leader of what could well have become a lynch mob. So in light of Mr. Merridew not inviting us to stay overnight at his residence after the exertions we have made on his behalf, I suggest we return to the Wheat Sheaf Inn and engage rooms there."

This was exactly what we did. I still suspected that Holmes knew more than he was telling me, but as usual I indulged him in his eccentricity of remaining tight-lipped and evasive.

After a late lunch, Holmes rose from the table and said, "There's nothing like an invigorating walk in the countryside to stimulate the grey matter, Watson. If I'm not back before evening, don't wait up for me."

For the second morning in succession, I was awoken by Holmes. This time it was not by the malodour of some obscure chemistry experiment, but by the man himself shaking me by the shoulder.

"Quick, Watson," he hissed, opening his watch to show me a time of twenty-five-to-eight. "We have an impromptu appointment with our reluctant host, Sebastian Merridew."

"It can hardly be an appointment if it's impromptu," I pointed out gruffly, but did as instructed and pulled on my less-than-pristine clothes.

We strode towards Ashbrooke House, the residence of Sebastian Merridew. As was Holmes's habit when on the scent, he was impervious to my inquiries, refusing to tell me where he had been or what he had done since I last saw him the previous day.

Ashbrooke House, on the edge of Elmswell, was a modern structure with steep gables, and it was surrounded by plain, though not unattractive, gardens. A gravel driveway, fringed with rhododendron bushes, approached the front of the house.

As we negotiated the driveway, Holmes checked his pocket watch, and I guessed that time was an important factor in whatever he had planned. "We must hurry," he urged. "It's only a quarter-of-an-hour before eight."

At Ashbrooke House's stone porch, Holmes gave the bell-pull a sharp tug, summoning Sebastian Merridew's butler. On learning that he was in the presence of the illustrious London detective Sherlock Holmes, the manservant showed us to the drawing room, where he announced us to his master before departing.

209

Sebastian Merridew, who was relaxing in an armchair with a cup of tea, was most annoyed at our unexpected appearance. "I thought the case was closed. What's your business?" he snapped.

"We've been put to some small expense," said Holmes, coolly.

Sebastian's lip curled into a sneer. The change from that snivelling wretch we first encountered in the Wheat Sheaf Inn the previous day was remarkable. "It was not I who called you here from London," said Sebastian. "Charles Dayton went to summon you."

"Yet your foreman was acting on your behalf, Mr. Merridew."

At this juncture, I became aware that Holmes wasn't actually concerned about being compensated for the few efforts we had exerted in tracking down Charles Dayton's killer. He was embarking on a ruse to expose the meanness and spitefulness of Sebastian Merridew.

"I owe you nothing," Sebastian insisted. "If you reckon you have a claim against me, take me to court. If not, good day, gentlemen."

Before another word could be uttered, a clock chimed, announcing the hour of eight. With it came the gallop of hooves. Through a bay window which gave us a view along the rhododendron-lined avenue, we saw the B-Wagon which had yesterday taken Bartholomew Merridew to Royston Gaol drive up to the front of the house.

"What's this?" yelled Sebastian, leaping to his feet as he watched Inspector Lestrade clamber down from beside the driver.

Seconds later, the Scotland Yard detective had joined us. His pinched face was a vision of contrition as he regarded Holmes, and he held his cap deferentially before him.

"If you would be patient enough to listen, Mr. Merridew," said Holmes, "everything will be explained."

Quivering with anger, Sebastian resumed his seat.

"This case has been dogged by lies and deceptions. Only by peeling away these lies and deceptions can we come to the truth of the matter. Firstly, we must look objectively at the evidence that has proved so damning to your brother. Randolph Gatts testified that he saw Bartholomew arriving at Elmswell Station – dressed in his rather unique greatcoat and hat – shortly after Charles Dayton. Secondly, we have three independent witnesses – myself, Dr. Watson, and a London cabbie – who saw a man wearing such singular attire attack and fatally wound Charles Dayton. Thirdly, while Dayton lay dying, he struggled to extract a penny and a farthing from his wallet in a desperate attempt to identify his assailant."

"The meaning here is obvious," said Sebastian. "Dayton meant the *Penny-Farthing* public house. It's owned by Bartholomew. Dayton was accusing my brother."

"Quite so," said Holmes. "However, this is just one possible scenario. Let us now suppose that Randolph Gatts is lying. You see, Gatts' appearance and demeanour fail to convey the impression of poverty so usually seen in one who begs for a living. In fact, for a tramp he appears rather too well-to-do. Furthermore, his insolent tongue is more apt to chase away donors than to elicit alms from them. So we now have the question of who is financing Randolph Gatts' extravagance?

"A second point is that Gatts mentioned to me that by habit, Bartholomew carries a riding crop. Indeed, I was threatened with it by Bartholomew himself. Yet Charles Dayton's murderer carried no riding crop, as Gatts went out of his way to mention. He did, however, carry a baling hook."

Sebastian Merridew shifted uneasily in his chair. "This is all very interesting, Mr. Holmes, but if Bartholomew didn't kill Dayton, then who did?"

"You did, of course," said Holmes simply.

Sebastian made a show of being taken aback. "This is preposterous! Where is your proof?"

"If you'll indulge me, I'll come to that." Holmes paced up and down, seemingly oblivious to those of us in the room as he arranged his ideas. "Let us continue with a second scenario which will completely exonerate Bartholomew. Although he is guilty of threats of violence, he is not responsible for vandalising your agricultural machinery, nor of poisoning of your cattle. The vandalism and the poisonings were carried out by you in an effort to implicate Bartholomew."

"Poppycock!" said Sebastian. "Why should I do such a thing?"

"On your father's death, each of his two sons received half of the Merridew estate. Your brother is still a bachelor. If he is found guilty of Dayton's murder and is executed, you will inherit his land and his property."

"As strong a motive as I've ever seen," said Lestrade.

"Thank you," said Holmes, dryly. "My suspicions were aroused when I discovered I was originally to have been consulted on a case of little more than threats and vandalism. These are matters that the local constabulary are more than capable of handling." Holmes turned his indefatigable gaze on Sebastian. "Your decision to consult Sherlock Holmes was a ruse by which you convinced your unfortunate foreman to take the early train to London. At the last moment, you told Dayton that you would not travel with him, but that you would stay behind under the pretext of protecting your property from Bartholomew."

Following Holmes's logic, I asked, "If Gatts was lying, and no one followed Dayton onto the train, why did he head for Waterloo to shake off someone tailing him?"

"Because he *was* followed onto the train, Watson. Only it was *Sebastian* Merridew who boarded the train, *disguised* as his brother, *Bartholomew*."

"My foreman would never have boarded at Elmswell Station if he had suspected any danger," Sebastian insisted.

"But you didn't get on the train at Elmwell," said Holmes. "You got on the train a short distance down the line at Blixworth Station. You then made sure Dayton saw only the clothing you were wearing, the same type and style of clothing as Bartholomew is wont to wear. So, following your instructions, Dayton headed to Waterloo, thus giving you time to arrive at Baker Street in preparation for your murderous attack."

"I'm sure I still have my unused train ticket about the house somewhere," said Sebastian, his voice increasingly desperate.

Holmes reached into his pocket, stepped forward, and placed three ticket stubs on the small table beside Sebastian Merridew's armchair. Two of the stubs belonged to one ticket and had identical numbers at either end. These Holmes pushed together. "This is Charles Dayton's ticket," he explained. "The return end of the ticket was found on Mr. Dayton's body, while the forward half I recovered last night from a large pile of collected ticket stubs at King's Cross Station." Holmes leaned across the table and picked up the remaining ticket stub. "This is the forward half of the second ticket that you and your foreman bought from the station master at Elmswell Station yesterday – the ticket that you just said is somewhere about the house. It is consecutively numbered, and has been verified against the numbered tickets at the station. I also recovered it from that pile of ticket stubs at King's Cross."

Caught out in his lie, Sebastian Merridew became silent. Meanwhile, Lestrade had walked over to the bay window. He waved to the driver of the B-Wagon, who in turn rapped on the roof of the police van. The back doors swung open, and two constables emerged. They were escorting a man dressed in a black greatcoat trimmed in sheepskin, his face obscured by a brown floppy hat.

"What's Bartholomew doing here?" Sebastian protested.

"It's not your brother," Holmes informed Sebastian. "He's still at Royston, on a charge of assaulting the arresting police officers." As the mystery man shuffled into the sitting room, flanked by the two constables, Holmes said, "I give you Mr. Thaddeus Chad, a gentleman of the road, our key witness, and a man whose acquaintance I so fortuitously made on my wanderings yesterday evening."

The man in question removed the hat covering his face, a hat indistinguishable from that of Bartholomew Merridew's, revealing the grizzled beard and wrinkled face of an elderly man.

"Do tell us your interesting story, Mr. Chad," said Holmes.

Falteringly, Thaddeus Chad began. "For years, I eked out a living at Elmswell Station. The rail travellers were not unkind to me and I received sufficient alms to survive well enough. Then, barely two weeks ago, Randolph Gatts came into my life. With threats and brute force, he sent me packing. Too old to start over somewhere new, I moved my pitch to the next station along the Great Northern Line, to Blinxworth Station."

Holmes rubbed his hands together in anticipation. "Can you tell us what happened yesterday morning?"

"Early yesterday, before the first train, I saw Sebastian Merridew, coming along the back road from Elmswell. I was sleeping under a hedgerow and, being a light sleeper by nature, Mr. Merridew's footfalls had awoken me."

"Would you describe what Mr. Merridew was wearing?"

"The very clothes I'm now wearing myself, sir. When he returned from London later in the morning, Mr. Merridew again didn't see me tucked up under the hedge. He threw this hat and coat into a nearby ditch."

Holmes gave his hands another vigorous rub and said, "Please reach into your coat pocket, Mr. Chad."

The old tramp put his hand into the front pocket of the greatcoat and pulled out a torn piece of card. "It's the return portion of a ticket from King's Cross to Elmwell," I ejaculated.

Lestrade pounced on the ticket stub. Its number matched the other half of the second ticket which Sebastian Merridew and his foreman had purchased at Elmswell Railway Station.

Addressing Sebastian Merridew, Holmes said, "You chose Blinxworth Station because yesterday there was no station master on duty who might later identify you as having got on or off the first train. Unfortunately for you, Mr. Chad was present. And you were doubly unfortunate in that you forgot to dispose of your return ticket before throwing away the clothes that you used as a disguise to implicate your brother in Charles Dayton's murder."

As if that weren't enough proof, Holmes took out a pristine white handkerchief and rubbed it across the material of the greatcoat Sebastian Merridew had worn on his murderous sally the previous day. The linen was soon dark and discoloured. "You see, Watson," said Holmes. "My experiment on the particulate content of London fog wasn't entirely in

213

vain. Whereas Bartholomew Merridew's greatcoat was unblemished because he hadn't been in the vicinity of London yesterday, Sebastian Merridew's greatcoat is literally laden with soot and grime."

Again Sebastian Merridew jumped to his feet. He pointed angrily towards Thaddeus Chad. "No one will believe this vagabond!" he shouted.

"He's more credible than Randolph Gatts," said Lestrade, "who's already confessed to obstructing a police investigation by lying on your behalf."

At that, Sebastian Merridew lunged desperately at Holmes, but was intercepted by the two constables. As the policemen dragged Merridew away to the B-Wagon, Holmes matter-of-factly opened his pocket watch. "If we hurry, Watson," he said, "we can make the next train to London."

Thus ended the strange and tragic case of Charles Dayton, our anonymous client, a man who was so treacherously murdered by his unscrupulous employer.

Capitol Murder
by Daniel D. Victor

For an educated human being to arrange an assassination,
he must have a streak of the monster in him –
even if the man he purposes to be slain is regarded by him
and by multitudes as an enemy of God and man.

– David Graham Phillips
"The Assassination of a Governor"
The Cosmopolitan, April 1905

I

I suppose the appearance of yet another American should not have been too surprising. After all, so many of them have played significant roles in some of the most personal adventures of my friend and colleague Mr. Sherlock Holmes. Why, our very first investigation together, the case I titled *A Study in Scarlet*, involved the American Jefferson Hope and the Mormons of Utah. And Holmes himself will never forget Miss Irene Adler of New Jersey, the female adversary whose successes earned from him the distinctive accolade of "*the* woman". For that matter, I myself was shot in the leg by one James Winter, the notorious "Killer" Evans from Chicago.

I might add that my literary agent, Arthur Conan Doyle, who knows a thing or two about successful publishing, has always encouraged me to promote the American angle.

"It's good for business, Watson," he constantly reminds me. "Sprinkling your adventures with Americans broadens the market." How else to interpret Sir Arthur's delight upon meeting William Gillette, the American actor famous for depicting Holmes on stage, and who at the time of the encounter was fully dressed in ear-flapped travelling cap and long grey coat?

According to the reports, Gillette approached Sir Arthur with magnifying glass in hand, and after examining him closely, proclaimed, "Unquestionably an author!"

Though I myself could never see the resemblance, it was the American Gillette who popularized for the entire world the inaccurate notion that Holmes smoked a calabash pipe and always donned a deerstalker.

And yet, in spite of the hyperbole surrounding such American influences, I continue to marvel at the large number of Holmes's investigations that truly did have connections to the United States. After all, with so many English trappings associated with the man – the Baker Street address, the London backdrop, *Bradshaw's Railway Guide* (not to mention his generally stoic nature) – it is difficult to imagine a figure that more fully epitomises the British character than does Sherlock Holmes.

One need only glance at some of our most celebrated adventures, however, to discover just how much of Holmes's career depended upon cases linked to the States. These include (to name but a few): "The Noble Bachelor", featuring the ill-fated marriage of Hattie Doran from San Francisco; "The Problem of Thor Bridge", dealing with a former American Senator; and "The Dancing Men", involving the peculiar stick-figure code employed by American gangsters. Two cases, "The Five Orange Pips" and "The Yellow Face", suggested the pernicious effects of Southern prejudice, and Holmes himself assumed the persona of an England-hating Irish-American before the onset of the Great War. And one must not forget two other cases, "The Red Circle" and *The Valley of Fear*, that brought within Holmes's professional circle Agents Leverton and Edwards, a pair of investigators from Pinkerton, the renowned American detective agency.

There is, however, a hitherto unknown investigation linked to this same Birdy Edwards that involves yet a third Pinkerton operator. Though much less dramatic than Edwards' clandestine work in Pennsylvania's Vermissa Valley, equally significant was the simple act he performed in referring a colleague to our Baker Street rooms.

In point of fact, it was this innocent recommendation that led to the conclusion of a political drama containing one of the most cold-blooded operations Holmes ever undertook. The less charitable among us might even say that the adventure I publish here for the first time lays at the feet of the world's first consulting detective the indisputable charge of premeditated murder.

The origins of the ugly business occurred in the middle of a wintry morning in late February of 1900. Holmes and I sat warming ourselves by the fire when Billy the page brought to our rooms a tall, thin, clean-shaven gentleman who seemed to be in his mid-thirties. He wore a long black coat over a dark suit, bowstring tie, and stovepipe trousers. Square-toed Western boots peeked out at the cuff, and his left hand was holding what appeared to be a dark-brown, wide-brimmed Stetson hat with a flattened crown. One did not need to hear him speak to conclude that yet another American was about to make his presence known.

"Wyatt Steele, Mr. Holmes," said our visitor, extending his hand. "I'm a Pinkerton agent." His flat intonations confirmed his provenance.

Holmes offered his own hand and then introduced me.

"Glad to meet you, Dr. Watson," said Steele, gripping my hand with an air of confidence. I must admit that with his strong square jawline, he cut quite a figure, every bit the straight-backed American that the Pinkertons were famous for hiring.

"I know it was a few years ago, Mr. Holmes," he went on, "but if you recall my old pal Birdy Edwards, it was he who said to look you up if I ever needed help in London. He wrote a quick note to me before he vacated Birlstone Manor. It was right after you investigated a murder there. He didn't sign the letter, but I knew it was from Birdy all the same."

Sherlock Holmes smiled. "I do indeed remember Mr. Edwards, a fearless Irishman with a singular mind. Lost at sea a few years back – or so the story runs – another victim of the late and unlamented Professor Moriarty." The smile waned as he contemplated the destructive power of his former enemy.

"Hold on," said Steele, raising his hat as a kind of stop-sign, "I had no intention of setting off so dark a mood. To tell you the truth," he announced, "I'm actually here on Pinkerton business."

Holmes took the man's hat and coat and hung them on a peg near the still-open door. Then, indicating to our guest a cushioned chair near the fire, he proceeded to shout down the stairwell at the pageboy. "Billy!" he cried. "Ask Mrs. Hudson to send up tea – on second thought, make it coffee in honour of our American friend."

I heard a murmur of what sounded like assent from below before Holmes closed the door and joined me in his own armchair opposite our guest.

"Now, Mr. Steele," said Holmes, "pray, tell us what sort of Pinkerton business has caused you to seek me out on so miserable a day. Other than the assassination of Kentucky's governor a few weeks ago, I recall no other recent crimes in America that would have sent you all this way."

Steele's mouth gaped wide. For a moment, the calm and cool Pinkerton agent seemed to have lost his composure. "Wh – how? How did you know?" he stammered.

I shared his amazement. Holmes's words were the first I had heard of any such affair.

"The newspapers provide all sorts of information," he said with the wave of his hand. "And when it comes to more vital issues of state, my brother Mycroft also keeps me informed."

"However you've come by the news, Mr. Holmes, you're quite correct. I am indeed on the trail of the killer of William Goebel, the governor of Kentucky. He was shot in Frankfort, the state's capital, and I have good reason to believe his assassin has come to London. But then you seem to know all this already."

"I make it my business to keep abreast of a variety of crimes, Mr. Steele, though I must confess that political assassinations generally fail to interest me. They're too prosaic. One politician doesn't like another and – *Bang*!" Holmes pointed his long index finger like a gun at Steele and pretended to fire. "Motives are obvious, and means are generally unimaginative. Not much to hold my attention, I'm afraid. This case, however, features some curious echoes."

I had participated in most of Holmes's investigations, yet I remained at a loss regarding the so-called "echoes" to which he alluded.

"Allow me to tell you what I know about the case," offered Steele. "Perhaps we might then combine our knowledge and reach some sort of conclusion. It's the sort of thing Birdy said you were so good at."

Just then Mrs. Hudson arrived with Billy in tow. He was holding a tray with her silver service and a few biscuits neatly arranged on a large plate. Mrs. Hudson herself placed the fixings on the low table near our guest, filled our cups, observed that all was in order, and finally – with a brief dip of her head – fairly pushed Billy out the door ahead of her.

Whilst we listened to the two of them thumping down the stairs, Holmes leaned forward to sample the coffee. Finding it to his satisfaction, he placed his cup back on its saucer and turned to our guest. "Now, Mr. Steele, pray tell us about this unfortunate William Goebel. What had he done to bring his death upon him, and, for that matter, what is there about his murder that is mysterious enough to have engaged the likes of the Pinkertons?"

As if to fortify himself, the American drank some of his coffee. Thus prepared, he began his tale. "First, one must understand William Goebel the man. Ironically for a politician, he wasn't a particularly likeable fellow – at least, according to those who knew him. Besides his brothers and sister, he seemed to have few friends. There was no woman in his life and, while he advocated reforms for working people, most folks believed that it was their votes he sought rather than their true well-being."

I grunted in agreement. I could name many a duplicitous politician in England who fit the same bill.

"Nor was Goebel much of a speaker. I'd actually been to one of his political rallies when I was travelling through Frankfort. Oh, he'd go through the motions, but his words didn't soar. You'd have to turn

218

elsewhere – to someone like William Jennings Bryan, who had, in fact, campaigned for him – if you wanted to get your blood flowing. His looks weren't much to speak of either. He had a pale skin, narrow eyes, and plastered-down black hair. To tell the truth, there was something reptilian about him."

Holmes and I exchanged glances. I knew that we were harbouring the same suspicions. The only person I had ever heard Holmes call "reptilian" was the cold-blooded Moriarty himself.

"And yet," continued the American, "despite such obstacles, Goebel successfully climbed the political ladder. In the name of the common people, he challenged the L&N – that's the Louisville and Nashville railroad, the major line in Kentucky. He called them 'blood-suckers', said their labour practices were unfair, their ticket prices too high, their interests only concerned with financial gain. It was a good sales pitch all right, and he rode it straight to the leadership of Kentucky's Democratic Party. He became quite the power broker. People called him Czar, King Goebel, even William the Conqueror."

"One presumes," observed Holmes quietly, "that in the process, he also collected some formidable enemies – the so-called L&N in particular."

"Precisely, Mr. Holmes. It was, in fact, the leadership of the L&N – Basil Duke and Milton Smith, to be precise – that hired Pinkerton to find out who killed Goebel. They want L&N's name cleared. You see, as Goebel's principal adversaries, they fear being held responsible for the assassination themselves – as, I can assure you, they already are by some. There are plenty of Kentucky Democrats who'd think nothing of shooting a likely suspect – especially if he runs a railroad."

"So I have read," said Holmes. "No, offense, Mr. Steele, but even before this latest outrage, a number of pressmen have already referred to Kentucky as the most violent state in your country."

"No offense taken, Mr. Holmes." With a chuckle, he added, "I'm originally from Montana," and proceeded to revisit his coffee.

"Kentucky's a dangerous place all right," he went on. "They have their own methods for working things out. It's funny. Though Goebel wasn't born there either, he seemed to fit right in. A while back, he was having some sort of dispute with a banker named Sanford. Planned or not, they happened to meet out on the street. Within seconds, guns were drawn, shots were fired, and Goebel's bullet struck Sanford in the head. The man died not long thereafter. That's how things get taken care of in Kentucky."

Frontier justice, I could not help thinking. To the average Englishman, myself included, Kentucky seemed no different from our opinion regarding the rest of the country.

"Which," continued Steele, "brings us back to that fateful day last month when Goebel was shot. The election for governor had taken place in early November."

"The election presumably won by Goebel," I noted. "You already told us he was the governor."

"If it only were that simple, Doctor. A Republican named William Taylor – 'Hogjaw' Taylor, they call him – came out ahead and was actually inaugurated in December. But, you see, Goebel had previously set up his own legislative committee to rule on the integrity of the election, and he appealed the results to them.

"Much to everyone's surprise, especially Goebel's, his handpicked committee confirmed Taylor's victory. Yet Goebel still wasn't satisfied, and he ultimately appealed the decision of the committee to his allies in the heavily Democratic state legislature. In fact, it was when Goebel was on his way to hear the final deliberations that he was cut down. Ironically, it was *after* he was shot that the partisan legislature overturned the election results and declared him the new governor. Mortally wounded – some say he was already dead – he was sworn in the next day, the 31ˢᵗ of January, 1900. He died three days later."

"My word," said I. "Quite a dramatic tale."

Holmes leaned back in his chair, steepled his fingers, and closed his eyes. "Describe the scene of the shooting, if you please."

"With your permission," said Steele, withdrawing a small pocketbook from inside his coat. He flipped through a few pages to consult his notes and then reported the following: "On the morning of Tuesday, January 30ᵗʰ – a cold, crisp day it was – Goebel set off with two friends for the state house from the Capital Hotel where he was staying. It was just a short walk – one block down Main Street and up St. Clair to Broadway.

"You must understand that due to the contested election, feelings were running high. This was Kentucky, after all, and most of Frankfort seemed an armed camp. Mountaineers from the south-eastern counties that supported Taylor – some called them '*desperadoes*' – had arrived with shotguns and rifles and pistols – presumably with the intent of intimidating the legislature into supporting Taylor. For their part, the Democrats responded with newly-sworn-in police to help maintain the peace. With all the talk of violence, of course, it was feared that somebody might even try to shoot Goebel himself.

"In fact, the two friends accompanying him that morning also served as bodyguards. Yet despite all the gunmen milling in the streets, when the three arrived at the Capitol grounds, they found the area almost completely deserted. Capitol Square takes up a full city block. The landscape is pretty flat, interrupted here and there this time of year by barren hackberry trees. The square is surrounded by an iron-rail fence. That morning, a thin layer of snow covered the ground. The water in the four-tiered fountain near the Capitol's steps had frozen. The Capitol building itself, a two-storey, brick and white-stone structure, stands at the centre of the square. Designed in the Greek revival style, it features a portico with six grand columns that hold up the gabled pediment."

Sherlock Holmes opened his eyes at this description, and Steele noted the change.

"I know what you're thinking, Mr. Holmes," said he. "An assassin hidden behind one of the columns could do some damage. But there wouldn't be enough cover, you see, and the front contains no windows and only a single entrance. A shooter in the portico would be easily detected."

Holmes nodded, and the fire crackled in accompaniment.

"At 11:16," Steele continued, "the three men made a turn into the square through one of the two open gates and proceeded up the wide stone walkway, their shoes crunching the leftover snow on the pavement. It's about a hundred feet from the street to the portico, and the walkway itself inclines slightly as you approach the building. One of the men went ahead to check that the interior was safe. the other dropped back a step or two.

"It was just then, right before Goebel reached the fountain, that shots rang out. Some say Goebel tried to draw his own pistol, but the wound was too great, and he fell to the ground. 'Get me away,' he's said to have uttered, 'I'm afraid it's all over for me.'"

"How many shots?" Holmes asked.

"Not certain. Maybe five. Maybe fewer. There were too many conflicting accounts. What *is* known is that a single bullet traveling downward pierced Goebel's right side – splintered a rib, passed through a lung, and exited his back. Mortally wounded, he was carried to his hotel room, where doctors were sent to his aid. Needless to say, the assassin escaped.

"A few days later, after having been sworn in as governor and visited by his sister and one of his brothers – the other couldn't get there in time – Goebel died. I suppose it's fitting that controversy dogs his last words. Democrats say that he told his friends to, 'Be brave, fearless, and loyal to the great common people.'"

221

"Quite noble in the end," I observed. "A lasting tribute to the man's social concerns."

"To be sure," said Steele, "if true. One of his doctors reported that his final words were really a complaint about his last meal. 'Damned bad oyster,' he's supposed to have said."

I shook my head in disbelief and changed the subject. "What did the police make of all this?" I asked. "Surely their investigation must have turned up valuable information."

Steele allowed himself another short laugh. "Well, Doctor," he drawled, "at least I can't say they didn't try. They did determine that a rifle had been fired from a window in the next-door Executive Building. It's a three-storey brick structure some forty feet to the east of the Capitol."

"You said 'from *a* window', Mr. Steele," Holmes pointed out. "Not from *the* window?"

"Good point, Mr. Holmes. Exactly *which* window wasn't so easy to identify. Remember that there were just a handful of people walking around at the time. A few of them pointed at the nearest open window in the southwest corner of the Executive Building – which, incidentally, just happened to be the private office of Caleb Powers, the newly-elected Republican Secretary of State. The shade was down most of the way, and the window was raised about six inches."

"There you have it," said I.

"Not quite, Doctor. You see, a number of other people maintained that the shot had actually come from higher up. A few said they'd actually seen a rifle barrel in a third-floor window."

"Certainly," said Holmes, "an immediate investigation would turn up the appropriate evidence to establish the facts."

Now anyone familiar with the investigative methods of Sherlock Holmes could predict that, had Holmes been there himself, he would have invaded both offices, fallen to his hands and knees, and begun peering through his glass in search of vital clues.

"So one would assume, Mr. Holmes. So one would assume." Here Steele paused – almost as if to draw keener attention to his next few words.

Holmes did, in fact, lean forward. "I sense that you're suggesting some impediment to the investigation."

Steele laughed again. "Indeed I am," said he. "You see, Bill Taylor, the soon-to-be *deposed* Kentucky governor, was paralyzed by fear. I should explain that with the arrival of Taylor's mountain men, Goebel's people had also been marching around with guns. Now, seething with anger at the assault on their leader, they began screaming about killing

222

Taylor in return. Fearing for his safety, not to mention that of his family, Taylor ordered in the state militia. Within minutes of the shooting, five-hundred strong of the Louisville Legion and the 2nd Regiment filled the square. Their bayonets at the ready, the fully uniformed militiamen stood positioned to prevent anyone from entering the area, which obviously included the scene of the crime. *'Anyone'*, of course, meant the police as well."

"Preposterous!" I ejaculated. The thought of soldiers hindering a criminal investigation – let alone blocking the state's elected representatives from convening in the Capitol Building – seemed unworthy of a democratic nation.

Steele merely shrugged. "The local authorities got no help at all from the Republicans. In fact, to the best of my knowledge, Taylor and his crew are still holed up in the Executive Building. By my count, it's been some three weeks now. Taylor told the Republican legislators to meet in the town of London – London, Kentucky, that is – and the Democrats are gathering in the Capital Hotel in Frankfort. It's like the state has two governments."

Holmes offered a single, sarcastic clap of his hands. "Wonderful!" he cried. "A regular comedy of errors."

"Don't get me wrong, Mr. Holmes," countered Steele. "Plenty of arrests were made. In fact, some twenty-seven people were rounded up at the start – clerks, politicians, even a state-police officer. But from what I've been hearing lately, suspicion has focused on three: Caleb Powers, the Secretary of State – "

"From whose office the bullet was fired," I interrupted.

"*Might* have been fired," Steele corrected. "Powers was thought to be the mastermind. A stenographer and notary public named Henry Youtsey, was charged with being the go-between. He worked in the state auditor's office just down the hall from Powers. Youtsey's the one they think hid a pair of rifles – a Marlin .38-55 and a Winchester .38-56 – behind a loose wooden plank in Powers' office. The last of the three, a Republican county assessor named Jim Howard, had previously been charged with some other murder. Apparently, *he* is now considered the gunman. I should add that Powers himself had conveniently arranged to be out of town at the time of the shooting."

Holmes nodded. "It sounds like the authorities have constructed a logical case, Mr. Steele. But you still seem to harbour doubts?"

"I do, Mr. Holmes – to a point. All these charges against Powers and the others may, in fact, be true, but I have to believe there's more. A full ten days after the shooting, the police discovered a .38 calibre bullet in the trunk of a hackberry tree, not far behind where Goebel had been hit. The bullet matched one of the rifles found in Powers' office. As a consequence, the police employed an engineer to show that one end of a taut string held at the bullet hole in the tree and the other end at Powers' corner-window would have passed directly through the point where Goebel had been standing, thus proving the origin of the shot."

"One moment," said Holmes. "How high was the bullet hole in the tree?"

"About four-and-a-half feet from the ground."

"And the distance between the ground and the bottom of Powers' window?"

"About the same."

"Hah!" Holmes cried. "Earlier you said that the bullet which struck Goebel had travelled *downward*."

"Exactly." Steele grinned. "You're an excellent listener, Mr. Holmes. What's more, you're also giving voice to the same thoughts I have."

Sherlock Holmes cocked an eyebrow.

"You see, I couldn't forget the witnesses – more than a dozen, actually – who'd mentioned a third-floor window. They all agreed the shots had come from somewhere between the Capitol and the office building, which I took to mean from the office building's west side, not from a front-corner window like Powers'. For that matter, I'm told that Howard, the alleged shooter, didn't seem a calm-enough type to have lain in wait and done the deed. Oh, some people did swear they'd seen him on the Capitol grounds near the time of the shooting, but he produced his own witnesses to say he was elsewhere.

"Assuming you're the sort of investigator I perceive you to be," said Holmes, "I imagine that you tried to confirm your doubts."

Steele smiled again. "On the second day of the occupation by the militia, I was able to check that third-floor office myself. I bribed one of the men – twenty dollars of L&N money was quite a sum to convince him to lend me his uniform for an hour or two."

"Excellent!" cried Holmes.

"Disguised as a soldier, I entered the Executive Building, climbed the stairs, and visited the room in question."

"What did you find?" Holmes asked, his grey eyes blazing.

"The room itself had been swept clean. And yet in front of the window stood two boxes, one on top of the other, reaching to the level of the windowsill. Need I say, a perfect place to rest a rifle? But there's more. The floor revealed scuffmarks in front of the boxes that suggested a person had been moving around at that spot. And that's not all. You see, there was something strange about the markings."

"Strange?" Holmes repeated. "In what manner were they 'strange'?"

Steele consulted his notes again. "Most were long, sweeps – as if a foot had been dragged along the floor rather than simply having stepped upon it – as if whoever made the marks had a bad leg."

"Well done, Mr. Steele!" cried Holmes. "At long last. Anything else?"

"One more thing, Mr. Holmes. I found *this!* It must have been brushed into a corner." As he spoke, he drew from inside his coat a long, white envelope, which he handed to my friend.

Like a starving man reaching for food, Holmes shot out his hand to receive it. Carefully opening the flap, he slowly drew from the envelope what looked to be a short, metal rod. It had a small wooden handle at one end and a tiny, round, bolt-like device at the other. Only after scrutinizing the entire piece, did he roll the thing between his thumb and forefinger.

"*Ein Hebel,*" he murmured.

"What's that, Holmes?" I asked.

"*Hebel* is German for *lever.*"

"You recognise it then?" asked Steele. "I figured it must be important, but I didn't know what it was."

"It is the lever," Holmes said, holding the rod vertically so Steele and I could examine it as he spoke, "used for priming the bellows within an air rifle. You'll remember, Watson, that back in '94, Sebastian Moran employed such a weapon – what the Germans call a *Bolzenbüchse* – for shooting at me – though in Moran's case, it had been modified by that tinker von Herder. I told you that this case offered familiar echoes."

Who could forget the horrible night when the dummy-likeness of Holmes that he had placed in our Baker Street window had taken the bullet meant for the man himself? It seemed like yesterday, though almost six years had passed.

"If I understand you correctly," Wyatt Steele addressed my friend, "you're suggesting that the assassin was, in fact, at the third-floor window of the Executive Building with an air-rifle."

"Quite so. I shouldn't doubt that, as you yourself have described, there were also shooters in the office of the Secretary of State. Let's not forget that there were gunmen running rampant throughout the city. Still, I'm willing to wager that the shooters in Powers' office were meant to be diversions. Oh, I have no doubt that they fired upon Goebel – one even hit a tree! – but whoever wanted him dead had put his true faith in the shooter with the silent weapon on the third floor. He's the gunman we're really after."

"A gunman with a gamy leg," I said.

"Exactly, Watson. And unless I am very much mistaken, I believe it is the same conclusion that has compelled Mr. Steele to continue his investigation."

"Indeed, Mr. Holmes. But not with the assuredness that your confirmation provides. While I was still in uniform, I asked some of the soldiers nearby if they'd seen anyone limping about."

"And?"

"'Now that you mention it,' said one, 'I do remember a beggar hanging around. A cripple he was. He had a bad back and twisted leg. He was wearing a pea coat and bell-bottomed trousers – you know, the kind that sailors wear. I remember his sea-faring clothes because I thought they looked pretty strange out here in the middle of Kentuck.'

"'And another thing,' a second soldier chimed in, 'even though he looked young, he walked with a cane. I guess 'cause he was all hunched over.'"

"A walking stick, Watson," said Holmes. "Do you mark that?"

I did, though I failed to make anything of it. That a deformed man required a walking stick did not seem unusual to me.

"Where was he seen?" Holmes asked.

"On Broadway in front of the Capitol grounds. Apparently, he was holding out a tin cup for money, but in all the commotion, he started hobbling east towards Ann Street. You should know, Mr. Holmes, that just past the corner of the square is the L&N railroad depot. It's quite close by actually – only a couple of blocks away. Once I got back into my regular clothes, I checked there myself. A ticket agent told me he'd seen a cripple begging out in Elk Alley next to the station. As far as I could tell, no one actually saw him get on a train, but you know how it is – once word gets around about a shooting, people start running every which way worrying about their own safety. I don't imagine they'd pay any mind to a beggar, not even a deformed one."

"You're suggesting," I said to Steele, "that this cripple boarded a train at the railway station and got out of town."

"I am," said the Pinkerton agent. "And depending on time and destination, he could have made connections to most anywhere. Say he got to Cincinnati. Then he could travel north. "

"Or west," I suggested, images of frontier gunslingers springing to mind.

"I wagered on New York," offered Steele. "The pea coat and flared trousers made me think of a seaport, and New York is the major point of departure – "

" – For ships sailing to London," said Holmes, completing the sentence.

226

"I figured it was worth looking into. I notified the agency to get some people out to the New York docks and keep an eye peeled for the twisted man."

"Excellent work, Mr. Steele," said Holmes. "I can only assume that someone saw him board a ship for London, which is why you are here."

"That's right. The Pinkerton Agency has had many dealings with the Metropolitan Police, and I cabled Scotland Yard to be on the lookout at the London docks for the suspect. An Inspector Lestrade was put in charge, but I guess that our man somehow managed to elude him."

"Fancy that," said Holmes drily, "someone eluding Lestrade." He allowed himself a brief chuckle and then said to the two of us, "Well, gentlemen, I suppose it will be up to us to track down the fugitive."

Steele's eyes widened. "Do you actually have someone in mind, Mr. Holmes?" he asked.

"By itself, I grant you that the naval attire doesn't tell us much. But when I match it to a deformed young man with the intent to kill, a certain profile most certainly comes to mind. What say *you*, friend Watson?"

There was indeed a ring of familiarity in the description, yet I could not place the figure in question.

"And if I tell you," Holmes continued, "that a trip to Sussex might be in order – to Cheeseman's in Lamberley just south of Horsham?"

"Bob Ferguson!" I cried.

"More properly, Bob Ferguson's son, Master Jacky."

Steele knotted his eyebrows. His confusion could well be understood, since I had not yet made public the case I planned to title "The Sussex Vampire". The narrative would dramatise for the reading public the young man to whom Holmes was referring.

"Jacky Ferguson is the son of an old friend of mine," I explained. "In our rugby days, the boy's father was known as 'Big Bob'."

Holmes cleared his throat to remind me to stick to salient facts.

"By 1896," I continued, "Bob's wife – that is to say, Jacky's mother – had died, Fergusson remarried, and soon they had a new son."

"Not long thereafter," said Holmes, "the trouble started."

"In November of that year," I went on, "Ferguson came to Holmes seeking an explanation for the apparently murderous intentions of his second wife towards the baby. As it turned out, however, it was not Bob's wife but the pampered older boy Jacky – I called him *boy*, he must be close to twenty by now – who had attempted to poison his tiny half-brother. His was a decidedly murderous plan intended to prevent the baby from coming between himself and his father. After revealing the crime, Holmes suggested that Jacky spend a year at sea."

The Pinkerton agent furrowed his brow. "I don't understand how – "

227

"Sorry," I said. "I failed to mention that the boy Jacky had suffered a terrible fall during his childhood. The result was – "

"Let me guess," Steele interrupted. "A twisted spine."

"Quite so," said Holmes. "Now, Watson, wire Ferguson with the news that we're coming to visit. We can catch an afternoon train at Victoria. No need to mention Master Jacky until we actually get there. Mr. Steele, I'm afraid we'll have to leave you to your own devices until we return. Three people descending on poor Robert Ferguson would be too many."

"Whatever you say, Mr. Holmes. I'm in your hands. I never expected to have identified a suspect so quickly. Birdy Edwards certainly had you pegged correctly."

A brief smile flashed across Holmes's face. He was never one to ignore a compliment.

II

As he had proposed, Sherlock Holmes and I took the afternoon train from Victoria to Horsham. Ashen clouds continued to bedevil the usually enticing Sussex countryside where one generally expects a floral palette rich with colour. Yet on this trip I had no desire to gaze out of the carriage window, and my lack of interest had nothing to do with the neutral tones provided by the greying skies. No, I preferred keeping my eyes riveted on Holmes as he revealed to me the various actions that had been going on directly under my nose, but about which I clearly knew nothing.

"Surely, Watson, once we discovered Master Jacky's vile role in that vampire business, you didn't imagine I'd let him go off into the world unobserved? One doesn't expect a sour temper to sweeten overnight. On the contrary, I requested your friend Ferguson to notify me as soon as a berth on some ship had been found for the boy. It took a few weeks, but the shipping agents at the father's firm, tea brokers Ferguson and Muirhead of Mincing Lane, were finally able to complete the task. A position 'before the mast', as it were, was secured for young Jack on the *S.S Heraldic*, a tea-carrying steamer in the Merchant Navy. What's more, from all reports, the boy appeared ready, if a bit reluctant, to perform his tasks to the extent that his physical abilities allowed."

"Most admirable," I said, pleased that my friend's son seemed to be falling into line.

"And yet, Watson, I needed to be certain. No sooner did I learn that Jacky would be setting out to sea from Gravesend than I put Sammy Trout and the other Baker Street Irregulars on his scent. With comrades all along the river, I knew that the Irregulars would have little difficulty keeping track of a flaxen-haired youth that exhibited a decided limp. I instructed Sam to inform me when they actually saw him boarding.

"Once Jacky had set sail, it was a simple matter to chart the *Heraldic's* comings and goings in the daily newspapers' accounts of commercial ship movements. My various contacts in European and American ports served to confirm what I had already learned, and such has been the case for the past three years."

Three years! – During which I had suspected nothing. The railway carriage swayed back and forth, and under ordinary circumstances the movement might have lulled me to sleep. Yet so intent was I upon hearing Holmes's story that drowsiness never threatened.

"How did young Jack fare as a sailor then?" I asked.

"As one might expect, Watson: He viewed anything required of him as punishment. Let's not forget that Master Jacky regarded his attempts to kill the baby as perfectly logical. As a result, his exile to shipboard labour must have seemed very unjust punishment indeed."

"And yet a moment ago, you described him as resigned to facing his sea adventure."

"Ah, Watson," Holmes sighed, "it only gets worse. As a not-too surprising consequence, the boy began to cultivate undesirable associates among his shipmates. One imagines that it took little effort on their part to interest him in firearms, and Jack soon extended his so-called 'tour of duty' aboard the *Heraldic*. Guns, you see, made no demands on his deformity – indeed, here were weapons that allowed him to gain the strength that he'd always felt he was lacking."

"Surely, Holmes, you didn't learn all this from the Baker Street Irregulars? Good watchdogs, so to speak, but mere children lacking the psychological insights you are reporting."

"Hah, Watson! Sharp as ever. No, the Irregulars merely presented the facts. I supplied the inferences. As it turned out, Jack had returned to Gravesend with an unsavoury group of friends. One of our lads followed them to the marshlands outside of town and watched them shoot at bottles and the like. Jack, it seems, had become quite proficient.

"Once I heard that he'd begun taking aim at stray dogs and cats, however, my concerns grew. In fact, I arranged for my associates with the German police to follow him on the occasion the *Heraldic* berthed in Hamburg. Sad to say, my intuition paid off. He had scheduled a meeting in the *Reeperbahn* with an elderly German with a knowledge of firearms – blind as it so happens – who, curiously enough, arrived at the rendezvous with two canes – and left with only one."

"Von Herder!" I exclaimed.

229

At that moment, like a warning cry, the train sounded its horn. We must have been getting close to Horsham.

"Quite so, old fellow," replied Holmes, oblivious to the noise, "Von Herder, the gun mechanic. It is he, I have come to believe, who furnished Jack Ferguson with an air rifle. Though not the most talented of gunsmiths, Von Herder is competent enough. Not only could he obtain the basics of the hollow walking stick from gun-makers like Townsend and Reilly, but he could also combine the structural framework with the mechanism of his own air gun. Jack would certainly not be the first shooter to employ a rifle that resembled a walking stick. But I hazard a guess that he may be the first to render the employment of *both* of its features a necessity."

"Of course!" I exclaimed. "A malformed assassin concealing his weapon in the guise of a dependable cane."

"Quite so, old fellow. It may have been no more than coincidence that the *Heraldic* was delivering a shipment of tea to New York in early January of this year, but I'm willing to wager that Jack was no longer part of the crew when it left a week later. He had honed his skills with the rifle and somehow presented himself as an accomplished shooter to the lawless elements bent on exploiting America's East Coast.

"Word travels fast within the criminal underworld, and Jack must have learned that his services could be put to use in Kentucky. It mattered little that the *Heraldic* had sailed before the deed was done. No doubt he earned plenty for his work and could easily book passage back to England. My hope in meeting with your friend Ferguson is simply to confirm my reasoning."

Though a closed carriage conveyed us the few miles from Horsham to Lamberley, we had to hire an open dogcart for the final leg of the journey. It began to drizzle as soon as we reached the road to Cheeseman's, forcing us to wrap ourselves more tightly in our long coats and pull our hats even lower over our brows. Only when we recognized the familiar winding lane of Sussex clay did we know our excursion was about to end.

No doubt, it was the unkind weather that made the seventeenth-century farmhouse appear more ominous than I had remembered. To be sure, the leaden skies and shadowy trees had darkened its redbrick walls, but I was certain that some element beyond the weather was rendering the atmosphere so oppressive.

"I have to admit to you, Mr. Holmes," said a sombre Bob Ferguson, who met us personally at the dark, oaken outer door, "that I'm of mixed minds talking with you. There's no two ways about it." He continued to

230

speak without so much as the briefest of smiles as he ushered us inside. "I will never forget the joy you restored to my life by revealing the causes of my wife's strange behaviour. And yet, though I know it was for the best, I cannot forgive you for compelling me to remove my Jacky from our family."

The reluctant host led us into a dimly-lit sitting room where bright flames danced in a cavernous fireplace, casting eerie patterns on the half-oak, half-plastered walls. Ferguson offered us each a brandy and seats on the leather couch, but his tone was anything but warm.

Recounting the recent history of his son Jack was obviously not to Ferguson's liking. After Holmes had asked what Ferguson knew of Jack's latest activities, the father required a pull of the brandy and began his report with a frown. "When Jacky returned home following his first voyage – it's been about two years now – I was hoping to see a positive change in the lad's attitude. Unfortunately, there was anything but. Oh, he did ask if we might go out shooting, not a sport in which he had showed a whit of interest prior to his putting out to sea. But he hit some grouse, don't you know, and seemed quite pleased with himself. I thought the outing might help us strengthen our friendship, but he remained here just a day or two. In point of fact, he collected his belongings and told us he would be taking a flat in London, thank you very much. Then he left, making off with my German dictionary for good measure. I haven't seen him since."

"Do you know his current location, Mr. Ferguson?" Holmes asked. "We have every suspicion that he has returned to London, and it is necessary for me to speak with him."

Ferguson scowled. "Is he in trouble again?"

"One can't be certain," Holmes replied. "That is why I need to find him."

I assumed that the boy's actual address was unimportant to Holmes. Certainly, the Baker Street Irregulars had dogged Jack Ferguson closely enough to identify his residence. Still, had his father known the boy's whereabouts, it would have made finding Jack that much more simple.

"No," said Ferguson, his voice laced with bitterness, "he's never shared that detail with me. If he had, I'm not certain I would want to share it with you. The boy has been through enough."

Holmes nodded. Later he would explain to me, "I wanted to learn just how estranged father and son had become. That the father doesn't know where his son is living indicates the severity of their break."

We saw no sign of Mrs. Ferguson during our visit and, having exhausted our topic, we finished our brandies, thanked a sceptical Ferguson for his help, and promised to keep him up-to-date concerning any developments that involved his son. Then, with the much-appreciated aide of Ferguson's carriage, Holmes and I made our way back through the rain and wind to the small railway station in Horsham, and ultimately home to Victoria and Baker Street.

Ringing in our ears throughout the journey, however, was Ferguson's final and unwarranted valediction: "None of this would have ever happened, Mr. Holmes, had we not followed your cruel advice."

I leave to my more fair-minded readers the question of premeditation. For my part, I have never been totally clear concerning the exact role Holmes played in the shooting that concludes this account. At the very least, however, we have arrived at the point in the narrative that, as I have already indicated, presents Sherlock Holmes at his most cold-blooded.

Unfriendly winds had been blowing throughout the night of our return to Baker Street, and yet, even as I was shuffling down the stairs for breakfast the following morning, I encountered my friend enveloped in cape and deerstalker, entering our sitting room from the outer hall.

"Out so early in this foul weather?" I asked.

"Indeed," he answered, hanging his cold-weather garments on the pegs by the door. "Windy or not, it seemed the right time for the Trout boy to show me Jack's lodgings. Sooner than later, I wanted to get the lie of the land. As it turns out, Jack has a flat in the Hanover Buildings in Tooley Street."

"Just south of the river – not far from the London Bridge Station?"

"Quite so," Holmes nodded.

I knew of the place, having ministered to a few of its residents while I was working as a houseman at Barts. Later to be renamed the Devon Mansions during the Great War, they had originally been constructed to house the working people who laboured on the nearby docks and warehouses. As far as Jack Ferguson was concerned, he could not have found a residence of lesser distinction – five identical six-storey blocks of yellow brick.

"The choice makes sense," I observed. "From nearby London Bridge Station, it's a simple train ride to Gravesend where his ship put out."

Not that I was overly familiar with the railway line that runs parallel to the Thames. But one could not forget the foul-weather trip that Holmes and I had made the previous year. We had journeyed by rail to Gravesend to meet the so-called "Baron of Brede Place", American writer Stephen Crane, who was returning to England following his adventures in Cuba during the Spanish-American War.

232

But the trip I remember most involving that railway line is the seemingly endless journey Holmes and I had taken a few years before. Holmes was hoping to resolve the business with Professor Coram and the golden pince-nez at Yoxley Old Place. With time of the essence, we had been reduced to catching the morning train, which stopped at every station along the way. At Charing Cross, the next station west of London Bridge, we had set out for Higham, the depot closest to Yoxley Old Place. But that infernal trip lasted forever – three long hours to reach Higham, which is just beyond Gravesend – and we knew for a fact that the day before, Inspector Hopkins had required only ninety minutes – *half* our time – to make the same journey. The thought still rankles.

Interrupting my memories, Holmes held up a small piece of paper. "I've taken the liberty to write Jack Ferguson a note in your name."

"In *my* name?" I replied. "Why not in *yours*? It is with you he has a quarrel, not with *me*. *You're* the one who suggested he go to sea."

"Precisely, my dear fellow. No love lost there, I'm afraid, which is quite the point. I don't think he'd agree to see *me*. A request from *you*, on the other hand, might make him curious enough to want to hear you out."

"And just what did I say in this note?"

"You've asked for permission to visit his flat."

"For what purpose?"

"To request that he invite *me* in as well."

I thought my friend must be losing his senses. Had Holmes not just suggested that Jack would not welcome him? For that matter, Holmes suspected him of being a killer. Would it be safe for *me* in the lair of an assassin? Unable to mask my fears, I cast a concerned look at Holmes.

"Nothing to worry about, old fellow," said he. "I'll be standing just outside the building. Once he gives his approval, your job will be to draw aside any curtains that might be in the way, open the window, and call me in."

I scratched my head in dismay. But knowing better than to question the rationality of my friend, I agreed to go along with his request. Still, as Holmes gave the pageboy the message for Jack Ferguson, I could not keep from wondering what trick my friend had up his sleeve.

"*Nothing to say to* you", ran the note that Billy returned to me. "*But I am curious about what you have to say to* me. *This afternoon. 2:00*". It was signed *JF*.

"Perfect," said Holmes, rubbing his hands together. "Now I have some last-minutes plans to put in motion. I'll be back at noon for lunch. Suggest beef sandwiches to Mrs. Hudson. That joint I saw in the kitchen looked quite inviting."

And then he was gone again.

A hansom brought us to the Hanover Buildings, just south of the Thames. The winds had died, but frantic traffic, laden with tea and coffee and hops and leather, bustled along Tooley Street as the nearby ships and warehouses and shops made their demands.

No sooner did we exit the hansom than Holmes pointed to the block nearest us. "That's his room," he said, indicating the second window in the first-floor line. "He'll be expecting you. Go." With that, Holmes turned his back and began to survey the other structures along both sides of the street.

A gate interrupted the short black railing round the building, and I made my way through it as well as through the unlatched outer door. Traversing a dark foyer, I climbed the equally dark stairs to the first storey and, in the light of a meagre gas lamp, managed to locate what I presumed to be the second flat facing the street. I knocked hesitantly and, receiving no response, knocked again more sharply. This time the door swung open, and I immediately found myself standing face to face with Jack Ferguson.

When we first had met, Jacky had been able to conceal the hatred he harboured towards his infant half-brother. His murderous intent showed only when Holmes had confronted him regarding the boy's foul plan. Now, however, with his thick, flaxen hair combed straight back, that same devilish look appeared permanently etched into his features. His knotted brow, curling lip, and narrow, brutish eyes conveyed a rage that he clearly felt no longer compelled to hide. Worse, as much as one might hope to deny it, his deformity added to his sense of menace. For though I would be the first to protest the casting of so general an aspersion, in this instance his twisted spine seemed to reflect his twisted nature.

"I welcome you to my home," said he, bidding me enter with an exaggerated sweep of his arm. He indicated an old armchair, which I took and, pulling out one of two wooden chairs nesting under a rickety table, he sat down with his bent-back to the window. I recognised the trick, one often employed by Holmes himself. With the window behind him, Jack's face became silhouetted by the brightness outside, the result rendering his facial expressions difficult to discern.

"I don't see my father much," he offered. "I should imagine that you came at his request – though I don't know how you discovered this place."

I thought of Sammy Trout and the Irregulars but, playing my cards close to the vest, I said rather cryptically, "As you know, I work with Sherlock Holmes, and when he wants to find someone, that person is found."

"Holmes!" Jack spat out. "The man who tore me from my family? The man who turned me into what I have become?" The more animated he grew, the more spasmodically his entire body jerked.

"Holmes wishes to speak with you," said I calmly, "but he fears that you wouldn't let him through the door."

"He's got that right. Quite the detective!"

"He anticipated you would react in such a fashion. That's why he asked me to pave the way. He was hoping I might talk you into letting him come up here. You see, he's just outside the building, awaiting a sign from me at the window to summon him in."

With some effort, Jack turned his body and glanced suspiciously at the window behind him. White curtains of gauze-linen barely covered the glass.

"What does he want with me?" Jack questioned.

"I'm sure I don't know. Why not let me signal that he can come up?"

Jack glanced at his bureau, a sure giveaway that something he wanted lay concealed within. Except for drumming his fingers on the table next to him, however, he sat motionless a moment or two. At last, with a sigh of resignation, he said, "Why not?" and waved me towards the window.

All I had left to do was carry out my instructions from Holmes. I spread the two curtains apart and then pulled up the sash. Holmes was pacing below, his eyes fixed on the window in search of any movement. I motioned for him to come up, at the same time being sure – as, for some strange reason, he had directed – to keep the window open and the curtains drawn.

No sooner had I completed the task than I turned round and discovered myself face to face with the revolver Jack was now pointing at my head. As if playing a chord on a piano, he had arched the fingers of his free hand on the top of the bureau, their obvious strength helping him maintain his balance.

"No need for the gun," said I.

"Just a precaution," he replied, pointing the barrel at the chair I had occupied. "Now sit."

I did, and with Jack still standing, we silently awaited the arrival of Sherlock Holmes.

Moments later came a quick rap.

"Enter," commanded Jack, the barrel of the gun now turned toward the doorway.

Holmes walked in cautiously, eyed the pistol, displayed his empty hands, and opened wide his coat to show that he carried no weapons.

Motioning with the gun, Jack gestured for him to sit down.

Holmes pulled the second wooden chair away from the table, placed it to my right – opposite Jack – and turned it slightly so it wasn't in direct line with the window. He then seated himself and faced the gunman.

"Now, Mr. Sherlock Holmes," said Jack, "be so kind as to inform me of the nature of your business."

Holmes flashed a brief smile, and then, after stealing a glance at the window, got straight to the point. "I merely wish to ascertain, Jack Ferguson, that it was *not* the L&N Railroad that hired you to assassinate Governor Goebel in Kentucky last month."

For a man holding a gun, Jack displayed an alarming lack of control. His eyebrows shot up and he lurched backward upon hearing Holmes's charge. "Who claims that I assassinated anyone?" he demanded.

This time Holmes's smile lingered. "Please, Jack, don't take us for fools. We know of your recently acquired talent with guns. We know a man of your description was seen in the Capitol grounds in Frankfort. We know you met with the gun maker von Herder in Hamburg when your ship put into port there last year, and thus we suspect that the walking stick you utilised in Frankfort was, in fact, an air rifle constructed by the German. Finally, we know that you boarded a railway in Kentucky after shooting the governor, secured a ship in New York, and ended up here in Tooley Street."

Jack Ferguson's demeanour grew darker with each point ticked off by Holmes. "If you know so much, Mr. Sherlock Holmes, how come you don't know who hired me?"

"That's why I'm here, Jack, to find that out – before we hand you to the authorities for shipment back to America."

"Ha!" he snorted. "That's funny, with me holding the gun. Though I don't suppose it matters all that much, since neither one of you is leaving here alive. When I explain to the police that I found two men burglarizing my flat and shot them dead, you won't be in a position to tell them otherwise.

Shooting us dead? Consider me foolish, but I had not anticipated so dramatic a turn of events. Though I realised Holmes had entered the flat unarmed, I earnestly hoped he had some sort of plan for extricating us from this dilemma. As I gazed at Jack's pistol, however, nothing popped into my head.

"I don't mind telling you," said Jack, "that L&N had nothing to do with the job in Frankfort. I was hired by a fellow called Rounceville – I doubt that's his real name, and I don't really care, because his money is good. He was a deputy to the Secretary of State in Kentucky, that fellow

Powers. But I tell you honestly that I don't know if Powers even knew what was going on. This Rounceville told me the Republicans didn't want Goebel stealing the election, and that to stop him once and for all, they wanted him dead. They told me when and where to lie in wait and promised diversionary gunfire when I performed the work. With my silent airgun, I knew I could shoot Goebel and escape undetected."

Holmes nodded. "As I thought," said he. Then he slowly stood and moved his chair to the right.

I suppose Jack could have shot him right then, but in point of fact he himself moved opposite Holmes placing his back squarely in front of the open window.

Holmes and I have been in some tight places together – but I cannot recall a moment that seemed more dire, a situation that seemed to offer no escape.

"Exit Sherlock Holmes," announced Jack, holding out his arm at full length as he pointed the pistol at my friend.

Suddenly – without a sound – a blossom of red erupted from Jack's white shirtfront. There was only a moment for a look of surprise to splash across Jack's face, and then he fell forward. In a sense, it appeared that he had exploded from within. but the truth, of course, was much less fantastical. He had been struck by a bullet fired through the open window. That I had heard no report accompanying the shot made it all the more perplexing.

Needless to say, I sprang to my feet to administer to the stricken young man. I felt for a pulse, but there was none. Jack Ferguson lay dead. The man who had killed Governor Goebel had been assassinated himself.

Sherlock Holmes stood by the window staring silently across the street. Only then did it dawn on me that he had set up the entire deadly scheme.

"Holmes," I said, but he hushed me with a forefinger to his lips.

"Come," said he, and together we exited, leaving the body of Jack Ferguson sprawled on the floor of his flat in an ever-widening pool of blood. When we reached the pavement, Holmes hailed a hansom, and we made our return to Baker Street.

"Not a word till dinner," said Sherlock Holmes in reference to our harrowing afternoon. "I have made plans with Mr. Steele to meet us in Simpson's at 7:00. We shall discuss the matter further then."

Leaving me to stand in wonder, Holmes retired to his bedroom, and soon I heard the strains of his violin as he attacked some concerto or other. For my part, I tried to pass the hours by reading the latest *Lancet*

237

and keeping up-to-date on medical matters. But it did little good. I could not stop myself from wondering whether Holmes had had the intention of shooting Jack Ferguson from the start. More practical queries coursed through my brain as well. The questions may appear obvious, but still I needed to learn who had actually done the shooting, and why I had heard no shot fired? For that matter, I also wanted to know what had happened to the body Holmes and I had left on the floor of the flat, and how Robert Ferguson would be told of the death of his son.

The answers to the first two questions came immediately upon my seeing Wyatt Steele enter the dining hall at Simpson's with the aid of a walking stick. Holmes and I were already sampling a pre-prandial sherry when the Pinkerton approached our table. As he settled into his seat, he carefully rested the stick against the chair's wooden arm. The significance of such a piece, especially in the hands of an accomplished agent like Steele, revealed all. The stick was the weapon fashioned by the gun maker Von Herder.

"It is a little-known fact, Watson," said Holmes, "that the original air-rifle we'd taken from Sebastian Moran in '94 and bestowed upon Scotland Yard for safe-keeping had been misplaced and ultimately stolen. It seems that, on his way to the Yard, Inspector Lestrade had alighted to quell some disturbance or other and left the thing in the hansom. [1]

"One of my Irregulars happened to be near the vehicle at the time. Happily, he managed to grab the rifle and bring it to me. As the one who had presented it to Lestrade in the first place, I concluded that the thing would be far safer in my hands than in his. Since then, I've kept it, along with the ammunition I bought, secure in one of my London hidey-holes. Today, however, when the business with Jack Ferguson materialised, I decided it might be needed to help extricate us from a delicate situation. Fortunately, Mr. Steele, who was positioned on a rooftop across the road, was up to the task. He is, just as I had surmised, an American sharpshooter."

Steele's face flushed. "This gun is a fine piece, Mr. Holmes. Make no mistake. You did your part by manoeuvring Ferguson to the window, but I never would have fired if he hadn't pointed that pistol at you."

"I believe I also speak for Dr. Watson when I say that we are both extremely glad that you did."

I raised my glass in appreciation, and the three of us drank to Steele's timely marksmanship.

"In anticipation of the other questions I assume you have concocted," Holmes said to me, "you will be pleased to know that I have anonymously notified the police of the presence of a body in the Hanover

Buildings. I leave it to the Yarders to inform Robert Ferguson of the death of his son. I don't believe he wants to hear anything more from you or me."

I felt a pang of guilt at not addressing Ferguson myself, but I have come to agree with Holmes's assessment of our intrusion into his life.

"I will also give to Mr. Steele," Holmes continued, "a note in my own hand to pass along to his employers at the L&N Railroad. To protect Robert Ferguson's good name, I've written that, whilst not offering the identity of the prime mover in the plot, the assassin exonerated L&N in the planning of Goebel's murder. I believe my reputation in the States is strong enough to alleviate any anxieties at the railroad. It is, of course, nearly impossible to put an end to the common gossip and speculation that will no doubt go on indefinitely."

"I'm much obliged to you for putting the record straight," said Steele. Holding up his glass once more, he added, "To Birdy Edwards. It was he, after all, who set me on the track that revealed Goebel's true killer."

"To Birdy Edwards," Holmes and I chorused, both of us in agreement that the late Pinkerton would have been duly pleased at the outcome of our investigation. No sooner had Holmes put down his glass than he signalled for the waiter to have one of the domed silver trollies brought to our table.

"One final question, Holmes," I asked before the carver arrived. "Do you not feel responsible for leading Jack Ferguson to his death?"

My friend stared into my eyes. "The man had become a hired killer, Watson, a paid assassin. However much I am to blame for his departure from this world, the regret does not give me much pause."

With that, we all turned our attention towards the trolley that was just then arriving before us.

Following Holmes's retirement in 1903, he and I saw each other only sparingly. Yet long after our involvement in the death of Jack Ferguson had ended, we continued to keep track of the latest legal developments regarding the assassination of William Goebel.

Thanks to the accounts of pressmen like Irvin Cobb and our friend David Graham Phillips, (himself the victim of an assassin's bullet in 1911), we could follow the evolution of the legal entanglements related to primary figures in the case. It was on 21 May, 1900, just a few months after Goebel's death, that the United States Supreme Court ruled on the legitimacy of Goebel's gubernatorial victory over Republican William Taylor. Citing the argument of states' rights, the Court refused to overturn Goebel's election that had earlier been upheld by the Democratically-inclined Supreme Court of Kentucky.

On the other hand, appeals courts dominated by Republicans nullified the convictions of Caleb Powers and James Howard. In point of fact, however, Powers would face three more trials. Although he was convicted twice, sympathetic courts demanded new trials both times, the last concluding with what the Americans term a "hung jury" – that is, the members of the jury were not in agreement.

Like Powers, Howard – the presumed gunman – also faced another trial, but though unlike his associate he was convicted, in 1908 both he and Powers were finally pardoned. For his part, Youtsey, the alleged go-between, was paroled in 1916 and pardoned three years later. In the end, Caleb Powers, who had been tried four times for murder without success, was elected to the United States Congress in 1911. He would go on to serve four successive terms.

One evening not long thereafter, Holmes came up to London for a visit. Whilst enjoying cigars together in my sitting room, we found ourselves discussing the contradictory resolution of the entire Goebel affair.

"If I recall correctly, Watson," Holmes observed, "in the case you titled 'The Abbey Grange', you recorded an observation of mine regarding the law. At the time, I said that I would rather play tricks with the law of England than with my own conscience. Is that not right?"

"Yes, Holmes," I said with a nod, "I believe you quote yourself correctly."

"Well then, " said he, stretching out his long legs and exhaling a plume of blue smoke, "allow me to also say that, judging from all we have learned in the Goebel case, it would appear that in America it is the law that plays the tricks and one's conscience that suffers."

I nodded, and both of us, ever contemplating the protean relationship between England and the United States, proceeded to fill the room with ever-thickening clouds of smoke.

NOTES

1 – In his essay, "Colonel Moran's Infamous Air Rifle", (*The Baker Street Journal*, Vol. 10, No. 3, 1960), Ralph A. Ashton corroborates the theft of Moran's weapon.

The Case of the
Dead Detective
by Martin Rosenstock

My story begins late one winter morning. I had gone to see a girl with whooping cough, but as I now walked towards Baker Street, my patient was no longer topmost on my mind. I was living through one of those periods in which Mary's dear face and the gaze of her blue eyes seemed constantly present in my mind. My heart was leaden as I considered and reconsidered what might have been. When I entered our lodgings, Holmes was finishing breakfast. We exchanged a few words, and then he disappeared into his room, a piece of toast between his teeth. I had a cup of tea and a boiled egg before pushing back my chair and reaching for *The Chronicle*. Mrs. Hudson gave me a disapproving glance when she cleared the table, but the good woman had come to know my moods after all these years.

I had worked my way through *The Chronicle* and was on to *The Times* when I heard light steps on the staircase. I lowered the paper. There was one perfunctory knock, and before I could so much as utter a word, the freckled face of Little Charlie, one of Holmes's Irregulars, looked into the room.

"Dr. Watson," he piped, stepping up to me with all the self-importance of an agent with momentous tidings. "I 'ave a message for ya." He uncurled his little fist and held out a crumpled piece of paper.

I smoothed it out and read a few words in a clear, functional hand:

If you are free, come to 89 Morton Rd – a strange sight.

Lestrade

I was struck by the lack of urgency in the message. The tone of confusion that generally attends the Inspector's communications was notably absent. I rose and dug tuppence from my pocket.

With a "Thanks, guv'ner!" the boy scampered off.

I went to see Holmes in his room.

We were on our way a quarter-of-an-hour later. During the night, the temperature may have dropped below freezing, and the wind blowing up from the Channel had a Siberian touch. People's cheeks were ruddy,

241

and the city's din, the clatter of hooves and wheels, the shouts and jingling of shop bells, reached one's ear with pristine clarity. Holmes remained silent as we headed towards Fitzrovia.

We arrived at Morton Road in twenty minutes. The houses to both sides were well-kept. They stood wall-to-wall, a terrace of flat-roofed, four-storey buildings with porticos and souterrains. The gate to No. 89 was open. As we stepped onto the property, a voice called to us from behind. "Gentlemen."

We turned and saw a man coming towards us. I guessed him to be in his mid-twenties. He had a well-groomed appearance. His light hair was parted fashionably at the side, and sideburns reached down to his jaw. He was wearing a single-breasted blue frock coat and matching trousers. A woolen scarf was slung around his neck. He now switched a shopping bag from his right hand to his left.

"Jacob Henslow." A flicker of amazement crossed his face. This reaction is not uncommon with people encountering Holmes for the first time outside the pages of *The Strand Magazine*, though unlike most, Jacob Henslow made no remark. "You must be Inspector Lestrade's associates," he continued blandly.

"Indeed we are," replied Holmes.

We shook hands. Mr. Henslow had the firm grip of someone who is no stranger to manual labour. He pointed to No. 89.

"My mother owns the building. Such a pity what has happened to Mr. Aherne. I will show you upstairs."

Henslow led the way, and we entered a bright stairwell and began to ascend. As we approached the third floor, a constable blocking a closed door to the right came into view. We heard another door opening, and a few more steps revealed an elderly couple in a door across the landing. She was wearing a tea gown, he a morning coat. They must have been waiting behind the door. Both were pale with grey, tousled hair; I noticed a florin-sized firemark on the man's right cheek.

Henslow tilted his head in exasperation. "Please, Mrs. O'Malley, Mr. O'Malley. The police need to do their work. You mustn't disturb them."

The couple stared at Holmes and me, but then the husband laid a hand on his wife's shoulder, and they retreated into their rooms. The door closed behind them.

"I will leave you here, gentlemen." Henslow nodded to us, as if to suggest we ready ourselves for a surprise, and then proceeded to descend the stairs.

The constable had turned and knocked, and now Lestrade's strident voice responded, "Come in!"

The door gave onto a short corridor, at the end of which stood the inspector, dressed as usual in a natty three-piece suit. "Ah, Mr. Holmes. Doctor." He made an inviting gesture. "Glad you could come. I believe you will find this interesting."

We passed along the corridor and into the sitting room. On first impression, the room appeared unremarkable. A well-stocked bookshelf lined the far wall, three armchairs and a sofa were grouped around a tea table. In the corner stood a walnut Davenport desk. A door next to the bookshelf led to a bedroom.

A further step or two revealed the body of a man. It was lying behind one of the armchairs. The body lay on its back, torso twisted, left hand half open, right clenched to the chest. The left sleeve of the man's shirt was rolled up. A loosened brace circled his upper arm. A syringe hung by its tip from the crook of his elbow and lay against his shirt. The man's face was a hideous grimace. His lips were peeled back, exposing clenched teeth, the skin on the ridge of his nose stood folded in steep creases. His clouded eyes stared at the ceiling. I put his age at no higher than twenty-five. His expression was one of horror, as if in his final moment he had understood a cruel truth.

Half-a-dozen puncture wounds dotted the inside of his lower left arm. The plunger of the syringe had been pressed down to the tip. I turned to the table on the right. A dark flask stood there. The label read *CO 7%*. My eyes traversed the room. An Inverness cape hung on a hook beside the door. On a mantelpiece lay a pipe and cleaner, beside them a Persian slipper. A black violin case stood beside a music stand with an open score on the rest. Through a doorway into another room, I could now see a workbench, on it a Bunsen burner and a rack with test tubes.

Holmes was looking at the dead man's fingertips. They were covered with acid burns and other discolourations, like Holmes's own. My eyes swung to the dead man's face. Death does strange things to a human being's features. Paradoxically, it both sharpens them and reduces their individuality, as if the type to which the person had belonged were laid bare. The dead man's head was round with a broad forehead and a curved chin. The nose too was broad and a little bent, as if it had been broken at some point. The eyes were set wide apart, the mouth was large. The impression of rotundity and ampleness though was counterbalanced by a lack of fleshy substance. The cheeks caved inward and the contours of the skull stood out clearly.

Naturally, the thought crossed my mind that the drug had been wasting away his bodily substance, but this was not the case. The exposed arm was muscular, the chest and shoulders were broad; in fact, he appeared to have been in excellent condition. There was something

243

incongruous about the whole figure, as if this man had with intense effort been shaping his body into a form at odds with its nature. I noticed another feature: His hair was cut in the same fashion as Holmes's, though the colour was somewhat lighter than my friend's.

"Well, Mr. Holmes, what do you say?" came Lestrade's voice.

"I take it his own Mrs. Hudson discovered him."

"She did. She has rooms on the ground floor. She brings . . . used to bring him his breakfast." Lestrade pointed to a tray on the table. A basket of scones stood there, next to a glass dish of marmalade, a teapot, and the usual breakfast utensils. "She found the body when she came in this morning."

I reached down and touched the back of the dead man's hand. It was cold. I closed his eyes. Feeling strangely agitated, I walked over to the bookshelves to scan the backs of the volumes. There was Faraday's *Experimental Researches in Chemistry and Physics*, as well as Frankland's *How to Teach Chemistry*, Gray's *Anatomy*, a few of Alexander Bain's writings, Lombroso's study on the female criminal, Mayhew's *London Labour and the London Poor*, and a whole array of writings that aimed to explain the natural world and the surroundings mankind has created for itself. This was the library of someone trying to understand both the times in which he lived and the unchanging laws of science and of the human soul. All of Holmes's publications, from his studies on cigar ashes and footprints onward, were also there, separated from the other volumes by a marble bookstand.

My own publications, so much fluff beside these scientific works, filled about a quarter-of-a-shelf at eye level. A glance sufficed to tell that every word I had ever presented to the public was assembled. Every issue of *The Strand Magazine* that had run one of my tales stood there in order of appearance. The issues of *Harper's*, where the same stories had appeared, were also there, as were my longer works.

I pulled out *Beeton's Christmas Annual* of 1887 with its yellow-and-red cover, which I have always found a trifle garish. The paper had acquired the softness that comes with many readings, though the volume had clearly been handled with great care. The spine was intact, the edges without cuffs, not a single dog-ear marred the pages. Yet they had been subject to some alterations. Occasionally two or three lines, sometimes whole paragraphs had been underlined with a pencil and a ruler. I scanned a few of the passages thus marked. Invariably, they addressed the methods by which Holmes solved his cases, what he himself has called the "Science of Deduction and Analysis".

244

I reinserted the volume and turned to see Holmes with the flask of cocaine solution in his hand. He lifted the flask to the window to gauge how much of the liquid was left.

"I believe I have not exaggerated, gentlemen." Lestrade's voice had a self-satisfied ring. "This is a strange sight."

I nodded.

"Perhaps an accident, but probably a suicide. The man was obviously a tortured soul."

At this moment, we all heard steps on the staircase and looked towards the door. The steps were fast; others, heavier and slower, were following. Whoever the first person was, his or her approach possessed the vigour to match a sense of vital urgency. We heard the constable at the entrance call, "Miss! Miss, you can't – "

There followed a crash and a cry of dismay, a few more steps on the boards of the corridor, and a young woman burst into the sitting room. Her mouth was open, her cheeks red. She took in the scene with one swift motion of the head, then her eyes fastened on the body. Her facial muscles seized up and her skin turned the colour of gypsum.

No outcry came, as I and, I daresay, the others expected. She made a few steps towards us. Her features regained animation and an expression of transcendent pain shaped itself upon them, of a pain that seemed to anticipate knowledge of an endless sadness that was to come. Lestrade made a motion to step in her way, but she brushed past him and then me as if we deserved no more attention than two potted plants and knelt down beside the body.

Her hands for a few seconds lay open in her lap as she looked at the dead man's face, and then finally a sob came, and she stretched out her right arm and traced her fingertips over the inanimate features. I am always at a loss in these situations. Even if one has experienced death in one's own small circle, one cannot in the moment feel the agony of the bereaved. Thus arises a sense of deficiency, almost of guilt, as if one were sorely lacking in common humanity.

She was twenty years of age perhaps, and was wearing a shop girl's black-and-white uniform. I noticed a pair of spectacles protruding from her chest pocket, and also a booklet of pins. Clearly, her place of employ was a haberdashery. She was pressing her lips together as tears quivered on her lower lids. Her dark blonde hair was tied into a *chignon*, but a few strands had escaped and lay against the nape of her neck.

I looked away. The constable had entered and was pressing a hand to his side. He regarded the kneeling girl with an expression of pique. Behind him, Jacob Henslow stood overlooking the scene. He caught my

245

eye and lifted his brows in apology; the second set of steps on the stairs had been his.

Lestrade now looked at me and then towards the girl. People generally believe that I am particularly suited to consoling people in their darkest hours. I helplessly turned my palms outwards, but then stepped over to the girl and touched her shoulder.

"Miss," I said. She did not respond. "Miss," I tried again. "Please, we must speak with you."

Still there came no reaction. The tears were streaming down her cheeks to her trembling lips. Yet I had the distinct impression that my words had registered. There was the sound of someone clearing his throat, and I saw that Holmes was holding out the handkerchief from his breast pocket. I proffered it to the girl. After a second or two, she took it and mechanically wiped her face.

Then she looked at me and also saw Holmes. She gasped as if she had seen a ghost.

"Please, Miss, let us sit down," I said.

I was relieved when she did in fact rise, though she remained next to the body and continued to stare at Holmes. Henslow at this moment appeared from the bedroom, holding a folded sheet. She nodded at him, whereupon he spread it over the body.

Turning, she walked over to the sofa with rigid steps, as if every movement required conscious effort, then placed herself in one corner. I considered sitting down next to her, but the girl now seemed enclosed in an invisible sphere, and so I, like Holmes, took one of the armchairs. Most people would not have described her face as beautiful. Her nose was freckled and a little too large. There was a certain fullness to her cheeks, her forehead was rather high, and her chin had perhaps more point than was becoming. Yet for some reason her features added up to an impression of endearing grace. She wiped her eyes again and blinked as she looked at Holmes.

"We would read your stories together," she said in a thick voice. "That's how we met. In The Little Kettle, near Piccadilly."

Both Holmes and I remained silent. "He was studying 'Silver Blaze'," she continued. "He didn't even notice me when I came in. He was bent over his copy, letting his tea go cold . . . ." Her voice petered out, and we were left to imagine how the scene unfolded. She had a London accent, but whether by design or not preserved her *h*'s and *t*'s. "I'm Fran Atkins," she finally offered.

"Miss Atkins," Holmes said, "how long had he been in England when you two met?"

She raised her eyebrows. "Mrs. Henslow told you he was American?"

"On his left hand, there is the kind of ring fraternity brothers at American universities like to wear."

"Chester would not have liked that you recognised him as American. He was from Boston. The family left during the Famine. His father was still a child." She cleared her throat. "He had only been in London a bit over a month when we met."

Holmes advanced a few more questions, all designed to have Fran Atkins delve into her memories. I thought this might in fact benefit her shattered spirits and did not interrupt. The story that emerged in halting words was that of a somewhat bookish English girl and of a young American unsure as to what path to pursue in life, and of how they had fallen in love over a shared passion for my stories. Chester Aherne was the son of well-to-do parents. America is unlike our own society and allows for a rapid rise through the ranks. Thus, the grandson of a poor lad from County Clare had been able to go up to university. Aherne, however, was of a retiring disposition, and though the family fortune was ample, it did not possess the patina of self-evidence that comes with many generations of existence. He had felt out of place with his classmates, whose ancestors had sometimes arrived two centuries before and who would have felt at home at Ascot.

The Ahernes had a business partner in London, and so at the end of his junior term, Chester decided to take a break from higher learning and to gain abroad some insights into the world of commerce. Or rather, this was what he had told his parents that he intended to do. In fact, he only put in token appearances at the office and spent much of his days walking the streets of the metropolis.

His interest in my writerly efforts appears to have predated his departure for the Old World. On his home shores, though, his consumption of Holmes's adventures had remained within the scope of the ordinary. I am proud to say that my narratives have been quite favorably received by the American public and that many readers there await with some eagerness the publication of a new tale.

On English soil, however, a transformation set in. When Fran Atkins encountered Aherne, this was already well underway. He had begun an in-depth study of Holmes's adventures. Some passages that addressed detective work he excerpted into a moleskin notebook and memorised as if they were scripture. He researched Holmes's methods, studied the sciences required, and conducted experiments. I can see Fran and him before me now, each holding a cup of tea, discussing excitedly the methods by which my friend nabbed the evildoers upon whose trail

247

Lestrade or a client had set him. I suppose it is any author's fondest wish that his writings may help his readers find a kindred spirit, and such it would be with me and Chester's and Fran's acquaintance, were this scene not marred by the future that issued therefrom.

A puzzled expression lay in Fran's eyes. "There was something about Chester. He wanted to be more than it was his lot to be. Maybe that is why he loved me," she added when neither of us spoke. "Because I believed this was possible. Perhaps that was a mistake."

"On the contrary," said Holmes. "The faith of others keeps us going. Tell me, Miss Atkins, apart from rowing, did he engage in any other sporting activity?"

"You could tell by the calluses on his hands." She smiled as if at an old trick. "Yes, he also went to a club to box and to practice that Japanese way of fighting – what do you call it?"

"Baritsu."

"Yes, that's it. He could break a board with one blow."

Holmes nodded towards the bottle on the table. "How often did he take that substance?"

"Maybe once a week. I was against it, so often he wouldn't tell me. You have taken it too, Mr. Holmes."

Perhaps I should never have mentioned Holmes's cocaine consumption, I thought, but how was I to imagine that anyone would regard him as an example when it came to this – anyone in his right mind, I could not help but adding.

"I used to, yes, I'm afraid. You mentioned a notebook, Miss Atkins," said Holmes, changing the subject. "Where did Mr. Aherne keep it?"

"I'm not sure. I did not come here often. We preferred to meet in my room." She looked towards the Davenport. "I saw it there once."

Holmes rose and stepped over to the desk. He lifted its top, then went through the drawers. Finally, he turned and shook his head. Fran raised her shoulders, as if to ask what it mattered now. Tears were again filling her eyes. Lestrade began scanning the bookshelves, Holmes wandered into the laboratory.

I also rose. The room's oblique familiarity produced an effect as if I were standing on a stage. Where would an avid reader of Holmes's adventures keep such a presumably treasured object? A cascade of images came rushing through my mind, before a notion struck me with a sense of complete certainty. Recalling an early case, one in which Holmes found his match – in a woman, I might add – I walked over to the bell-pull. The wallpaper above the bell-pull appeared unmarred, but when I passed my hand over the wallpaper and exerted a light pressure, a

248

rectangle of about five inches by ten moved inward with a click. Then this rectangle slid noiselessly aside, exposing a small aperture.

"Well done, Doctor!" exclaimed Lestrade, walking over and patting me on the shoulder.

Henslow appeared next to the Inspector. The young man's eyes were wide. Evidently, the notion that a tenant could have effected such an alteration to the property came as a surprise. Fran raised herself from the sofa.

Lestrade meanwhile had reached into the aperture and extracted a moleskin notebook on which lay a thick packet of American money. Holmes now appeared from the laboratory, and I caught a glimpse of him letting something slip into his trouser pocket.

"Your friend has learned a thing or two from you, Mr. Holmes," said the inspector.

"He certainly has."

The inspector laid the money aside, then flicked through the notebook.

"What a hand!"

"May I have a look?" said Holmes.

"Of course. I can't let you have it, though. This is still a homicide investigation."

"I understand, Inspector."

Holmes scanned a page, then another. Fran stood next to him. She now pulled the spectacles from her chest pocket. Henslow and I had also sidled up to Holmes and were peering over his shoulder.

"Yes, this is it." Fran touched the page, when a sharp bang came from the laboratory and we all spun around.

"Oh dear!" exclaimed Holmes. "I'll have a look." He handed Lestrade the notebook. "This will certainly merit scrutiny if the autopsy reveals anything untoward."

"I doubt it will. But we will take all proper measures." This latter Lestrade had directed at the girl. He turned to me. "I hear, Doctor, there is a lot going on these days in the field of psychology. Not your bailiwick, I know, but what do you think of the matter?"

"You're right, I'm just an old sawbones . . . ." I paused to arrange my thoughts. "Most of us have heroes," I finally said. "Especially when we're young."

"Are you going to quote Carlyle to me now?"

"I'm wary of quoting Scotsmen. All I'm saying is that aspiration needs a goal. In this case . . . ."

"Things went a little far!"

"In this case," I repeated, "one might say there was a genuine desire to do good."

Lestrade harrumphed and turned to Henslow.

"What do you think, young man?"

"Mr. Aherne was a pleasant tenant," Henslow replied, choosing his words carefully. "A little peculiar, but I have nothing bad to say about the man. I suppose he was a scientist at heart. They have their idiosyncrasies. I understand next to nothing of these matters."

Holmes had reemerged from the laboratory and was standing next to the tea table. Now he rejoined our group. "Yes, they do. Mine is fiddling with other people's chemicals. My apologies for the ruckus. This has been a remarkable morning, Inspector."

Evidently Holmes wished to be underway, and I had no objections. Fran now appeared somewhat composed. She was still pale and her eyes were red, but she had regained control of her features. She had, it seemed, absorbed the first shock and steadied herself. Where was her home? What losses had she sustained and recovered from before this present one? The flood of sorrow, I knew, crests well after the first breaking seas have come ashore. But maybe she knew that also, I thought.

As Holmes and I descended the stairs, we saw through the window on each landing two women and a man in conversation by the gate that separated the property from the street.

"That's the old lady and her husband who were standing in the door when we arrived," I remarked.

"Yes, I saw them from Aherne's rooms. They were just coming down the street."

"What was their name?"

"O'Malley. The Irish seem to have taken over the place . . . ."

We stepped outside and all three turned to face us. The O'Malleys appeared less disheveled than upon our first encounter. She was wearing a dark bonnet and a dark kersey cape, he a scuffed pea coat. They both still looked rather sallow, and an expression of what I could not but think of as worry lay upon their features. The woman with whom they had been in conversation appeared roughly their equal in age, though in stature the three could not have differed more dramatically. While the O'Malleys were rather short and on the full-figured side, their interlocutor stood around five feet ten inches, and appeared as thin as a dysentery patient a week after leaving the ward. She too wore a cape, but no bonnet. Her hair was pulled back into a bun. Unlike the O'Malleys, she had not gone entirely grey, and some blonde strands glimmered in the sunlight.

If the woman's appearance could have raised questions as to her constitution, these were dispelled when she spoke.

"Good day, gentlemen," she said in a voice that rang with robust health. "I am sorry we meet under these circumstances."

We expressed the identical sentiment and introduced ourselves.

"Henslow," she said, bowing her head. "I understand my son showed you upstairs. Terrible what happened with young Mr. Aherne. I shouldn't have thought it possible."

"The realm of the possible is large," Holmes remarked.

"We will now go to church to commend his soul to our Lord." She looked at the O'Malleys, who nodded obediently.

Holmes passed over the remark. "How long had Mr. Aherne been living with you, Mrs. Henslow?"

"This was his fourth month, if I'm not mistaken." She turned to the O'Malleys. "You came in September, right?"

"Yes, that's right," Mrs. O'Malley said.

"He came the month before you," declared the landlady. "So yes, four months."

"And you noticed nothing unusual about his behaviour?" Holmes asked.

"Not exactly. He did keep odd hours. Sometimes he returned home rather late. On account of this, he would not take his breakfast until ten. He is not the first young gentleman I've had as a tenant, Mr. Holmes," she continued in a tone of self-justification. "I do not condone such behaviour. I offered to introduce him to our church. But I can only offer. I am not their parent."

"He wus a gran' lad," Mr. O'Malley now interjected. "A gran' lad, out on de town every once in a while, that's al' . . . ." A stern look from Mrs. Henslow silenced him.

Holmes turned to the landlady again. "Did you know of his drug use?"

"Most decidedly not! I was shocked to find him the way I did. But was I surprised, Mr. Holmes? No! He had this friend, a girl. She came by two, three times." Mrs. Henslow nodded upwards to Aherne's rooms where Fran still was. "She is trouble, I can tell. I made myself quite clear. She was welcome to stop by for afternoon tea, but I wanted her out of my house by sunset."

Holmes lowered his eyelids in deep understanding. "Well, I'm afraid we must be off," he said. "Inspector Lestrade will see to it that all proper steps are taken."

With that we took leave of Mrs. Henslow and the O'Malleys and retraced our steps down Morton Road. I looked back once and saw them walking in the opposite direction.

"Did you notice anything about Mr. O'Malley?" asked Holmes when we were out of earshot.

"He seemed upset."

"Anything else?"

I shrugged, and Holmes shook his head in desperation.

"Watson, Watson. How often must I tell you, don't see. Observe! Didn't you notice the edge of a telegram receipt sticking out of his coat pocket?"

"So he and his wife were coming from the telegraph office. And crossed paths with their landlady, who buttonholed them, so as to persuade them to accompany her on commending a soul."

"Precisely."

"Accompany her to the wrong kind of church, according to the O'Malleys, I would assume."

"Hence the need for persuasion, perhaps."

"But to whom did they send a telegram?"

"Later, Watson. Think. Anything else about O'Malley?"

Holmes tapped his cheek with his fingertip.

"His firemark!" I exclaimed. "It wasn't visible. He must have covered it."

Sherlock Holmes nodded, but said no more. Rather, he stomped along, staring into the distance. My friend's energetic mind was sifting through possibilities, discarding some, setting others aside for further contemplation, considering various avenues for proceeding. The question of the firemark lingered in my mind, but was then pushed aside by another line of thought that had been preoccupying me.

I have always striven to render lifelike the scenes or characters I was describing. Though I believe that by and large I have succeeded, it cannot be gainsaid that my efforts have been helped immensely by the work of a young gentleman by the name of Mr. Sidney Paget. He is a very pleasant individual, with a keen perception and an enviable artistic talent. When *The Strand* began running my tales, the editor sent Paget by my practice in Paddington. We all thought Holmes dead at the time, his body irrecoverable at the bottom of the gorge of the Reichenbach Fall. I showed Paget photographs of Holmes, which Paget used as the basis for his sketches. Over the years, Paget then on his own initiative visited some of the locales where Holmes and I had been and created drawings of crucial scenes based on my descriptions. His drawings, I have come to believe, have established the image of Holmes more firmly in the public's mind than my words could have done, had they been unaided by the visual arts. The efforts Aherne had gone to so as to approximate his own appearance to Holmes's would have been impossible without these drawings as models. But yet, my responsibility . . . .

At this point, Holmes thrust a moleskin notebook out in front of me.

"Could you please go through this, Watson? I need to conduct a little experiment when we get back."

I took the notebook, looking rather dumbfounded, I am afraid.

"I saw you giving it to Lestrade."

"Not this one. Your mnemonic mind almost got us into trouble this time, Watson. In passing, I would like to mention that the case that inspired Aherne's construction of a hiding place is one I should not altogether mind forgetting. Be that as it may, you will recall that I was in Aherne's laboratory when Lestrade congratulated you so warmly on finding the object in question. Luckily, beside Aherne's Bunsen burner there lay a moleskin notebook, which he had been using to keep track of his experiments. There was also a dish with a little mercury fulminate. I quickly set up a contraption with the fulminate and some hydrochloric acid. When I joined you all in the sitting room I saw to my relief that the notebook you had discovered was of the identical manufacture as the one from the laboratory. I ensured that I had the sitting room notebook in my hands when the explosion occurred. Of course, everyone's attention was momentarily diverted, and it was easy to give Lestrade the laboratory notebook." He pointed to the one in my hand. "That one may turn out quite interesting."

"I wonder if my readers would believe such a lapse by Sherlock Holmes. Beaten to the treasure by me."

Holmes raised a wry eyebrow, but did not comment. Instead, he waived for a passing cab.

Once we were rattling towards Baker Street, Holmes reached into his coat and extracted the flask of cocaine solution.

"I also had a chance to lay a hold of this."

"Lestrade will surely notice that it has disappeared."

"Let him. He can have it again very soon."

Back in our quarters, Holmes set to work at his chemistry bench. For a moment, I wondered whether he would be tempted by the substance now in his possession. Our addictions stay with us for life, even if we no longer heed them. Then, however, my mind was set at rest by the notion that Holmes was now in thrall to his other addiction, a mystery that demanded a solution.

I sat down with Aherne's notebook. There were many quotes from my narratives addressing detective work. There were also quite a few passages unrelated to my writings. These passages, I soon realised, formed a tale, in parts both strange and frightening. Before returning the notebook to Lestrade, who passed it on to the evidence room of Scotland Yard, I transcribed them and some paragraphs that added flavour into my scrapbook. These excerpts I now present here:

Aug 22
Think I found a place finally. Like the arrangement of the rooms. 18 guineas a week! Not cheap this city. Landlady a little humorless, but nice enough. Runs the place together with her son. Decent fellow. Offered to help me lug up my stuff. Might buy some furniture. Pretty much made up my mind. Sometimes you just get the feeling, this is it. Taken up boxing again. Very British in a way – hit the other guy, but be a gentleman.

Aug 29
Set up lab. Pushing myself with the weights. Have lost almost a stone over the past month, would like to lose another. London, what a city! The world is here. Could walk around forever. Wish I knew more people. The work at the office would bore anyone to tears. How do people do this for decades? They stand around debating weather reports from Egypt and worry about the price of cotton. I don't give a fig about the price of Egyptian cotton, nor about that of Russian grain or Swedish iron ore. Nor for that matter about the cleverest way to avoid paying import duties. Reading quite a bit, lots to learn.

Sept 1
Set the alarm today. Not used to this anymore, but wanted to be first in line at the W.H. Smith to get the new Strand Mag. Wasn't the first, two guys ahead of me. But got my copy. Fantastic chapter of "The Hound of the Baskervilles" – can't wait for Holmes to show up!
Worked on "Irene's safe" very quietly. Should be ready tomorrow.

Sept 3
What an evening! Just in the door. Meant to go to the theater, but ended up in a show of dancing girls. Well, I suppose it's something I had meant to do. Then walked

around the West End. Was passing a side street and saw three louts heckling an old homeless woman. One of them poured a bottle of beer over her head. Suddenly found myself walking toward them. One of them pushes me with both hands, tells me to "piss off". Don't know how it happened, just put a straight right on his chin. Next one rushes at me. Blocked his punch, followed with an upper cut, and he's on his pants. The last one backed off. The other two were scrambling to their feet. They start cussing me, but then disappear round a corner. The old woman thanked me. Felt very awkward. Gave her a few shillings. Can't sleep now, my heart is still racing.

Sep 9
Reading people on the Tube again today. Two gentlemen, bowler hats, suits, clean shoes, about fifty. They got off at Marble Arch. Had them down for bankers. Decided to follow. They ended up going into a law office. Close!

Sep 12
Making progress with chemical studies. Will never achieve H.'s level of ingenuity, of course, but really think I've got some talent. Irish couple moving in across from me. Just talked to them. He's more chatty. Henslow was helping, his mother also there. That woman would have been right at home on Plymouth Rock in 1649. Grumbled about how I've been coming home late. None of her business, and she got her rent. That's all she cares about anyway. Pretty sure she's overcharging me. Anyway, surprised the Irish would want to live on the third floor. Must be pushing seventy, seem in good shape though. Left the old country decades ago, he said. Hope they won't mind when I torture the violin. No hope for me there. But I can see why H. does it. Easy to let the mind drift.

Sept 16
Saw them both today! Was walking along Baker Street, tried shortly before noon this time. Was wearing a hat, different coat from last times. In any case, might just be someone who often runs errands in the area. Was maybe eighty yards from 221, on the opposite side, when the door opens. H. steps out, W. follows. They get into a cab. Maybe one day I'll pay my

255

respects, doubt it though. Last thing I want is to be a nuisance.

Sept 21
Can't read the cases often enough. You learn something every time. Just had another look at 'The Adventure of the Speckled Band.' Amazing how H. did it, but absolutely logical.
So glad I'm away from Boston. Another prim tea party at my parents', think I might have burped and picked my nose. Also the college crowd. The nonsense that goes on there! If I want to drink, I'll drink, happily. I'm Irish. But those stupid games, not sure I could have taken it much longer. Wonder what they'd all be thinking if they knew I'm two generations away from a papist spud farmer. But of course they know! We must be the only Unitarian Ahernes on the planet. The power of the Silver Dollar makes a lot go away. No matter how it was made . . . .

Sept 25
Asked Henslow for a good pharmacy. Gave me the address. Only fifteen minutes away. Run by a father and son team. Very British John Bull types, complexions like broiled lobsters. Sold me the stuff, no questions asked. Didn't want to get it through the wholesaler, though it's all above board. It's sitting here now. Holmes no longer takes it, of course, but I'm curious. Not sure what I'll do.

Sept 30
Second time I'm seeing something like this. On the way back from Piccadilly, I passed a stretch where the sewer is still open, stinks to high heaven. Looked down and saw a dead cat in the garbage. But it hadn't died there. Could tell because there was only a stump where the front left paw had been. Clambered down some steps, used a stick to push the body. Stiff as a board. A tomcat. Poor critter. He looked strong, in his prime. Someone had also driven a nail through his other front paw. Was suddenly sweating. Probably whoever had done this had hoped the sewage would wash the body away. Or maybe it had washed up here. This has to be connected with what I saw two weeks ago. Also the body of a tomcat, under some bushes in the park nearby. Someone

256

had hit him over the head with a blunt instrument. Bloody, one ear almost shorn off. Looked like he'd dragged himself there to die. Maybe some stupid boys, kids can be cruel. Dad would have given me the thrashing of a lifetime if he'd caught me doing something like this.

Oct 2
My hands feel electric, watching my right moving the pen. It took two, three minutes or so after I injected myself. Only 600ml. Could feel there was something in my blood. Then the charge in my brain. For a moment like the sound of chalk over a blackboard. Jumped up. Not sure how long I've been pacing around. Can't write now, need to go outside.

Oct 6
Met O'Malley in town by accident. Invited me over for tea. They're from Limerick originally. Worked as a shipping agent, seems to have made good money. Said they owned a small house in the East End, but sold it when the children moved out.
Should write to mom. Had a letter from her yesterday: Hope you're keeping well, dress for the weather, etc. She thinks I'm still twelve. Just couldn't face the office today. Dread the day when I have to go into Aherne & Sons.

Oct 8
I met a girl! Was in The Little Kettle, studying "Silver Blaze" – very important case. When I looked up, there she was, sitting at the table across from mine. She was holding her cup of tea in both hands and looking out the window, a smile on her face. Before her on the table the last Strand Mag! Felt a ball of warmth in my stomach. Tried to go back to "Silver Blaze" but couldn't. Had to do something, it was a sign from the fates. Maybe there was still some of the drug from yesterday in me. She turns her face and I catch her eye. "What did you think of the Holmes?" She grins. "I think the man on the tor is Holmes." "How so?" "Female intuition." And then: "I hope you're also enjoying the sights of London Town. Holmes might give you the wrong impression. It's really quite peaceful." It gets on my nerves that I can't open my mouth here without people knowing where I'm from. "I have all the time I need, I'm not a tourist." "Do you work

257

*here?" "Yes, I do." "What do you do?" and I thought I now
detected some curiosity in her voice.*

*Still can't believe what I did then. Got up, stepped over to
her table, and sat down opposite her. "Miss, I'll be happy to
tell you all I know about myself, but I won't shout it across
the room." Her eyes open wide. "Why, yes, sir. Please, do sit
down by all means." She wasn't flustered at all. Her name is
Fran, short for Francis. She works in a haberdashery. She'd
been making deliveries and had popped into The Little Kettle
for a cup of tea and to read "The Hound of the
Baskervilles". I've never met a girl I found so easy to talk to.
The waiter brought over my tea set, and we chat away.
About Boston and where she's from, Norwich. Will have to
look it up. Her father is a sheep farmer. I felt bad telling her
about where I'm from and all, but oddly I knew she wouldn't
think the less of me for it. She's been in London for almost
two years. Her life can't be easy. But she's full of spirit. And
she sure knows her Holmes! She never believed he was dead
after "The Final Problem" – like me! When the clock on the
mantelpiece chimed, she gasped. "I must go." "Oh, yes,
why?" I stutter, stupidly. She puts some coins on the table,
takes her magazine. "How . . . when can we meet again?"
She bites her lower lip. "Well, Mr. Yankee, I take it this is
your favorite London saloon. I'll meet you here." With that
she's walking to the door. Once outside, she looks back
through the window and gives me a wave.*

Oct 9
*Was in The Little Kettle till they closed. She didn't come.
Think they'd love to fire me in the office. Of course, they
won't. Not that I'd mind though. Can't sleep. She didn't tell
me which haberdashery she works in, but I suppose I could
find out.*

*Just heard something, like a child wailing. Looked out the
window, but the sound came from farther away, hard to say
which direction. It's never completely quiet here, but this
sound was odd. Debating whether I should make use of the
pharmacist's dispensation. Then I'll be lucky if I sleep
tomorrow night, but it would take my mind off things. Not in
the mood, really. Wonder what that cry was. Maybe she was
busy the whole day.*

Oct 10

Rowed ten miles this morning. Fingers almost fell off. By one, I was in The Little Kettle. Tried to read, but caught myself looking at the same sentence over and over again. Once, I thought I saw her in the crowd outside. Looked down because I didn't want her to see I was waiting for her. But must have been mistaken, for when I looked again she wasn't there. Think she's not going to come . . . .

My mind isn't working right. Case in point: When I came back from rowing my door was open! Thought Mrs. Henslow was in, but it was O'Malley. Said my door had been open. Must have forgotten to close it. Good thing I always hide the CO among the chemicals. O'Malley ribbed me a bit. Asked what it's like to have such a loudmouth as president. As if it's my fault! A small dosage. Going to work in the lab now. Definitely getting better at proving blood residue on fabrics. Things can't go on like this.

Oct 11

She came! She tapped me on the shoulder while I was staring out into the street. When I spun around, there she was, a grin on her lips. "Mr. Yankee," and looking down at my cup: "Are we turning you into a tea drinker?" "You leave me no choice, your coffee is so awful." I have my moments. She laughs, sits down. "I didn't notice you coming in." "How would you, engrossed in your reading as you were?" She can raise her left eyebrow independently, which she now did. "Yes . . . I guess . . . I just thought . . . ." "Actually, I came in through there." She nods to a half-open door at the back of the room. "I know one of the women in the kitchen. Speaking of work, yours hardly seems to leave you a free minute." "I am thinking of changing my career." "I see. Some people here make a living tasting tea. So keep developing your palate." "That might be too nerve-wracking for me. Are you coming back from making deliveries?" She rolled her lips inward, which I've noticed is something she does when there's a thought going through her mind. "I work for a nice elderly lady. She lets me take a break if there's nothing much to do and there's an American who needs some help with the local customs." She ordered a cup of tea and some chocolate cake. We chatted for almost an hour, then she had to leave. She told me a few things about

259

herself. She's the oldest of five siblings, her mother died in childbirth three years ago. I wanted to reach across the table and touch her hand. We said we'd meet again on Monday. She's taking the train to Norwich tomorrow and will stay the weekend. I can see her face in front of me now.

Oct 13
Didn't really want to, but ended up taking 700ml in the afternoon. Worked like a fiend till almost eleven. Completed two series of tests for alkaloids. Then just had to get out of these digs. London at night is very different from Boston. In Boston after a certain hour, you feel you're the only person awake in the entire city. Not here. After the pubs close you hardly see anyone, but there's always light behind some curtains. Life, at least in some quarters, is continuing. Walked through Hyde Park, then Westminster. My temples were still beating after all these hours, but the cold and damp were slowly bringing me around. The substance is amazing! You feel not quite human, like the ancient berserkers must have felt going into battle. Near Trafalgar Square I ran into a bobby. Asked if I was lost. "Just can't sleep." "Have a nightcap when you get home, lad." The law encouraging you to drink! The Abigail Bunyans of Beacon Hill would be chattering in their corsets, if they only knew! Then something happened that will be with me till my dying day. Was about half-a-mile from home when I heard what sounded like someone being sick. The sound came from an alley I'd just passed. Hesitate, walk back. The alley narrow, can't see a thing. Then the sound again, more purposeful if that makes any sense, followed by a scraping sound. Take a few steps into the alley and can now make out some low shapes at the rear of a house. Garbage cans. The sounds seem to have come from behind them, and I see a shadow moving in spasms. The scraping noise was of shoes against pavement, I suddenly understand, and the sound of someone being sick, that of a person gasping for breath. I run forward, idiot that I am. The guy was crouching, and just as I reach the garbage cans he lunges forward and rams his fist into my stomach. Been training my stomach muscles, but wasn't prepared. Now I know what it means to have your breath knocked out of you. The air bursts from my mouth and I'm on the pavement. Couldn't breathe. The figure

260

*coming for me. I'm pushing backward. He gets ready to kick
me in the face, I lunge to the side, his boot rushes past my
ear. Then he takes off. I turn, and he's disappearing round
the corner. In no condition to follow. Get to my feet and
manage to breathe, though I tasted blood. Walk toward the
garbage cans. Behind them a figure. Dead, I think, but when
I bend down I hear breathing, and then: "Who in blazes are
ya? Are ya going to stick me. I'll give ya a good fight
awright." "You've got the wrong guy. Whoever put you on
your pants took off." "Now has he, the yellow bastard! I
showed him, by the living jingo! Help me up, if ya please."
He sways back and forth. "Let's go back to the street," I say.
He holds on to my shoulder. A lamp on the corner, and when
we reach it I can see he's some toff as they call them here,
silk cravat and all. Has a shiner. I think there were
strangulation marks around his neck, and he was bleeding
from a cut at the side of his throat. Lipstick on his cheek and
I could smell lady's perfume. "Did you see the guy's face?"
I ask. "We should call the police and you might need a
doctor." "No, no, my good man. Too many questions I
shouldn't like to answer." He presses his cravat against the
cut, then looks at the blood like it's something he's never
seen before. Grabs the lamppost and points down the street.
"Let's go back to Madame Rose's, my dear fellow. It's all on
me." And he's laughing so loud I think windows will start
opening. Luckily, a hansom is coming along. Cabbie says
he'll take one last fare. Bundled in Madame Rose's patron.
He drawls out a Mayfair address and off they go.
My stomach hurts. Threw up twice during the night. The
more I think about it, the stranger the whole affair seems.
Think he had a beard, though not even sure about that,
average height. That was no ordinary robbery, maybe I
saved a life.*

Oct 14
*Told Fran about everything. We were in her garret room. I
like the place, it's tiny but cozy, and you look out over the
roofs. She made me open my shirt, and when she saw the
black and blue below my sternum she gasped. "Wait," she
says and runs downstairs. Five minutes later she's back with
a lump of ice wrapped in cloth. Makes me lie back on her
bed, places the icepack on the bruise. "How do you feel, Mr.*

261

Yankee?" "Like a million pounds." She laughs and leans forward and kisses me!! I can feel it now! Unfortunately, then she saw where I've been injecting myself. Told her I was experimenting with glucose, but I think she didn't believe me. She may have had some suspicions anyway . . . .

Went back to the alley after lunch. It's cobble stone, but found a foot print beside a puddle. A sturdy boot would be my guess, could have been his. Took measurements. Then checked by the garbage cans. Found a button, inch in diameter, black, clean – can't have been there long. Certainly not from the toff's outfit. A thread through two holes, ragged edges. Where do I go from here?

Oct 15
A wire from the parents. The usual, hope you're learning a lot, also having a good time, etc. Can tell though something's on their mind. Probably they've heard that I haven't been showing up to work . . . .

Oct 22
Something going on in this neighborhood. Was walking to the bookstore this morning when I saw some kids standing in a in a yard. "What have you got there?" I call.

"Someone's killed Rupert," one shouts. Walked over. There before his kennel lies a German Shepherd with his tongue hanging out in a pool of half-dried blood. Someone had slit his throat. Shook my head and walked on. Didn't want the kids to see how upset I was. There is a connection between everything that's happened. H. would see it immediately.

Fran said I need to quit smoking. Maybe she'll be okay if I lay off the shag tobacco, only cigarettes. Ran into O'Malley on the way back home from her room. Like the old geezer. Told him my girl thought smoking a "beastly habit". He just throws up his hands. "Give up, son. No man has ever won that fight." She didn't mention my injections. Will wire the parents. No intention of going through life without Fran. Don't think I could anyway. Maybe I shouldn't even write. Not sure I can handle any back-and-forth. Just let them know afterward, fait accompli.

At this point in my reading the sound of voices made me look up, and I saw Holmes at the door with Phillips, current captain of the

Irregulars. Phillips took off his cap and entered, then followed Holmes to a cupboard that houses part of Holmes's archive, which over the years has grown to occupy every available space in our rooms.

Holmes pulled out three boxes and placed them on the floor. He opened them and nodded.

"Yes, these are the right ones."

He handed the boy a slip of paper. "This is the name. I'm afraid you'll have to go through every one of them. We'll be over at Dombey's."

"Yes, sir."

Holmes turned to me. "Well, Watson, what insights bring your reading?"

"More questions than insights, but you should give this notebook some attention."

"No doubt. Let me have a synopsis on the way. We need to pay a visit to a local tradesman."

As I rose to fetch my coat and shoes, I saw Phillips settling himself cross-legged on the floor and begin pulling old newspapers and magazines from the first of the boxes. I knew that one reason why he had risen to his present rank was his ability to read. What name had Holmes given him, I wondered, but I did not ask.

A few minutes later, we were again walking towards Fitzrovia. It was past four o'clock by now, and the shadows were lengthening. As best I could, I provided Holmes with the salient points of Aherne's narrative. Holmes interrupted me a number of times to ask questions and then listened silently while puffing at his pipe. We stayed on the main thoroughfare and did not turn off in the direction of Morton Road. Soon we reached a pharmacy with a sign *Dombey & Son* in green letters above the door.

"Let's see what the purveyors of rapture have to say, shall we?" said Holmes and pulled open the door.

The tinkling of a bell announced us, and a heavyset man with a mass of tangled white hair looked up from a ledger that lay before him on a mahogany counter. I have always liked the atmosphere of a pharmacy, the warm brown of the paneling, the rows of porcelain jars on the shelves, the scents of cloves, sage, salts, and alcohol. I think of the pharmacy as a place where people go who have left the worst stages of suffering behind, the opposite of the ward with its ceaseless misery.

"Good afternoon, sir," said Holmes, stepping up to the counter.

"Good afternoon, gentlemen."

Holmes extracted the flask of cocaine solution from his coat pocket. "I believe you sold this."

Mr. Dombey took the flask and peered at the label. "Indeed, that's from us." He had the gravelly voice of a regular smoker. "Would you like another?"

"No, thank you. This one has come into my possession in the course of an investigation." Holmes indicated the label. "Seven percent, it states."

"Investigation? Are you with the police? There is nothing wrong with the bottle. It is properly labeled."

"No, we're not members of the force. Please be assured, you stand accused of nothing. However, something is wrong with the label. It does not match the content."

Mr. Dombey eyed the flask with approval, then us with skepticism.

"It is not a seven-percent solution, but a twenty-percent solution," Holmes said.

The pharmacist's eyebrows rose. "Are you sure?"

"You needn't take my word for it. Please, conduct your own tests. Meanwhile, you will appreciate that a mistaken label bears certain risks . . . ."

Mr. Dombey had turned. "Joseph! Joseph!" he called through an open doorway. "Come here for a moment!"

There was some commotion, and a man stepped through the door who appeared Mr. Dombey reincarnated as a thirty-year old. Dombey Junior had his father's build, the same features, round face, and florid complexion. The only striking difference was the colour of his hair, a chestnut red, in contrast to his father's white.

"Joseph," said Dombey Senior with curt authority. "The gentleman claims this bottle is mislabeled and contains a twenty-percent solution."

Dombey Junior's face blanched and he took the flask from his father. "That . . . that . . . that can't be. That would be very dangerous."

"Quite," said Holmes.

"But look, how could it be mislabeled? The bottle is half empty, so it has been in use . . . ."

"'Tis a mystery. What is the highest cocaine solution you sell?"

"Ten percent."

"Are there higher percent solutions that are unavailable to the public, for the use of the professional?"

"There are fifteen- and twenty-percent solutions available from the manufacturer."

"I understand. May I see your workshop?"

Dombey Junior looked to his father, who shrugged while in the process of lighting a cheroot. The younger man lifted a falling board that formed part of the counter and bade us step forward. Then he led the way through the door by which he had entered. It opened immediately upon a badly lit room. The window blinds were drawn almost to the bottom, a gaslight burned in a corner. There were shelves with rows and rows of labeled glass bottles on the back wall. A pill-making machine lay on a sideboard. A massive oak table occupied the centre of the room. On this table stood a good dozen white ceramic bowls, each with a pestle leaning against the side. I glanced into the bowls. All contained powders or crystals of various colours. Evidently, the business of Dombey & Son was thriving.

Holmes's eyes traversed the room. They fastened on a door with six dull glass panes forming its upper third. He crossed the room and I followed. Through the glass rectangles an overgrown garden became visible in the dusk. The garden stretched back for perhaps thirty yards and ended in a mass of bramble bushes. A path of flagstones wound its way towards them.

Dombey Junior had reached up to a shelf for what looked like a quarter-gallon bottle. He placed it on the table.

"This is our seven-percent solution."

Holmes stepped back to the table and eyed the bottle with hands crammed into his pockets. "Is this how it comes from the manufacturer or do you produce it yourself?"

"We dilute the twenty-percent solution from the manufacturer." The chemist had already bustled back to the shelf. He reached down another bottle and now placed it beside the seven-percent solution.

"This is the twenty-percent solution."

Both bottles were two-thirds full. I have been tempted, but have never tried the drug. I had seen its effects on Holmes in the early days of our friendship and had developed a sense of dread with regard to the substance. There was enough of the poison here, I realised, to kill dozens of men outright.

"I take it the solution, as it comes from the manufacturer, is exactly twenty percent?"

"I believe so."

"But your own seven-percent solution could be a little higher or lower?"

There came an intake of breath on the part of the junior pharmacist and he looked over my shoulder to his father. "Not at all, sir! Our product is exactly seven percent. I will vouch for that."

I could tell that Holmes was evaluating the young man's response, and my friend now nodded, thoughtfully.

"Do you ever sell the twenty-percent solution?"

"We do not."

"Has anyone ever asked for it?"

"Not to my knowledge." Again Dombey Junior looked towards his father, who shook his head.

"No one's ever asked," he affirmed gruffly.

Abruptly, as if he had made up his mind, Holmes turned and pointed towards the backdoor. "I should like to have a look around your garden, if you don't mind."

"Dear me," said Dombey Senior. "No one's been through that door since my wife died. The key must be somewhere upstairs."

Holmes returned to the door and pressed down the handle. It squeaked, he pulled, and the door opened with a scraping sound. A rush of fresh air entered the room.

I looked at the two pharmacists. Both seemed aghast, the younger one more so than the older. Dombey Junior walked over to the door.

"I can't believe this."

Dombey Senior exhaled smoke like an ill-tempered dragon. "You must have opened it at some point, Joseph. And then forgotten to lock it again." His voice had dropped half-an-octave with disappointment.

"No, no, I didn't. It's impossible."

The father waved away his son's protestations.

Despite what he had just said, Holmes initially seemed little interested in the garden. Rather, he bent forward to peer at the lock. After a second or two, there came a "Hmm . . . ." It was not hard to see what had prompted this sound. Both the doorknob and the lock were covered with a thick layer of rust, but around the keyhole scratches were visible that exposed the underlying steel.

"Someone picked the lock!" exclaimed Dombey Junior.

"It would appear so."

Holmes righted himself and stepped outside. We all followed. Holmes kept to the flagstones. Twice he stopped to look at a patch of grass to the side, but then moved on without closer inspection. After perhaps ten yards, a black iron gate in a redbrick wall to the side came into view. We walked up to the gate. It was around five feet high and composed of bars and crossbars. Holmes pressed down the handle. The gate was locked. He passed his forefinger along a section of a crossbar and some crumbs of dry earth fell off. Absentmindedly he repeated the movement on the top of the gate, with the same result.

At this moment, we all heard a voice calling from the direction of the house. "'Ello! 'Ello! Anybody 'ere?"

Dombey Senior returned to the garden path. "Boy, this is private property! Get back into the shop and wait your turn!"

"I believe he might be looking for me," said Holmes, joining the pharmacist. "Phillips, what have you got?"

"I think I found 'im!"

I joined Holmes and Dombey Senior and saw the boy running towards us. He was holding a tabloid paper. As he handed it to Holmes, I recognised it as an issue of that most regrettably melodramatic of press organs, *The Illustrated Police News.*

"That was quicker than I thought."

"Maybe I was jus' lucky, Mr. 'Olmes," said Philipps, beaming with pride. "Look on page five, Mr. 'Olmes!"

Holmes did as directed and nodded, quietly. Then he passed the paper to me. There was an image of Mr. O'Malley. The face was much younger, but the firemark on his cheek was unmistakable.

I was still looking at *The Illustrated Police News* after we had left Dombey & Son. The two pharmacists had come to the door with us. Dombey Senior had returned the bottle of cocaine solution to Holmes, who had given Philipps sixpence, and the boy had run off, presumably to rejoin the other Irregulars and spend this unexpected boon on sweets and lemonade.

"Have you ever had a professional encounter with O'Malley?" I asked as we marched along the pavement.

"Never met him before this morning. That's why he wasn't in my files. But I remembered the face. And that *nom de guerre.*"

"Merely from this?" I lifted the tabloid. The picture in question was in fact only one of a good dozen, admittedly well-executed, drawings. They were grouped under a shrieking headline, *Cracksmen and Fences of London.* O'Malley's portrait had a caption: *Red Paddy, Menace of the East End.*

"Memorable, no? I was rather taken aback when I could not recall the exact publication. Middle-age is upon us, Watson."

I did not comment. The paper was from 1882, which made it almost twenty years old.

My eyes dropped to the box of prose that accompanied O'Malley's picture:

> *A crafty Irish rascal, well-known to sell any kind of loot, also a smuggler and cracksman. Spent two years in The Steel*

267

before breaking out. Probably he skedaddled to Ireland. Scotland Yard made our city too hot for him.

The street lamps were on by the time we once again turned into Morton Road. As we walked up to the door of No. 89, it opened and the gaunt figure of Mrs. Henslow stood on the threshold.

"Ah gentlemen, good evening. I just happened to be looking out the window, and there you were coming along the street. It is nice to see you again. Inspector Lestrade has gone, I'm afraid."

"We're not looking for the inspector," said Holmes.

Mrs. Henslow laughed nervously. "Well, you can't be looking for me."

"Perhaps we are."

She pulled her black shawl tighter around her shoulders and reluctantly stepped back into the hallway. A door at its end stood open, presumably leading to the rooms she herself occupied. I thought she would ask us in, but she now drew herself up with an almost military bearing.

"What can I do for you, gentlemen?" Her voice had regained the stentorian quality I had noticed earlier.

"Your tenant, Mr. O'Malley," said Holmes. "How long have you known that he was a crook?"

The woman startled at the brusqueness of Holmes's question, but at the same time I thought I saw an expression of relief cross her face.

"What nonsense! Mr. O'Malley is elderly, as you well know."

"I must ask you to listen carefully, Mrs. Henslow. I did not say Mr. O'Malley *is* a crook, I said he *was* a crook. And I will tell you how you found out."

"I'm listening, Mr. Holmes."

"You bring your tenants their breakfast, and at one time, or maybe more often, Mr. O'Malley had forgotten to cover his firemark. But he always covered it before going outside. He is not unduly given to the sin of vanity, and thus you started reflecting on the reason for this behaviour. The conclusion was obvious. He did not want to be recognised. Why? Again, the conclusion was obvious. Perhaps you did some research, and you soon confirmed your suspicion."

"And what if it were so?" Mrs. Henslow tilted her head back. "Should I have played the informer? Ours is a merciful God, Mr. Holmes. They are papists, it is true, but I hold out hope that I will see them onto the path of our Lord. It is not too late for them both."

"What if I told you that Mr. O'Malley recently fell into his old ways?"

An expression of consternation formed on her face.

"How about we talk with him?" asked Holmes.

Mrs. Henslow stepped aside and made an inviting gesture towards her rooms. Then, however, she took the lead and marched ahead of us.

"These gentlemen here would like a word with Daniel," she said, crossing the threshold.

We entered directly into a large kitchen that also served as a dining room. Mrs. and Mr. O'Malley were sitting on straight-backed chairs at a table, cups of tea and a plate of bread in front of them. The gas light cast an orange penumbra over everything. To the right, the room gave onto what appeared to be a garden, to the left lay the living room in darkness. A cross hung by a fireplace. I discerned chintz-covered chairs and a cabinet with some knick-knacks on the shelves. A stretch of Morton Road was visible through the window.

Mr. O'Malley nodded to us. "Pleased ter see yer again, gentlemen."

His firemark sat like a bloodstain on his cheek.

Both Holmes and I remained silent. O'Malley wound his hands around his cup and looked at Mrs. Henslow, who had taken up station by a sideboard. The landlady's features were a study in impassivity.

O'Malley's by contrast were working as if a host of worms were squirming under his skin. Finally, he looked Holmes in the eye. "It's naw use, Oi guess. Oi heard yer out dare. Yer right, Mr. Holmes. Oi'm an auld jailbird, one that flew de coop. Filed me way through de bars, den down de drainpipes an' into the sewer. A gran' mess Oi wus. It was spillin' rain dat night it wus, and they mighta thought I drowned like a rat an' spilled out into de river. Spilled out Oi did alright, but auld Daniel O'Malley swims like a cod. And so Oi got away. Lived an 'onest life since den, more or less."

He looked to his wife and she nodded. "We should've gone away, Bridget an' me, but we didn't. Stupid, but London is wha yer can make a livin'. I did me best ter disguise meself, and it's worked for years. Thought age had solved de problem, but Oi couldn't get rid of dis." He jabbed a forefinger at his firemark. "And Oi'm not as careful as Oi used ter be. Oi don't put dis on first thing when Oi swing me legs outa bed." Reaching into the pocket of his cardigan, he extracted a flat metal box. He opened it and pulled out what looked like a thin flap of impregnated fabric. He flicked open a compartment within the box and revealed some grease. With a practiced motion he smeared some onto one side of the flap and pressed it to his face. A few careful touches with his fingertips followed, and when he removed his hand the firemark had disappeared and his skin looked like that of any old man. He cackled. "Before Oi met Bridget, Oi knew a lassie on de stage. Taught me a few things she did,

269

not only dis. But ter get on with me story. One mornin' Mrs. Henslow saw me without me patch. Oi could tell dare and den dat somethin' had started in 'er mind. I tol' Bridget we oughta leave, but we cudn't, now cud we . . . ?"

"You had given your word to the Ahernes that you would watch over their son."

"Yer a clever fella, Mr. Holmes. His father and me, we wus lads together back in Limerick. Dat telegram Oi sent him this mornin' was de 'ardest one Oi ever sent. Yer man was like me older brother, till the whole family up and lef' for America. He did come over here ter London three, four times in later years. Me and himself did some business together. And when Chester came over, he asked me ter keep an eye on'im. We were just sellin' our place in Spitalfields, so it worked out dandy. Oi liked Chester. A gran' lad he was. Though he didn't have 'is father's . . . ." Here he clenched his fist and made a grunting sound.

"What did you tell his father over the past months?"

"Told 'im de truth, Oi did, dat Chester wus wastin' 'is time mixin' chemicals instead of goin' ter work, and dat he wus gallivantin' out late at night. Never mentioned dat lassie of his though. Dat wus no one's business. But I did say he seemed ter 'ave a problem o' sorts."

"Of what sorts?"

"Of wantin' ter be like you!"

Holmes contemplated his shoes. "Did you tell him that Chester was injecting cocaine?"

"Oi didn't know till dis mornin', Oi didn't! Oi swear! Mrs. Henslow tol' me how she found' im. Oi . . . ."

Holmes silenced O'Malley with an impatient cutting motion. "Do you know what you were stealing in the pharmacy, Mr. O'Malley?"

All blood left the old cracksman's face. His eyes flickered, looked to Mrs. Henslow, to his wife, and then back to Holmes.

"Please, Oi didn't even . . . ."

"Do you know what you were stealing?!"

There came no response.

"You were stealing a murder weapon."

I saw puzzlement and comprehension struggle in O'Malley's eyes as his mind raced back over his memories, and they took on a new complexion.

"A few days ago," Holmes continued, "Jacob Henslow informed you that he knew of your past. His mother must have mentioned it." The lady in question silently raised her chin. "He's a charming individual, but I'm sure he can put some fear into his interlocutor. Not exactly the fear of God, but something similar. But he didn't ask much in exchange for

270

keeping quiet, merely that you put your old skills to use and break into a pharmacy . . . ."

"Me an' himself went together dat night! Oi didn't even go in! Just fixed de door, Oi did, an' kept a lookout. Yer man took me lantern an' wus in dare and out again in foive minutes. Oi didn't even know what he stole . . . ."

Holmes motioned to the four tea cups on the table. "It would appear we just missed him. Or rather, Mrs. Henslow delayed us long enough for him to escape."

The landlady's eyes were pinned to Holmes with an expression that most reserve for loathsome insects.

"What gives you the right to cast aspersions on my son?" she now hissed. "In my own house." Her arm shot out to indicate the door by which we had entered. "Leave! I demand that you leave."

"What gives me the right, Mrs. Henslow? Reason gives me the right . . . ."

At this moment, we all noticed that Mr. O'Malley was looking towards the backdoor that gave onto the garden.

"Dare," he said quietly. "He left through dare . . . ."

A shriek of rage issued from the landlady as she attempted to throw herself on O'Malley, but his wife, with surprising agility, jumped up and pushed Mrs. Henslow back against the wall.

"Leave him alone, you hag!"

Holmes had gripped O'Malley by his cardigan and was pulling him in the direction of the backdoor.

"Come, Watson. Enough time wasted. I'll never forgive myself if we're too late."

Holmes yanked open the door and pushed the old cracksman outside.

"Oi don't know wha' he went," protested O'Malley.

"I do," said Holmes. "What I don't know is the address. You followed Aherne around, though."

We hurried through the garden and into an alley that ran parallel to Morton Road, then rushed towards the main thoroughfare.

"You don't happen to have your old service revolver on you, Watson, do you?" Holmes called.

"Afraid not."

We were in luck. As we reached the thoroughfare, some gentlemen were alighting from a growler. Holmes pushed O'Malley to the fore.

"The girl's address!"

"Oi, Oi, let me tink . . . ." He pressed his fingertips to his forehead and took a deep breath. Then he blurted out an address in Lambeth.

"Hurry," said Holmes to the driver as we all climbed aboard. I remember casting a look at the nag in harness and my heart sinking. A crack of the whip rang out, and we were on our way.

The nag, however, proved only partly to blame for the slow progress that followed. Another reason was the traffic. Every year this seems to worsen; by now it all but comes to a standstill in the evenings. With every expansion of the Tube, London is promised that this marvel will alleviate the situation. I cannot say that I have ever noticed any improvement.

Fran's face was before my mental eye as we moved towards the river in fits and starts, occasional yells by our driver testifying to his frustration with the other occupants of the road. She would surely have gone home after the morning's ordeal. Most of us require solitude when we are bereaved, to gather ourselves before we again face an indifferent world.

"Last night Oi 'ad ter git up," said O'Malley, who was sitting next to me and across from Holmes. "Needed ter git meself a glass o' water. Oi went into de kitchen, and while Oi'm dare drinkin' me water, Oi hear someone goin' down de stairs, quiet like. Thought it wus Chester, but Oi also thought it wus a wee bit strange, 'cause Oi'd met 'im earlier in de evenin' whaen he came home, and he says ter me he wants ter work in his laboratory, he says."

"You heard Henslow," replied Holmes. "He was checking on his handiwork."

O'Malley pushed his hand through his hair. "Oi still don't understand . . . ."

"It is quite simple. After you had picked the lock, Henslow stole a quantity of twenty-percent solution of cocaine. He has keys to all the rooms, so when Aherne was out, Henslow poured away Aherne's seven-percent solution and replaced it with the twenty-percent solution. When Aherne administered this to himself, his heart failed, as the drug was almost three times the strength to which his system was accustomed."

The old cracksman was shaking his head. "Oi thought he wus stealin' something for 'imself . . . ."

The remainder of the ride passed in agonised silence. I do not know how often I looked out of the window, which always seemed to reveal a melee of vehicles and pedestrians. We crawled across Westminster Bridge amidst a hullaballoo of cries and whip cracks, and suddenly, as we reached the south side, began to gather speed.

"We're nearly dare," announced O'Malley after a short while.

Sure enough, a minute later our cab came to a halt in a lane off St. George's Road and we all jumped out.

"Dare." O'Malley pointed at a run-down tenement building. "That's wha' Chester went in. But Oi don't know whaich floor."

"The garret," I said.

Holmes was already bounding towards the front door. I pressed a half-sovereign into the driver's hand. By the time I entered the house, Holmes had disappeared around a bend in the staircase. I could not hear his steps and made sure to be as quiet as possible myself. This was not easy as the stairs were worn, steep, and prone to squeaking.

By the time I had made my way up four flights, my heart was pounding. All was silence. Gingerly, I moved up the next flight. I had reached the top floor and saw to my left an even narrower set of stairs continuing upward to the garret. Only the weak light that always seems to emanate from the city came through a small roof window. I tiptoed onward, rounded a bend in the staircase, and Holmes was staring me in the face.

"No time to lose," he whispered.

There were three doors in the garret, all made of rough wood, all closed. I could barely stand upright without grazing the beams, but Holmes had to stoop. He motioned to the door on the left. A sliver of light issued from beneath it. I leaned forward and could now hear someone pacing and a murmur of voices, but could not make out any words.

I put my eye to the keyhole, but the key was in the lock. Holmes lifted his index finger. We had only one chance. Then he made a motion of putting his shoulder to the door. I looked at it again. It appeared old, but sturdy. What awaited us on the other side? Fran in the hands of that madman? What if we failed to break through? I thought of the girl's sorrowful features, and of the determination with which she had pulled herself together.

We retreated a few steps to the other end of the landing. Holmes looked at me and then nodded. We rushed forward and crashed our shoulders against the door. The wood split and the upper half burst out of the frame, but the lock held.

"Again!" shouted Holmes, pulling me back.

We rushed forward again and slammed all our weight against the door. This time it fell inward, and we stumbled into Fran's garret room, just as Jacob Henslow was helping her to escape through the window.

His face, as he turned, was strangely empty, pale and expressionless like a Venetian mask. Out of the corner of my eye, I saw – rarest of occurrences – an expression of surprise take shape on Holmes's features.

Yet it vanished in an instant and was replaced by one of resolve, as Henslow reached into his trouser pocket. His hand emerged holding a black cylinder. There came a snapping sound and a blade shot out. This was the blade, I understood, that had grazed the neck of Madame Rose's patron and cut the throat of Rupert the German Shepherd. None of this, however, was now of any importance. Henslow came charging towards us. Holmes and I, both of us still off balance, stumbled backwards. The next moment it was Henslow who was stumbling backwards, a cry of dismay issuing from between his teeth. The knife clattered to the floor. Holmes had flung the bottle of cocaine solution and hit our attacker on the forehead.

I rushed forward, determined to capitalise on our advantage, and received a kick against the upper thigh for my recklessness. Fran had turned around in the window, lowered herself onto a dresser, and jumped from there to the floor. As I fell to the side, Henslow dealt me a blow against the ear that sent me head first into the metal frame of a bed in the centre of the room. For a second or two, I was dazed. When I turned, I saw Holmes and Henslow locked in a struggle over who would reach the knife that had slipped under a wash basin. Neither of them would. Fran was stepping over them and would momentarily have the object in her possession. Holmes reached out and grasped her ankle, whereupon she stumbled. In the instant, however, he released his double-handed grip on Henslow, the young man wrenched himself free and struggled to his feet. Meanwhile, Fran had reached the knife. She spun around, brandishing it, her eyes full of hatred.

"Leave us be!" she screeched.

Henslow grasped her by the wrist and they were rushing for the door.

Perhaps I should have let them escape; they would not have got far. But in the heat of the moment not every man's mental faculties are a good judge as to the best course of action. Fran had stepped past the wreckage of the door and Henslow was right behind her when I reached him. This time I ducked his blow and rammed my head into his torso. A rickety balustrade separated the landing from the stairwell, and as his weight crashed against the wood, it splintered. There followed a thud that almost rendered inaudible a simultaneous cracking sound.

The knife in Fran's hand glimmered in the dark, oddly foreshortened in the perspective as she raised her arm to bring the weapon down upon me. And then the knife froze in midair, swayed left and right, and fell to the landing.

"It's naw use, lassie," said O'Malley as he pinned her arm behind her back. "De peelers are on their way."

She groaned, but did not say a word.

"Redemption becomes you, O'Malley," said Holmes, emerging from the room.

Indeed, the police arrived only minutes later as we were walking the young woman down the stairs. For the second time that day she came into proximity with a dead man. This time I saw a shiver pass through her frame, and I believe her knees shook, but that was all. She straightened her back and stepped past the twisted body.

The wind cut into our faces as Holmes and I made our way back to Baker Street. My hands felt clammy in my coat pockets and there was a throbbing sensation behind my forehead. I longed to lie down and let the world sink away.

"Quite an impressive showing back there, Watson," Holmes suddenly ventured.

I nodded. Indeed, I myself had been reflecting on the precipitate nature of my actions.

"Almost as if you were on a vendetta."

"I don't know what came over me," said I. "One thing, Holmes. Were we not quite rash to break through the door? What if the situation had been what we both imagined, and Fran had been Henslow's captive? He might have had enough time to . . . ." I left the sentence unfinished.

"We were, but I conjectured that in a moment of surprise he would hesitate. Think of his victims, Watson. All male, human or animal, every single one. He killed within his own sex, not the opposite, unlike in other cases that have occurred."

"I suppose. In fact, he might not have been ready to kill a human being with his own hands yet. That's why Aherne could save the man in the alley."

"Probably. Aherne and Henslow both stood at the beginning of their careers. One wonders what each of them would have done in the future, had they not encountered each other this early in their lives."

We walked for a few minutes in silence.

"You know, Watson," Holmes then said, "there is one aspect in which Henslow was quite truthful. That is, when he mentioned that he did not understand anything of scientific matters. The theft of the twenty-percent solution was entirely unnecessary. He could simply have bought a seven- or ten-percent solution and let it stand open. The solvent would have evaporated and the strength of the solution would have increased until it had reached a deadly level."

"How did you come upon his track so quickly?"

"There were only two possibilities. Aherne could have administered too large a dosage to himself, either deliberately or accidentally, or the cocaine had been tampered with. A test confirmed the latter. The obvious first suspects were those with easy access to his quarters: Henslow and his mother. She was hoping to see Aherne onto the right path. She would not have presumed upon the Lord's prerogative to punish a sinner."

"Do you think that's what Henslow was trying to do? Punish a sinner?"

"We'll never know what he told himself he was doing. But he was following a compulsion. When the police look through his possessions, they will find a dark coat, maybe with a button missing, a fake beard. He was creating another person he could turn into as he so desired."

"Fran Atkins," I reminded Holmes. "She was also in Aherne's rooms."

"Indeed. And it must have been she who told Henslow that Aherne was injecting cocaine. It would appear the fair sex led astray my powers of explanation. Not for the first time, either."

"It is all very strange. What drew them together, Henslow and Fran?"

"Oh, one might conjecture that they were hoping to lay hands on the money Aherne kept in his secret compartment. Lestrade will construe things that way. A clear motive, a tidy solution. She might hang, but probably she will spend her days in a Dartmoor prison."

"But what is the truth?"

"Who knows? Maybe a liaison animated by shared murderous impulses. Or she was seduced by his warped desires. Or he by hers. Maybe he was becoming jealous. You could conduct some research and write a nice little story."

Sherlock Holmes's voice had been losing animation. He seemed to be slipping into a mood of dejection and not to feel any further need for exchange.

"Any other explanation?"

He shrugged and quoted Shakespeare. "*Hell is empty. The devils are here.*"

The Musician Who Spoke From the Grave
by Peter Coe Verbica

Chapter I
The She-Wolf

Holmes stood at the bow window of his flat at 221b Baker Street. The late morning light illuminated his hawkish nose and the frontal lobes of his ample forehead. Mrs. Hudson cleared a small octagonal table of dishes, but the lean consulting detective remained in private reverie, ignoring the commotion. I gave her room to pass and nodded. She gave me a brief look, the corner of her lips moving slightly as if to signal her stoic consternation toward her boarder's eccentricities.

Walking near the fireplace mantel, Holmes retrieved his old briarwood pipe from a rack and raked some tobacco from a Persian slipper. He lit the pipe in silence, took a few puffs, and then turned toward me. His sharp and piercing eyes showed that the inner springs of his highly complex mind had just seized upon an epiphany. He beckoned me open-handedly to one of the padded wicker chairs.

"Please, Watson, have a seat and rest a minute. I have an interesting case brewing and you could be of great assistance. It involves a popular young music teacher who recently died. He was a bit of a prodigy, and taught aspiring violinists, cellists, pianists, and harpsichordists. His tutelage mostly extended to the children and adolescents of the well-to-do and those with royal lineage. His father achieved a modicum of fame in Vienna before he married a Scotswoman. The family subsequently moved to the outskirts of London."

"The news seems somewhat familiar," I offered.

Holmes scooped up a crumpled newspaper from next to a cockeyed stack of chemistry and medical textbooks. He extracted a yellowing page and handed it to me. I looked down at the print and realized I was being supplied with the obituary from a month prior. Three entries down, I noticed the block-print of a distinguished-looking young man wearing a tilted top hat, regal tie, and ten-button white vest. His cape languished over his shoulders, held by a braided silk rope. Under his likeness were the words, *"Bernhard Ainsley Fischer"*.

277

"Impresses me as a bit of a dandy, but, of course, I'm sorry the fellow passed," I said. "The death reportedly was from natural causes. He fell ill one morning after posting some letters, preparing for a lesson, and eating a light breakfast."

"If I'm not mistaken, his much-bereaved mother is making her way up the stairs presently," Holmes said as he strolled to the door and admitted a frail, elderly woman dressed in black. A veil covered her face. Atop her head, she wore a plain black hat adorned with a pearl-ended pin. Her shoes, more akin to boots, were worn, but still had a shine. She shuffled them on a small rug at the entrance to the room, as if determined not to bring in any fall leaves from the street.

"Welcome, Mrs. Fischer," Holmes began, showing the lady polite attention and guiding her to a chair.

"No need to help me, Mr. Holmes. I may be old, but I'm not helpless," the woman chided with a curt brogue. "I trust you received my telegram?" she asked, gripping his arm. Her thin lips stretched over widely spaced teeth.

"Yes, Mrs. Fischer. Our sincerest condolences on your loss. Please allow me to introduce my trusted colleague, Dr. Watson."

Mrs. Fischer lifted her veil and studied me with tired, gray eyes. Her wan cheeks were lined with vertical striations in patterns one might find in the thin bark of a tree. She dropped into the chair closest to her, as if relieving her feet of a weight far in excess of her diminutive figure.

"Thank you," she murmured, then acknowledged me with a slight nod. "Doctor." She gathered herself, then began.

"Gentleman, I am here because my dear son, God bless his soul, was healthy as a draft horse before he began to fall ill over the final two weeks of his life. To say he died of 'natural causes' defies common sense. The flame of youth shone in his countenance until his passing. Inspector Lestrade refuses to listen to me. He insists that the case officially has been closed. He assured me my son's breakfast and beverage were checked for poison, and none was found. He also said my son's body showed no evidence of unusual marks either – not so much as a pinprick."

Mrs. Fischer worried the bulb of one of her knuckles. Her jaw muscles contracted as she clenched her teeth in genuine distress. Bouncing her knees involuntarily, she fidgeted as she sat.

"Let us not worry about Mr. Lestrade, Madam. He will bask happily in the notoriety when we deduce what really happened, and let him take the credit."

The lady brightened marginally with the prospect of Holmes's assistance and straightened in her chair. "As my father would have said, that inspector is just 'bum and parsley'."

"I would offer you some tea or a brandy, but you strike me as someone who would like to get on with the task at hand," Holmes said. "Would you be kind enough to let us look through your son's personal effects? If you could familiarize us with his list of clients and friends, it might be of great help to Dr. Watson and me."

"Certainly, Mr. Holmes! Certainly," she responded. She reached for her purse and began digging for coins.

"Don't worry about payment, just yet, Mrs. Fischer," he said. "Give us time to prove our merit, and we can discuss compensation when the matter is concluded. May I ask you a personal question, madam?"

"If it's helpful, of course."

"Did your son ever borrow money from you? How were his finances?"

"Borrow? No, no. The opposite, Mr. Holmes. He would insist on providing *me* with funds. Sometimes a bit *too* generous . . . ."

"Despite his taste in clothes, Mrs. Fischer?"

"He was careful with how he spent his earnings. He rarely ate out, was not one to hang out at clubs, and would grit his teeth when sick rather than spend money on a doctor. He abhorred gambling, though he did enjoy numbers. I always thought that if he hadn't gone into music, he would have done well as an academic, perhaps in mathematics."

"He didn't seem to dress like a professor," Holmes offered.

"His attire, though fashionable, was never purchased during the height of a season. I'll confess where he often obtained his clothes, but you must swear never to tell a soul."

"Upon the King James Bible," Holmes answered, looking at me as if to ensure my silence. He then returned his gaze toward the grieving mother.

Mrs. Fischer leaned forward and quietly said, "The mortuary, Mr. Holmes."

"Unorthodox, but eminently practical," Holmes replied with a raised eyebrow. "Before we review your son's belongings, may I ask what he had for breakfast before he passed away?"

"Though I hate anchovy paste, my son would usually have Crosse & Blackwell spread on toast, an egg, and some black tea."

"Thank you for taking time with us this morning," Holmes concluded. "We look forward to calling upon you shortly."

The elderly lady leaned forward in her seat and lifted an old needlepoint pillow from Holmes's divan. She grimaced and bared all of her teeth like a she-wolf. In a flash, she deftly removed her hatpin, bared its six-inch needle and drove it into the cushion with menace.

I started involuntarily and nearly tipped over in my chair in reaction.

"Justice for my son," she snarled. "Get me justice for my son."

She stood and shook both of our hands firmly. "No need to show me the door," she declared with the same immediacy of her arrival and she left as abruptly as she had arrived.

My eyes returned to the hat pin. Holmes grabbed the pearl end with his long, slender fingers, removed the pin, and set it upon a bookshelf next to a wooden box filled with small note cards, indexed by numerical dividers.

"Never underestimate a woman," Holmes said in a *sotto voce* to himself, as he resurrected his extinguished pipe.

Chapter II
Flushing a Fox

The following day, we pressed our way to Clapham, a lower but genteel neighborhood dotted with a few professional offices, as well as furnished lodgings, including the former residence of the deceased musical teacher.

I removed my hat and let my eyes adjust to the morning light as Holmes rapped upon the door of the bachelor's quarters. The ashen-faced lady we had met earlier opened the door to reveal a small hallway and a dim drawing room.

She was still dressed somberly in black and shook our hands with resolve. Now, without a hat and veil, I observed wiry ringlets dropped to each side of her wrinkled face, with the balance was pulled back into a bun. She wore mother-of-pearl earrings, and I was somewhat relieved that she was without a decorative hatpin.

After greeting us, she began with a *non-sequitur*: "Gentlemen, critics are the lowest forms of life. Ignorant, jealous, and devoid of any skill of their own, they nip like flies wherever they land." She brushed her arms at imaginary insects and shuddered.

"Some see only the thorns rather than the blossoms, Mrs. Fischer," Holmes responded, wiping his feet on the floor mat.

"What is the wellspring of your antipathy?" I asked, trying to discern her thoughts.

"But for a scathing article early in Ainsley's music career, I'm certain that my son would have risen to greater heights," Mrs. Fischer continued, with a noticeable rasp in her voice. "He played at Covent

Garden, the Philharmonic Society, and the Queen's Hall to great acclaim – often selected as a deputy musician."

Holmes, in the meantime, made a discreet bee-line past an array of simple wooden chairs and stacks of violin cases to an undersized secretary. He began carefully examining the contents of its drawers. He picked up a mechanical, double-sided pencil from off of the desktop and fanned through sheets of music with it. "I've looked through his correspondence already in search of clues, Mr. Holmes," the elderly lady stated, "even pulling out the drawers completely in search of hidden compartments or cubbyholes. All that I could find was a portable ledger book where he tallied student lesson charges and his orchestral earnings. You can see the initials of each student penciled in a column just after the date."

"Given your familiarity with your son's work, do you mind providing the names of each of his students if possible?"

"That would be child's play, Mr. Holmes." She retrieved a notebook from a shelf, flipped open a brass-topped, glass inkwell, doused a quill tip pen, and neatly wrote the following:

JA – Jennifer Atkinson
MP – Molly Penworth
TU – Thomas Upham
RT – Robert Turnbull
CS – Clarice Sonnell
GH – Gertrude Huber
FB – Fannie Bottson
JS – Jayne Smith
MA – Maurice Appleblossom
MN – Mary Naglee
SR – Samuel Rothert
AN – Anne Newberry
DW – David Wright
MA – Maddie Artisanson
JB – John Beggs
RF – Ronald Firth

Mrs. Fischer ripped the page from the bound book, pressed it against a felt blotter, and handed it to Holmes, who pocketed the list after reviewing it quickly.

He proceeded to unsnap the various wooden violin cases one at a time, carefully removing the instruments and their bows. He unscrewed containers of rosin and examined them briefly with a jeweler's loupe.

After inspecting the case interiors one by one, he returned the items to their cases, nestling the instruments into their burgundy-colored velvet recesses. He closed and carried each case by its brass handle and returned it to its original location.

Holmes returned to the sheaves of music with renewed interest, holding them up to light from the window, as if searching for watermarks. Mrs. Fischer and I stood patiently to the side, like apostles waiting on a high priest. Holmes appeared to be systematically separating pieces, including the *Contrapunctus* from Bach's *The Art of Fugue*, as well as his *Canonic Variations on "Vom Himmel hoch da komm' ich her"*. He also removed a piano solo by Robert Schumann, entitled *Carnaval*, and Froberger's *Tombeau de M. Blancrocher*. Lastly, he segregated some additional pieces by other composers, including several by Mozart.

Holmes raised a sheet of Bach's music and once again held it in his gaze. His eyes seemed to glisten with nearly imperceptible excitement. But for my extensive experience with him over the years, I wouldn't have noticed the emotion.

"Mrs. Fischer, these may be helpful," Holmes said, organizing the items into a leather and board folio. "May I borrow them and his billing ledger for a number of days?"

"You may, Mrs. Holmes. My son had eclectic taste in music, but I'm not sure how sheets of musical scores will help you solve his demise . . . ."

Holmes gently placed his hand upon the woman's shoulder. "Music, it has been said, soothes the soul. I'm confident we will soon flush a cunning fox from the underbrush."

Chapter III
A Loud Shriek

Days passed before I saw Holmes again. I attended to a number of patients at my small medical office, including a severe case of phosphorus necrosis of the jaw which made even my worst day as an Assistant Surgeon with my regiment during the Second Afghan War seem like a lark in comparison. Run by Quakers, the match factories using white phosphorus were a blight to English society. Holmes had been quietly working with his brother, Mycroft, to press upon even His Majesty to get the manufacturers to switch to a less lethal red phosphorus. In character, Holmes never took credit when the worst of these workshops finally were shuttered.

It had rained the night before as I made my way down a baptized Baker Street. The cobblestones were still shimmering. A shiny hansom cab dotted with beads of water passed me. The clippity-clop of horseshoes echoed against the townhouses. Clouds covered the sky overhead, darkening the spaces between tree branches despite the hour.

Suddenly, I heard a man's loud shriek issue from a window just above the street entrance to Holmes's flat. I mobilized myself up the narrow stairway of 221b to find a flushed shopkeeper in his early forties standing at the top. His coat had a Swiss-canton emblem on one of the pockets – a key in fields of juxtaposed red and white. The result was a man with the appearance of a plump schoolboy. He grasped at his chest, his fleshy face twisted in terror, and a crown of perspiration adorning his brow. A salesman's leather stationery case lay at his feet. Despite the disadvantage of coming toward him from a lower elevation, I blocked his exit until I could ascertain what was amiss.

Holmes stood behind him with a white turban on his head. The oddity gave him the intimidating appearance of being a foot taller. Over the shorter man's shoulder, I noticed that Holmes held a lidded basket at his breast. From Holmes's stance, I was reminded of a player braving a scrum, protecting the ball. Akimbo on the Persian carpet, I spied a peculiar musical instrument. At first, I thought it was a clarinet, but it lacked complex valves. It was fluted at one end and lined with a series of holes.

"Dr. Watson, I assure you everything is all right," Holmes assured. "There is no need for alarm. Everything is under control."

"You are a madman!" the flustered guest declared, still catching his breath.

"Doctor, may I introduce you to the proprietor of one of London's finest stationery stores."

"I need no introduction!" the man admonished. "Now, sir, kindly allow me my leave!"

I looked to Holmes, who nodded. I stepped aside. The businessman rushed past me, his square case in tow.

Holmes retrieved a thin leather strap from the couch and affixed it round the woven basket. After joining the end pieces to form an "X" on the lid, he finished with a mooring hitch and set the object upon the floor. I could swear that I saw it move, but unsure if my eyes were deceiving me.

Holmes moved to his favorite chair, chuckling and lit his pipe.

"I've been studying various poisons, Watson, relating to our musician instructor's death. One I wanted to re-familiarize myself with is a cobra's venom."

"Goodness, Holmes. I would have thought you had your fill after the Speckled Band. Don't tell me that's what you have trapped in that basket!"

"I wouldn't say 'trapped', Watson. The reptile was raised in it. It's more akin to the snake's residence. This lethal creature comes to me by way of the Indian subcontinent."

"Mrs. Hudson wouldn't be pleased to house this sort of a lodger, I should think."

"True, Watson. I plan to return it to its snake-charmer owner shortly. I have been wrestling not as much with what poison might have been used on Mr. Fischer. Given his rapid decline, I've narrowed it down to three probable toxins. Still to be clearly resolved are three questions: How was the poison delivered? Who would want to harm the victim? And, what was the evil-doer's motive?"

"Are you planning to exhume the body, Holmes?"

"That might prove difficult, given Lestrade's convenient conviction that the death merits no further investigation. It would also be stressful for our victim's mother. Perhaps more at hand, such activity confirms nothing which I haven't anticipated. We can tender that it is the highest probability that evidence of the poison will remain in the mouth of the victim's corpse."

Chapter IV
Music in the Silence

We took a hansom back from the docks to Holmes's flat. We had traveled there in order to deliver the snake to a ship, ready to steam to Bombay by way of the Cape of Good Hope. I hoped that the unusual cargo wouldn't raise havoc with the journey.

Mrs. Hudson had thoughtfully prepared tea and twin pillars of finger sandwiches, despite her dismay with a tenant whose behavior included untidiness, noxious chemical experiments, unsavory guests, playing of music at odd hours, and even in-door target practice with his pistol at playing cards. To his credit, Holmes offset his liabilities with prompt and regular payment of generous rent.

"Holmes, it seems as if you're making progress, but I'm having trouble following along," I confessed.

"Watson, let's look at the facts as you understand them. What do you glean to date?"

"Well," I responded, clearing my throat, "if we assume that a mother knows her son better than most, we can accept he was, until two weeks before his death, in robust health. His being felled in his prime speaks to some sort of poison being employed, perhaps in his food or drink. And since killers who use poison are nearly always female, we can theorize the killer was a woman – perhaps a student – involved somehow with her teacher, and scorned."

"An arguably reasonable logic, Watson. I agree with you on certain points, but in this instance, I believe the killer was a man rather than a woman."

"Is that not improbable, given the choice of weapon?" I countered.

"There are other means by which an individual can be dispatched quickly without leaving a trace. One need only turn to Edinburgh, to William Burke and William Hare, who suffocated their victims to enrich their own coffers. But, since our musician was in good health, it's my belief that even if there were two assailants, Inspector Lestrade would have taken note of a struggle occurring at the young man's premises. There was no evidence of such. So, I agree that poison undoubtedly was used. We can further deduce the method of poisoning. While cyanide acts quickly, it produces the easily traceable side-effects of convulsions and nausea. Strychnine, while also effective, is improbable, as there is no evidence of Ainsley Fischer's frothing at the mouth or having muscle spasms. This leaves arsenic as the most likely culprit."

"So I'm on the right track, then, Holmes?"

"In many ways 'yes', and in some 'no', Watson. Women are just as capable of being as heinous as men, but an overwhelming majority of homicides are committed by males. Moreover, if one reviews killings by poison over the past five decades, more than half were perpetrated by men, from both higher and lower stations. Examples include Edward 'the Human Crocodile' Pritchard, Thomas 'the Lambeth Poisoner' Neill Cream, the disowned Quaker John Tawell, William 'the Rugeley Poisoner' Palmer, and numerous others. Naturally, a woman poisoner provides a more salacious story for journalists who are in the business of exploiting others' misfortunes. Husbands who beat their wives would be wise to change their ways, or be prepared for the permanent consequences of tainted soup."

"I'm still uncertain as to where you are headed with this, Holmes. We don't seem to have much in the way of clues, though you have the man's ledger with his students' initials. Why aren't we actively interviewing suspects? You seem as deskbound as your brother, Mycroft, despite the urgency of the research needed," I stated with uncharacteristic reproach.

"Watson, I appreciate your desire for sweat and industry, which I'm never one to shun when necessary, but clear clues are abundantly evident. I believe that I know the name of killer. It is now a matter of tightening the noose, or in musical terms, bringing the matter to a crescendo."

"How is that possible?" I asked, perplexed.

"Did you notice anything unusual about Mr. Fischer's musical choices?"

"Not in particular."

"Does the name '*Blancrocher*' remind you of anything?" he asked, extracting a page from the victim's folio.

"No, I can't say it does . . . ."

"It's by Froberger, and considered by some to be the embodiment of sadness. It's meant to mimic the sound of his friend, Blancrocher, a lutenist, who fell down the stairs to his death. Froberger witnessed the event, and it undoubtedly affected him profoundly. Remembering this haunting piece played on a harpsichord, I began to wonder if Ainsley Fischer might have been secretly communicating something via music to one of his students – perhaps a love interest."

Holmes stood, adjusted the edge of his shirt cuff, and began improvising a conductor's motions.

"The selection by Bach which I showed you in front of Mrs. Fischer was chosen because if you examine the notes, you'll find '*B-A-C-H*' embedded in the third line."

"Bach," I repeated, beginning to understand. "The '*BACH*' motif – "

"Precisely, Watson. When I saw Schumann's *Carnaval* in the stack of Fischer's scores, I realized that I was onto something. Schumann relished embedding his pieces with puzzles. In fact, he taunts the listener by placing musical cryptograms within music about a masked ball. If you attend to what's played, you will detect references to the town where his fiancée was born, the composer's name, and more."

"By modifying the music played with a student, Fischer could communicate with the pupil surreptitiously in front of a parent or chaperone . . . ." I suggested.

"Indeed. That's when I began looking for anomalies. One limitation at first is the series of notes available to spell words, namely "*A*" through "*G*", but there are ways around this, including one technique referred to as 'the French Method'. In this technique, the encipherment is achieved by using many-to-one mapping, referencing the original "*A*" through "*G*" diatonic notes with naturals, sharps, and flats – to provide a musician cryptographer with additional letters."

"And, you found an unusual cryptogram within the notes used?"

"No, Watson, I did not," he replied matter-of-factly.

"Then why did you take the sheaves of music?" I asked, somewhat crestfallen.

"I remembered a quotation from the 1700's attributed to Mozart. *'Die Stille zwischen den Noten ist genauso wichtig wie die Noten selbst.'* This may be translated literally as, 'The silence between the notes is as important as the notes themselves.' Others have elevated this statement further, interpreting that the composer argues, 'The music is not in the notes, but in the silence between.'"

"The silence, Holmes?"

"Brilliant, Watson. You've hit upon it. I began looking for the pauses in the pieces. I spied what I thought was a minor error: A *fermata* on a note which shouldn't be there."

"*Fermata*," I responded, blinking, and admiring Holmes's aptitude for music, but remembering my years spent more comfortably on a rugby field.

"A note played just a bit longer, Watson. Normally, it wouldn't be much to think about, except for Mr. Fischer's love of music that involves puzzles and games."

Holmes drew a box in the air with his index finger and made a slicing motion, cutting it in half.

"After this initial cue, I discovered in a Mozart piece, out-of-place *minim* rests added after the ninth and twelfth notes of a phrase. Then, after another series of two *fermata*, errant *crotchet* rests occurred after the second and ninth note. The errors continue after another out-of-place *fermata* later in the piece, followed by half rests after the seventh and eighth notes in a measure."

Mrs. Hudson interrupted Holmes's tutorial, announcing that a gentleman caller had arrived. She presented Holmes with a thick, crème colored card. The font upon it was bold and angular.

Chapter V
A Music Lesson Interrupted

A tall man in his forties entered the doorway, holding an alpine-style hat in his hand. He was balding on the top of his head, and his close-cropped hair was a salt-and-pepper gray. His ears were oddly shaped, nearly triangular, and his nose was sharp and thin. He wore garish white socks and woolen pants held up by suspenders too wide to be made domestically. He looked dressed for a hike in the mountains, rather than an amble through London streets.

"Mr. Huber, thank you for visiting us this afternoon. I trust that your stroll was a pleasant one?" Holmes asked.

"I have no trouble getting out for a brisk walk, Mr. Holmes," he responded. "I grew up hiking hills steeper than any in this country," he responded, clipping the ends of his words.

"Your calling is appreciated, sir. Dr. Watson and I are hoping that you can provide us some insights into the death of Mr. Fischer."

"After the stunt with the snake you pulled upon my cousin, Mr. Holmes, I want you to understand that I am in no mood for pranks. You said that you had some important information regarding my daughter. I find your notice unnecessary. She's at our home with my wife, completely safe."

"Mr. Huber, I assure you that your visit will be a productive one. Doctor Watson and I were just enjoying a debate." Holmes retrieved his violin and bow. "Perhaps you can help us out. Indulge me with some musical fun from Mozart's *Verzeichnis aller meiner Werke*, which Köchel numbered 522."

"Mr. Holmes, that piece is one of my least favorites. It is an unamusing abomination."

"I've added a few pauses which I think give it a better rhythm. Tell me what you think, Mr. Huber."

Holmes began playing the piece with vigor. It reminded me of fiddling and struck me as repetitious, but pleasant on the whole.

"Did you hear that I first added two *fermata*, and a pause at the ninth note?" Holmes asked the gentleman.

"Yes, but that proves nothing."

"And a pause after the fourth, ninth, and fourth again?"

"Too soon clever, Mr. Holmes, and too late smart, especially for some who think that they are ingenious. Your game proves nothing."

"I prove that you're an unintelligent coward, Mr. Huber."

"A man isn't a coward for protecting the reputation of his daughter, Mr. Holmes. But, I will grant that you are a formidable nuisance."

"I will be apprising Scotland Yard of the facts shortly. In fact, an inspector is on his way," Holmes said as he checked his pocket watch. "Your cousin has already confessed to providing you the arsenic, as well as the stamps and stationery you sent to Ainsley Fischer, purportedly from your daughter, urging him to write to her as often as possible."

Huber pulled a pug-nosed revolver he had kept hidden in a holster underneath his arm and pointed it at Holmes's chest. Aghast, I realized I was without my trusted Webley, and too far from the culprit to be of any utility. The outcome appeared unavoidably dire. I was in a position to save neither Holmes nor myself.

"Not before I take care of you med – " Huber began, before being interrupted by the report of a gun. Huber spun and dropped his weapon, clasping his right shoulder. I seized the moment and tackled him to the floor, driving a knee into his ribs. I turned to Holmes and saw smoke rising from the palm of his hand, but, inexplicably, no firearm.

Lestrade and a policeman burst through the door. The policeman joined me in restraining Huber and affixed cuffs to the man's wrists, behind his back.

"'*Meddlers*', I believe, is what Mr. Huber was thinking of calling Dr. Watson and me, Inspector."

Lestrade turned his ferret-like face to Holmes and said, "Well, Mr. Holmes, you've succeeded in making more work for me. Once again, I'm having to clean up your mess."

"Thank you, Inspector, for arriving in the nick of time. Once again, you've saved the day."

"So, what gives, here, Mr. Holmes?" Lestrade asked, pulling a small note-book out from his vest.

"Simple, really. Nothing that you couldn't have figured out for yourself. Mr. Fischer, the music teacher, was wooing one of his brighter pupils, Gertrude Huber, via encoded music. I've taken a sheet from Ainsley Fischer's music books, a piece by Mozart. The key to the code was in the spaces between the notes. He used a cypher with twenty-four letters, rather than twenty-six, in two rows. He threw out the "*M*" and the "*Z*" which made following it slightly more difficult. The *fermata*, shall we say, in *errata*, were keys to when to listen for the silence. I've taken a red pencil and circled them for you, as well as provided a transcription underneath. To stimulate a discussion with this blackguard, I played a cypher of my own."

Huber moaned quietly and his face had paled.

"Inspector, may I suggest you get this criminal to a surgeon?" I said, pointing to the slumped man's shoulder.

"Yes, yes, there'll be plenty of time for that," he replied, staring at the sheet of paper in Holmes's hands. In red pencil, Holmes had written at the bottom, "*I love u GH*".

The policeman grabbed Huber by the left elbow and got him to stand. Together, he and Lestrade walked him through Holmes's door and they headed down the stairs, toward the street.

"One of these days, we're going to have to teach Lestrade how to close an open door, Watson," Holmes said.

Chapter VI
A Quiet Whiff

Holmes was reclining, enjoying a quiet whiff from his pipe, as content as a coastal seaman back from a successful fishing expedition. Mrs. Fischer had been apprised of the apprehension, but I still needed elucidation.

"You have some questions still, Watson?"

"Cracking the musical cypher early in the game made the case easier, I presume?"

"Yes. One difficulty, however, was the absence of any poison at Mr. Fischer's domicile. This completely blunted the scent of Lestrade. I then began thinking not about what was present, but instead about that which wasn't. I hit upon the idea that the poison could have been applied to the back of a postage stamp and the glued backing of newer envelopes. The victim could be baited, via a ruse – in this instance, the writing materials supposedly coming from Huber's daughter. But, my initial problem was with the dosage. Easier to poison a man with food or drink in higher quantities, where he keels over at once. This explains Mr. Fischer's decline over a period of two weeks."

"Thus the encouragement to 'write often', eh? Remarkably simple, Holmes, once you explain it."

"True, but I was still at a handicap. I needed to see if I could trace the stationery to a particular store, then capitalize on a weak link who would have less of a stake in the game. Knowing that immigrants often have strong affinity groups, I hoped that Huber would purchase stationery from someone within the Swiss community, and preferably, someone living in London."

"And so, you looked for stationery store owners who were Swiss?" I said.

"Precisely! You're following wonderfully. And, I discovered only one, who, as luck would have it, was Huber's cousin."

"The gentleman with the emblem on his jacket and aversion to snakes . . . ."

"One and the same, Watson! If Huber had kept his cool and feigned ignorance over the musical cryptogram rather than pulling out a pistol, it would have made our work more difficult. Luckily, my bait of the musical message in Mozart's ditty incited his anger."

"Such as 'You did it,' I presume?"

"Lacking your spelling skills, Watson. Rather, '*U did it*'," as he made the shape of a "*U*" with his index finger.

"How did you manage to shoot Huber in the shoulder with a bare hand, Holmes? That's a trick I would appreciate you teaching me!"

"Happy to, Watson. It's an unusual device called a 'Lemon Squeezer', which I had sent to me from Chicago. I modified it by affixing a *faux* watch-face on one side to enhance the deception."

Holmes opened up his palm and displayed a large pocket watch with a protruding tube. He wedged the device between his two hands and unscrewed it. Inside, I spied a wheeled ratcheting mechanism with seven blunt spines. Just as quickly, he reaffixed the twin edges.

"Seven rounds, I note. You were prepared for violence."

"Clearly the man had no regard for human life," Holmes replied.

He emphasized his point by extending his arm away from me and fired four times into the burgundy wallpaper. I looked through the gun smoke across the room, feeling a slight sense of pity for Mrs. Hudson. When the blue haze cleared, I noticed the addition of an *!* to the right of the *V* and *R*-shaped bullet holes (which one may recall from my mention of them in "The Musgrave Ritual").

While I have criticized Holmes's untidiness in the past, as the sunlight streamed in through the bow window on this particular afternoon, I was grateful for his eccentricities. His shrewd preparation and marksmanship had saved us both.

The Adventure of the
Future Funeral
by Hugh Ashton

A pair of muddy shoes was on the doorstep as I arrived at 221b Baker Street. The minor mystery of who might have left their shoes outside the house was resolved when I took the seventeen steps to the rooms I shared with Sherlock Holmes and discovered him deep in conversation with a stranger, seemingly a client seeking Holmes's services.

"No, Watson, I would not have you leave for the world," Holmes told me, as I apologised for my intrusion and hastened to back out of the door. "Mr. Urquhart has been telling me of a most interesting circumstance."

I regarded the visitor with some interest, attempting, in the manner of my friend, to deduce some facts from his appearance. His black mourning clothes marked him as someone who had recently suffered a loss, and his generally lugubrious aspect confirmed my suspicion. My professional training informed me that he appeared to be an asthmatic, and I noted with some interest the signet ring, which bore the initials *S.O.* His feet were missing their shoes, presumably to be seen on the doorstep, with the left great toe protruding through a hole in the sock, but the heel had been darned. I therefore deduced that it was his wife had quit this world, following the repair to the heel of the sock, but prior to the more recent damage at the toe.

"I must commiserate with you on your loss, Mr. Urquhart," I said to him. "It is indeed hard to lose one's wife."

Holmes's visitor looked perplexed. "What in the world are you talking about, er – ?"

"This is Doctor Watson, my friend and colleague, who is kind enough to write small fanciful romances based on some of my more interesting cases," Holmes answered him. "Tell me, Watson, by what process did you arrive at this conclusion?"

"The fact that Mr. Urquhart is in mourning points to a loss, probably recent, as the garments are relatively new. I must apologise, Mr. Urquhart, but the state of your left sock indicates that at one time there was someone in your life who would mend your socks for you, but that state of affairs has sadly ceased to be."

Holmes clapped his hands together. "Bravo, my dear Watson! You are coming on splendidly."

"Then I am correct in my deductions?"

"Wrong in every particular. For example, why does a man wear mourning weeds?"

"Because he has lost one who was dear to him?"

"Indeed, that is one possible reason."

"There are others?"

"Naturally. Let us suppose Mr. Urquhart to be an undertaker – that is, a man whose professional dress is one of mourning, and which must, moreover, always be in a state of good repair so as not to cause offence to the bereaved mourners."

"I see. And the sock?"

"You may have noticed that it has been raining heavily for the past week."

"So?"

"This has made it impossible to dry the laundry, and I am drawing a bow at a venture here, but I would guess that Mr. Urquhart, when he donned his socks this morning, was reduced to a pair that he would not normally have considered appropriate."

Urqhart chuckled. "You're right there, sir. The missus was not well pleased that this was the only pair left to me, but needs must, eh?"

"Quite so, quite so. The rain is also responsible for the last clue in the identification of Mr. Urqhart's profession."

"The boots on the doorstep?" I enquired. "The rain has made them so muddy that they were not fit to walk on Mrs. Hudson's carpets?"

"Indeed so. And the mud, or rather the leaves adhering to them that I noticed when I opened the front door to Mr. Urquhart, confirmed my immediate suspicions. That species of broad-leafed oak is to be found only in Highgate Cemetery, or in a small arboretum on the outskirts of Shrewsbury. I chose the nearer location as being the more likely."

"And once more you are right, sir," said Urqhart. "It's a wonder to me how you can see these things."

Holmes waved a languid hand. "I see only what other men see," he explained. "It is what happens in here," tapping the side of his head, "that is different. But tell me, what is your reason for coming here?"

"Well, sir, it was last Tuesday that this gentleman came to see me. Well, not quite a gentleman, perhaps. Though he spoke well enough, there was something about him that didn't quite ring true."

"His boots, perhaps?" suggested Holmes.

Our visitor started. "Why, that was exactly it," he exclaimed. "I was just about to say that it was his boots that gave him away, as you might say, and you put the words into my mouth. Well, then, this man – "

"He has a name?" Holmes asked.

The other smiled. "He gave me the name of John Blenkinthorpe, and requested that I collect the body of his wife."

"Hardly an unusual occurrence, I would have thought?" I interjected.

"Indeed not. It is, after all, the way in which I earn my living," replied Nathaniel Urquhart. "In such cases, we naturally enquire what time will be the most convenient for us to make the collection. In this instance, I was given a date and time a year from now."

Holmes raised his eyebrows. "Indeed? That would seem to be an unusual development."

"Not merely unusual, Mr. Holmes. Absolutely unheard-of. Why, you can imagine the state of a body after a year, can you not?"

"Indeed so. Most singular. There is more?"

"Yes, the whole business is confoundedly queer. I was taken aback by his request, but asked for the name of the deceased. He thereupon informed me that he was unmarried at present."

"And yet he had asked you to collect his wife's body?"

"That is correct."

"You would appear to have been the victim of some form of practical joke," I suggested.

Our visitor smiled. "It goes further than that," he explained. "As you may guess, I had been given an address from which to collect the body of this non-existent wife, before I had even been given a date on which to perform the operation."

"And the address was a false one?" suggested Holmes.

"Not quite. When I passed by 23 Belvedere Gardens some time later on my way home from my business premises, I noticed that a sign proclaimed that it was to let. Out of curiosity, I went to the nearest letting-agents and enquired regarding the lease of the property, describing to them the man who had given his name as John Blenkinthorpe. Not only was the name unknown to them, but they had no knowledge of a man who answered the description which I presented to them, and, even stranger, the property was not to let through them. They recommended several other agents in the vicinity, given that I had expressed an interest in the property, but I likewise failed to obtain any information about Blenkinthorpe or the property."

"Most curious," remarked Holmes. "But I fail to see where my services may be of value to you. In what capacity do you wish to engage me?"

"Why, none, sir," replied our visitor. "I knew that the unusual held some interest for you, and remembered you from the time of poor Lady Frances, and thought you might find my story to be worth the hearing."

Holmes threw up his hands in exasperation. "I am a busy man, Mr. Urquhart, and even though your story may be interesting of itself, unless you set the puzzle for me to unravel, with a definite solution and goal to attain, I consider the telling of it to be a waste of time. Goodbye to you." With these words, he turned away, and thereby brought any further conversation to an end.

Urquhart turned to me, but while Holmes was within earshot I was unable to offer him any advice, or to do other than to usher him silently to the door.

"I have no doubt that Mr. Holmes has an interest in your story," I told him, when I judged us to be out of my friend's hearing. "However, it is hardly reasonable to expect him to take on any kind of investigation without a definite end in sight. I can assure you that it is not the financial aspect of the matter that is of concern – I have known him to take many cases without fee – but it is the intellectual challenge that stimulates him to action. I therefore wish you a very good day."

I saw him down the stairs and returned to the room.

"Thank you, Watson," Holmes remarked to me, without turning or raising his head. "You have an admirable gift of tact on occasion, a gift which I all too often seem to lack."

"And what of our friend's story?" I asked.

"Do you believe it?" my friend asked me in reply.

"Why, yes. What possible reason could he have for telling us such a fable?"

"I can conceive of at least three reasons why we have heard this story," Holmes told me. "You surely have not forgotten the story of Mr. Jabez Wilson, with the remarkable head of red hair. His story to us seemed too preposterous to be true, but it ended in the very satisfactory capture of Mr. John Clay, who had been a thorn in the side of Scotland Yard for some years. Could not this story be a similar ruse to lure Mr. Urquhart from his business?"

"And the other two reasons?"

"I am reminded of a case in Baden in 1865, where a Herr Hufschmidt made a similar request for a coffin for person or persons unknown, to be filled in the future. The motive in that case was to deflect any suspicion of murder, for what murderer would signal his motives in advance in so brazen a fashion? In this instance, the murderer is himself the maker of the coffin to contain his future victim."

"But surely you do not consider Mr. Nathan Urquhart to be a potential murderer?"

"All men, even you, Watson, may be said to be capable of that crime, given appropriate circumstances and motivation. However, I do not say that I consider this to be a likely probability, merely one of several possibilities."

"And the third?"

"That Mr. Urquhart is not of sound mind, and has recounted a dream or some other delusion to us, in the sincere and firm belief that this incident really occurred."

"That last should be easy enough to check," I laughed. "It is a simple matter of making our way to Belvedere Gardens and examining the premises."

"And if they turn out to be empty, pray, what would that tell us? Merely that Mr. Urquhart has passed an empty house in his everyday journey and had remarked the fact that it was empty somewhere at the back of his mind. He then proceeded to spin an elaborate fable around the fact."

I sighed. "It is a shame that we are not able to take the case further."

"Case, Watson? Case? There is no case. There is merely a procession of bizarre and *outré* events related to us by a stranger, which may or may not have a basis in reality."

"At all events, I propose to take myself to view the premises in question."

"By all means do so, though I fail to see what you will discover of interest there. In the meantime, it is of importance to me that I should finish these notes on the derivation of harmonies in the motets of Lassus."

I therefore took myself off, and proceeded to Belvedere Gardens. No. 23 proved to be at the end of a red-brick terrace, and presented a forlorn aspect. One of the front windows, bare of any curtains or hangings, was cracked, and the paint was peeling from the front door.

Since the house stood at the end of the row, it was a comparatively simple matter for me to make my way to the rear of the building, where I entered the back yard through an unlocked gate. The back of the house was, if anything, more unprepossessing than the front, but it was noticeable that the handle of the back door appeared clean and free of grime.

On a whim, I turned the handle, and to my surprise, found I was able to open the door, which moved easily and silently on its hinges, allowing me to enter the small room that served the house as a primitive kitchen. Though I am well aware that I lack Sherlock Holmes's powers of observation, it was clear to me that this place had been used in the very recent past. There were vague imprints of feet on the dusty floor, and there were signs that the range had been in use not too long before. A half-burned scrap of newspaper bore a date of only two weeks before.

There were few other signs of occupation, and on my trying the door that led to the other rooms of the house, I discovered that it was locked. I was therefore forced to the conclusion that whatever had taken place in this house had taken place only in this room.

I returned to find my friend engaged in looking through the voluminous scrapbooks that formed such a large part of his working tools.

"This case is almost unique in the annals of crime," he remarked, glancing up from a page of newspaper cuttings. "I now recall a similar event in Brussels in 1876, and the one in Baden in 1865, as I mentioned previously, but as far as I am aware, this is the first time that such a thing has occurred in this country."

"You believe there to be a case, then?"

"Indeed I do. Of its precise details, I am as yet unable to say, but we may take it as certain that some devilment is afoot, and that of a strange nature. But tell me, what have you discovered?"

I informed him of the nature of the house and its internal arrangements.

"Indeed, most singular," he commented.

"What, then, are we to make of this funeral ordered for a year hence?"

"For me to answer that, you must inform me of what the neighbours had to say about this house and its inhabitants."

"I feat that I did not talk to any of them."

"Tut, Watson. Was there no twitching of the net curtains, as a stranger walked through Belvedere Gardens?"

"I did not observe."

"And you entered only the kitchen from the rear of the house?"

"That is correct."

"You have been most confoundedly careless about the whole matter, Watson. No matter. Prepare to leave here in twenty minutes."

"Where to?"

"Why, Belvedere Gardens, of course."

"You regard this as significant, then? I have discovered a clue?"

"In the sense that you have discovered some parts of this business which have whetted my appetite, yes. In the matter of clues leading to the solving of this mystery by the forces of justice, no. I must therefore conduct this investigation myself. I can ill-afford to take time away from my investigation of the Duchess of Hampshire's diamonds, but the case is almost at an end, and I believe that even Lestrade will be able to apprehend the criminal with the hints that I shall give him." So saying,

Sherlock Holmes turned to his writing-desk and proceeded to write a few lines on a scrap of notepaper, which he folded and sealed in an envelope before ringing for Billy, our page, with instructions to hand it to Inspector Lestrade personally.

"And now," he announced, entering his bed-room, "I shall make myself ready to visit Belvedere Gardens."

It was precisely twenty minutes after Holmes had announced his intention of visiting the house that we caught a cab to Southwark. I guided Holmes to the back of the house, where I once more entered the back door into the kitchen.

Holmes cast a quick eye over the scene, as if to confirm for himself what I had previously communicated to him, and made for the door connecting the kitchen to the rest of the house.

"It is locked, as I told you," I informed him.

"No matter," said he, and indeed, his ever-present picklocks were already in his hand as he spoke. "Ha!" he exclaimed as the lock sprang open.

The hallway likewise was bare of furnishings and furniture, presenting a dismal aspect.

"Curious," I remarked.

"Let us look further," Holmes answered me, and led the way to the other room on the ground floor. This, too, proved to be a room empty of all furniture, with bare floorboards. "And upstairs," Holmes added, bounding up the bare boards of the staircase. The rooms at the front of the house on the first floor were also bare and empty, but those at the back were furnished, albeit meagrely, with a bed and washstand, and on my drawing my finger across one of the ledges, these rooms appeared to have been used and cleaned relatively recently.

Holmes bent over one of the beds and removed something from the pillow, which he placed carefully in an envelope.

I observed a strange crunching feeling under the soles of my boots, and on closer examination, I discovered that a part of the floor was covered in places with small round globes, less than one-tenth of an inch across. I picked up one of these, and examined it, but could make nothing of it. I therefore picked up a few of these, and folded them in a piece of paper torn from my notebook, and passed them to Holmes for his perusal.

He examined them carefully through his high-powered lens before bringing the paper to his nose and sniffing cautiously.

"Birdseed," he pronounced.

"Birdseed?" I repeated incredulously. "I see no trace of any birds here."

"In that case, Watson, what would you make of this?" he asked me, smiling.

"I cannot tell," I answered. "This is most curious – I have never encountered anything of this nature before. To find a house with but a few rooms and the entrance hall fully furnished, and with some birdseed on the bare boards – it passes all understanding."

"Well, well," smiled Holmes. "Shall we pay a call on the neighbours?"

We left the house by the way in which we had entered, Holmes carefully re-locking the door leading from the kitchen to the hallway, and made our way to the front.

"See, Watson," said Holmes, gesturing with his stick towards the windows of the house we had just left, "there are no curtains in the window, and no sign of habitation from the street. Would you not swear, from this aspect, that the house was uninhabited?"

"I would indeed."

"And now," said Holmes, knocking at the door of one of the houses opposite. "Let us see what we can discover."

The door was opened by a maid, who listened to Holmes's request to talk to the mistress of the house. This personage transpired to be an elderly lady, who regarded Holmes through a pair of thick spectacles.

"Excuse me, madam," Holmes addressed her. "I have a rather delicate question to ask. I am a complete stranger to London, but I am the only nephew – indeed, I believe I am the only relative – of my aunt, who passed away two days ago. I received the telegram this morning, sent by her neighbour, Mrs. Parker, and came from Hampshire right away, together with my friend here."

"I am sorry for your loss, Mr . . . ?"

"Johnson, madam. I apologise for not presenting you with my card, but in the heat of the moment . . . ."

"I quite understand, Mr. Johnson. As I was saying, I am sorry for your loss, but I fail to understand what your aunt's death has to do with me. Do you know of some connection between her and me?"

"No, no, no. It is nothing of that nature, I assure you. My query is a more general one, though of a delicate nature, as I say. It is the matter of the funeral. I have no knowledge of the undertakers in this part of the world, and I was wondering if you had any knowledge of firms who provide these services?"

"My dear husband passed away some years ago, and his funeral was arranged by the firm of Nathaniel Urquhart, whose business is not far from here – on the Kennington Road, in fact."

"My condolences on your loss, madam. Thank you for the information." Holmes bowed slightly by way of thanks.

"However," our interlocutor told us, "if you would like to know more about these things, you should ask over there," and she pointed towards the house from which we had just come.

"Indeed?" Holmes raised his eyebrows.

"Well, it's a strange thing," she went on in a conspiratorial whisper, "but that house hardly ever seems to have anyone entering or leaving it, and as you can see, it is marked as being to let, and appears empty, but there have been at least three funerals from there in the past eighteen months. I am not sure, but I think there may have been four."

"That does seem to be an excessive number," Holmes agreed. "And you have no knowledge of the undertakers who carried out these services?"

"I couldn't tell you that, but it did seem more than a bit strange to me that there should be so many funerals in such a short time."

"Perhaps they were children who had succumbed to some common malady," I suggested. "Diseases such as chicken-pox can be very contagious, and often prove fatal to young infants."

She shook her head. "These were not children's coffins. I had half-a-mind to tell the police about it, but then I said to myself that I was just imagining things. It does seem strange, though."

"I agree that it is more than a trifle peculiar," Holmes confirmed. "I thank you for your information regarding Urquhart. I will take your recommendation. Thank you for your time, and goodbye."

"What in the world did you hope to gain from that conversation, Holmes?" I asked, as we walked away.

"We have been informed, have we not, that there has been an extraordinary spate of funerals conducted from that house."

"But that is impossible," I expostulated. "We have seen for ourselves that no-one lives there."

"Indeed they do not. But we should consider the possibility that they die there, or at least, that their bodies are taken from there."

"I begin to understand you, Holmes."

One aspect of our findings continued to puzzle me until we returned to Baker Street, and I asked Holmes, "By-the-by, what do you make of the birdseed that I discovered on the floor of the room?"

"Oh, that is common birdseed, such as is used to nourish caged birds. There is little remarkable in the seed itself, merely in its presence."

"Caged birds? In an empty house? There were no feathers or any other sign that there might have been a bird in there. At any event, I observed none."

"Then, my dear Watson, I would recommend that you secure the services of a good optician." So saying, he leaned across and plucked something from the back of my right shoulder, which he proceeded to scrutinise.

"What is it?" I asked.

"A feather. I believe it to be a wing feather from a specimen of *Serinus canaria*, the common domestic canary. I can only assume that it escaped your notice as it drifted onto your coat."

I was more than a little crestfallen that I had failed to observe what was clearly an obvious sign that a bird had, in fact, at some time been present in the room. "You are certain it has come from a canary?" I asked Holmes.

"I am as positive as I can be without a microscopic examination," Holmes told me. "The shape of the feather, its colour, and the barbs on the tips are almost conclusive, however."

"But how would a canary find its way into an empty house?" I asked.

"I do not believe that it found its own way. The presence of the food on the floor would seem to confirm that. I fear, Watson, that we are about to find ourselves rubbing shoulders with one of the more detestable specimens of the London criminal. Would you be good enough to reach down the volume of the Index that deals with the letter '*W*', and read for me what you find regarding Edward Wilson."

I perused the scrapbook in question, and under the relevant entry, read out the following words, which had been written in the sprawling and near-illegible hand that Holmes used for such matters, "*Edward Wilson, born –* "

"Yes, yes, Watson," Holmes exclaimed patiently. "The meat of it, the nub."

I read on and reported, "You have written here that he is one of the most vile men plying his trade at present. This is strong language, Holmes."

"Indeed so. I have my reasons for believing this. Read on."

"His offences are such that he has so far escaped the attentions of the police, it would seem."

"So they have, but I have had my eye on him for quite some time now. This may be what I need to arrange the fate for him that he so richly deserves."

"Good Lord, Holmes. You have written here that his business, at least as far as the law is concerned, appears to be breeding canaries, and training them to sing. But you have good reason to believe otherwise?"

"Indeed so. I believe him to be one of the most villainous of all the criminals in London at present. He will stop at nothing to achieve his ends, which are, I believe, evil incarnate."

It was unlike Holmes to use such terms to describe those against whom he had set himself, and I could not help but enquire further.

"Ah, Watson," was his reply, uttered in tones of sadness and compassion. "He preys on vulnerable young women, of the poorest and most defenceless kind. They are shamelessly exploited in ways I do not care to expound upon, and when they appear to be of no further use to him, they are disposed of, brutally, and without remorse. These he also refers to as his 'canaries', and he treats them as if they were indeed beings of a lower standard than humanity."

"He is a man to be avoided, then?"

"On the contrary, Watson, I wish to meet him, and put an end to his activities."

"Why is this villain still at large, and why is he not behind bars?" I expostulated.

"He is damnably cunning, and uses his skills to cover his tracks in such a way that none of his tricks can be traced to him. Young Stanley Hopkins has had his suspicions for some time, ever since I informed the police of Wilson's activities, but even he has been unable to find the proof that would satisfy a jury, and Hopkins is one of the best of the bunch at the Yard. However, this hair that I removed from the pillow in the house, while perhaps not constituting a legal proof, may yet form a strand in the noose that winds itself around Wilson's neck."

"How do you mean?"

"I told you that Wilson cynically refers to the young women whom he exploits as 'canaries'. This is partly a cynical allusion to their caged nature, but also, I have heard it said, that all of them are fair-haired, or blonde, as our French cousins would have it, if not by nature, by artifice. And so," he added, bending to one of the microscopes that graced the table by the window, "this hair, naturally dark, has been treated to give it a fairer appearance."

"So you believe the man who ordered the funeral a year hence from Mr. Nathaniel Urquhart was this Wilson?"

"I believe that to be the case."

"And his purpose for doing such an extraordinary thing? For showing his hand, so to speak?"

"Ah, that is something that at present I have been unable to deduce. There is something confoundedly mysterious here, Watson, and I am unable to determine it."

302

For a few days, I was busy with my practice, and Sherlock Holmes was engaged on other cases, but it was with some excitement that I received a telegram from my friend, requesting me to call on him at the rooms at Baker Street.

"I believe we are to attend another funeral from Belvedere Gardens," he remarked. "We are not invited, but I feel we should at any rate view the cortège as it leaves the house."

"Wilson?" I enquired.

"Indeed so. Word has come to me – through sources that I prefer not to reveal at present – that one of his 'canaries' has departed this life, and he is ready to dispose of her."

I shuddered. "There is something monstrous about this, Holmes."

"I agree."

"But why does he not dispose of the bodies in Whitechapel?" I asked.

"I cannot tell, but I agree with you that this business of carrying them across the river to Southwark seems a deucedly long-winded way of doing his foul business. But come, are you ready?"

We set off on our journey, and paid off our cab as soon as we had crossed Blackfriars Bridge.

"It is best if we proceed on foot from now on," Holmes told me, but failed to provide a reason for this.

We reached Belvedere Gardens and took up our positions opposite the house where we had discovered the birdseed and the other mysteriously furnished rooms.

A hearse, drawn by a pair of black horses, was already standing outside.

"There is no coffin inside at present," I whispered to Holmes. Indeed, not only was there no coffin, there was a complete absence of undertaker's mutes or any other person who appeared connected with the funeral.

"Strange," muttered Holmes. "By whom and for whom was this ordered?"

"It was ordered by myself, for your benefit, Mr. Holmes," came a rough voice from behind us.

I turned to behold a face, the likes of which I hope never to see again. The brow was bestial, beneath which a pair of dark eyes glared, and the lips curled in an animal's snarl exposing jagged and crooked teeth.

I started, and even Holmes seemed taken aback.

"I surprised you there, I think, Mr. Sherlock Holmes," the apparition said, with an unpleasant chuckle. "But I had been expecting you as soon

303

as I was told you had visited my little hideaway." He nodded towards the empty house. "I can see you are still wondering who I am and who informed me of your doings."

"Not at all. You are obviously Edward Wilson, and the woman who told us of the funerals here was in your pay."

The man threw back his head and laughed. "You have me placed to rights," he said. "I'll give you that, Mr. Holmes. But you are mistaken if you think I would pay money to my dear old mother for her work in helping bringing you to meet me. Now, if you don't mind, you two gentleman are going to pay me a visit at my place, and we will have a little talk." He had hardly finished speaking when two roughs came from the shadows, and before Holmes and I had fully grasped what was happening, our arms were twisted behind our backs, and I could feel rope being placed around my wrists, binding them together.

"In you go," Wilson said, gesturing to a baker's van. "We're going for a short ride."

The two bravos pushed us into the closed vehicle, and Wilson presumably acted as driver, or sat with the driver. We could see nothing of the road as we rattled and swayed our way through the streets of London. I started to speak to Holmes, but was instantly checked by a heavy hand on my shoulder and the gruff words, "It'll be better for you if you say nothing. Try to speak again without being told you can, and you'll regret it."

I held my peace, as did Holmes. For my part, I was racked with apprehension regarding our possible fate, but as far as I was able to judge in the semi-darkness that surrounded us, it appeared that he was unconcerned.

After what I estimated was about forty minutes, the jolting and rattling stopped, and the doors of the van were opened. Holmes and I were unceremoniously escorted by our gaolers to what appeared to be a warehouse, where Wilson was already seated behind a rough table. A faint sound of birdsong was audible from a darkened corner of the room.

"So, Mr. Sherlock Holmes," Wilson sneered. "I hear that you have been looking into my affairs, and as you might imagine, since you have the reputation of being an intelligent man, I am somewhat averse to others poking their long noses into the business of my canaries without my permission."

Holmes smiled wanly. "I can quite understand that," he remarked in an easy tone of voice.

"My problem now is how to proceed. Your reputation does not lead me to believe that a financial inducement will cause you to drop your interest in my canaries."

My friend seemed to be seized with a fit of coughing. "You are correct," he spluttered out, in the midst of his paroxysms.

"In that case, I must take measures to ensure that you do not meddle any further in my business, or indeed, the business of anyone else. That goes for your friend here," he added, nodding in my direction.

Holmes, who was still coughing, nodded. To my horror, I heard him say, "I quite understand your position, Mr. Wilson. I would probably feel the same way myself were our positions to be reversed. However, may I trouble you for a trifle?"

"Why not?"

"My handkerchief is in my pocket. Would you permit me – " here his coughing interrupted his speech for a full thirty seconds. "Would you permit me," he resumed, "to have my hands untied so that I might at least be a little more comfortable as regards my throat?"

Wilson laughed, not altogether pleasantly. "See to it," he ordered one of his henchmen. "Slowly, and no tricks," he warned Holmes, as my friend rubbed his hands together, and slowly extracted his handkerchief from his pocket. "Excellent."

Holmes raised the handkerchief to his face, and coughed twice. "Thank you," he said, removing the cloth from his face briefly, before replacing it.

The room was suddenly filled with the noise of the police whistle, concealed in the folds of the handkerchief, which Holmes was blowing with all his might. Before Wilson or his bravos could react, the door crashed open, and four police constables entered, truncheons drawn, with Inspector Stanley Hopkins at their head.

The scuffle which ensued was brief, thanks to the element of surprise enjoyed by the guardians of the law, and Wilson and his men were quickly overpowered and handcuffed. Hopkins himself released me from my bonds, and I thanked him sincerely for his efforts.

"Search the place," Holmes instructed the police-agent. "You are likely to find some canaries, and not all of them will have feathers."

That evening, Inspector Stanley Hopkins called at Baker Street, where Holmes greeted him warmly.

"My congratulations, Inspector, on a remarkably fine piece of work."

Hopkins shook his head. "The credit is all yours, Mr. Holmes," he said to my friend. "We needed you to allow us to enter his premises and search the place. We cannot thank you enough. Over twenty of Wilson's 'canaries' are now free to live their own lives, poor things, and I am positive that Wilson and his men will not see the outside of prison for many years once they have been sentenced."

I was still in the dark. "It is clear that you baited the trap to catch Wilson with both yourself and me," I said, "and that you knew that all this was going to take place."

"I apologise, Watson," said Holmes. "Though I never feared for our lives, I did expect a certain amount of discomfort in the time that Wilson had us in his power."

"But you knew that he would be there to meet us?"

"Of course. Consider the facts, Watson. Though the house was marked as being to let, our friend Nathaniel Urquhart was unable to find any letting-agent, and I was likewise unsuccessful. The notice was therefore a blind, to persuade the neighbours that the property was unoccupied. As you and I discovered, Watson, this was not the case. The place was used by Wilson's 'canaries' to carry out their trade. Their customers would use the back door. You will note that the front rooms of the house remained unoccupied, and all comings and goings were through the rear of the house."

"But the funerals that we were told took place there?"

"Tush. Pure fiction, as I suspected from the first. Wilson's mother . . . ."

"Whom we now have in custody," Hopkins added, "as an accessory to Wilson's crimes. She acted as caretaker and guardian to the 'canaries' who plied their trade from that address. She has already told us that she was installed in the house some months ago, and told to report the story of funerals to anyone who asked about them."

"It was clear to me that no funerals had taken place from that house," Holmes said. "What undertaker would ever have calmly removed a body from an empty house without asking questions? And as you yourself wondered, Watson, if Wilson were to dispose of bodies, why would he take the trouble to take them over the river? Indeed, why would he pay for a funeral? I therefore started my investigations following our visit to Belvedere Gardens with the conviction that that the woman who had informed us of them had been less than truthful in her account. I therefore made enquiries of all the undertaker's businesses in the area, and, as I had expected, there had been no such funerals."

"And then?"

"I had little alternative but to consider that the story was a trap designed to ensnare me. The order for a funeral in one year's time presented to Mr. Urquhart would almost certainly bring the mystery to our door sooner or later. We explored the house, and I am sure that the birdseed and possibly the canary feather that attached itself to your coat were left there deliberately to lead us to Wilson. The account of the false funerals would confirm the suspicions in my mind."

"And then Wilson spread the rumour of another such funeral in order to lure you to the spot?"

"Precisely. I did not, as you saw, go unprepared. Once again, though, I must apologise if the results of my actions caused you any discomfort, or seemed to place you in any danger. I had previously alerted Hopkins, who was waiting with his men in another house, unobserved by you or by Wilson. As soon as we left in the baker's van, he followed at a discreet distance, and stationed himself outside the warehouse to which we were taken, awaiting my signal."

"Remarkable," said I. "You would appear to have anticipated Wilson at every move."

Holmes shrugged. "The credit shall all go to Hopkins here. We were merely the bait, he the hunter who snared the prey."

"Uncommonly good of you to say so, sir," said the police inspector. "We have wanted this villain behind bars for some time now, and I am sincerely grateful to you for your help."

"And I am sure that gratitude is shared by Wilson's 'canaries'," I added. "You have performed a noble service, Holmes."

"However," my friend added, "I trust you will not give this account to your adoring public. The details of the crime are too unsavoury for general consumption."

Even so, I have secretly recorded the details of this case, and will place it carefully at the bottom of my dispatch-box, to be deposited at some future date with Cox & Co. It may be that in years to come, it will be discovered, and felt to be interesting enough to justify publication.

The Mystery of the
Change of Art
by Robert Perret

One of the principal dangers of becoming a practicing physician is that, as soon as one hangs his shingle, he discovers that patients choose the most inconvenient times to be in urgent need of a doctor's care. I hesitate to even mention this, but since much is made of my willingness to abandon, as the accusation goes, my patients to aide my friend, Mr. Sherlock Holmes, I feel it is only fair to observe in turn that the ill, the injured, and the incapacitated never feel compelled to consider the hour when pounding upon my door. Worst of all are newborn infants, who seem to take a puckish delight in entering this world in the wee hours of the morning, preferably in a torrential rain or a blizzard, with not a cab to be found.

So it was that I found myself, having once again facilitated the miracle of birth and been thanked for my pains with a ruined shirt and a mother's gratitude, sloshing ankle-deep up Baker Street, my mack soaked through, in hope of a cup of Mrs. Hudson's formidable coffee and an hour of respite at Holmes's hearth before facing whatever awaited me back at my surgery. I was disappointed to see that Holmes already had an early caller, for there was a beautiful carriage standing at the kerb, with impeccably polished golden accents shining against the black body. The contraption was so flawless that I would have believed this was its maiden voyage into the hardscrabble streets of London.

A coachman stood at attention in the squall as stoically as Her Majesty's own Royal Guards. Up on the first floor, I saw the light of the very fire where I had hoped to dry my feet, flickering and dancing in defiance of the gloomy atmosphere. All of the sudden, Holmes himself was at the window. I thought perhaps he had anticipated my approach, as he had so many of our clients. Instead, I was surprised to see him slash at the window and then hold up the instrument of his assault in order to consider it in the light. He then began to pontificate to whomever his august audience was, there in the study of 221b. It was one of his complexities that he so often evaded public commendation for his efforts, and yet he would seize with relish these opportunities to pantomime for clients. Even I, who had seen my friend perform a thousand such routines, was ensnared in the flourishes of his hands and the drama of his postures.

308

The spell was only broken when a lady, hidden in a high collared coat underneath a smart umbrella, came bursting from the door before me. The coachman expertly bumped me out of her path as he opened the door to the cab. Neither deigned to acknowledge me, but I suppose I looked like little more than an itinerant idler in my sodden state. As the carriage clattered away, Mrs. Hudson called to me.

"Dr. Watson, Mr. Holmes asks that you come in. I would have opened the door earlier and saved you a bout of pneumonia, but the Lady was quite insistent that she not be disturbed."

"My apologies, Watson," Holmes called from upstairs. "Lady Longetine is rather skittish, in the way that all of her type are, and it would have been tiring to regain her candor with a new person in the room. I think she was inclined to put Mrs. Hudson herself out on the street, but a minimum level of decorum prevailed."

"It's none of my concern . . . ." Mrs. Hudson began.

"And yet – " Holmes countered.

"I was surprised you took the Lady as a client. It is a trivial enough matter, even to me. It is not like anything but her pride will suffer, and I reckon that can only improve her disposition."

"It is true that the case itself offers little of interest, but her little trinket interests me."

"Holmes!" I said. "That is hardly a sentiment worthy of you, nor is it fit for the ears of Mrs. Hudson."

The landlady just *tsk*'ed as she helped me shed my outer garments. By the end of the procedure, I was still soaked at the cuffs and shins and left in stocking feet, but was otherwise much intact.

"I'll hang these by the stove," she said.

I entered Holmes's study to find him running a jeweled necklace between his fingers in a serpentine motion, endlessly looping round and round.

"A little sleight of hand I picked up in Morocco," he smiled. "This, of course, was the trinket I referred to."

"Holmes," I declared, "that 'trinket' is worth as much as this flat."

"Hardly," he said, tossing it to me. "It is paste."

"Paste?"

"Hence Lady Longetine's embarrassment. She has worn it proudly at any number of society gatherings. Worse, it is a family heirloom, worn by four generations of Lady Longetine's, and appraised at the time of her marriage. Isn't true love grand?"

"Which means the legitimate article was lost on her watch."

"And she didn't even notice, until the paste stones began to spoil. Look. In the light, they have developed a prismatic sheen."

"Like a pool of oil."

"Beautiful in its own way, except that it proves a forgery."

"I've never heard of such an effect."

"Neither have I. There are a dozen easy ways to confirm a stone is paste. You saw me scratch it against the window. A diamond, or indeed any gemstone, would cut the glass. Paste does not. That proof was for Lady Longetine's benefit. Such an unusual flaw suggests a novel means of forgery, and that is what interests me. Everything else about these paste replicas is flawless, the best I've ever seen. A new hand is at work which is deft at science and art."

"How will you go about finding this new hand?"

"I suppose you are imagining boiling beakers and damning chemical reactions and the like."

"That does seem your forte."

"In a perfect world, I would welcome such a battle of scientific wit and guile, but I fear the next step is rather pedestrian. At some point, the authentic jewels were swapped for the replica. An examination of the Lady's jewelry box is called for, just as it would be with any case of a light-fingered maid. Will you come with me?"

"Of course. But will Lady Longetine allow it?"

"She does not want to be inconvenienced by my investigation, and I do not want to be inconvenienced by her zealous secrecy, and so it has already been arranged that I will examine the scene while she is out, doing whatever it is that society mavens do during the day. It will be a trivial matter to overcome the objections of whatever butler or maid may greet us."

So once again my critics can accuse me of abandoning my patients, if only for a few hours, but having added one new soul to the city this morning I felt I had earned the right to wander a little. As my own clothes were still hopelessly soaked, Holmes lent me a few items from his prodigious wardrobe.

"It is for the best," Holmes said. "Lady Longetine has not revealed her disgrace even to her own servants. I am meant to appear in the guise of an engineer plotting the installation of a personal telephone. You can play the role of my handiest linesman, to whom I am giving explicit instructions."

"Why can't I be a second engineer?"

"Do you know how a private telephone line functions? Can you convincingly sketch the blueprints of a room on first sight? Have you memorized the names of the legitimate telephone agents in case they come up in conversation? No, as a linesman all you need do is grunt disagreeably, carry a toolbox, and watch for my signals."

310

Despite my misgivings I went along with Holmes's plan. To my surprise, when we stepped outside, a workman's cart laden with spools of telephone wire and other bric-a-brac was waiting for us. Holmes hopped into the driver's seat as if nothing could be more natural, and we were off to the Longetine Estate through a gentling sprinkle.

Even as we pulled the cart to a halt, an imperious butler came stomping out of the house, furiously waving us around the side. It took me a moment to realize what the fuss was about, for doctors are always welcomed by the front door. In the guise of tradesmen, we were shunted round to the servants' entrance. When we stepped inside, a startled scullery maid scuttled away without so much as making eye contact.

"Mr. Matthews, I presume?" The butler was addressing us from a door to the main house, set several steps above the servants' work area. "I take it you are not accustomed to clients of the Longetines' calibre?"

"To the contrary," Holmes replied with a rolling lilt, "all sorts are taking to the telephone, sir. Mark my words, there will be one in every home one day."

"Absurd," the butler said. "What does the common fool have to natter on about, and who would want to hear it?"

"You may be right, sir. In any case, a telephone is *de rigueur* for a personage like Lady Longetine."

"Just mind where you park your cart. And wipe your feet. I'll not spend half my day cleaning up after the likes of you."

"Ta, Mister . . . ?

"The name is Goldstone – not that it will be much use to you. I expect this to be our one unfortunate meeting. Follow me to her Lady's chambers."

With that, Goldstone turned on his heel and disappeared.

"There's a pleasant chap," I said.

"No doubt it takes a certain force of personality to withstand the Lady herself."

Goldstone was up the main stairway by the time we entered the foyer. Holmes took three stairs at a time to close the distance. I, lugging a toolbox that weighed at least two stone, resigned myself to ascending at the prescribed rate. By the time I had gained the landing, Goldstone had already returned from where he had deposited Holmes. He turned his nose up at me as he passed as if I had come straight from working in the sewers.

"Never mind that, Watson," Holmes hissed from down the hall. "Come here."

A short hallway opened up into Lady Longetine's chambers, which appeared to be as large as 221b. The mistress of the house was very

311

much present, in that her likeness met my gaze at every turn. A great oil painting, nearly life-size in its depiction, took pride of place. It depicted Lady Longetine in the bloom of youth, posed like a queen, gazing across the Longetine grounds with a beatific look that I feel safe in wagering had never appeared upon her actual face. Around this were a dozen photographs, some posed, some in fancy dress, all seemingly placing her in important company. Littered about were a few pencil sketches, a striking charcoal piece, and several studies in watercolor.

"Make some noise over here," Holmes said, indicating a spot of wall next to a fine cherry-wood end table.

"Make some noise?"

"Bang your tools around, knock on the wall, give the definite impression of manual labor. That should keep Goldstone at bay."

"And you?" I asked, making a production of measuring and remeasuring the wall.

"I will ply my own trade."

Through the passage to the bedroom, which had as many mirrors as this room had portraits, I could see Holmes begin by careful examination of the floor and then the windows. He then stepped to an ornate vanity and produced a vial of powder from this pocket. This he gently dusted over the contents of the vanity's top. He then produced strips of paper that became adhesive when moistened. Running them delicately across his tongue in turn, he took impressions of the dust he had sprinkled. When he was satisfied, he blew the residual powder away and gently opened the Lady's jewelry box. With an expert eye, he quickly appraised the contents, and then he closed it again.

"Well?" I asked when he returned.

"There are exactly two sets of finger marks on that vanity. One a woman's and one a man's. I think it is safe the assume the woman is Lady Longetine."

"Could the man be Goldstone?"

"Perhaps. The rugs only show one set of marks large enough to be a man, while at least three women have recently been in that room. I would hazard that her *boudoir* is off-limits to Goldstone, and the vanity is off-limits even to her maids."

"But if there are a man's finger marks, then couldn't it be Goldstone?"

"More likely to be the Lord of the manor. At the same time, only one of the smaller sets of marks appears directly in front of the vanity, but there are dozens of such impressions about the room. Those I take to be of the Lady herself. Come, Watson."

312

To my surprise, Holmes plucked a silver candlestick from the table beside the chamber door and laid it atop the pile in my toolbox.

"What is this, some vital piece of evidence?" I asked.

"A means to an end, Watson. Shall we?"

Quietly Holmes led the way downstairs, where he proceeded directly to the front door. He knelt down and blew his vial of dust against the inside of the door around the handle. Nodding to himself, he now let out a tremendous cough, and began fiddling with the lock on the door. As an expert lockpick, he surely could have sprung the thing without a creak, but now he was cranking the handle about like he meant to snap it off.

"Hold it right there!" Goldstone shouted from behind us. "What are you doing?"

"Nevermind the rest of it now, just grab the toolbox and run!" Holmes said, throwing the front door open and letting a lump of putty fall to the ground. He dashed off and left me stammering as Goldstone gathered his nerve and stared me down. In a state of utter confusion, I fumbled for the toolbox at my feet and ran after Holmes. As I did, the silver candlestick tumbled free.

"Thieves!" Goldstone called as he chased after me. I had almost made it to the street when a bullet whizzed by my head. I looked back and saw Goldstone at the front door with a rifle. From the way it swayed in his uneasy grip, I could tell he was not used to the gun. He shuffled forward onto the drive in hopes of bettering his aim. The horse drawing our cart roiled when the butler fired his second shot. As he fumbled to reload, I leaped up into the seat and Holmes, already with reins in hand, whipped the startled beast into a brisk trot. We were barely around a bend in the lane when Holmes brought the cart to a halt and hopped off.

"Where are you going? We barely escaped with our lives."

"That's exactly why Goldstone won't expect my sudden return. Besides, the man is no crack shot."

To my consternation, Holmes sprinted back to the Longetine Manor. When he entered the gate, he disappeared from my view. A few moments later, another shot rang out and Holmes came flying towards me. Goldstone stepped out into the lane, cursing the good name of the imaginary Mr. Matthews. He leveled his gun and gave one last blast.

"Tally ho, Watson!" Holmes said as he swung himself up into the driver's seat. With a flick of his wrist, we were off, the furious Gladstone quickly disappearing in the rain behind us.

"What was all of that business?" I asked.

"I was taking the measure of the man, metaphorically and literally."

"Oh?"

"Yes. The finger marks on the jewelry box and the front door, where I had seen him place his hands as he chastised us upon our arrival, did not match. Further, Mr. Goldstone has the distinct amble of a victim of rickets."

"Absurd. I saw none of the hallmark deformities."

"The signs were subtle, I admit, and further I believe Mr. Goldstone takes great pains to hide them. Nonetheless, the nascent angles of *caput quadratum* could be seen about his temples, and the footprints he left in the mud don't lie. My first conjecture would be that the deficiency was congenital, and that a corrective diet was not supplied until after infancy. I suspect we would find that Mr. Goldstone was put into an orphanage at an early age, and from there taken into household service. Besides the signs of a deprived nativity, he demonstrates that unique combination of haughtiness and contempt found only in those lifelong servants accustomed to dining off of their master's silverware. No matter. He was admirable if ineffectual in defending Lady Longetine's belongings."

"From you."

"From what he perceived to be a pair of robbers. If he himself were the thief, it would have been the perfect opportunity to let us go about our business and implicate us for any past crime he may have committed. He may be an ill-tempered lap dog, but he is at least a loyal one."

"So we have cleared him of suspicion."

"Indeed, the whole household, for Goldstone and Lord Longetine are the only men in residence, and the Lord would have little reason to sneak into his wife's jewelry box. Even if he meant to convert the jewels to currency, he surely could have simply taken the necklace at any of a thousand opportunities. More to the point, there were half-a-dozen pieces more valuable at hand, and the Lord would have known that."

"Then we have little to go on. The necklace might have been switched at anytime since the marriage."

"I am uniquely well-versed in the art of counterfeit. This method is new, and so must the theft be."

"So we may yet catch the villain."

"The possibility remains," Holmes replied, a lupine grin stretched taut across his clenched jaw. What seemed to me utter defeat was to him the very scent of the game. He retreated into the depths of his mental process for the duration of the trundle home, and I was left to turn up my collar and lament the sodden cigarettes in my pocket.

Mrs. Hudson met me at the door of 221b as Holmes handed the cart off to a rough looking fellow who seemed to materialize from the shadows when we halted.

314

"Oh, Dr. Watson, this is the second time today you have dripped all over my floor. I shan't be surprised if the boards are warped tomorrow. Nevermind that, your own clothes have dried, and cleaned as much as a soap and brush can manage. You'd best resume your traditional attire. Mr. Holmes has a client waiting."

Keenly aware of the good landlady glaring in my general direction from the heart of her kitchen, I exchanged my workman's togs for my suit, which she had restored admirably, behind the cover of an open cupboard door. I hung the soaked costume up myself and shuffled up to Holmes's parlor with much the posture of a chastised schoolboy. By the time I arrived, Holmes was sat primly in his chair, as if he had been sat there all day pondering the papers and smoking his pipe. In my own chair was an agitated man turning his top hat round and round between his hands. His side whiskers were eccentric but impeccably groomed, and he wore a fine green velvet jacket atop a silk cravat, pinned with some kind of heraldic crest too fine to make out in the gloom.

"My associate," Holmes gestured to me, "Doctor Watson."

"Doctor." The man touched his brow as if to tip the very hat that was dancing in his lap.

"I'm afraid I do not investigate matters of a purely domestic nature," Holmes said. "There are any number of agencies better suited. I know Barker to be a good man and can supply you his card."

"This isn't a simple domestic matter . . . ." The man glanced at me.

"I assure you that Doctor Watson can be relied upon absolutely," Holmes said.

"The drawing was one thing, but as far as it went, it was a perfectly fine hobby for a girl."

"The drawing?" I asked.

"Mr. Reynold's daughter has an artistic bent and has long been sketching about town."

"I would prefer she focused on still-lifes, of course," Reynolds said. "Or even landscapes, but she has always been fascinated by the people of London, and by drawing what she calls 'scenes from life'. She wanders down the shabbiest streets as if that were nothing extraordinary."

"I sympathize with your concerns," I said, "But I quite agree with Holmes. There is little he can do about that."

"I have long since resigned myself to her stubbornness. Her mother is much the same and, to be honest, it is one of her better qualities. I don't want a meek little mouse for a child. That said, we did come to an agreement that she would limit her wanderings to broad daylight, and remain in plain view. That, at least, she has heeded."

"Then how do you expect us to be of service?" Holmes asked.

315

"Her habits have changed recently. Where once she made studies of the common Londoner, street scenes and depictions of the harbor workers and so on, which could be argued to have social and artistic merit, she now draws portraits of rich idlers and heiresses. Worse, she accepts payment for it."

"There's nothing wrong with having an industrious spirit," I replied.

"She is toiling for shillings when she is on the cusp of a marriage that would give her security for life."

"She has a fiancé?"

"No, but she is of age, and there has been definite interest from more than one suitor. I have had more than my fair share of success, gentlemen, and am in a position to see that marries well."

"Perhaps she prefers her independence," I said. "Some do, these days."

"I could provide for that as well, and would if it would make her happy."

"That isn't really independence," I observed.

"Tut, Watson," Holmes said. "The girl resides with her parents, takes her meals at home, relies upon the servants for her needs. This is no radical reformer."

"Yet she gathers coppers," I mused. "After seemingly abandoning her concern for the poor."

Holmes sat far back in his chair and drew from his pipe deeply. A prodigious billowing of blue smoke poured from his lips. He seemed to watch it twirl and climb, to be dashed against the ceiling, before he spoke. "Women often keep their secrets for good reason, though admittedly girls sometimes keep them injudiciously. I shall make a preliminary inquiry, Mr. Reynolds. If I deem that your daughter is in danger, or that there is something rotten in the business, I shall take the case in hand."

"Thank you, Mr. Holmes!"

"Yet," Holmes held up a cautioning finger, "If I find this is a silly nothing, whether on her part or yours, I shall immediately retreat. Such decision will be entirely at my discretion, as well as what, if any, findings I will report back to you. If I tell you there is nothing to it, that is to be the end of it."

"Very good, Mr. Holmes. I trust your judgement completely."

I showed the excitable Mr. Reynolds out before turning the Holmes. "Why take on a new case, one very much beneath you, when we have just begun the other for Lady Longetine?"

"Just as the first tantalizes me on a scientific level, this matter intrigues me on a human level. Besides, it will be an hour's work to decipher the riddle of Miss Reynolds."

As he spoke, Holmes disappeared into his bedroom. Moments later, he returned in crisp suit and tie.

"Whatever are you dressed up for?" I asked.

"Why, for tea at the Meadowlark, of course." He produced a gilt invitation from the mantel.

"What is the Meadowlark?"

"A charming country retreat, the summer home of some ancient duchess or some such. A classic example of Tudor architecture, with all of the modern amenities, of course. Mr. Reynolds' daughter, Emily, has been spotted there, applying her vocation."

"By whom?"

"As he himself indicated, he has been casting his daughter about town in hopes of finding a good match. She is a bit of a celebrity at the moment in certain circles, as all eligible young ladies are in due course."

"That's a bit of a cynical view, Holmes."

"Nonetheless, we are charged with extracting her with a minimum of scandal. Reynolds is going to wire ahead to make arrangements for us as American business prospects out for a weekend at a real English country manor. He assures me it is the perfect camouflage."

"I can hardly pass for American, Holmes, particularly if there is are genuine Yankees present."

"No, but you shall serve quite well as my British secretary. Someone who knows the ins-and-outs of business practicalities here."

"And you?"

"I have had some small practice. We will put it to the test."

As we rode out to Meadowlark, clattering along on one of those rural lines that seems to be maintained almost as a hobby of the locals, I began to seriously wonder about Holmes's mental state. He had been eccentric as long as I had known him, but his behavior at the Longetine Manor had been foolhardy at best. Then to pivot on his heel to this bit of frivolity was most unlike my friend.

As the train made its way up to the station, which was hardly more than a garden shed with an extended roof, Holmes righted himself again, executed a brief series of contortions to limber himself up, and snatched his travelling bag from the shelf above. After I had stiffly levered down my own bag, we stepped down onto the dirt. I had not realized how stale the air in the train had been, but the clean scent of warm soil came as a kind of shock. We had managed to leave the rain behind us and that, at least, was a relief. A little way off sat a landau, the Meadowlark crest

317

painted garishly in gold upon the doors. A pair of ladies were directing the coachman as he secured their luggage at the rear of the vehicle.

"I could not ask for better accessories to our disguise," Holmes whispered to me.

"Accessories?"

"A group of men are, by nature, viewed, however subconsciously, as a kind of invasion. The company of women tempers such instinctive suspicions. Besides, as you yourself have often proved, a beautiful woman is the best distraction, or at least the surest."

His whole body suddenly assumed a new posture and Holmes bellowed out, "Hold on there, friend! Don't forget about us!" It seemed that Holmes's had conjured the ghost of Buffalo Bill Cody, whom we had both seen at the American Exhibition. He sauntered over to the carriage with a kind of movement I would not have thought possible of my friend. Once there, he slapped the back of the unfortunate driver and dropped his bag on the fellow's toes. "See that you find a good spot for my luggage, my good man." He then pivoted on his heel and seized one hand from each of the women. He lifted each in turn and kissed their knuckles with too much familiarity and for far too long. The ladies blushed and playfully batted Holmes away, only to titter to each other.

"I have never been so charmed," said the one on the left. Her dress was covered with elaborate frills of lace, as was her hat.

"May we ask whom we have the pleasure of meeting?" said the other. While at first her outfit seemed much more conservative, upon closer inspection it was studded with black pearls, as was her hair.

"Colonel Raymond Colburn at your service," Holmes said, leading them up into the carriage.

"My sincerest apologies," I said to the coachman as I approached. The man had a grimace of pure spite aimed right at Holmes's back.

"There's no more room for luggage," he spat at me. "You and your friend will have to ride with your bags in your lap."

"I quite understand," I said, stooping to retrieve Holmes's bag. When I tried to hand it up to Holmes, I found him hunched deep in conspiratorial conversation with the two beauties. It was one of life's incongruities that Holmes, who had such little desire for the affections of women, was so apt at ensnaring them. With no help from anyone I fumbled my way into my seat, where I found the view much obstructed by the pile in my lap. Holmes pounded upon the roof, and, with what seemed like an excessive cracking of the whip, we were off.

"Somewhere under there is my man in London, Nigel Greenstreet," Holmes said. "What are you up to under there anyway?"

"There was no more room," I managed before being cut off by the peals of laughter.

"We're in luck," Holmes said. "The girls here practically run the Meadowlark, and they are going to make sure we have a real good time."

"Now, Colonel," chided the one in pearls, "you mustn't say things like that, and certainly not with that tone."

"Just because we are French in our fashion doesn't mean we are French in our behavior," said the other. "We are proper ladies, and you, sir, are going to act like a gentleman."

The four of us sat in serious silence for a moment before the three of them began cackling again.

"Of course, my darling Arietta," Holmes said. "Anything for you."

"As always, they pledge themselves to my sister."

"On the contrary, beautiful Minuet, I fear any pledge to behave myself with you would be tantamount to a lie."

They carried on in this fashion the whole way, and to say it was a relief when at last we arrived at the Meadowlark would be an understatement. The hotel was breathtaking. There were a dozen peaked gables and a dizzying array of pattern work on the exterior. The top floor was completely ringed in glazed glass. When the carriage came to a stop, Holmes clamored out over me to help the ladies down. Again I was left to manage the bags. By the time I had extruded myself from the carriage, Holmes was disappearing inside with one of the women on each arm. Members of the hotel staff had appeared to carry the luggage inside, and mercifully a man in pristine uniform at last relieved me of my burden. Just before whisking the carriage away again, the driver gave me a momentary look of sympathy. At my elbow, then, was a maid.

"You are Colonel Colburn's companion?" she asked.

"Yes. Mister, uh, Greenstreet, of London."

"Very good. I can show you to your room."

The stairway was remarkably constrained and, by the time we had gained the second floor, I was quite glad that I did not have to carry the bags up. While the room was small, it had a commanding view of the hedge maze out back – a view ruined only by the sight of Holmes cavorting with the ladies we had met on the way here, as well as a number of other merrymakers.

The maid had left me with a pitcher of clean water, and after some ablutions and a cigarette, I felt restored enough to face the garden party below. Holmes was looking on as the sisters posed for a sketch by a woman who must certainly be Emily Reynolds. As I approached, Holmes stirred and took me by the arm, leading me a discreet distance away from the other revelers.

"I don't know what you are playing at, Holmes, but this charade is too much."

"I quite agree. I abhor vacuous small talk and empty pleasantries, and if I do not speak to anyone, including you old friend, for at least a week after this has concluded I hope you won't think ill of me."

"You seemed to like it well enough when you had Arietta and Minuet cooing over you."

"Ha!" Holmes said. "Nonetheless, it has borne fruit."

"Yes, I see we have found the young Miss Emily. We hardly needed those women for that."

"No, but I was able to commission a sketch of them, and that has revealed at least three items of interest. Observe for yourself."

I stepped closer to peer over the artist's shoulder. Her depiction of the insufferable socialites was quite good. She clearly had a quick eye and a clever hand. In fact, she had captured something in black and white that I had failed to decipher in life. I stepped back to Holmes.

"Egad!" I cried. "They aren't just sisters, they're twins!"

Holmes sighed.

"With one so fair and the other so dark, I hadn't seen it before," I said.

"Again you are looking at the women when you should be looking at the facts."

"What do you see, then?"

"One: Miss Reynolds labels the drawings with names and addresses. A strange practice when she surrenders the drawing to her clients on the spot, wouldn't you say? And yet she never signs her own name. I have yet to see the working artist who does not sign her own work."

"She is an amateur, despite what her father thinks. You make too much of little things. What else do you see?"

"While her portraits are certainly serviceable, her skill only really shines in her depictions of jewelry."

"What do you mean?"

"I mean she spends more time on their adornments than their faces, and the result is practically schematically perfect."

"So she is better at drawing things than faces. What of it?"

"I find that doubtful, considering that she has spent the bulk of her career drawing people. Moreso, the motive becomes clear in conjunction with the next point."

"Which is?"

"She is using stylographic paper."

"You mean the self-copying kind?"

"Precisely."

320

"To what end?"

"That we know for a certainty."

"We do?"

"Think back, Watson. Where have you seen her work before?"

"Nowhere, before today."

"That is probably true, but not in the sense you mean."

"You are speaking in riddles, Holmes."

"Let me put the question to you another way. Where else have you seen portraiture today?"

"You don't mean Longetine Manor?" I peered at the sketch on the artist's easel again. "Why, I think you may be right, Holmes."

"It is all but a certainty, but remains a conjecture until I hold the proof in my hands."

"We won't be able to show our faces at Longetine Manor anytime soon. Particularly if you still mean to keep the Lady's secret."

"I have made the acquaintance of a score of burglars who might be up to the task."

"Holmes, you simply cannot burgle one of your own clients."

"It would be an easy thing. I took a plastic impression of the lock on the front door."

"I thought that was a ruse to goad Mr. Goldstone. Besides, you let the clay fall to the ground."

"I let the excess fall to the ground. It was as easy to take the impression as it would have been to pretend to do so."

"Perhaps we should leave the matter to Scotland Yard and keep our hands out of shackles."

"A dreary solution, but perhaps Athelney Jones wouldn't make a complete hash of it."

"That's better, Holmes. I'm sure a prison cell would drive you to destruction."

"You have convinced me, Watson. I shall return to the station to wire Jones, while you stick to that copy of the drawing like a stamp."

"Why you? Surely I, as your secretary, would handle such banalities."

"Undoubtedly, but I fear I have been far too effective in ingratiating myself with the Whitshire sisters. If you were to leave me alone with them, you might well return to find me engaged, perhaps twice over. They have no such affection for you."

"What a relief," I groused.

"They are beginning to stir from their perch. I'll be back by dinner."

Before a protest could escape my lips, Holmes had disappeared and Minuet and Arietta were upon me.

"Where has the Colonel gotten to?" Arietta asked.

"We wanted to show him our charming portrait," Minuet said.

"I'm afraid he had to see to some pressing and personal business," I said.

"Oh, dear!" Arietta said. "He is returning, is he not?"

"Quite soon, I'm sure," I said. "In the meantime, I would be happy to be of service."

In response, the sisters simply wandered away. After a long moment of consternation, I snapped to attention when I realized I had already failed to keep an eye on the duplicated drawing. Emily Reynolds had packed up her supplies, and her satchel and easel were propped against the side of the hotel. I chanced to see the girl disappearing into the hedge maze with her portfolio precariously clutched under one arm. If the thing hadn't slowed her down, I might never have seen her at all. Having, by some instinctual means, been deemed beneath the notice of this august company, I easily slipped through the throng and stepped into the maze. The hedges were expertly manicured to be rigidly plumb, and so dense that it was markedly darker and cooler inside. I could hear a gentle rustling ahead and so, as quietly as I could manage, I stalked along the narrow passages.

More than once the path doubled back and Miss Reynolds passed near me, separated by only a thin wall of leaves and branches. I hoped my movements were more silent to her than hers were to me. After what seemed to me an improbably long journey, I found myself at a dead end and, having met no diverging paths for at least a minute, I found that I had lost the sound of her dress dragging along the branches. I cast about for any foothold that might allow to look above the maze, but no such cheat manifested itself. I took a moment to consider the possibilities. Miss Reynolds could be passing through the maze to the opposite side, or she could be progressing towards the garden at the center. For that matter she could be making a rendezvous at any prearranged point within the maze.

Hesitant to fall any further behind in my pursuit, I determined that the garden at the center was the most likely goal, and should that prove false, it was the spot from which I had the greatest chance of pursuing her further. In a moment of pique I tried to push through the nearest barrier in hopes of passing directly through to my destination. The hedge was surprisingly impermeable. Decades of patient horticulture had nurtured a formidable barrier. So I relied upon my sense of direction and moved ever towards the center. With each silent moment that ticked by, I became more sure that I had bungled the entire endeavor. At last, I came to a row where sunlight trickled through and I discovered a gap that allowed a view of the central garden.

Within, I saw Miss Reynolds *tete-a-tete* with a figure turned away from me. They each had their hands on the portfolio and Emily seemed reluctant to surrender it. The man was whispering something to her, to which she gave brief, perfunctory responses. At last, she let the portfolio fall away from her grasp, her stance shouting resignation. I thought that this rogue was somehow blackmailing the girl, but then he cupped her chin and kissed her. I had just laid my hand on the stock of my Webley when she drew the man in with both of her arms. I stepped back from my peephole and waited until I heard movement again. When I resumed my observation of the scene, I saw the two departing from opposite sides, the stranger going away and Emily returning to the hotel.

She stopped at the threshold of the maze and turned to watch the man go. He did not so much as pause. Even I could read the looming heartbreak for Miss Reynolds. I made every effort to pursue the man to the far side of the maze, but he had long departed by the time I found the path through. I looked out upon the rolling hills as the sun hung low in the sky. I was ill-equipped to go out onto an unfamiliar countryside in the dark. With no small trepidation, I returned back through the maze. Perhaps having gained some understanding of its design, I soon found myself at the Meadowlark again, with the warm light of the dining room beckoning.

I had crossed the lawn and was just about to step inside when I was seized from behind. My good arm was pinned behind my back and my other hand clawed helplessly at the immobile elbow crooked round my throat. As I was being dragged back into the darkness, I felt my revolver dangling uselessly against my side. My heels scrabbled against the grass, failing to find any purchase. In a last fit of desperation, I threw all of my weight to one side. My assailant simply seemed to disappear from under me and I found myself on the ground. Quickly, I pushed myself up on my knees and went for my gun, which was now missing completely. I heard a familiar laugh.

"I'll admit I expected a warmer welcome, Watson," Holmes said, my Webley dangling by the trigger guard from a wagging finger.

"What do you mean by attacking me from behind like that?" I said, snatching the gun back.

"I do apologize, old friend, but the moment you were seen, we would have been committed to see the dinner through."

"We aren't going to the dinner?" I said, the aromas coming from the dining room now swelling around me and causing a hollow ache in my stomach.

"No need, thankfully."

"Oh."

"As I suspected, in these kind of bucolic hamlets, the telegraph operator and the postman are one and the same."

"What does that have to do with roast capon and saddle of mutton?"

"A postman is better than a vicar for knowing every last tittle of information in a village. It seems there is a recent immigrant by the name of Mr. Nigel Horne, who has set up shop in the old tannery."

"Indeed?"

"The postmaster finds him to be a most remarkable specimen in that he has received no correspondence of any kind."

"Surely any number of men move out into the countryside for a bit of solitude."

"Yes, but this man was quite particular in directing the postmaster to hold all mail rather than deliver it."

"Yet he has received no mail."

"Nor ever even inquired."

"Seems a strange way to run a business."

"Hmm. The locals are not sure what he does, but they are emphatic that he is no tanner."

"What does this Mr. Horne do then?"

"I mean to see for myself. As to the results of my telegraph, I'm afraid I owe Inspector Jones a new hat. It seems Lady Longetine reacted with some vigor when he asked for the sketch of her drawn at the Meadowlark. She expressed, in no uncertain terms, that Inspector Jones had best forget whatever I had injudiciously revealed to him, which of course was nothing but the very word that earned him a beating. That confirmed the locus of the crimes, and of course we already suspected the means. I still expect that a judge will find the Lady's charcoal sketch most interesting."

"So Miss Reynolds' sketches are being used to create fraudulent replicas, by her accomplice who I followed out to the woods?"

"Where a mysterious Mr. Horne abides for no apparent reason."

"You are suggesting this Nigel Horne's enterprise is set up to rob the guests of this one isolated hotel? That is madness surely? How could he not be caught?"

"I suspect he thinks his counterfeits to be flawless. Besides, hotels are the perfect feeding ground for criminals. The guests come and go, they are distracted, all of their routines are disrupted, and things like jewelry can easily be lost along the way. In this case, he even provides a substitute so that any suspicion is allayed until later. Weeks in the case of Lady Longetine, perhaps forever in others. Remember, she suspected nothing until the forged jewels began to disintegrate. If not for some minor inconsistency in his method, she would have never known."

"This is enough for Scotland Yard to make the arrest, surely."

"Lady Longetine will not register an official complaint, and I doubt any other victim will either. Their reputations are worth more to them than a given valuable, which is exactly the arbitrage Mr. Horne is counting on. In a way he allows his victims to blackmail themselves with vanity and pride. Besides, I came to see his process and I mean to do it."

As good as his word, Holmes immediately set off as I hurried to keep pace. The moonlight did little to penetrate the hedge maze, and yet Holmes passed directly through as assuredly as if he had nurtured the thing into being himself.

"This horticultural puzzle was designed to deceive," Holmes said in answer to my silent ponderings. "Yet even the best gardener cannot hide the scars of decades of wanderers wearing paths into the ground. The greatest erosions and most elaborate restorations are as good as signposts."

I could hardly see the ground in the moon cast shadows myself, but there was no arguing with the way Holmes dissected the maze in minutes.

"Ha!" Holmes barked when we arrived at the rolling hills lying before the trees. "A clever man indeed. Had he always followed the same path, he would have worn a tell-tale trail. Here, you see the faint traces of at least two comings and goings. More have surely been lost upon the resilient heath in the recent rains. No matter, but one trace is all I need."

Following some track that was invisible to me, we crowned the hills and passed through the trees. The stench was the first sign Holmes was on the right track. It was not that of a tannery, but rather a chemical scent, almost industrial in nature. When Holmes paused for a moment and cocked his head, I was sure he had discerned many of the components of Horne's concoction already. We continued until the trees ended. A distance away, we saw a ramshackle building, the stonework and large timbers largely intact, but the thatch work long since collapsed. There was a faint flickering visible through warped wooden shutters. Holmes crept up to peer in. I followed on his heel with my Webley at the ready. More than once a villain had gotten the drop on us in his own lair. Holmes seemed transfixed, yet for me there was little but dwindling fortitude and the oblique sounds of a craftsman inside at his trade. As the moon crossed overhead, I slumped against the wall, and finally sat with my gun across my knee. At some point I must have dozed, for Holmes was gently shaking my shoulder and gesturing that we should retreat into the woods. The pink fingers of dawn were just peeking over the canopy.

"Remarkable," Holmes whispered. "Mr. Horne is truly an artist in his own right. It is a shame he has abused his talent thusly."

"We have him dead to rights, at least," I yawned.

"I'm afraid the law is ill-equipped to understand the implications of his laboratory, and he burned the incriminating diagram upon completion of the piece. At the moment, all he has upon him is a bit of costume jewelry."

"What was the meaning of our vigil then?"

"It was a master class in forgery. I've learned as much from observing Mr. Horne for a night as I might have in a year of study on my own. It is a rare pleasure for me to be the student."

"My aching bones beg to differ."

"Fear not, Watson. The criminal will be in shackles within the hour. In the meantime, let us return to the hotel."

Holmes surprised me by making his way out to the road rather than trailing Mr. Horne directly.

"We know precisely where he is going and I mean to be there first," Holmes said.

"Surely this is the longer route."

"Yet quicker nonetheless."

We stepped out of the trees to find a sour-looking man with a rifle across his lap sitting atop a sturdy hay wagon.

"Constable Juno, I presume?" Holmes said.

"So you are the famous Mr. Holmes," the man spat from beneath a bristly mustache. "I don't much appreciate you stirring the pot around here. And without so much as a by-your-leave either."

"My apologies, sir. I left word for you at the earliest opportunity, as soon as I knew there was a situation worthy of your attention."

The constable seemed to ponder for a moment before spitting in a great arc towards the far side of the road.

"We don't have time to waste," Holmes said. "If you do not find this morning's endeavor to be worth your while, I shall gladly stand you a few rounds at the Meadowlark."

Juno made some kind of clicking sound deep within his jaw. "Get on."

Holmes instructed the country constable to park his wagon round the far side of the hotel. Quietly, we slipped through the servants' entrance and had the room opposite the Whitshire sisters unlocked. All of the guests were at breakfast, and so the guest rooms were completely silent and void. Holmes was peeping through the curtains he had just closed.

"There he is!" Holmes hissed.

Juno took his place at the crack in the window dressing. "All right, Mr. Holmes. You have produced a mysterious figure in black creeping from the maze. You have my attention."

We crossed the room and put our ears to the door. There was a slow creaking upon the main stairway, and then silence for several moments. The next sound was the tumble of the lock across the way.

"He has a key!" Juno whispered.

"A trivial matter for a criminal fabricator of his talent," Holmes said. "Give him a few moments more."

Holmes ticked off the count to three with his fingers and then we burst forth into the hallway. There, framed in the open doorway as pretty as a picture, was Nigel Horne with his hand in Minuet Whitshire's jewelry box. Quickly he yanked the genuine necklace out and tossed in the replacement before frantically glancing about the room. He turned and began wrenching at the window.

"Please, Mr. Horne," Holmes said. "It is a sheer three story drop to the ground. You may not survive it, and you surely won't escape that way."

Horne turned to face his captors, calm seemingly washing over him.

"This is it, then?" he asked.

"There are but few criminals who have impressed me, Mr. Horne. I count you among them."

"And yet it will be the shackles for me."

"The gallows more likely," Holmes said.

"You can spare the girl," I said.

"What girl?"

"Why, Emily Reynolds!"

Horne snorted. "Why bother."

My fists were clenched and my aspect red. "Is she not dear to you? You certainly kissed her thusly."

"I kissed her because I could. She is in my power completely."

"*Was* in your power," Holmes corrected. "How?"

"She is a naive idealist, blind to the ways of the world. She was so eager to help the downtrodden, particularly a fellow artist. It was easy to win her affections with my tragic story." Horne smirked at me.

"Which was?" I managed through clenched teeth.

"Mr. Horne was a jeweler, or at least a jeweler's apprentice," Holmes said. "That much is clear from his craft. He enjoyed an education far beyond his means, as is evidenced by his art, his manners, and his dress. He was cast aside unfairly, and by a young woman, perhaps a fiancée, as is evidenced by his self-loathing, and his choice of enterprise."

"Simple," Horne sneered. "I thought you were meant to be clever, Mr. Holmes."

"So you compromise Miss Reynolds and then use her disgrace against her?" I said.

"Steady, Watson," Holmes said. "Mr. Horne is playing a bigger game. You involved Miss Reynolds in one of your thefts, knowingly or unknowingly on her part, and then used that to drive a wedge of control deeper and deeper."

Horne's smirk faltered a little.

"I'm guessing you told her a tale of a family heirloom, a wedding band that was both sentimentally and monetarily irreplaceable to you perhaps. Maybe that was even true?"

Horne's mouth was flat now.

"In any event, it was the perfect romantic wound for Miss Reynold's to heal, and it allowed you to impress her with your own, not inconsiderable, artistic skill. Now you were in control, and you drew her further and further into illegal behavior, inch by inch, until she was fully enmeshed in your scheme. You used her good nature and independence to turn her against her own father, her own art, and her own best interests. Like a snare, everything she did just allowed you to squeeze tighter."

"That's right, I've had my fun with her. Let the law take its course, and let the devil take me," Horne said to a very befuddled Constable Juno.

"I appreciate your discretion, Mr. Holmes," Emily Reynolds said. To see her now, perched upon the chaise at Baker Street, restored in affect and appearance, was to appreciate how much she had wilted in the shadow of her oppressor.

"It was a personal satisfaction to me to catch the man in the act, and thus strike him where it would pain him the most, in his twisted pride. Unlike his other victims, the Whitshire sisters reveled in the infamy and were delighted to allow a case to be brought against the man. There was no need to draw you into it."

"I'm sorry to be so much trouble to everyone," Emily sipped her tea. "I feel like such a fool."

"There, there," I said. "It is a sad fact that people of conscience are always vulnerable to people without conscience."

"Who was Nigel Horne? Why did he torment me?"

"The name is an alias, of course. Some wearisome afternoon I may delve into my lumber room and tease out his particular identity from my

328

library, but for now it suffices that he was a man at loose ends and apparently without recourse to his specialized trade."

"Why ever not? For all of his horribleness, he was truly gifted."

"While I hesitate to guess, I do find his cruelty towards wealthy young women to be suggestive, but not definitive. I suspect that you were caught in a reenactment of sorts, though perhaps with the roles reversed. Mr. Horne was a man fixated on the past. My polar opposite in a way, and that was my blind spot."

"How do you mean, Holmes?" I asked.

"After observing him at work, I now believe that his original vocation was in fact art restoration. What I took to be a new technique was in fact a very old one. It seems he took the art of Roman dichroic glass and applied it to paste."

"I'm afraid I don't follow, Mr. Holmes," Emily said.

"Nor I," I said.

"Another test for paste is to examine the reflections within a jewel," Holmes explained. "A natural gemstone, once cut, will reflect like a kaleidoscope, each face in a different direction. Paste, even when cut, does not share this property. All the reflections will be aligned."

"Remarkable!" Emily said.

"And useful in detection for those times you can't handle an item directly. However, the ancient Romans discovered that integrating gold powder into glass restores the kaleidoscopic effect. As you know, I spent a few years knocking about the British Museum before I found my calling. That collection holds several remarkable examples. Horne must have learned this old trick during his apprenticeship and then hit upon the idea to apply it to paste. Impurities in his gold dust interacted poorly with the lead oxide and potassium carbonate, causing a visible separation."

"Too clever for his own good," I said.

"At every step," Holmes nodded.

"What have you told my father?" she hesitated.

"Nothing at all. I was quite clear that I would only give him such information as was needed to secure your safety."

"Without calling upon him to pay you, which would betray my secret, I'm afraid I can only give you what little Nigel left of my earnings," she produced a small purse.

"I'm sure you will meet people during your artistic rambles through the city that need that more than me," Holmes said. "Another client will be padding my coffer presently."

"Perhaps I might offer you a drawing, then?"

"There are quite enough portraits of me in *The Strand*."

"What of your beloved Baker Street?"

I was surprised to see Holmes retreat wistfully into himself for a moment. "I would be glad to see it."

As I escorted Miss Reynolds out, I warned her, "Mr. Holmes is most particular about details. Most particular."

When I closed the door I noticed the post had arrived. As had become usual, there were two envelopes, one ivory, another a deep speckled grey. Each was perfumed, and each was written in an eccentric yet undeniably feminine hand. It seemed both Arietta and Minuet Whitshire remained quite charmed with Holmes, even after his ruse had been revealed. If anything, discovering the famous detective's true identity only whet their appetites.

"Are you quite sure neither of them has the slightest interest in your biographer? I am a war hero, you know, and a bit of a sensation in the literary world."

"Take them both, as far as I'm concerned," Holmes embraced his violin and began sawing aimlessly. "As for me, I've been thinking of a Continental retreat. Do you believe two or three years would be long enough to throw them off my scent?"

The Problem of the
Bruised Tongues
by Will Murray

It is the rarest of occurrences when I enter a mystery before my esteemed friend, Sherlock Holmes, has stepped into the picture. More commonly, I am drawn into his adventures – not entirely against my will, I readily confess.

On the morning of October 31, 1902 – mark the date – I was summoned to the home of Nathan Chalmers, who had been discovered in his bed, unresponsive. I hurried over to Chalmer's residence, where I was greeted by a flustered housekeeper, who shakily told me, "When Mr. Chalmers failed to present himself at breakfast, I took the liberty of knocking upon his bedroom door. Receiving no response after numerous vigorous entreaties, I became concerned for his welfare and so took the liberty of entering. The poor man would not wake up. Since you are his physician, Dr. Watson, my first thought was to summon you."

"I am sure that it is well that you did so," I replied hastily as we mounted the stairs to the bed chamber.

The flustered maid stood outside the room while I entered and began an examination. It proved to be very short indeed. I had only to observe the pallor of my late patient and touch his brow and cheek to determine that he had been deceased for some hours.

Covering his face with the bed quilt, I turned gravely to the woman and enquired, "Had Mr. Chalmers been unwell of late?"

The maid was staring, her thin face stark. She did not appear to be of very high intelligence, but the meaning of my respectful gesture struck her with great force.

Her thick voice was a croak. "Not in the least, Dr. Watson. Not in the least. He – he has departed?"

"Sometime in the night," I told her.

Although I last examined Chalmers three months ago, he had been in exceedingly good health at that time.

Turning her face away while attempting to get hold of her trembling arms, the poor maid replied as she stared up at the ceiling blankly, "Nor had he given me any reason to question his vitality."

"Inasmuch as this is an unattended death, I must summon the coroner before the body can be removed from this house."

Shaking, the poor woman pointed towards the telephone stand in the hallway and withdrew.

The medical examiner arrived within twenty minutes. He threw back the quilt, observing the dead man's set features critically. Chalmers' eyes were shut, his expression composed. His mouth lay open, but not excessively so.

The coroner moved the man's head back-and-forth, evidently to determine if *rigor mortis* has set in and to gauge how long the deceased had been dead.

The head moved easily, but when the open mouth moved toward the morning light streaming through one window, a peculiarity was revealed. Sight of it caused the medical examiner to gasp.

"What is this?" he blurted to himself.

I had only a glimpse of what he had clearly seen, perforce I drew nearer to observe the yawning cavity of the open mouth, for the jaw dropped open under the coroner's manipulations.

The poor man's tongue had protruded as far as his bite, and the tip of it was as blue as if it had been bruised. It was a distinct blue against the dull enamel of his teeth.

Seeing this, I remarked, "I have never heard of a human tongue displaying signs of bruising."

"Nor have I," admitted that medical examiner. "I did not think such a thing to be possible," he added.

"I daresay it is a rare sight," said I.

"Grotesque," snapped the coroner. "Nothing less. And fitting for a Halloween morning."

I produced a tongue depressor from my medical satchel and offered it. The man accepted the tool wordlessly and used it to press down on Chalmers' tongue, while simultaneously prying the jaws open. I assisted insofar as shining the beam of a pocket torch into the dead cavity.

Only the tip of the tongue showed blue. There seemed to be no injury, no laceration, no abrasion. The man had not bitten down on his tongue in a death agony, as sometimes happens. There was absolutely nothing to indicate what had discolored the member.

The medical examiner pried open the lids. The eyes were thus examined. There was nothing remarkable there, just a glassy sheen common in the newly dead.

"Most peculiar," said he. "I have attended many deaths, but this symptom is out of my range of experience."

"It's new to me as well," I confessed. "What do you make of it?"

The coroner was a long time in replying. "I can make nothing at all of it without going more deeply into the matter. But I am wondering if this might be a freak occurrence worthy of your good friend, Holmes."

I was taken aback, admittedly. I blurted out, "Do you suspect foul play?"

The man turned to me and his expression was one of chagrin. "I only suggested that this may be a puzzle worthy of a greater brain than my own."

"Well, if you are so firm in your opinion, I will summon him, if he deems the matter worthy of inquiry."

"Well, tell him I am the most senior man in my field in all of London, and this is beyond my understanding."

I attempted to ring Holmes, but received no answer. Reporting this to the medical examiner, I said there was no telling if Holmes was out for a stroll or off on some fox-and-hounds affair of his own.

"In that case," said the official, "I must have the body removed to the morgue. Let us hope that Holmes returns in time to peer into this man's mysterious mouth."

At that, I took my leave.

It was evening before I caught up with Sherlock Holmes.

I found him in his usual preserves, and at first he seemed abstracted to the point of disinterest as he puffed way at his briar pipe, filling the room with the bluish smoke of black tobacco.

Beside him lay a calabash pipe unfamiliar to me, and next to it a small brass dish in which lay a cold bit of dottle, presumably knocked from the bowl of the pipe. The unburnt plug of tobacco was crumbled into the ashy remains of the rest. A scattering of slobber next to a pipe tool suggested that the bowl had been scrupulously scraped clean.

I have barely begun my recounting of the matter when Holmes cut me off and snapped, "Men die in bed every day. The fortunate ones at least. You say this fellow was a patient of yours?"

I nodded patiently. It was a patience that I did not keenly feel. "Nathan Chalmers. Not quite fifty years in age, healthy as the proverbial horse. An unlikely candidate to pass in his sleep."

"And yet he did," said Holmes. "Would that we be so fortunate in our own hopefully distant futures."

Sherlock Holmes's countenance was a severe mask, his austere grey eyes unfocused, as if attempting to peer into another world – the world perhaps of pure and untarnished mental machinery. For I could see that he was focused on another problem than the one I was attempting to lay before him.

Bluntly, I demanded, "Holmes, have you been engaged on another matter?"

He nodded. "One has been brought to my attention. A most puzzling case. I do not yet know what to make of it."

"Perhaps the one I have in mind pales in significance against the one that is already on your plate," I averred. "Perhaps it must wait."

As if half hearing my words, Holmes murmured, "Perhaps, perhaps . . . ."

"It is just that the medical examiner requested that I make clear to you that he had never seen such a thing in all of his professional years."

Holmes waved my statement away with a careless gesture. "There is nothing new under the sun, Watson. Each man rediscovers what those who came before him first uncovered."

"No doubt," I said. "But a bruised tongue seemed to me to be to rise to the level of a mystery."

My words did not appear to immediately impinge upon Holmes's consciousness, so deeply was he immersed in his own problem. I was in the act of turning to go when his eyes seem to spring back into clarity, as if taking his notice of his surroundings in earnest. His head lifted and his gaze locked into mine.

"Would you repeat that, Watson? I am not certain I heard you properly."

"I merely remarked that the deceased was found to have a protruding tongue whose tip was an unusual blue color."

Those grey eyes were snapping now. His sere features swiftly shook off the fog of a restive night and deep contemplative thought.

I was shocked by the pointedness of his next question, not to mention its essential character. "What color blue?"

"I beg your pardon?" I retorted, somewhat taken aback by Holmes's sudden vehemence.

Impatiently, he said, "Was the blue the color of a robin's egg, or the hue of an unclouded sky? Quickly, Watson! Do not ponder it too long. Give voice to your initial impression. There are many shades of blue, both natural and unnatural. What shade was this?"

It was not something to which I had given any consideration prior to this. I hesitated. "Why, I would judge it to be on the order of an exceedingly pale blue."

Holmes was rising from his chair. An eagerness seized his countenance. It was as if a fox was concentrating all of its being on what lay before it.

"Come, come, Watson. Name the exact shade of blue! Out with it!"

"Why, I would judge it to be in an Egyptian Blue."

334

"Are you certain?"

"As certain as memory would permit certainty. I was so aghast at the sight I did not attempt to classify the exact coloration. It did not remind me very strongly of a bruise blue, nor did it have any purple or green attributes. It was if the tip of the tongue had been dipped in dye."

"It was not a Prussian Blue?"

Irritation coming into my own tone, I responded, "I have already asserted that it was closer to an Egyptian Blue. Why do you press this point?"

"Because," replied Holmes calmly, "before you entered this apartment, I was engaged in a problem. The problem had to do with a man named Arthur Chambers. Chambers was found dead late last night. He was at his writing desk slumped over. There was not a mark on him, Watson. Not even a bruise upon the forehead that had forcefully encountered the ink blotter. Yet when he was examined, it was found that the tip of his tongue was exceedingly blue. I have had the opportunity to examine it myself, and I can attest to the exact shade. It was a deep Indigo. Nothing less."

"My word, Holmes that makes two men found in identical circumstances!"

Holmes shook his head violently. "No, no, certainly not identical at all. One man discovered at his writing desk, the other in his bed the following morning. There is nothing identical about either circumstance, except for the matter of the tongue. And the tongues in question were not identical either. Could there exist two shades of blue farther apart than Indigo and Egyptian Blue?"

"Two dead man found within hours apart with the tips of their tongue discolored blue strikes me as virtually identical," I retorted.

"Similar, I grant you, Watson. But not identical. You know better to that use the word improperly."

I was becoming agitated at my friend's brusk manner. But his next words soothed my rising wrath.

"Watson, as you know, I have sometimes questioned you with asperity, but today you are a godsend. I have been up half the night pondering this question without results."

"I rang you up earlier this morning."

"I seem to recall the telephone ringing, but I was too absorbed in thought to heed it any mind."

"Had you answered," I pointed out, "you might have spared yourself some wasted effort, for only now are you learning that this matter of yours is assuming a greater significance. My only question is, what does it portend?"

Holmes was striding towards the door, where he put on a coat and hat. "It portends, Watson, a visit to the London morgue. Are you up to the rigors of such a visit?"

"I am undeterred by the prospect of dead bodies," I replied coolly.

"Capital. Then be good enough to follow me. We are going to compare tongues."

"I beg your pardon?"

"Of course, I do not mean our own, for Mr. Arthur Chambers is also reposing in the London Morgue. No doubt the two men can be found in adjoining compartments."

London's great morgue was not unfamiliar to us. Holmes and I had visited it more than I care to recall. It was a cool, dank foreboding place. The Chief Medical Examiner, whose name was Curray, welcomed us in his rather dour manner.

His smile was on the grim side, but it was welcoming, even if it was not noticeably warm.

"Ah, Mr. Holmes! I assume you are to here to examine the remains of Mr. Nathan Chalmers."

"And Mr. Arthur Chambers. Would you be so good as to lay them out side by side for us?"

The medical examiner looked momentarily nonplussed.

I intruded by saying, "Evidently, you were not informed that the late Mr. Chalmers was discovered with a discolored tongue."

"I will speak to my associates about the oversight," he replied shortly. "But first I will make the arrangements you request. Be so good as to wait here."

While we waited, I asked Holmes, "Do you imagine that Chalmers and Chambers were acquainted in any way?"

"I imagine nothing of the kind. I prefer to leave such a rash conclusion unjumped upon, as it were."

Holmes appeared irritated. I suspected he had put so much effort into mentally masticating the problem of the first dead blue tongue that when I arrived with a second example, he was having difficulty tearing his mind away from his original train of thought. I had no doubt that I'd brought unwelcome tidings, but Holmes is a man who likes to reason out his own problems by himself in the austere solitude of his brain.

When the two corpses had been arranged on dissection tables side-by-side, we were called in.

Having already familiarized himself with the tongue of the late Arthur Chambers, Holmes went immediately to Mr. Chalmers and used a steel implement to examine the tongue, as well as the interior of the mouth. He was at this some time.

336

When he straightened, Holmes said, "You are correct, Watson. My apologies for doubting you. This is an Egyptian Blue."

I nodded my head in recognition of the apology.

Then Holmes went to the other dead man and, using a forceps, pulled out the flaccid tongue and showed that it was clearly a richer shade of blue.

"What would you call this hue, Watson?"

"Indigo."

"What does Indigo suggest to you?"

"Various subtropical plants yield Indigo, such as woad and Dyer's Knotweed."

"And Egyptian Blue?"

"Natron, such as the ancient Egyptians employed in the course of their mummification procedures. More commonly called sodium carbonate. But what do the two distinctly different shades signify to you? Murder? Poison?"

"Without a doubt both, but there is a third element present."

"Yes?"

"Experimentation!"

With that startling word, Sherlock Holmes fell silent. He examined the bodies for marks and other clues, but found nothing. At least, he offered up nothing.

Grim of face, Holmes turned to the medical examiner and said, "Be on the watch for more such tongues."

The man became aghast of expression. "Do you suspect a plague of some sort?"

"A plague, most definitely. But a man-made one. A plague of poison. Exactly what motivates the author of these outrages is at this point obscure. Perhaps an examination of the Chalmers residence will unearth something interesting."

As we left, I asked Holmes, "Had you examined Arthur Chambers' living quarters for traces of poison?"

"Thoroughly," replied Holmes. "Yet I found nothing. Perhaps the Chalmers domicile will yield something more tangible."

"Will you inform Lestrade of your findings?"

"I have no doubt that the medical examiner is doing exactly that at this moment. I would not be surprised if Inspector Lestrade beats us to the Chalmers house."

It was exactly as predicted. I was not in the least bit surprised. Inspector Lestrade was already questioning the housekeeper when we arrived at the Chalmers' modest home in Earls Court.

337

The woman in question answered our knock and, by all appearances, was even more flustered then she had been during the difficult morning.

"So it is you again, Dr. Watson?"

"Yes, and I have brought my friend, the esteemed Sherlock Holmes."

From inside the dwelling came Lestrade's sharp tones. "Mr. Holmes! Is that you? Enter, please."

The maid permitted us to go inside and we made our reacquaintance with Inspector Lestrade of the Yard.

"I have been questioning this woman, but to no special conclusion," he said solemnly.

"Will permit me to look around the residence?" asked Holmes.

"As you wish, Mr. Holmes."

Sherlock Holmes addressed the flustered housekeeper and asked, "Take me to your late employer's store of tobacco."

The woman blinked. "Why sir, Mr. Chalmers did not take tobacco in any form."

Holmes seem slightly taken aback by this declaration. "Are you certain?"

"Quite certain, sir," the woman said levelly. "Why, you have only nearly to take a turn around his study and have a sniff yourself. It is as fresh as Surrey air."

Not being one to take a statement at face value without investigation, Holmes moved about the first floor, his sharp nose lifted like that of a sleuth hound, finally arriving at the late Chalmers' study.

After sampling the air with twitching nostrils, Holmes examined the man's desk and bookshelves. All seemed in order. It was exceptionally neat and tidy.

Turning to the woman, Holmes demanded, "Did Mr. Chalmers avail himself of his writing desk last night?"

"Yes, he wrote letters before he retired. He directed me to post them in the morning, but owing to his sudden demise, I did not get around to it till this afternoon. Not that that matters a jot now."

"Had he any known enemies?"

"Not known to myself, sir," replied the housekeeper.

Holmes frowned. "It was the same with Chambers. Only Chambers smoked a pipe. I had expected to discover the same with Chalmers. Or at least that he indulged in the odd after-dinner cigar."

Inspector Lestrade spoke up, giving voice to the thoughts rising in my own mind. "Is it your theory that both men were done away with through tainted tobacco?"

338

"It was one of my theories – now discarded, I admit frankly," replied Holmes.

I spoke next. "It is a sound theory, if I may say so myself. For a man's tongue to be so severely discolored at the time of death suggests that the appendage came into contact with a virulent poison."

Holmes shook his head furiously. "Not so virulent that the victims succumbed immediately after coming into contact with the agent of death. Otherwise, we would discover said agent. Instead, there is nothing." Disgust tinged his last utterance.

I could scarcely believe my ears. "What are you saying, Holmes? That you are utterly baffled?"

"No," said Holmes tersely. "I am stating what I know to be the facts in the matter. Had food or drink been responsible for either man's demise, it would have stood at hand. Were tobacco the cause, the pipe or cigar would be an evidence. It is absolutely clear that Chalmers did not smoke. The fact the Chambers did is no longer of significance."

My good friend was clearly frustrated. I could hear it in the sharp edge in his voice. He had given deep thought to the matter of Arthur Chambers during the day and now that that day was exhausting itself, his lengthy ruminations had proven futile. It was common for Sherlock Holmes to arrive at conclusions before all others. But not upon this unique occasion, it seemed.

"Well, it is back to the beginning for all of us," commented Lestrade.

Holmes began pacing, his eyes searching the titles of the books neatly arrayed upon the shelves. I could not tell if he was reading their spines, or merely seeing past them. He was again deep in thought and his nervous energy suggested controlled agitation.

At length, he began speaking.

"The nature of the poison can be narrowed down through autopsy. No doubt it will be. But no poison with which I am acquainted – and I am familiar with virtually all of the devilish cornucopia of murder – fits the salutary problem of the blue tongues."

Lestrade interjected, "I, too, am familiar with most poisons employed to do away with innocent persons," he mused. "And I know of none that will turn the tongue a vivid blue."

With a nearly savage ferocity, Holmes turned on Lestrade and barked, "The organ is not blue. Only the tip. This suggests a poison that acts upon contact, not upon ingestion. Hence my initial suspicion that a common tobacco product has been tampered with."

"Sound reasoning," I remarked.

"Not sound enough," snapped Holmes. He resumed his pacing.

Lestrade ventured, "Could a venomous insect have bitten either man?"

Holmes laughed dismissively. "Upon the tongue? In both cases? Surely, Lestrade, you can do better than that. Why, I fancy Watson here can summon up a better theory."

His hooded eyes turned in my direction, and I rose to the challenge as best I could.

"Let me think," I mused. "A man's tongue comes into contact with his food, his drink, and anything else that he dares to put in his mouth – "

"False!"

I started. Holmes's tone was extreme. I stared at him.

"You disappoint me, Watson. Have you forgotten that tongues also protrude?"

"I have not, for I had not completed my catalog," I countered. "Of course tongues protrude from the mouth, but a sane individual is fastidious about what he brings into contact with the organ of taste."

"Some examples?"

"Perhaps sweets," I suggested. "A man may touch his tongue to some form of dessert before eating, if he fears it to be too sweet."

"Few would," returned Holmes dismissively. "If cherry pie is set before him in, he will either eat it or not, according to his lights."

"What if the food was unfamiliar to him? Say, a candy confection or an exotic fruit."

"If you are suggesting that either man was poisoned by lychee nuts or some foreign berry, I reject your suggestion out of hand." Catching himself, Holmes added, "But I thank you for that suggestion nevertheless."

With that, he lapsed into silence.

Inspector Lestrade and I exchanged glances, and neither one of us had anything to offer.

Suddenly, Holmes asked, "Do you recall the addresses of those letters you posted earlier today?" His eyes were fixed on the hovering housekeeper.

"I may have glanced at them, sir, but I paid the addresses no special heed. I am not the prying sort. Mr. Chalmers' correspondence was his own affair, not any business of mine. I simply posted them as he asked."

Holmes went to the late occupant's desk, and examined the ink blotter minutely.

"Was it Chalmers' habit to write directly upon his desk?"

"Yes, but not upon the blotter's surface. He preferred to stack papers and write upon the top sheets."

Holmes barked, "Show me that stack – what remains of it."

340

"I put it away, sir. Let me fetch it."

Forthwith, the housekeeper brought forth a sheaf of stationery from the right-hand top drawer, and set it down upon the ink blotter.

Holmes lifted the top sheet and held it up to the light. Eyes narrowing, he shifted the blank sheet of paper this way and that, as if attempting to divine something written in invisible ink.

"May I borrow this?" he asked the housekeeper.

"You may keep it, sir, if you think it will be of use in your investigation. You are welcome to it."

Very carefully, Holmes bent the sheet without folding it and kept it firmly in hand rather than place it in a pocket.

"I believe we are done here," he announced abruptly.

"I have some further questions of this good woman," Lestrade said.

"Carry on then, Inspector. I will inform you of my findings, if any."

As we departed, we turned up the street in search of a hansom cab, and I asked of Holmes, "Do you see any significance in the similarity between the last names of both individuals?"

Sherlock Holmes it was so deep in thought I had to repeat my query.

"I have noticed the similarity, Watson. As to its significance, there may be none. I defer judgment on that score. This is an oddly confounding situation. From my study, I am unable to identify the poison or the means by which it was delivered, not to mention the killer's motives."

"What do you imagine that blank sheet of paper will give up?"

"Impressions of the last piece of correspondence Nathan Chalmers wrote in this world."

"Well, let us hope than that it was more significant than a note to the greengrocer."

We failed to find a hansom cab, and Holmes abruptly announced, "I believe, Watson, that I will walk home. I suggest that you do the same."

"Very well. I imagine that you will be working on this matter through the night and wish no company, nor any evening meal."

"You imagine correctly," said Holmes with a trace of coldness that I ascribed to his mood and not any fracture in our friendship.

I went my way, and Sherlock Holmes went his.

"Watson, I am an imbecile!"

"I would hardly agree," I replied civilly.

It was the next morning, and I had dropped around to visit with my friend. Curiosity, as much as solicitousness for his state of mind, motivated me.

341

Holmes was at his briar again. "I have been racking my brain, seeking among the appointments of the victims the source of the poison. In vain. Conceivably because the instrument of murder had been in both cases disposed of in the most clever and I daresay elegant manner."

"I fail to follow, Holmes."

"Come, come, the absence of poison should have proclaimed the truth. I was too focused on uncovering the hidden, to consider the absent."

"Now I am thoroughly confused."

"No poison, nor instrument of delivery, was found because it had been disposed of in a unique manner. The killer is no doubt a fiend in human form. But a fiend who devised a method of murder so ingenious that it nearly caused me brain strain."

I held my tongue. Holmes continued.

"By the careful application of emery dust, I brought out the impressions made upon the blank sheet of paper inscribed by the late Nathan Chalmers. I present them to you, Watson, for analysis."

I took the sheet, and studied it carefully. The method by which my friend had brought out the writing was not unique, but it was certainly novel. Certain words were very clear while others somewhat obscure. I read carefully, but to little profit.

"These appear to be merely scattered, disconnected words," I decided. "I can construct no sense, nor discover any train of thought in these rambling jottings."

"That is because there is none. Mr. Chambers was not writing a letter. But answering questions with unusual brevity."

"I see the word '*yes*' several times. One '*no*'. And another word I might assume to be '*perhaps*'."

"There are also circles and checkmarks," pointed out Holmes.

"What do you make of it?"

"An unknown person or business entity sent Chalmers an unsolicited questionnaire. Chalmers duly obliged by filling it out. More than that we do not know, since we can safely assume that the questionnaire was promptly mailed by the housekeeper."

"So it is a dead end then?"

Holmes responded thoughtfully. "A blind alley, perhaps. For motive remains elusive and the perpetrator unknown."

"And the method of murder as well, I daresay."

Holmes's eyes grew bright. Well did I know that look. It told that he had broken through the impenetrable cobwebs that had hitherto constrained his investigation.

"I fell victim to a simple assumption," he related, "That the tongue is used primarily to taste. But in that I overlooked something so elementary that I hesitate to confess my failure."

"Go on, Holmes," I entreated. "I am eager to hear more."

His bright eyes glanced up and seized my own. "Surely, Watson, you can deduce the truth from the point to which I have led you."

"I confess that I cannot. I remain baffled."

"Well, reason it out, my good man."

"From what point? There are so many."

He puffed at his pipe. "Very well, I will take hold of your restraining intellectual leash and drag you to a conclusion. That it is obvious to me does not necessarily mean that it is obvious. Only that it should be. Consider the questionnaire, Watson. If you had received one from a medical association, what would you do?"

"Why, fill it out, of course."

"Of course, of course," Holmes said impatiently. "Follow the necessary train of actions. What would you do next?"

"Post it, I imagine."

"And in between?"

I hesitated. Holmes's impatience grew apace.

"Visualize it, my dear friend." There was an edge in his voice, but I did not take it personally. "It might assist your efforts if you close your eyes and imagine that you were doing it in fact. Leave out nothing, no matter how routine."

I did exactly as bid. I imagined myself filling out the document, folding it, and inserting it into an envelope, addressing the latter and applying a stamp.

After I had related all of this to Sherlock Holmes, he asked, "Would you lick the stamp?"

"I would have to, unless I applied a moist sponge, which would seem to me to be an excessive tool for such a modest task."

Holmes regarded me in silence.

A sudden thought flared up in my brain. I gave it voice. "Do you mean to say, Holmes, that the stamp was in some manner poisoned?"

"The thought had crossed my mind," he said dryly. "But I dismissed it almost immediately."

"Why is that?"

"Do you realize that you left out a step in your mental reenactment?"

"If I did not know you better, Holmes," I returned. "I would insist that I had not."

"Well said. You know me too well." The briar came into play briefly. "To answer your first question: No, the stamp was not poisoned. Why would it be? There is little doubt that the questionnaire arrived with a folded envelope addressed to the originating party, and doubtless a stamp for convenience already affixed to the envelope."

"I struggle to glean the step you claim I have left out."

Holmes's tone became almost mockingly thin. "You would have had to seal the envelope, Watson."

"A minor trifle," I scoffed.

"Men have lost their lives over trifles," he retorted. Holmes's enunciation turned flat and emotionless. "The envelope flap," he said simply, "was unquestionably poisoned."

When this theory sank in. I fairly shouted, "Upon my word! Why, this has the makings of the perfect crime!"

"And there you have it, Watson. At last you have wrenched a successful conclusion from the morass of facts. The gum in the envelope flap was in some way impregnated with a poison that, when it came into contact with the tip of the tongue, turned the moist tissue blue, and set into motion the onset of death, however long delayed. There was sufficient time for the letter to be posted to the sender, taking with it all clues to the killer's identity, along with the method of murder and instrument of death, which were one. And all for the price of a stamp."

"Then we have no way forward?"

"The fact that two separate shades of blue bloomed upon the tongues of two victims suggests a man experimenting with a poison. Such experimentation further suggests someone with the knowledge of a chemist, if not a chemist by trade."

"A slim enough clue, given the number of chemists in greater London."

"Greater London and beyond," snapped Holmes.

"Have you any notion as to the nature of the poison?"

"Again I feel rather stupid, Watson. The discoloration of the victim's tongues caused me to grope in exotic directions. In fact, I have little doubt that the autopsies will show that the agent of doom was a salt of ferrocyanic and carbonate. But such pharmacological knowledge gets us only a little further along the path to the truth."

"Perhaps the housekeeper who mailed the sheaf of letters might be interviewed again. Her memory might be subject to jarring in the matter of the addresses of the fatal envelope."

"Sorry to disappoint. But I hardly think that would be a profitable endeavor, Watson. Such a clever schemer could hardly be expected to use his true address, in the event that the expected order of events went awry."

"So where did the return envelopes end up?"

To my mild astonishment, Sherlock Holmes seemed not to have followed his thinking to its logical point. He rose from his chair, suddenly innervated.

"In the dead letter office, of course!" he cried. "Let us go there at once."

It was not far, so we walked briskly.

Holmes paid a visit to the postmaster's office, laid out as much of his concerns as practical, and received an encouraging reply.

"Two envelopes have been brought to my attention which are outside the normal range of stray mail. In most cases, an improperly addressed envelope is missing a digit, or two or more numerals are transposed. In this case, neither the address nor the addressee can be found in any directory."

"May I see these letters?" Holmes requested.

The items in question with swiftly produced, and laid out on the postmaster's desk for Holmes to inspect. They were ordinary envelopes, and the addresses had been tapped out on a machine. Holmes's black brows crowded together when he saw that there would be no handwriting to analyze.

The addresses were identical.

Institute of Hermetical Science
55 Greenlawn Way
Brixton

"There is no such institute!" snapped Holmes. "Of that, I am certain."

The postmaster concurred, saying, "We have been unable to locate any such enterprise."

"May I borrow these?" asked Holmes.

"How are they of interest to you?"

"If I am not mistaken," Holmes said gravely, "they are instruments of murder. I would like to analyze one and offer the other to Inspector Lestrade for his good opinion."

The postmaster became shockingly pale of countenance, as would anyone coming into contact with cold-blooded murder. "In that case, Mr. Holmes," he said crisply, "I will dutifully commend them to your good care, asking only a letter of receipt in return."

345

"And you shall have it," returned Holmes, accepting pen and paper from the postal official.

Once we were out on the street, Holmes remarked, "Let us visit Lestrade and compare notes."

"Do you think the inspector has made progress in the intervening hours?"

"Unlikely," said Holmes. "But it would be more politic to suggest otherwise when we encounter Lestrade."

"I will keep that injunction in mind," I said dryly.

We were fated never to reach Inspector Lestrade's office.

Upon turning a corner, a hansom cab trundled by and out poked the police official's head. "Mr. Holmes!" he cried. "There has been another!"

It was pointless to ask another what. The inspector urged the cab to a halt and threw open the door. Holmes climbed in, leaving me to call for another.

I was soon bringing up the rear in my own cab.

Both conveyances pulled up before a neat and respectable-seeming house in Kensington. The name of the mailbox was "Gideon Chandler."

Sherlock Holmes and Inspector Lestrade had already entered. I naturally hastened to follow.

The door has been left ajar for me and, when I slipped in, two men were engaging another individual earnestly.

"She seemed perfectly healthy," this man was insisting in an agitated manner. "On awakening, I found her as cold as a stone."

Lestrade asked, "Did she have any complaints in recent days?"

"None, none! Mrs. Chandler was the picture of health."

I took this man to be Mr. Gideon Chandler.

Lestrade continued his interrogation. "Were you aware of the fact that her tongue was discolored prior to the arrival of the family physician?"

"Well, no sir, I was not. In fact, I was not aware of this fact until Dr. Allgood brought it to my attention."

Lestrade asked several other questions which seemed pertinent, and Sherlock Holmes appeared content to observe and take silent note of the answers.

When at last the inspector had exhausted his questioning, Holmes spoke up. His first question brought all eyebrows into highest elevation.

"What, may I ask, what was your wife's maiden name?"

The bereaved husband was so taken aback that he was momentarily speechless. In fact his inability to answer dragged on for more than a minute. Eventually, he got his tongue untangled and operating in correct gear.

"Why do you ask?"

"Why do you hesitate to reply?" countered Holmes. "Certainly you know the answer full well. Do you not?"

The fellow continued to hesitate, but finally he gave forth. "Mrs. Chandler was known as Virginia Dowling when we first met. But I do not see where that fact has any bearing on what has transpired this morning."

"No doubt you are correct, but the query came to mind, so I gave it voice," returned Holmes smoothly. He next asked, "Was your wife recently engaged in answering correspondence?"

At this, Inspector Lestrade's eyes grew baffled. But he held his tongue.

"That is a peculiar question, if I may be so bold as to put it plainly."

"The question stands, sir," said Holmes calmly.

"As is a matter of routine, she invariably attended to any correspondence in the hour before taking to her bed. It was no different last night. I believe there are several letters on the kitchen table that have yet to be posted."

Something in the unfortunate fellow's eyes seem to catch fire like a bit of coal set to smoldering. It was resentment there. Resentment, and a dash of anger.

With his wife lying dead one floor above, no doubt he was feeling helpless and besieged.

Holmes said, "I would like to see them, as would, I am sure, the inspector." This last was evidently calculated to mollify the widowed man. And it seemed to work to that end. Whereupon, Mr. Chandler immediately launched into the kitchen and came back clutching a sheath of envelopes, his features a sullen brick-red.

Chandler handed them to Inspector Lestrade, who rippled through the lot and remarked, "I see nothing out of the usual here."

"Allow me," interposed Holmes. After accepting the envelopes, he examined them quickly and, without asking permission, he tore one end off the sealed envelope.

"Oh, I say!" thundered Chandler. "Of all the nerve!"

"Mr. Holmes no doubt has his reasons," Lestrade reassured the man.

Shaking out the contents, Holmes unfolded a single sheet of stationery, handing it to Inspector Lestrade after the briefest of perusals.

Lestrade took a full minute to read what was on the sheet. I had already formed an opinion. The inspector announced it for me.

347

"This is a printed survey of some sort."

Holmes showed the address on the envelope and remarked coolly, "I have already ascertained that the address on this envelope is imaginary. A falsification. There is no such institute, nor any address corresponding to it."

"How the devil did you determine that?" demanded Lestrade.

"The postmaster can vouch for my assertions," said Holmes. "I have in my pocket two envelopes just like it. And if you take them both back to Scotland Yard, your forensic scientists will swiftly confirm that the glue on both flaps are impregnated with a salt of ferrocyanic and carbonate, as well other substances, including one which reacts with the saliva coating the human tongue to produce vivid colorations."

Inspector Lestrade seemed at a loss for coherent words. "This smacks of black magic, Holmes!" he cried.

"The only black art involved in this grisly matter," corrected Holmes firmly, "is the dark art of cold-blooded murder."

Mr. Chandler intruded at that point. Evidently, his brain had assembled the facts floating about the room into something sensible.

"Are you saying that my wife was murdered? And by a poisoned envelope flap?"

"She was not the first," supplied Holmes.

The man staggered backwards, leaning his back against the fireplace mantel. I thought he might swoon. Certainly, he blanched noticeably.

"But who would do such a dastardly deed? My wife is – was a commonplace but good soul."

"Whoever engineered such perfidy," assured Sherlock Holmes, "will be brought to book in short order."

Lestrade demanded, "If what you say is true, Holmes, and this address is a false one, how may we track backwards to the perpetrator? We do not even have a motive."

"It may be that a madman is at work," said Holmes carefully. "Yet it is my experience in these matters that most pre-meditated murders have in back of them a cold, logical brain. Something connects the death of this woman with the other two victims. It will be brought to light, one way or the other."

In a stiff voice that was seething with repressed anger, Mr. Chandler said, "I am certain my late wife would find cold comfort in your words, sir."

"No doubt," said Holmes, taking no visible umbrage. "What is your occupation, Mr. Chandler?"

This time there was no hesitation. "I am a chemist by trade."

"Ah, a chemist. Very good. Did you happen to notice the discoloration of your late wife's tongue?"

"Did I not already say so?"

"I believe you did," said Holmes calmly. His grey eyes appraised the man who had stepped back from the mantel and was visibly reasserting his self-control.

"What color was it?"

"Blue. A particularly livid blue."

"Could you be more specific?"

"If I could, I would judge the hue to be Prussian Blue."

"And what substance would produce such a specific shade of blue?"

"I – I am not quite certain, sir. Nor do I see the point of your question. In fact, if I am not mistaken, you have no true standing in a murder investigation, except by leave of Inspector Lestrade. So if you do not mind, I will entertain any further questions from the lawful authority present and bid you a good day."

Having finished his speech, Mr. Chandler turned his attention to Lestrade. But at the next pronouncement from Sherlock Holmes, his face fell like a brick wall under the wrecking ball.

"Inspector Lestrade, I suggest you arrest that man in the murder of his wife."

"Are you mad, Mr. Holmes? Upon what evidence?"

"Upon no direct evidence, but I point out to you that a common housewife is unlikely to receive a survey from a scientific institution. Nor is she in the same class as the other two victims. Therefore, she was singled out by someone close to her."

"That is rather thin," Lestrade said flatly.

Undaunted, Sherlock Holmes went on. "Consider then that it would be a very poor chemist who did not know that Prussian Blue is produced by the reaction of salts of iron with potassium ferrocyanide, from which the pigment was first derived. Looking at Mr. Chandler, I judge him to have been in his trade for several years. So elementary a fact could not possibly have escaped him. Therefore, he is temporizing, as well as prevaricating. I have no doubt that if you search this dwelling, you may find certain pernicious poisons. If not here, then in his place of work. Either way, I guarantee his guilt. Place him in handcuffs now, or risk his flight before your investigation is over."

I tore my eyes from Sherlock Holmes and studied the accused.

Various expressions crawled across his wide, meaty face. His features flushed, and his yellowish teeth were bared as if he were a human cur. Fire was in his eyes, but it was not the flame of anger now –

349

instead, it was the red rage of thwarted ambition. The transformation of his countenance was swift and unsettling.

"Sherlock Holmes, is it?" he snarled. No man ever voiced a snarl that was so bestial, so charged with malicious passion. "The consummate sleuth. The master investigator. I do not know how you stumbled upon your facts, sir, but I congratulate you. Yes, I congratulate you – but I would rather rip your throat out with my naked teeth."

"Mr. Chandler!" cried Lestrade. "What has come over you?"

By a visible effort, the man took hold of his nerve and his passion, and heaved a prodigious sigh. Reaching into a vest pocket, he produced a hunter-case pocket watch. Clicking open the cover, he consulted the dial.

"I see that I have been awake less than an hour. Less than one hour of my final day on earth has already elapsed . . . ."

Hearing these ominous words, Sherlock Holmes launched forward – but, alas, too late.

Gideon Chandler brought the timepiece up to his mouth, and swiftly touched his tongue to the concave inner surface of the watch cover. It came away turning a vivid blue.

Holmes wrenched the pocket watch from the men's grasp, spilling the contents upon the floor. It proved to be a pale powder having the semblance of dry snow.

"The telltale poison, Lestrade!" he crowed. "There is your definite proof."

As if his legs had turned into water, Mr. Chandler sank to the floor, his broad back to the mantelpiece. His expression was that of a defeated man, and his eyes were dazed.

"It is done," he croaked out. "I am poisoned. In less than six hours, I shall be dead. And no one will know my motives. For they no longer matter in this world. Whether or not they will matter in the next one, I will shortly learn." He gave out a dry little cackle of a laugh. It struck me as a trifle demented. "I daresay you gentlemen will have to await your own passing before you can uncover the truth. For I have interred it rather deeply."

With that, he closed his eyes.

Turning to Lestrade, Sherlock Holmes said, "Summon an ambulance, Inspector, although I doubt the physicians at the hospital can do much good. But perhaps it is worth a try. And while you are at it, kindly alert the postal authorities to be on the lookout for any other letters emanating from the sinister Institute of Hermetical Science."

Hearing this, Mr. Chandler laughed anew. This chortle was ghoulish in a way that made my skin crawl. I shall never forget it, although I would like to.

We forthwith repaired to Holmes's quarters, where he produced an envelope from his pocket and laid it on a side table.

I could not fail to notice that it was addressed to him in a flourishing hand.

"Wherever the devil did you find that?" I exclaimed.

"It was among the last letters written by the late Mrs. Chandler."

"It was among those found on the kitchen table?"

"Fortunately, no. It arrived only this morning, having been posted the day the deaths of Chalmers and Chambers were reported in the newspapers. The timing is unfortunate," Holmes added dryly.

"Did Mr. Chandler not realize this astonishing fact?"

"Evidently not. No doubt he forebode from rifling through his wife's recent correspondence, lest he leave his own finger marks on any incriminating envelopes."

Holmes produced his oily black clay pipe, filled it with black shag, and applied a match. Soon he was smoking thoughtfully and peering it up at the ceiling with an increasingly dreamy expression.

I enquired, "Are you not going to open the letter?"

"No, not at this time," replied Holmes in that distracted tone I knew so well.

"I imagine that it may contain the ultimate solutions to this maddening mystery."

"No doubt you are correct, Watson. But I prefer to apply my own intellect to the remaining skeins of the problem at hand. To open this envelope now would be to cheat me of one of the most challenging schemes I have ever attempted to unravel."

"Understandable, I suppose. But to open it later would be anticlimactic."

"Perhaps. But if it contains what I suspect it might, any threads that escape me will be tied up neatly. But I prefer to do my own spinning, just as does the lowly spider."

With that, Sherlock Holmes fell into a reverie of intense contemplation. Seeing the direction in which his attention trended, I quietly bid him a goodnight, promising to return if summoned before then.

"I do not think I will require it, but I thank you for your kind indulgence, Watson."

I left without another word.

Holmes rang me up less that twenty-four hours later. His tone was a trifle disappointed, I thought, as he asked if I would come round to see him.

"I shall be over directly," I promised.

Upon my arrival, I discovered Holmes seated in the identical posture as the day before. His attire was different, although his thin hair was somewhat unkempt. I imagine he had not slept in the interim, but I could never determine the truth of that assumption.

"You appear to be in a less-than-enthusiastic mood," I suggested as I took a chair facing my friend.

"It is all dreadfully dreary," he proclaimed in a subdued voice.

"The fact of murder?"

"The now-tattered cobweb that underlies this particular chain of useless destruction," he returned, offering the now open letter written by the deceased Mrs. Gideon Chandler.

Before I could read it, Holmes offered, "The key to the whole thing lay in the detestable lie that Mr. Chandler told during our brief association. Namely, that his wife's maiden name was Dowling."

"You suspected otherwise?"

"Only in the sense that I am always on the lookout for deceit, even in the most innocuous statements. It did not take me a very long prowl through official records to determine that Mrs. Chandler had, during infancy, briefly borne the last name of Chalmers."

"Ah! She is related to the first victim then?"

"And the second. It appears that Nathan Chalmers and Arthur Chambers were brothers, who were separated at a very young age, as was Virginia Chalmers, who happened to be an infant at the time. When they were separated, their names were changed, apparently by the parent who surrendered them to the orphanage. Chandler was the last name assigned to the brother who in time became Gideon Chandler, chemist."

"Peculiar."

"Sordid," corrected Holmes. "Merely sordid. The mother had died of consumption after giving birth to four children, all of whom were scattered to the winds by their father, an importer named Crowninshield, who did not care to raise them alone, nor bestir himself to find a proper wife to carry on in the stead of his first spouse. As is often the custom in these matters, the newly renamed Virginia Chalmers was given the name of her adoptive parents, and grew up never suspecting that her last name was not Dowling."

"Then Chandler did not lie."

"He lied, for he had lately discovered the awful truth – namely, that he had accidentally married his own sister."

"My word!"

"Yes. It is a tragedy from start to finish. But it grew more horrible in the unfolding, for when the recalcitrant father had at last slipped into his dotage, he commenced a search for his abandoned children. Unfortunately for all concerned, he uncovered Gideon Chandler first. Learning of his true origins, Chandler plunged into the dusty records of a certain orphanage and was staggered – and no doubt horrified – to discover that he had wed his unsuspected sister, whom he had not beheld since her infancy. But that was not the worst of it. He and the other three Crowninshield siblings stood to come into a great deal of money once the repentant father rewrote his will accordingly.

"Promising to help locate the other three former foundlings, Mr. Chandler instead formulated a rather diabolical scheme to do away with them all, leaving him the sole Crowninshield heir – and incidentally burying from public discovery his acute marital embarrassment, which, I suspect, was his overriding motivation."

"Ghastly," I gasped out.

"Merely sordid," reminded Holmes. His tone was listless. I imagine he had suspected more exotic motivations underlay the situation, before it had resolved itself.

"But how did the wife uncover the truth?" I enquired.

"It is all in her letter. You may read it for yourself. For myself, I am both sickened and bored by the whole grotesque affair. Would that the criminal mind be as ingenious as I sometimes imagine it to be. In this case, the ingenuity at work is overwhelmed by the banality of the parties involved, as well as by their respective motivations."

"What of the poisons? You can scarcely deny the cleverness with which the poisoner operated."

"Nor do I. The problem was as engaging as any I have ever encountered. That it led to such ugly doings is what I object to. The poison was, as I suspected, a salt of ferrocyanic and carbonate. The clever chemist had merely added differently colored dyes to the gum mucilage in order retard the poison's effects long enough for the doomed recipient to post the completed survey. This was where experimentation played a significant role. The choice of blue substances was doubtless intended to create an effect that the villain hoped would confuse the inevitable police investigation."

"He reckoned without Sherlock Holmes," I commented.

"I have learned that Gideon Chandler died without speaking further. Not that there is any significant loss attending his passing. Now, you may read the letter Watson. If you are so inclined."

I remain captivated and intrigued, so I did exactly that.

It was a tangle, one not worth recapitulating in full.

Mrs. Chandler had been oblivious to her own origins at the start. It happened that her husband belonged to that group of people who are afflicted with nightmares. Once, she was startled to be aroused in the deepest part of night by Chandler's thrashing about wildly, crying out on his sleep, "Sister! I married my own sister!"

She woke him and repeated the blurted outcry, but Chandler professed ignorance, dismissing the words as the product of a bad dream.

Thereafter, she noticed a creeping aloofness in his manner, which gradually shaded into a sullen coldness. In short order, insomnia overtook them. One night, Mrs. Chandler awoke to discover herself alone in the martial bed. Creeping downstairs, she found him pacing his study, muttering over and over, "My own sister – my lawful wife! How could such a queer fate befoul my existence?"

Unnoticed, she crept back to the bed chamber, where she resolved to seek her own origins, in which she had hitherto showed scant interest, having lived up until then a fortunate life.

Virginia Chandler's private investigations concluded just days before Arthur Chambers was found dead. The matter of the blue-tinted tongue suggested to her an exotic poison, and her thoughts inevitable careened in the direction of her chemist spouse. Naturally, she could scarcely credit her theory. Then Nathan Chalmers was done away with. Straight away, she resolved to write Sherlock Holmes and lay all facts before him – but alas, too late. She sensed that she might be the next to turn up with a discolored tongue, and took precautions with her food and drink, but did not imagine that an innocent survey might be the deliverer of her own doom – as it had for the others, her unsuspected brothers.

The rest was merely lamentations and questions. She, too, was aghast at the realization that her husband was in truth her oldest brother. In her despair, she wrote to Holmes, requesting assistance in the queer affair.

Folding the note, I wondered, "Why, on that murderous morning, didn't Chadler post the fatal letter, thus disposing of the murder weapon?"

"Evidently, the wife attended to her correspondence very late, presumably well after her faithless husband's bedtime, for he was a working man who rose at an early hour, and she a late riser. As with all schemers, his brain was filled with mental rehearsals of how he would act upon discovering the cold corpse in the morning. Chandler neglected to consider the possibility that his carefully-executed scheme would have been penetrated in its essential details."

354

"He expected an opportunity to post the deadly letter after the body was carried off, I take it."

"Goaded by me, in his agitation Chandler handed the evidence over," noted Holmes with satisfaction.

"I suppose that no other fatal letters were intercepted."

A slow, tired sigh carried with it the essence of pipe tobacco. "No, Watson. Presumably, there are none. The circle has been closed."

"What of the repentant father?"

"Mercifully, Mr. Meldrum Crowninshield passed away in his sleep the very night his last surviving son succumbed to his own diabolical poison. I am informed that the tip of Crowninshield's own tongue was also an exquisite Turquoise."

"Remarkable. The circle has indeed been closed. There will be no need for Fleet Street to learn all the dreary details."

"Why add to the common misery?" murmured Holmes. "Especially when so many are so industriously dedicated to multiplying it."

I could think of no suitable rejoinder, and so let my silence speak for me.

The Parsimonious Peacekeeper
by Thaddeus Tuffentsamer

The winter of late 1902 was a particularly brutal and nasty affair that plunged many into violent moods of depression and despair. My practice saw a noticeably propitious incline of clientele due to the general mood overhanging the city. While that did well for me, my friend Mr. Sherlock Holmes was not so fortunate.

His consulting had seen decline both personally, as well as from the Yard. The general consensus was that it was simply too cold for the nefarious lot of the greater London area to engage in such said activities.

I found these times to be the most harrowing, as I knew all too well his need for mental stimulation, as well as the depths he would plunge to in order to relieve himself of the burden of boredom.

I decided to close my practice for the day and impose myself upon him, hoping to provide a suitable distraction, if only to get him outside.

As I entered 221 Baker Street, Mrs. Hudson was just coming down the steps leading from my old flat.

"Good to see you, Doctor."

"And you as well, Mrs. Hudson."

"The breakfast table is set with an extra place for you this morning."

I stopped short, surprised by this. "Why is that?"

"Mr. Holmes told me to. He said that you would be round this morning for breakfast."

I must have looked a sight to her with my eyebrows furrowed so tightly together. I then let out a short sigh and, relaxing my eyebrows, smiled. "Of course, he did," I replied.

She turned her head away and then quickly looked upon me again. "Something looks different about you, Doctor."

"Indeed, something is."

She continued to study my face and then gave way to a smile, as what she had been looking for revealed itself. "You've restyled your moustache. You've gone and trimmed the side tips off."

"You are correct, Mrs. Hudson. I decided to try a straight edged look for the time being."

"You look like an American," she said and went back into the rear of the house.

356

I traversed the seventeen steps leading up to my dear friend. No sooner had I reached out for the doorknob then I heard his voice from the opposite side.

"Come in, Watson."

I did as I had been instructed and gladly removed my coat and bowler, hanging them on the hooks. I walked to the mantel and looked to see if there was anything of interest jackknifed to it. Satisfying myself that there wasn't, I joined Holmes at the table.

He gestured grandly to the food before me. "Help yourself to breakfast, Watson, as you have not yet eaten."

I did not question as to how he knew that. I simply acknowledged the fact that he did. I made a plate of eggs and meat and poured myself a cup of coffee to accompany it. I ate happily.

"You have plans for today?" he asked.

I leaned into the back of the chair. "Nothing special," I said, trying for the entire world to seem nonchalant. "I was simply passing by and decided to drop in."

"That, my dear Watson, is untrue. Let me expound. You have made plans for spending time with me today. You have, in fact, closed your practice and have no doubt planned to present some little problem for me, hoping I would become intrigued so as to go off with you and thereby avoid turning to my . . . box."

"Why ever do you say that, Holmes?"

"Simple. Your shoes give you away."

"My shoes?"

"Indeed. Those are not the shoes you wear to your practice. They are old, though not worn through. You would never present them to your patients in a professional setting. You aren't ready to discard them just yet, as there is still life in them, so you have relegated them to the ones you wear when you plan to spend the day walking. So be it. You have decided to come see me and drag me away from here," he said, gesturing the expanse of the sitting room.

"I admit that you are correct on all accounts, but may I ask how you knew that I would be here today? How did you know to have Mrs. Hudson set a place for me?"

"You are predictable."

"Indeed, and how so exactly?"

"We have not communicated for the past several days. Yesterday, you sent me a general note to express your wishes and inquire about my well-being. I have not ignored you, by the way. I simply saw no need to respond. Since I did not, you would have no choice in your mind but to

357

follow through with your concerns and come to see how I'm doing in person."

I simply stared at him.

"I am fine, by the way," he added.

"Again, you are correct on all accounts. With that so, can I get you out of these rooms?"

He stretched out his long legs turned his face away from me, looking toward the window. "No."

"So be it. But I dare say, my dear fellow, that your observational skills are suffering at the moment . . . ."

He cut me off with a wave of his hand. "There was no reason to mention the manner in which you have groomed your moustache. You are aware that you have trimmed it, and looking at you, I am likewise aware of it. Why waste either of our words in a superfluous observation over your personal hygiene?"

"There are times when your logic can be infuriating!"

"I will not challenge that," he said, a wide smile spreading out over his lips.

"So, you will change your mind then and accompany me?"

He slowly turned his head back round to look at me. "No."

"I give up!" I said with frustration in my tone.

"In that case, you have gotten the point."

I leaned forward and continued my breakfast, made up of the usual morning delicacies that Mrs. Hudson so lovingly makes, I nibbled at them and again leaned back in my chair. "At least we will enjoy each other's company for the morning."

Holmes rose, walked to his chair by the fireplace, reached out to his pipe, and picked it up gingerly. He slowly twirled it between his long fingers, not committing to filling and lighting it. "For a few more minutes, at least," he said finally.

"How is that, then?"

"I am expecting a client in a moment."

"And here I came to distract you, Holmes."

"Rather, you came upon my request to assist me with a client."

I began to ask him how that could be the case, since he could not possibly know I was coming. But, looking at the plate of food in my hand, combined with yesterday's note that he'd just mentioned, I knew better than to even ask the question.

No sooner had the thought run through my mind than Mrs. Hudson ushered in his client.

He was a short, thin, nervous-looking individual. He came in bowing and wringing his hat in his hands. He was not a peasant, but

358

neither was he a man of means. Though not slovenly in appearance, his clothing had seen better days. It was also obvious that shaves and haircuts were few and far between.

Holmes pointed to the chair opposite his. "Pray, good fellow, sit down and tell me what is troubling you."

The man did as he had been instructed. He had a meek demeanor and sallow countenance. He placed his hands in his lap. "Thank you, Mr., 'Olmes. Me name's Neuburry, Reginald Neuburry. I am in sore straights, Mr. 'Olmes. Sore straights, indeed, sir."

"You are a flower seller in the lower Islington district."

Neuburry looked up, startled. "Yes, guv'nor, but how could you be in knowledge of that?"

Holmes smiled reassuringly at him. "Your vocation is obvious, as you have pollen all over your coat. That does not come from someone who has purchased a bouquet to bring home to his wife, but rather from someone who constantly has flowers clutched to his breast. It is winter, and yet you have been around flowers – a great deal of them. Finally, you have dried petals under your lapels which also add to the confirmation of your career."

Neuburry nodded in acknowledgement. "Yes, sir. But how could you know that I work in Islington?"

"Your trouser cuffs have multiple mud splashes on them. As a flower seller, you need to go to a busy intersection is order to attract the most clientele. The intersection at Islington is notoriously known for being bustling with pedestrian and vehicular traffic. It is also notoriously wet and muddy. Many carts have turned the corner quickly, causing you to jump away, while not quite escaping the splash of distinctive Islington mud."

"Oy, they told me you was a clever one, and they wasn't wrong, sir. I hope you can help with my sorrows, sir."

"Yes, we'll see. Pray tell what your sorrows are."

"I've been arrested three times, sir. Public nuisance is what they's saying 'bout me. I ain't no nuisance, sir. I don't make much money, barely more than to force a smile over an extra shilling. But I am a hardworking man, sir."

"Three times you've been arrested, you say?"

"Yes, sir. It happened once last week, once the week before that, and another time two weeks before that. I seen the constabulary there just today looking at me funny from 'cross the street, so I ain't waited for them to come nab me again. I ran away and sent a message here to you."

"Each charge was for being a public nuisance?"

"Right you are, sir."

"What has been the outcome of your arrests? What has the jury decided on each of these charges?"

"There's never been no jury for me, sir. I just stand before the magistrate 'imself."

"The same one each time?"

"Yes, sir, each time. Blackborn is his name, sir. Though '*Black Heart*' be more fitting for him."

"And what is the outcome when you stand before him?"

"He tells me I's guilty of being a public nuisance and fines me two shillings and four pence. That don't sound like much money, but it's a whole week's wages for a humble man such as me self."

"Are you aware of others in the same circumstances as yourself?"

"Aye. All the lads working the street vending has been telling stories of their own plights, sir."

Holmes clapped his hands together so suddenly that we both jumped in surprise. He launched out of his chair and across the room to stack of newspaper clippings. He dug through them until he found the article for which he was looking. He scanned it quickly and then stuffed it into his pocket.

He turned to face Neuburry. "Be of stout heart, dear fellow. I will have a chat with the magistrate this evening, and I can assure you that you will not be molested further."

Neuburry's countenance changed from a man distraught to one filled with new strength. "Are you certain, Mr. 'Olmes?"

Holmes took his hand a shook it vigorously. "Have every confidence that I will be successful."

Neuburry began to pat down his pockets. "I don't have any shillings, sir, but bear with me and I'll pay you your wages."

Holmes waved him away. "Do not worry over it. I will handle this for my own personal satisfaction."

Neuburry smiled, but shook his head. "No, sir, an honest man I am. I am in debt, and so I will pay."

He reached into his pocket and pulled out a small cluster of tulips that had likewise seen its better day. He handed it to Holmes. "It's all I can offer you, sir, but surely it will go over well for you with your misses downstairs." He then left the flat.

After his departure, I could not restrain myself from a laugh at Holmes's expense. "I say – to think that you . . . and Mrs. Hudson could be – "

His irritated gaze was enough to reprimand me into silence.

A moment went by before he again spoke.

"We will go before Justice Blackborn this evening, Watson, and clear the matter up."

"You believe that you can insist upon an audience on such short notice?"

"He'll see us. After we're arrested, that is."

That evening, after Holmes had spent several hours out on errands of his own, he came walking out of his room. He had made himself up in his usual theatrical makeup. He looked like a recently dispatched sailor that was down in his luck and searching for some honest work. He had a thin wispy beard, two blackened teeth, and a severe squint to his left eye. Had I not known he had been in the room preparing himself, I wouldn't have recognized the man who walked out and now stood before me.

He held out a fish wrapped in paper. "Mackerel, guv'nor? Fresh from the boat today, it is," he said in a Cockney accent.

"I say, Holmes. You've outdone yourself this time."

Holmes tossed the fish upon the table. "It's time that you were prepared as well," he said, and before I could protest, the warm theatre adhesive of spirit gum began to be brushed upon my own chin.

Within a span, I myself looked the part of Holmes's assistant, a low-ranking sailor who sold fish when in port.

In short order, we were walking the streets approaching Islington. A telegram received just before we left told us where we needed to be this night.

We walked up Hampstead Road towards Downshire Hill and all became clear as we rounded the corner and came upon Wiggins, the leader of Holmes's band of street urchins that he refers to as his Irregulars.

As he laid eyes upon us, he looked sharply left to right and, with a learned discretion, he made his way over to us. "Evening, Mr. 'Olmes," he said.

Holmes returned the greeting. "Have there been any arrests tonight?" he asked the boy.

Wiggins nodded. "Yes, sir. There's been three so far since we got 'ere."

"Excellent. Thank you," he said to the boy. He took four shillings from his pocket and handed them to him. "Here is one for each of you for your work tonight."

He then handed him another. "And here is an extra shilling for your troubles," he added.

Wiggins crammed them into his pocket and speedily fled the scene.

"Why are we here, Holmes?" I asked him.

"We're at Hampstead Road and Downshire Hill. What is near our current location?"

I took in the scenery. I had not often frequented this side of London, so nothing immediately leapt upon me; however, slowly I put the location's importance into perspective. "There is Parliament Hill."

"And there have only been three arrests tonight. Not so many that suspicions would be aroused, and yet enough to satisfy the greed of he who is issuing the arrest warrants." Then, in a loud voice, he called out, "Mackerel for sale! Only the freshest from the port! *Mack-e-rel*!" he stretched the word out to all three of its syllables.

We were watched closely by a few men of various professions on the street. Though it looked as if some might wish to enquire about the fish, they kept respectful distance.

"Do you find this odd?" I asked Holmes as he continued to announce our wares for sale. He didn't bother to respond with more than a quick shake of his head.

A few more minutes and a bobby approached us, his baton held firmly in hand as he meandered his way towards us.

"What have we here?" he asked.

Holmes held the fish up for his inspection. "We're just selling a few o' the fish we caught on our last ride, officer," he said.

The police man looked sternly at him. "Let me see your selling license."

Holmes patted the coat pockets on his left side. Then, transferring the fish to his left hand, he patted the right side down. "Sorry, Officer. I seems to have left it on the boat, I did."

"Then you had better come with me."

I began to protest and dispute the arrest, stating that we were hard-working men and deserved to be treated with respect. I was likewise grabbed up and herded off, along with Holmes.

In less than a half-an-hour, we were in a small, cold, holding cell that wasn't intended for more than one occupant. I was sitting on one side of the bench with Holmes on the other.

"What will become of us, then?"

Holmes continued his troubleless stare at the side of the cell. "That is not nearly as important as what will become of Blackborn."

"Whatever do you mean?" I asked, but before he could answer, the heavily rusted metal door creaked open. Two guards reached in, collected us, and shuffled us down the cobbled corridor leading to an adjacent chamber.

Holmes leaned in to me and barely above a whisper said, "The game is afoot!"

362

When presented, I did not feel that this was the atmosphere of a game.

The room was as cold as the holding cell, grey stone comprising the walls and dark mahogany comprising the benches, witness stand, and everything else.

We were shuffled to the defendant's bench and heavily sat down, the jolt of it reminding my leg of the time that I had I spent in Afghanistan.

The magistrate entered the room and sat down behind the opulence of his desk and reached out towards the court clerk, who quickly stuffed a slip of foolscap into his hand. He opened it and read aloud its contents. "You are charged with selling without a proper license and being a public nuisance. How do you plead?"

He stared down at Holmes and me. Holmes casually, crossed his legs and placed his hands in his lap.

"I plead contempt," he said casually as if asked about the current weather.

"I beg your pardon?" said Blackborn, for it was surely he, with heavy tones of irritation in his voice.

"Believe me, sir, it's not *my* pardon for which you will be begging."

The man's face flushed a deep crimson. "I'll ask you again, and I suggest you weigh your response carefully, sir. How do you plead against the charges brought forth against you?"

Holmes scratched the side of his long aquiline nose and centered his grey eyes into a deep stare. "I plead contempt. Contempt for you personally as one who abuses the office which you should hold sacred, and contempt for a likewise corrupt system that has ignored your misdeeds for far too long!"

Blackborn, now fully furious, slapped his palms out flat on the table, the heavy thud sounding throughout the room. He stood up, towering over myself and Holmes in a hope to intimidate us. His approach might have worked on me if I were guilty of something, but Holmes, as usual, sat unperturbed.

"How dare you!" Blackborn screamed at us.

Holmes also stood up and faced him eye to eye. He calmly and quietly reached into one of his pockets and pulled out several newspaper clippings. He began to lay them out on the bench, one at a time.

"You make many social appearances around town. For instance, you were seen at the Mayor's Ball. Here is another describing a social event which you attended, Miss Marristown's opening performance of *That Which Calls* only two weeks ago.

"According to witnesses from all walks of life, you were spotted in new suits from M. O'Neil and Company, a very expensive choice in haberdashery. And you've been seen all over town in a new carriage with an equally new steed pulling it – both much finer than a man with your finances should allow. I have researched your accounts. I know your salary, and what you should be able to afford. The carriage and horse were purchased by you just short of two months ago. I wonder where you found the funds?"

Blackborn was no longer of crimson countenance. Rather, his face had begun to pail as if drained of all blood.

Holmes continued. "I have a few more items to discuss if you wish, but I think the point is well enough made that you seem to be living entirely above your means."

Blackborn was unable to speak. He feebly cleared his throat.

"There have been a substantial amount of arrests for all types and varieties of petty 'crimes' for the past three months, and not without irony, all of the increases in such arrests happen during the evenings that you hold court."

The official tried to reclaim his bluster and his dignity. He balled up his fists and clenched them tightly. "I'll remind you, sir that you are under *my* jurisdiction, and it is yourself who stands accused!"

Holmes actually chuckled at this. "I believe that I have done a very sufficient job in making my own accusation towards you, sir."

Blackborn bristled. Without waiting, Holmes pushed forth in his final assault. "You and your officer have been arresting hard and honest working men and women for months now on trumped-up charges. Your 'fines' equal a week's wages for these citizens. You have no thought or care for the turmoil you place upon them and their families. You only care about lining your own pockets with shillings!'

Holmes was speaking in terse, firm tones. In the time that I had known him, this was one of the closest occasions that I had seen that he had ever come to an expression of rage.

Regaining his wits, Blackborn stood to his full height. "You will have trouble proving any of this from your cell, you . . . you . . . you worthless vagabond!"

Holmes tore the whiskers from his face and chin. He opened the squint from his eye and drew a handkerchief from his pocket, which he used to wipe away the blackened teeth. "Vagabond? Indeed not, sir. Allow me to introduce myself. I am Sherlock Holmes, independent consulting detective. You may not know me. However, I am quite sure that you will know my brother . . . . ."

364

As if on cue, the doors burst open and the rotund form of Mycroft Holmes walked in, accompanied by a police constable. He tapped the floor heavily with his walking stick with each step. He walked up and glowered at the magistrate.

Blackborn was reduced to a jumble of nerves. "Mr. Holmes. You honor me with your presence."

Mycroft stared deeply into the man's eyes, never once breaking away from his stare. Slowly and wordlessly he shook his head side to side. "You are a disgrace to the King," he admonished.

Blackborn fell heavily into his chair, unable to speak.

Sherlock turned to Mycroft. "Thank you for coming, brother mine."

Mycroft sighed. "Next time, don't send a street urchin into my club as a messenger."

"Desperate times."

"Times were so desperate that you sent a street waif to the Diogenes Club?"

"I was on my way to being arrested."

Blackborn remained quiet during the interchange. Mycroft turned to the constable. "Arrest Blackborn and that officer with him and put them into a cell."

Blackborn began frantically to protest. "You cannot arrest me! I am a magistrate! I demand to be heard!"

"Heard, as if by trial?" Mycroft asked.

"I demand it!" Blackborn stated.

Mycroft turned to stare directly at him. "Then I find you guilty! Constable, take him to an especially damp cell. I'll come and check on him in six months . . . perhaps."

Blackborn began to plead for mercy but it fell upon deaf ears. The constable grabbed hold of him as Mycroft led Holmes and me outside.

As we stepped out into the street, Holmes turned to Mycroft, "Dinner?" he enquired casually, as if nothing of significance had just happened.

Mycroft nodded and turned to me. "Doctor, where do you recommend we eat tonight?"

I admit to having been taken completely off guard by the question. One moment we were being sent to a prison cell, and then the next we were casually making dinner plans. However, flattered to have my own opinion heard, I said, "I believe there is a new Polynesian restaurant that has opened a few streets away," my head still spinning from it all.

Mycroft turned to Holmes, who nodded his approval of the suggestion. Mycroft nodded as well and walked on in silence towards the eatery.

I determined that later I would chastise him, telling Holmes that I find such instances of his leaving me in the dark utterly unacceptable. But I knew that my words would fall upon ears that, while not deaf, were completely unable to distinguish anything wrong in the manner in which he conducts business towards me.

With that, my determination faded and I consigned myself to letting it be.

All in all, it was fine with me. Such is the cost of being in collaboration with so honorable a man.

The Case of the
Dirty Hand
by G. L. Schulze

Before retiring to Sussex, I became involved in a most baffling of cases. I contemplated whether to put to pen the events that transpired over the course of a mere two days. But as Watson would have reminded me, "The world needs to know!"

He accompanied me less often upon my cases, having taken upon himself a new practice situated in Queen Anne Street, the front sitting room of his residence serving as his office. We saw one another on occasion, but as life has a tendency to move forward and away, so did our association of old.

I do not have his flair with vocabulary, but I do yet retain a keen observation and memory of all the facts. It was a Thursday evening, the eleventh of June, 1903. I sat with my pipe, staring into a cold fireplace, the weather being much too hot for a flame. I had no case to ponder, no villains to pursue, no scoundrels to apprehend. It was, in fact, a most boring evening.

This had been the circumstance for several days. But on this evening, late as it was, I heard the wheels of a carriage on the street below, the slamming of the downstairs door, and a thunderous stomping of hurried footsteps on the stair.

"A-ha!" I thought. Boredom alleviated! I rose, for immediately there was a pounding upon my door. As I opened it, a great bulk of a man breathing heavily pushed passed me and cried out, "Good heavens, Sherlock! It's about time! And close that bloody door!"

I was somewhat taken aback but recovered quickly. It was not an angry look that I first observed on my brother's face as he rushed passed me. On second glance, I saw it to be anxiety – even fear – such as I've never encountered from Mycroft before.

He paced the room for a moment but the exertion soon caused him to pause. "A brandy!" he exclaimed.

I poured out two glasses. He took the first, drank it down in one swallow, and then took the second.

"Better?" I queried.

"Wipe that priggish look off your face, Sherlock. This is a matter of the utmost urgency."

"It generally is when you pay me a visit. It means that you have gotten yourself into a sticky mess and wish me to clarify it."

"Not I," Mycroft said. He swallowed the second glass of brandy and then leaned back heavily in the chair. His cheeks were flushed to a brazen pink, but underneath the skin was the color of bleached parchment. A vein at his neck pulsed rapidly. I sat opposite and waited for him to explain. His demeanor told me all that I needed to know regarding the gravity of his visit, and I knew this was more than a sticky mess.

"I cannot help if you do not tell me," I said to him.

Mycroft ran a hand through the scant few strands of hair remaining on his nearly bald head. He patted the beads of sweat with an already sodden handkerchief, and then finally turned his attention to me.

"As you know," he began, "these past few days Crown and Country have been celebrating the end of this horrendous South African War. The Boer War, as it is will be called in the books, will go down in history as the fiercest bloodiest clash of all time! And God only knows how we were thrust into the middle of things! It will be an unhealing scab on the Crown for years to come!"

I merely nodded. What could I say? He was correct. Murder and worse atrocities had been committed on both sides of that conflict.

"So you can understand when I tell you the King was more than reticent when he was called upon to act as an intermediary in their dispute."

"A dispute? With whom?"

"Don't interrupt, Sherlock. Allow me to finish. As you know, for some time now King Alexander Obrenovic of Serbia has been attempting to get into bed with Russia, for protection purposes. We all know it. Obrenovic is aware of what is happening in his own country, the dissent of his people regarding his marriage to his Queen Draga. It was a farce and done in an underhanded manner. The people will not forget his treachery and deceit any time soon. An alliance with Russia would give him the peace of mind that he has an ally, should one be needed at his side.

"But Nicholas II has been keeping him at arms' length, refusing to meet with him. He, too, understands Obrenovic's ploy and does not wish to become embroiled in a family dispute that will spill onto the populace."

"What has King Edward to do with all of this?" I asked.

"Everything! The King was approached by Obrenovic's emissary to play host to a meeting between Nicholas and Obrenovic here in London. The emissary played on the King's recent triumph in the Boer War and his relief at its end, pointing out that should another conflict, possibly between Serbia and Russia, arise, it would be nearly at the King's own doorstep. 'The King wouldn't want that, would he?' The emissary queried."

"And so he agreed?"

"Yes," Mycroft sighed. "The King agreed."

"And Emperor Nicholas and King Alexander Obrenovic will be coming to London for this meeting?"

"They will. They arrive this Saturday. Sunday will be a day of pleasantries, but the real meeting is to begin on Monday."

"It all sounds as though you have things well in hand. What am I to do about it?"

"This." Mycroft pulled an envelope from his inside pocket and handed it to me. "This is what you're to do, Sherlock."

I took the envelope by my fingertips and, using forceps, extracted the scrunched piece of brown wrapping paper from inside. Laying it beneath my lamp, I opened it and read one single line: *The King will die.*

"You must find who sent this. Find him and stop him."

But I wasn't listening to Mycroft. Something was amiss with the envelope. It wasn't in keeping with the note. "What of this?" I held it up to him.

"Never mind the envelope. It is one of mine. That crumpled up note was brought to me by the butler at the Diogenes Club exactly as you see it. I put it into the envelope simply as a means of bringing it to you. What do you make of it?"

"I'm surprised at you, Brother," I said to him. "Your instincts are keener than mine, as you have told me time and again."

"I have enough on my mind, what with the King's security, as well as the protection and running of the government. I've brought this to you for your full attention."

"Of course. I have several questions. First, how many people are aware of this meeting?"

"Good lord, Sherlock! Hundreds! The kings of each state, their guards, the hired help, the chamber maids . . . ."

I held up my hand. "Too many. Next, when did you receive the note?"

Mycroft looked at his watch. "An hour past. As soon as I read it, I rushed over here immediately!"

"And you say the butler gave it to you? Exactly like this?"

"Yes, crumpled like a ball in his fist is exactly how he handed it to me. He stated a young woman with a veil was at the front door, and when he went to see her away, she thrust it into his palm and said for Mycroft Holmes. Then she was gone."

"I see." I looked once more at the paper. It was ordinary brown wrapping paper, a piece torn from a larger section. The words appeared to be crudely written in ash. "Hearth ash," I muttered.

"What? What's that you said?"

"I said it is hearth ash. Soot from a fire place. The granular texture of the wood or coal burned is rough and thick due to the coarseness – not at all like the delicate residue of tobacco ash. It means that the writer used what he had at hand."

I stood up abruptly, indicating that Mycroft need stay no longer. "You don't give me much with which to work, nor much time, Brother, but I am up to the challenge. You see to our King. I will see to this." At the door, I mentioned, "There is one question we haven't asked, Mycroft."

He turned, a glint of fear flickering across his face once more. "What is that?"

"We haven't asked the most important, the most crucial, the most critical question. *Which king is it that will die?*"

I saw immediately the question did nothing to allay Mycroft's agitated demeanor. He gasped as though his breath had caught in his throat, turned abruptly more pale than before, and then slammed the door behind him.

I instantly chose to disregard the King's safety. After all, that was Mycroft's affair, and I left him to it. Instead, I held up the brown paper and studied it once more.

It was a scant three by five inches, jagged on three sides, and with a razor cut clean edge along the fourth. This in itself wasn't much, as every shop used this type of paper to wrap their customers' items. But it was the three ragged edges that intrigued me. The note had obviously been torn from a larger piece, and as I scrutinized it beneath my microscope, I noted a faint print in one of the corners.

I went immediately to my stores of chemicals and mixed a combination of powders in minute portions. Once completely blended, I darkened the room and then added several drops of hydrogen peroxide. With a gentle breath, I blew a fine mist of the mixture onto the stain.

It wasn't long before the chemical reaction of the iron in the stain reacted with my solution, and within seconds, the spot began to glow a luminous blue. It became clear that this was blood. What shop would wrap goods that might involve blood? A butcher shop, of course.

It was late, I knew, but Mycroft had received the note no more than two hours ago. The butcher shops were closed at this hour, but that didn't deter me. Three butcher shops later, much to the dismay of the owner,

Marcot Strange, I found what I was looking for. A roll of brown paper was sitting atop his counter, where the edge met the razor, was a segment where a piece had been torn free.

Strange had recently hired a young man, he told me, a foreigner who barely spoke the language and was down on his luck. He'd desperately needed the work, he said. And so for three days the young man appeared promptly, worked diligently all day, and left in good spirits at each day's end.

Except for today.

"What was different today?" I asked of Strange.

"The young man came in as usual and worked as usual, but at closing time, a young woman entered and whispered something to him. I saw him tear off a scrap of paper from the roll there. He dipped his finger into the cold ash of the hearth and, after marking the scrap, he gave it to the woman."

"Can you describe her?"

"No, sir. She was dressed all in black, her face covered by a dark veil."

"Can you describe the young man, then?"

"He is of average height, and as I said, a foreigner. He has a swarthy complexion, dark hair, dark eyes, dark facial beard, and mustache. Always wears a knit cap pulled low to his brow."

"And his name?"

"Sam was what he said, but I knew that wasn't right. Still," Strange shrugged, "who am I to question?"

"Who, indeed?" I thought upon leaving the shop.

It was mid-Friday when I met Mycroft at the Diogenes Club. I gave the butler a note for him to meet me in the Stranger's Room, the only location within the establishment where conversation is permitted.

Soon I explained to Mycroft all I had discovered thus far. To the butler, when he joined us, I asked, "The woman said nothing more?"

"No, sir."

"Do you recall anything special or different about her?"

"No, sir."

"No hair out of place? The smell of a perfume perhaps?"

"No, sir."

"No rings, or jewelry of any sort?"

"No, sir. She wore gloves."

"Ah!" I exclaimed at last. "The man does have a vocabulary!"

371

"There is no need to be flippant, Sherlock. These fellows are trained to be unobservant." Mycroft chastised, then waved the butler to dismissal.

"Of course. I quite forgot how completely unobservant most people are."

"Is that all that you have accomplished?"

"Why, Brother, you do me foul! Of course I have my street eyes and ears out. I'll have messages waiting once I return to Baker Street, to be sure."

Mycroft rose to leave. "Be sure!" he commanded, and waddled away.

I did have messages when I arrived. My urchins were on the tail of several women in black, and others were shadowing the man described by Strange. A full report would be in soon. But the knock at the door surprised even me. Mrs. Hudson entered, a most perplexed look on her face.

"What is it, Mrs. Hudson? I am much too busy for trivialities today."

"A young lady at the back door told me to wait five minutes, then give you this." She held out her hand and there, in her palm, was another crumpled piece of brown paper. I snatched it up and raced to the back door, but there was nothing to indicate that anyone had been there, for Mrs. Hudson had been sweeping the back steps when the young woman approached her. Any signs or clues had been swept away.

"I'm sorry," she said behind me on the stair. "It was such a silly request. I finished my sweeping and then came up."

"It's all right, Mrs. Hudson," I soothed, my tone as cool as I could muster, despite the seething anger that boiled inside of me. The young woman! At my very door step! And I was too late!

I returned to the sitting room and carefully unfolded the crumpled brown paper. And I must admit that this time I was completely taken aback. The sooty scrawl on the paper was smudged but readable. *Leave it alone, Holmes,* it said, *or Dr. Watson dies.* And there, at the bottom, was a black sooty imprint of a hand

I read the note again. The handwriting was the same as that of the first note when I compared them side by side. I determined that the blood smudged finger mark on the first matched that of the second. The same man!

Watson, of course, was my immediate concern, but who were these new fanatics that threatened the life of a king, yet played with such childish threats as that of a hand print?

I missed Wiggins, my Baker Street detective of old, but he'd grown up and moved on. But there were always wayward and homeless urchins

372

on the streets willing to earn a fast shilling, and it was Toby's step I heard upon the stair. Just in time.

"I came in the back way, Mr. Holmes. We found the woman in black. She met up with the man of your description and they be lodged at – "

"Very good, Toby. Your crew is still on watch?"

"Yes, sir," Toby answered smartly.

"Good, good," I said. "Then I have a new assignment for you. I want you to – "

"But – " Toby interrupted. "Sorry, Mr. Holmes, but that man with the beard didn't return to the lodgings alone, sir. He had Dr. Watson with him."

"I see. That changes everything." I thought for a moment. Toby's message clearly told me they already had Watson, which indicated that someone was watching me as certainly as I was watching them. I feared that if I made a move to rescue Watson, it might just push them to murder.

I quickly wrote a note for Toby to deliver to the telegraph office, and then told him, "Quick, boy! Downstairs, and ask Mrs. Hudson for a scrap of brown paper just like this!"

Toby scurried quickly, returning just as fast.

"This was all she had, sir."

"It will do." I tore the paper to the same size as that sent to me, dipped my finger in the ash of my own cold hearth, and scrawled: *The King is not coming - Pull back.* I had Toby lay a hand to the ash and imprint his palm on the note. After crumpling it, I told him, "Deliver this to the man or woman at the lodgings. And be quick!"

"Sir!" Toby cried, and disappeared while I shouted, "Telegraph first!" at his retreating back. I could only hope that my ploy would work and that Watson would be released unharmed. It was some time later that a paper slipped beneath my door simply stated "*Done*".

Not too long after, I heard the heavy tread upon the stair.

"Sherlock!" My brother cried from the door. "Sherlock! It is finished!" He came in with a heavy relieved sigh.

"To what are you referring?"

"It is finished. There is no further need of your assistance. I have just come from a meeting with the King. He is angry, to say the least, in his feeling that he was been played the fool."

"What are you babbling on about?" I asked, peeved at his avoidance of getting straight to the fact.

"The meeting, what else? Nicholas has changed his mind. He is refusing to come, citing internal issues of his own."

"Ah!" I thought to myself. My telegram to Russia had arrived on time.

"Needless to say," Mycroft continued, "King Obrenovic, the hot headed Serb that he is, turned his ship around mid-way across the Channel and returned to the Continent. The meeting is canceled. The King is safe!"

"But Watson is not," I retorted. I showed Mycroft the note.

"But this cannot be!" he exclaimed. "I myself saw Watson through the open kitchen door downstairs, having a tea with Mrs. Hudson!"

I jumped from my chair and rushed downstairs. Sure enough, there was Mrs. Hudson with Watson.

"Hello, Holmes!" he called out to me. "I was on my way to call when Mrs. Hudson insisted I try her new blueberry scones, fresh from the oven!"

"Watson! You are safe! You are unharmed?"

"Why, what has gotten into you? You see me standing here with your very eyes. Ah! But I did have an urgent sick bed to attend to, and I have a message to deliver. Quite out of the ordinary, I might add, but here it is old chap."

Watson took from his pocket a crumpled piece of brown wrap paper and, as he handed it to me, Mycroft crept up to read it over my shoulder. The only thing on it was a black hand print.

"Strange," Watson remarked. "Who would use such a childish symbol for a message?"

"Who indeed, Watson? Who indeed?" For he had chosen the very words that I would have used.

It was just a little over a year later when news spread from the Continent of the assassination of Serbia's King Alexander Obrenovic and his wife Daga in their private palace, done by a secret organization of insurrectionists on the rise. It was several years later into my retirement, as I tended my bees in Sussex, that the full implication of this was realized when the headlines screamed across the world of another assassination, that of Archduke Franz Ferdinand and his wife Sophie, in the same manner – an assassination at the hands of the militant insurrectionist group that called themselves *The Black Hand*, an assassination that would start a bloody conflict that would encircle the globe.

The Mystery Of the
Missing Artefacts
by Tim Symonds

Date: *August 1916*
Location: *A dungeon under the Dolmabahçe Palace, Constantinople*

I stared up at the patch of blue sky visible through a tiny grille high up on the wall. I was a prisoner-of-war in Constantinople, left to rot in a dank cell under the magnificent State rooms of Sultan Mehmed V Reşâd, my only distraction a much-thumbed copy of Joseph Conrad's *The Secret Agent*. Near-permanent pangs of hunger endlessly recalled a fine meal I enjoyed with my old friend Sherlock Holmes at London's famous Grand Cigar Divan restaurant some years earlier. What I would now give for such a repast, I reflected unhappily. Every detail came to mind: The Chef walking imposingly alongside the lesser mortal propelling a silver dinner wagon. Holmes ordering slices of beef carved from large joint, with a portion of fat. I chose the smoked salmon, a signature dish of the establishment. For dessert, we decided upon the famous treacle sponge with a dressing of Madagascan vanilla custard. And a Trichinopoly cigar to top it off.

I should explain how twists and turns of fate had brought me to my present state. I shall not go into exhaustive detail. It is irrelevant to the bizarre case soon to unravel in a small market town in the English county of Sussex. Suffice it to say that, at the start of the war against the German Kaiser and his Ottoman ally, I volunteered to rejoin my old Regiment. The Army Medical Corps assigned me to the 6th (Poona) Division of the British Indian Army, which had captured the town of Kut-al-Amara a hundred miles south of Baghdad, in the heart of Mesopotamia. I had hardly taken up my post when the Sultan retaliated by ordering his troops to besiege us.

Five desperate months left us entirely without food or potable water. Our Commanding Officer surrendered. The victors separated British Field Officers from Indian Other Ranks and transported us to various camps across the Ottoman Empire. I found myself delivered to the very palace where, ten years earlier, the previous ruler, Sultan Abd-ul-Hamid II, received Sherlock Holmes and me as honoured guests. [1] Now I was confined to a dungeon under the two-hundred-eighty-five rooms, forty-six halls, six *hamams*, and sixty-eight toilets of the magnificent building.

It was clear from the despairing cries of my fellow captives that I was to be left in squalor and near-starvation until the Grim Reaper came to take me to Life Beyond.

The heavy door of my cell swung open. Rather than the surly Turkish warder bringing a once-daily bowl of watery grey soup, a visitor from the outside world stood there. We stared at each other. I judged him to be an American from the three-button jacket with long rolling lapels and shoulders free of padding. The four-button cuffs and military high-waisted effect reflected the influence of the American serviceman's uniform on civilian fashion.

The visitor spoke first. "Captain Watson, MD, I presume?" he asked cordially. He had a New England accent.

"At your service," I said warily, getting to my feet. I was embarrassed by the tattered state of my British Indian Army uniform and Service Dress hat. "And you might be?"

Hand outstretched, the visitor stepped into the cell. "Mr. Philip," he replied. "American Embassy. A Diplomatic Courier came from England with a telegram for you. I apologise for the time it's taken to discover your whereabouts. At the American Embassy, we are all acquainted with the crime stories in *The Strand* magazine written by Sherlock Holmes's great friend, Dr. John H. Watson. None of us realised the Ottoman prisoner of war 'Captain' Watson was one and the same." The emissary's gaze flickered around, suppressing any change of expression at the fetid air. The pestilential hole had been my home-from-home for more than a month. "Not the finest quarters for a British officer, are they?" he smiled sympathetically.

I pointed impatiently at the small envelope in his other hand. "Is that the telegram?" I prompted. Mr. Philip handed it to me with a nod. The envelope carried the words *"From Sherlock Holmes, for the Attention of Captain Watson MD, Constantinople. To be delivered by hand."*

"I have no doubt," Mr. Philip went on, "that it's to inform you that your old companion is working energetically through the Powers-that-Be to have you released and returned to England."

Nodding agreement, I tore open the envelope. My jaw dropped. I glanced up at my visitor and returned my disbelieving gaze to the telegram. *"My dear Watson,"* I read again, *"Do you remember the name of the fellow at the British Museum who contacted us over a certain matter just before I retired to my bee-farm in the South Downs?"*

I remembered the matter in considerable detail. Towards the end of 1903, a letter marked *Urgent & Confidential* arrived at Holmes's Baker Street quarters. It was from a Michael Lacey, Keeper of Antiquities at the British Museum. Some dozens of small items in the Ancient and

Mediaeval Battlefield department had gone missing, artefacts ploughed up on ancient battlegrounds or retrieved from graves of tenth or eleventh Century English knights and bowmen. They were of no intrinsic value. The artefacts had spent some years in storage awaiting archiving, but due to a shortage of experts, no work had been carried out. Would Mr. Holmes come to see the Keeper at the Museum and investigate their disappearance? Holmes waved dismissively. "Probably an inside job – perhaps a floor-sweeper hoping to augment a pitiful salary. It would hardly prove even a one-Abdulla-cigarette problem." My comrade clambered to his feet, reached for his Inverness cape and announced, "I plan to spend today at my bee-farm on the Sussex Downs, checking my little workers are doing what Nature designed for them, filling jars with a golden liquid purloined from the buttercup, the poppy, and the Blue Speedwell."

He looked back from the door. "Watson, don't look so crestfallen. It's hardly as if the umbra of Professor Moriarty of evil memory has marched in and stolen the Elgin Marbles. Kindly inform this Keeper of Antiquities that I haven't the faintest interest in the matter. Refer him to any Jack-in-office at Scotland Yard." His voice floated back up from the stairwell. "No doubt Inspector Lestrade will happily take time away from chasing horse-flies in Surrey to check on an owl job of such little consequence." With a shout to our landlady of "Good day, Mrs. Hudson!" Holmes stepped into the bustle of Baker Street and was gone.

Now, inexplicably, ten and more years later into retirement, he wanted to know the man's name. Not one word on my desperate situation. I turned the telegram over and wrote, *"Dear Holmes, The name of the Keeper at the British Museum was Michael Lacey. Why do you ask? I recall how rudely you refused to take up the case. You said that after 'A Scandal in Bohemia', no ordinary burglary could ever be of interest to you."* With blistering sarcasm I added, *"Would you do me a small favour? When you can find a moment away from whatever you're pursuing, get me out of here as quickly as possible? If the rancid slop doesn't do for me, cholera will."*

The days passed with agonising slowness. At last, Mr. Philip returned. He told me the American Ambassador would shortly be making a demarche to the Sublime Porte to get me released. He handed me a second communication from England. I wrenched it open. The envelope contained a cutting from a Sussex newspaper, *The Battle Observer.* Below an advertisement for the Central Picture Theatre (*The Folly of Youth*), Holmes had marked out a photograph of a corpse lying in a field below ancient ruins. The photograph was attributed to a Brian Hanson, using a Sinclair Una De Luxe No. 2 – a camera I was myself planning to purchase using the savings from my Army pay, forced on me by my incarceration. The headline blared *"Strange Death of Former British Museum Keeper"*.

The report continued:

> *Early this morning, a body was discovered by local resident Mrs. Johnson, walking her dog across the site of the Battle of Hastings. An arrow jutted out of the deceased's left eye. The dead man has been identified as Michael Lacey, former Head of Antiquities at the British Museum. The police were called and the body removed to the Union Workhouse hospital. It is not known what the deceased was doing in the field in the night. It is a spot seldom frequented after dark. Local legend holds the land runs crimson with blood when the rain falls. Ghostly figures have made appearances – phantom monks and spectral knights, red and grey ladies. Furthermore, each October, on the eve of the famous battle, a lone ghostly knight has been reported riding soundlessly across the battlefield.*

The article ended with:

> *The police describe Mr. Lacey as a well-known if controversial and isolated figure in the area since his retirement to a house on Caldbec Hill, over ten years ago. He was rumoured to hold to the widely-discredited theory that the Battle between William of Normandy and Harold Godwinson of England did not take place on the slopes below the present-day ruins of Battle Abbey, but at a location several miles away. What remains certain is that William's victory and Harold's death from an arrow in the eye changed the course of our Island's history, laws, and customs.*

An accompanying note in Holmes's scrawl said, *"Come soonest. SH."*

A week later, a Turkish Major-General fell into the hands of British forces outside Jerusalem. A prisoner-exchange was agreed. By early October, I was back in London, greeting the locum at my Marylebone surgery. In a matter of hours, the Chinese laundry on Tottenham Court Road restored my Indian Army uniform, topee, and Sam Browne belt to pristine condition. I would wear the uniform for my visit to Holmes to avoid the attention of the ladies of the Order of the White Feather.

I tarried further in the Capital just long enough to visit Solomon's in Piccadilly to purchase a supply of black hothouse grapes, and Salmon and Gluckstein of Oxford Street, where I stocked up with a half-a-dozen tins of J&H Wilson No. 1 Top Mill Snuff and several boxes of Trichinopoly cigars. The train deposited me at Eastbourne. I boarded a sturdy four-wheeler to engage with the mud.

The ancient County of Sussex is rich in historical features and archaeological remains, including defensive sites, burial mounds, and field boundaries. Holmes's bee-farm was tucked in rolling chalk downland with close-cropped turf and dry valleys stretching from the Itchen Valley in the west to Beachy Head in the east. Some miles later a lonely, low-lying black-and-white building with a stone courtyard and crimson ramblers came into view. Holmes was waiting to greet me. At the familiar sight a wave of nostalgia washed through me.

While I fumbled for money to pay the cabman, Holmes drummed his fingers on the side of the carriage. The payment made, at a touch of the driver's whip the horses wheeled and turned away. Holmes reached a hand across to my shoulder. "Well done, Watson," he said, adding in the sarcastic tone of old, "Prompt as ever in answering a telegraphic summons."

"Holmes!" I cried. "You might remember I was rotting in a dungeon in the Sultan's Palace two-thousand miles away when your invitation arrived. I was lucky to find a British warship in Alexandria, or I might have been incarcerated a second time. The Mediterranean bristles with the Kaiser's dreadnoughts and battle-cruisers."

To mollify me, Holmes said, "We must ask my housekeeper, Mrs. Keppler, to bring you a restorative cup of tea. You will be offered a very civilised choice of shiny black tea or scented green."

We seated ourselves in the Summer-house. I handed over the tray of Solomon's black grapes and a share of the Trichinopoly cigars. My comrade passed across a large copy of the newspaper picture I had first seen in the Turkish cell. "I obtained this at a modest charge from *The Battle Observer*," he explained. "Now, Watson, you're a medical chap. I need your help. My knowledge of anatomy is accurate, but unsystematic. Tell me, what do you think?"

"Think about what precisely?" I queried, staring at the corpse in the picture.

"The arrow in his eye, of course," came Holmes's reply. "The local police say he must done it to himself," he continued. "King Harold was

379

shot in the eye by a Norman arrow. They suggest Lacey chose to die the same death, maddened by his failure to disprove the true site of the battle. The citizens of the town are in a hurry to close the case. They most definitely do not wish for unfavourable publicity ahead of the commemorative events."

"Which events?" I asked.

"The eight-hundred-and-fiftieth anniversary of the Battle of Hastings," Holmes replied. "In a week's time. Hundreds of visitors are expected. *Le Tout-Battle* wishes to make a lot of money from them."

"If you mean did the arrow cause his death, I can answer that straight away, Holmes. No, the arrow was not the cause of Lacey's death. The angle of entry is quite wrong. It would have slipped past any vital part of the brain. In Afghanistan, I administered to one of our Indian troops who caught an arrow in the eye. He lived on for months and probably years."

"Could it have been self-inflicted?" Holmes asked.

"Unlikely," I replied. "In my opinion, he was already dead when the arrow was pushed into his eye."

Holmes asked, "So the fear and horror on his face?"

"Already frozen into it."

"Therefore the real cause of death?"

"Undoubtedly a heart attack," I replied. "From fright," I opined. "Something spine-chilling must have happened to Lacey on that isolated spot. Whatever it was, a rush of adrenaline stunned his cardiac muscle into inaction. Think of Colonel Barclay's death in the matter of the Crooked Man. He died of fright. There's a close similarity here." I went on, "Dying of fright is a rather more frequent medical condition than you may imagine. I estimate one person a day dies from it in any of our great cities."

Holmes rose quickly. "You have me intrigued, Watson. We must hurry. Drink up your tea. I may not have displayed the slightest interest in the Keeper of Antiquities and his little problems while he was alive, but in death he presents a most unusual case."

"Hurry where?" I asked, bewildered.

"Why, to the British Museum, where else! It'll be like old times. The last time I was there, I read up on voodooism."

We went into the house. Holmes picked up the telephone receiver to order a cab. As he waited, he remarked, "A small point but one of interest, Watson. The police outside London often asked for my assistance whenever I was in the neighbourhood. I am a mere twenty miles from Battle. The inspector knows I am here, yet despite a mysterious death on his patch, no request to meet me has arrived at my door. What do you make of that?"

Within the quarter-hour a carriage arrived. As we jolted along, Holmes pulled out a packet of Pall Mall Turkish cigarettes and lit one, eyes narrowing against the smoke. He reached into his voluminous coat for the photographic print purchased from *The Battle Observer*. He stared at the image, puffing in thoughtful silence. "What is it, Holmes?" I asked at last. "Why the knitted brow and repeated drumming on your knee?"

"There's something odd here, Watson. Something I quite missed at first. You have my copy of *The Observer* in your side-pocket. Can you pass it to me, please?" Holmes reached once more into his coat, withdrawing a ten-power silver-and-chrome magnifying glass. For a while it hovered over the newspaper. I was irresistibly reminded of a well-trained foxhound dashing back and forth through the covert, whining in its eagerness, until it comes across the lost scent . . . .

Holmes gave a grunt. He passed the print and magnifying glass to me. "Tell me what you see," he ordered. I stared down through the powerful glass.

"Nothing unusual, Holmes," I said, looking up.

Holmes asked, "What about the grass under the corpse's head?"

"The ground around the body gives no indication of a deadly struggle," I replied. "Is that what you mean?"

He passed the newspaper back and commanded, "Now look again at the grass around the body as it appears in *The Observer*."

Once more I looked through the magnifying glass. "Why, it's nowhere near as clear as in the print, Holmes," I replied. "In fact it's quite grainy."

"Precisely, Watson. Why would the grass be quite clearly defined in the print but look grainy when the same photograph appears in the newspaper? This is a three-pipe problem at the very least, Watson. I beg you not to speak to me for fifty minutes."

Holmes flicked the cigarette butt out of the carriage window and produced his favourite blackened briar. I threw my tobacco pouch to his side and looked quickly out of the carriage window, blinking away a tear of happiness. The Sherlock Holmes of yesteryear was back.

After only one pipe, Holmes pointed at my Indian Army uniform. He shot me an unexpected question. "Watson, I presume sun-up would have had a vital role in your Regiment's confrontation with Ayub Khan at the Battle of Maiwand. Isn't that where you received an arrow in your right leg?"

"Left shoulder," I replied. "And it was a Jezail long-arm rifle bullet, not an arrow."

"My point is, Watson, did you become something of an expert on the daily motion of the sun?"

"I did," I responded.

"To the point you can calculate the very moment of sunrise?"

"Yes, Holmes, but it's far from as simple as you might think. First, you must decide upon your definition of sunrise – is it when the middle of the sun crosses the horizon, or the top edge, or the bottom edge? Also, do you take the horizon to be sea level, or do you take into account the topography? In addition, what of the Earth's atmosphere? It can bend the light so that the sun appears to rise a few moments earlier or later than if there were no atmosphere."

Holmes's expression turned from one of interest to irritation. He tore the briar from his mouth. "Yes, Watson, yes," he flared. "Take the arrow which stuck in your thigh. I consider a man's brain is like an empty attic. We must stock it with just such furniture as we choose. I merely want to know whether – given a while with a note-book and pencil – you can calculate the exact time this photograph was taken?"

I replied, "If we say sunrise refers to the time the middle of the disc of the sun appears on the horizon, considered unobstructed relative to the location of interest, and assuming atmospheric conditions to be average, and being sure to include the sun's declination from the time of the year – "

"Yes, yes, yes!" Holmes bellowed. "Take all of that into account, by all means!"

A telephone call from Holmes's bee-farm ensured we were greeted at the Museum's imposing entrance by Sir Frederick Kenyon, the Director. Sir Frederick was a palaeographer and biblical and classical scholar of the Old School. Our host led us to a small antechamber. The first drawer he opened revealed a glittering array of gold hoops and gold rivets, several silver collars and neck-rings, a silver arm, a fragment of a Permian ring, and a silver penannular brooch. Each was meticulously labelled. Sir Frederick picked out a sword pommel. "Mediaeval battles," he announced. "This was Lacey's life's work – the Battle of Fulford, the Siege of Exeter . . . . Never have I had a colleague who worked with such application. For years at a time, he would hardly leave to go home at night – that is, until . . . ." He paused.

"Until?" I echoed.

Sir Frederick looked at Holmes. "I don't know how else to put it –
until Mr. Holmes failed to come to his help in finding the missing
artefacts." A flush of colour sprang to Holmes's pale cheeks.

I interjected quickly, "Was it also from this drawer that the items of
no intrinsic value were disappearing?" The Director shook his head.

"Not from here, no." He pulled open a second drawer. "From here."

The drawer was empty except for an envelope. It contained the letter
I penned years earlier to the former Keeper of Antiquities, apologising
for Holmes's refusal to become involved in the investigation. I had
reconstructed Holmes's own words to read: "*Mr. Sherlock Holmes sends
his regrets. He is attending to his bee-farm in the South Downs and will
not be taking cases for the foreseeable future.*"

"The missing artefacts were in this drawer," Sir Frederick
continued. "Here's where Lacey kept the more common or garden pieces
found at various battle-sites. Broken sword-blades and the like.
Miscellany too lacking in value or utility even for the local peasantry to
pick up. Nevertheless he took the theft very hard." Sir Frederick looked
sympathetically at my companion. "Mr. Holmes, I understand your
refusal. There wasn't a gold or silver item or precious jewel among the
lot." Our host hesitated, then added, "Despite this, Lacey did seem
unusually affected by Dr. Watson's letter. His behaviour changed. He
grew secretive. Now I reflect on it, it was as though he was developing a
plan."

Sir Frederick continued, "I noticed one other change . . . . Other
people's fame began to obsess him. For example, when the antiquarian
Charles Dawson declared the human-like skull he had uncovered near
Piltdown to be the 'missing link' between ape and man, Lacey muttered
something about making a discovery one day which would make his own
name just as famous – not in anthropology but in the annals of English
archaeology."

I asked, "Did you have any idea what he meant?"

The Museum Director shrugged. "One day I came in upon him
unexpectedly. He was bent over that table studying a drawing. Beyond
saying it involved electrical theory, he would elaborate no further."

"Electrical theory?" I heard Holmes repeat, asking, "Do you recall
anything from the drawing itself?"

The Director shook his head. "I chanced only a quick glance before
Lacey slipped it under some other papers. There were wires. I spotted a
few words in French. I remember there were two large wheels, one at
each end of the legs of a bipod. Oh yes, something about the wheels was
odd. They weren't upright like a dog-cart or other means of conveyance.
They were flat on the ground."

383

"What were the words in French?" I asked.

"'*Faisceau hertzien*'," came the reply. "I'm told that means *wireless beam*. My curiosity overcame me. "'Lacey," I said, 'I'd be grateful if you kindly let me in on this secret of yours!' But all he muttered was something about unexploded bombs. Then he got up from the table and said he'd been meaning to talk to me. About retirement. He said if Europe's greatest Consulting Detective couldn't be bothered to look into the theft of artefacts from the British Museum, his faith in human beings was gone. A month or so later, he handed in his resignation and quit."

The great doors of the Museum shut behind us. I hailed a motorised hackney. "Waste of time coming all the way here, wasn't it, Holmes!" I remarked, "I can't say we learnt much about anything."

Holmes's eyebrows arched. "To the contrary, Watson, I think we learnt a very great deal. Take Lacey's violent reaction when he received your letter. Even to hand in his resignation! I'd have expected him to be exercised if the priceless gold and jewelled artefacts had been filched. None of those went missing, despite being right next to the drawer containing quite ordinary relics. You'd have thought even the most common or garden sneak thief in something of a hurry can spot the difference between a gold torque and a rusty link from a dead Saxon's chain-mail armour."

The cab turned in response to my wave and halted at the kerb in front of us. Once seated, Holmes continued musing. "Why would the loss of a few worthless battlefield gew-gaws generate such a clamour from the Keeper?"

"Monomania perhaps?" I answered. "As you know, there's a term the French novelist Honore de Balzac invented, '*idée fixe*', describing how an obsession may be accompanied by complete sanity in every other way."

Holmes asked, "What do you make of the other curious matter, the machine depicted in the blueprint? A bipod with two large wheels flat against the ground?"

"I haven't the faintest idea, Holmes, nor why the subject of unexploded bombs would come up at the British Museum."

"True," Holmes responded thoughtfully. "It's certainly an odd subject for a Keeper of Antiquities."

We reached Victoria Station. The train trundled over the Thames. We were on our way back to Sussex. The last low rays of the setting sun sparkled against the cross atop the great dome of St Paul's Cathedral.

384

After a lengthy walk in Holmes's woods and fields that evening, we returned to the farmhouse. I struck a match on my boot and put it to the fire laid earlier by Mrs. Keppler to ward off the country damp. The ancient hearth blazed up as heartily as in our days at 221b Baker Street, fuelled from the abundant oak, the Weed of Sussex, rather than the sea-coal in our London fireplace. I opened my note-book and said, "Holmes, you asked where the sun was at the instant the camera shutter was released. Judging by the shadows in the photograph, I believe the photograph was taken when the geometric centre of the rising sun was eighteen degrees below low hills to the south-east. Around 6:40 a.m. was the first moment there would have been enough light."

My companion absorbed this in silence. A few minutes later he asked in a sympathetic tone, "If Captain Watson of the Army Medical Department were to consult Dr. John H. Watson, MD, at the latter's renowned medical practice in Marylebone, would Dr. Watson tell the Captain he has fully recovered from a frightful ordeal in Mesopotamia, followed by incarceration in a Turkish dungeon?"

"Thank you, Holmes," I replied, touched by this rare concern. "You may take it the Captain's heart would be certified as strong as that of the proverbial ox. Daily walks on the warship returning Captain Watson to these shores, combined with the fine food of the Naval Officer's Mess, completely restored him."

"Excellent!" my companion exclaimed, a trifle enigmatically. He leaned with his back against the shutters, the deep-set grey eyes narrowing. "Watson, we hold in our hand the threads of one of the strangest cases ever to perplex a man's brain, yet we lack the one or two clues which are needful to complete a theory of mine. Ah, I see you yawning. I suggest you retire. I shall tarry over a pipe a while longer to see if light can be cast on our path ahead."

The country air and the warmth of the log-fire had taken their effect. I hadn't the slightest idea what Holmes was up to or whether or how the strength of "Captain Watson's" heart could have anything to do with the present perplexing case. I fell into a comfortable bed and a restful sleep.

I was dreaming of I know not what when a loud rat-tat-tat came on the bedroom door. "Watson!" Holmes called out. "We must throw our brains into action. Dress quickly!" I opened an eye. Through the window, Venus and Mars were in close conjunction, bright in an otherwise cloudy night sky. "What is it, Holmes?" I returned indignantly. "Can't it wait till dawn?"

The door flew open. My impatient host entered, dressed for the outdoors in Norfolk jacket and knickerbockers, with a cloth cap upon his head. "Watson, the *genius loci*. As you know, I'm a believer in visiting the scene of the crime. It is essential in the proper exercise of deduction to take the perspective of those involved. I have just returned from Battle. I must return there with you straight away. Just one thread remains, my dear fellow. You are the one person who can provide it."

Scarcely an hour later, Holmes and I stood side by side on the spot where William the Conqueror's knights crushed King Harold's housecarls and his Saxon freemen. Holmes flapped a hand over a patch of grass. "I estimate the body lay here. Watson. How long before the geometric centre of the rising sun reaches eighteen degrees below the horizon?"

I looked to the south-east. "Not more than five minutes," I replied, adding, "May I say I'm at a complete loss to know what in heaven's name we're doing here, Holmes. The dawn hasn't even . . . ."

"Then Watson, you must have your answer!" Holmes shouted. "Turn to face the Abbey!"

I whirled around. A terrifying apparition burst upon my startled gaze. With no sound audible above my stentorian breathing, a knight in chain-mail astride a huge charger was flying down the slope towards me, a boar image on his helmet, on an arm a kite shield limned with a Crusader cross and six *Fleur De Lis*. Behind, half-a-dozen cowled monks rose out of the ground, menacing, crouching, uttering strange cries. I broke into a cold, clammy sweat. My muscles twitched uncontrollably. I felt I was about to crash to the ground. The immense horse and rider passed by in a second, dashing on until the pair merged with the spectral mist rising from a clump of bushes a hundred yards down the slope. I turned to face the ghostly monks. There was no-one there. It was as though a preternatural visitation had returned to the Netherworld with the first shafts of the rising sun.

I dropped to all fours, dazed. Holmes's voice came to me faintly, as though from a distant shore: "Watson, my dear fellow, are you all right? You've had a terrible shock." The familiar voice brought me back to sanity.

"We can agree that I have, Holmes," I panted. In the same reassuring tone, Holmes went on, "The phantoms have gone, my dear friend. They've returned to their rest. They will not be back until the next anniversary of the Battle of Hastings."

I looked around the empty sward. "Where on Earth . . . ?" I began.

"Tunnels, my dear fellow," Holmes answered. "Monks and other ecclesiasticals. Landed Gentry. Knights Templar. Abbots. All particularly given to tunnels."

The terror I endured for those few seconds was dissipating. Holmes looked at me closely. "Again I ask, are you all right, my dear fellow?"

"I am nearly recovered," I said. "I appreciate your evident concern, Holmes, but you are clearly not an innocent party to this strange event. I deserve and demand an explanation."

Holmes seated himself on the ground at my side. "Two clues put me on a scent, Watson. First, the trace evidence around us here." His finger described an ellipse following the trajectory of the ghostly horse as it galloped down to the swamp. "Look there, and there," he ordered.

I stared at the series of depressions in the grass. "But Holmes," I protested, "while those indentations may fit where a horse's hooves would have landed, they are both too shallow and too square for the marks of a horse ridden at speed!"

"My dear Captain Watson, I take it even in your service in the Far East you failed to hear of mediaeval Japanese straw horse-sandals known as *umugatsu*? They were tied between the fetlock and hoof to give traction on wet terrain and to muffle the sound of the hooves, and to deceive by eliminating the deep cuts hooves would inflict on damp earth. I think we can credit the local schoolmaster for his scholarship."

"Nice touch. The Crusader shield too," I remarked sarcastically, "when you consider the first Crusade didn't commence until thirty years after the Battle of Hastings."

I fingered my pulse. It was returning to normal. "And the second of two clues, Holmes?"

"The second lay in the difference between the print I purchased and the same photograph as it appeared in *The Battle Observer*. The editor wanted only the corpse's face and the arrow. Therefore, Hanson enlarged the middle of the print. This brought out a granulated effect in the grass under the head. But why? Why was there any graininess about the background at all? Why weren't the blades of grass as much in focus as the face and arrow?"

"Holmes," I responded, "I have given it some thought. Forgive me if what I'm about to propose sounds absurd, but I'm very far from being unacquainted with cameras, as you know. The only explanation is the camera must have been positioned much higher up than if held by someone standing on the ground in the normal way. Getting the face in precise focus at the greater distance would mean anything deeper would be less in focus. This effect would show up most when the photograph was enlarged."

"The very conclusion I came to myself, Watson!" my companion exclaimed, rubbing his hands in delight. The *occipitofrontalis* muscles of my forehead wrinkled. I asked, "But why would Hanson stretch his arms high over his head to take the photo?"

"He wouldn't," came the response. "He didn't need to. He was seated on a horse. The knight was none other than *The Observer* photographer himself."

I waved at the field stretching away above us. "Holmes, how in Heaven's name did you get them to cooperate?"

"Not eight hours ago, I paid Hanson a visit," Holmes replied. "He admitted everything. I told him he and his co-conspirators could be in mortal danger, accused of murder, and that my silence was not safeguard enough – others may yet make the same deduction. He said 'I'm the one who thought up the caper. If anyone is to meet the hangman, it should be me.' I told him I had something in mind. He and the monks were to reassemble here before dawn today." Holmes tapped his watch and raised and dropped an arm. "At my signal, the knight was to charge straight at the man in a captain's uniform at my side. The monks were once again to spring up like dragon's teeth, yelling any doggerel they could remember from schoolboy Latin."

The explanation jolted me to the core. "Holmes!" I yelled. I broke off, breathing hard. "Holmes," I repeated, "I once described you as a brain without a heart, as deficient in human sympathy as you are pre-eminent in intelligence. Are you proving me right? Are you saying that despite Lacey's frightful death, you deliberately exposed me to an identical fate?"

"Yes, my dear Captain," Holmes broke in, chuckling, "I did. You must remember I took the precaution of checking on your health with a Dr. Watson famed on two continents for his medical skills. He pronounced your heart strong as an ox. Who am I to dispute his diagnosis?"

"And if the good Dr. Watson had made a misjudgement?" I asked ruefully.

"High stakes indeed, Watson," came the rejoinder. "I would have lost a great friend, and a hapless crew of locals their best witness, leaving me bereft and them open to a second charge of murder!"

My legs still felt shaky. "Holmes," I begged. "Why are you so adamantly on these people's side?"

"Think of this small town, Watson," my comrade began. "Eight-hundred-and-fifty-years ago, when Duke William crossed the Channel, there was no human settlement here, just a quiet stretch of rough grazing. Look at it now! Without the battlefield, it would be nothing, a backwater, a small and isolated market-town. Imagine Royal Windsor without the

388

Castle, Canterbury without the Cathedral. Visitors to this battleground provide the underpinning of every merchant on the High Street, the hoteliers and publicans, even *The Battle Observer* itself, dependent on advertising Philpott's Annual Summer Sales and the like. The mock monks and a spectral knight on horseback can fairly be accused of one thing – trying to protect their livelihoods. If visitors stop coming, the hotels die. The souvenir shops die. The cafés and restaurants close.

"Napoleon greatly incensed the English by calling us 'a nation of shopkeepers', and England remains a nation of merchants. All her grand resources arise from commerce. What else constitutes the riches of England? It's not mines of gold, silver, or diamonds. Not even extent of territory. We are a tiny island off the great landmass of Eurasia."

Holmes pointed to where ghostly horse and rider had disappeared. "Have you recovered enough to walk down to that clump of bushes? I anticipate we shall find something there of extreme interest."

At the bottom of the slope, a small bridge took us to a patch of marshland dotted about with bushes and reeds into which horse and rider had disappeared. Holmes's former quick pace slowed like the Clouded Leopard searching out its prey. With a grunt of satisfaction, he darted forward, calling out "Come, Watson – give me a hand!" A pair of wooden spars jutted from the mud. A spade half-floated on the mud a few feet beyond. We dragged the contraption to a patch of dry ground. It was the physical embodiment of the blueprint the Keeper of Antiquities had tried to hide at the British Museum. Held upright, the bipod was perhaps three feet in height. It was exactly as described by Sir Frederick: The two wheels were not wheels of a small cart, but circles of wood and metal lying flush with the ground, some twenty-four inches apart. A set of wires led to a half-submerged metal box filled with vacuum tubes and a heavy battery.

I pointed. "Holmes, those are Audion vacuum tubes. I've seen them used in wireless technology. This must be the secret invention Lacey hinted at."

"If he had not built it, Watson," Holmes responded, "Lacey might still be alive." He continued, "I pondered long and hard about '*Faisceau hertzien*', and the reference to unexploded bombs. Then by chance, my brother Mycroft called to say he had been seconded to the War Office for the duration. In the greatest confidence, he told me the French 6th Engineer Regiment at Verdun-sur-Meuse has been developing a machine using wireless beams to detect German mines. Somehow Lacey must have heard about it. He realised he could adapt it to search for metal artefacts at ancient battlegrounds."

"But, Holmes," I asked. "Why use it on this field? After all, if Lacey's intention was to *disprove* the battle took place here . . . ."

"It was Lacey's '*idée fixe*'," my companion interrupted.

He pointed at the spade. "He criss-crossed these fields at night using a device which could spot even a silver penny dropped nine centuries ago. With it, he was able to detect and remove every metal artefact left by Duke William's and King Harold's men. Lacey may have found nothing whatsoever, not even a piece of rusty chain-mail, proving the battle never took place here, or he was clearing it of anything traceable to 1066 – in short, planning a great evil against the noble profession of Archaeology. At a moment of maximum publicity, he intended to denounce the town's claim to the battle-site. He did not give a thought that the town's prosperity would come to an abrupt end. Even *The Battle Observer* would go out of business. But one recent moonlit night, Brian Hanson saw this phantom-like figure slowly across the landscape. He recognised Lacey. He guessed what he was up to. The townsfolk had to work fast."

"Should we go to report our findings to the local police, Holmes?" I asked.

"By no means," came a firm reply.

I turned to stare at my companion. "But . . . but surely, now we know – "

"Watson, we need do nothing but wait to see if the matter progresses or simply dies away. If the latter, a kindly fate has taken its course. If the former, thanks to you no jury of twelve good men and true will convict for murder."

"How can that be, Holmes?" I asked, "when indisputably their actions caused the death of a man. How can they escape the hangman's noose?"

"Bear in mind," Holmes began, "our motley crew of locals didn't have murder in mind. They rose up out of the ground dressed as the disquieted souls of long-dead Benedictine monks and inadvertently caused Lacey's heart to give way. Their plan was to frighten him off and fling his infernal contrivance and spade into the swamp. That that was their intent is the more credible, thanks to your survival. They now have a good case to plead *Mens rea* – no mental intent to kill. At worst manslaughter, not murder."

"The arrow?" I asked.

"Admittedly a barbarous act," Holmes replied, "but the man was already dead. Hanson hoped to confuse the coroner, to make him conclude the arrow caused the stricken expression on the corpse's face. Otherwise, alarm bells would ring, and a case of murder arise."

Now mollified, I asked, "And who would want to associate the vile crime of murder with these dear old homesteads set in a smiling and beautiful countryside?" I continued lyrically, "I could hardly bear the thought such a peaceful and pleasant English market town could harbour a murder gang. Another case resolved, Holmes. Let us leave the good people of Battle to their commemorative preparations and repair to our favourite eatery deep among the Downs – in short, visit the Tiger Inn and partake of a hearty lunch."

We heaved the spade deeper into the marsh, and marked the unexploded-bomb detector's location for retrieval by Mycroft Holmes's agents at a later time. As we walked back across the small bridge, I said, "There's a matter you have not explained. Why did the Keeper of Antiquities react in such a choleric way to your refusal to investigate?"

"It was quite worthy of arch-criminal Moriarty of old, Watson, a most devious ploy. A snub was precisely what Lacey wanted. I should have smelt a rat by the way he worded his request – '*I shall of course understand if this case is of little interest to you, Mr. Holmes, the missing articles being of no intrinsic value whatsoever*'. That's hardly as compelling as '*Mr. Holmes, while the relics are of scant intrinsic value, from the historical point of view they are very nearly unique*'. Your letter informing him of my refusal came like Manna from Heaven. He could show Sir Frederick he'd tried to bring in Europe's most famous Consulting Detective. No-one would ever dream the larcenist was Lacey himself. He would be able to use the pilfered artefacts to 'salt' the field of his choosing."

"Thereby," I added, "becoming one of the most famous men in England."

"Yes," my companion nodded. "As famous in the archaeological world as Charles Dawson has become in the world of the palaeontologist and anatomist."

Together we walked across the historic fields. A line of horse-drawn cabs was forming at the Abbey entrance, the fine arrangement of bays and cobs snorting into their nose-bags, ready for the day's influx of visitors. We went to a Landau driven by a pair.

"Cabbie, the Tiger Inn," Holmes instructed. "An extra guinea for you from the captain here if we arrive before their kitchen runs out of that well-armed sea creature, the lobster."

NOTE

1 – This was a case published under the title *Sherlock Holmes and the Sword of Osman* (2015, MX Publishing).

About the Contributors

The following contributors appear in this volume
The MX Book of New Sherlock Holmes Stories
Part X – 2018 Annual (1896-1916)

Hugh Ashton was born in the U.K., and moved to Japan in 1988, where he remained until 2016, living with his wife Yoshiko in the historic city of Kamakura, a little to the south of Yokohama. He and Yoshiko have now moved to Lichfield, a small cathedral city in the Midlands of the U.K., the birthplace of Samuel Johnson, and one-time home of Erasmus Darwin. In the past, he has worked in the technology and financial services industries, which have provided him with material for some of his books set in the 21st century. He currently works as a writer: Novelist, freelance editor, and copywriter, (his work for large Japanese corporations has appeared in international business journals), and journalist, as well as producing industry reports on various aspects of the financial services industry. Recently, however, his lifelong interest in Sherlock Holmes has developed into an acclaimed series of adventures featuring the world's most famous detective, written in the style of the originals, and published by Inknbeans Press. In addition to these, he has also published historical and alternate historical novels, short stories, and thrillers. Together with artist Andy Boerger, he has produced the *Sherlock Ferret* series of stories for children, featuring the world's cutest detective.

Brian Belanger is a publisher and editor, but is best known for his freelance illustration and cover design work. His distinctive style can be seen on several MX Publishing covers, including *Silent Meridian* by Elizabeth Crowen, *Sherlock Holmes and the Menacing Melbournian* by Allan Mitchell, *Sherlock Holmes and A Quantity of Debt* by David Marcum, *Welcome to Undershaw* by Luke Benjamen Kuhns, and many more. Brian is the co-founder of Belanger Books LLC, where he illustrates the popular *MacDougall Twins with Sherlock Holmes* young reader series (#1 bestsellers on Amazon.com UK). A prolific creator, he also designs t-shirts, mugs, stickers, and other merchandise on his personal art site: *www.redbubble.com/people/zhahadun*.

Derrick Belanger is and educator and also the author of the #1 bestselling book in its category, *Sherlock Holmes: The Adventure of the Peculiar Provenance*, which was in the top 200 bestselling books on Amazon. He also is the author of *The MacDougall Twins with Sherlock Holmes* books, and he edited the Sir Arthur Conan Doyle horror anthology *A Study in Terror: Sir Arthur Conan Doyle's Revolutionary Stories of Fear and the Supernatural*. Mr. Belanger co-owns the publishing company Belanger Books, which released the Sherlock Holmes anthologies *Beyond Watson, Holmes Away From Home: Adventures from the Great Hiatus* Volumes 1 and 2, *Sherlock Holmes: Before Baker Street*, and *Sherlock Holmes: Adventures in the Realms of H.G. Wells* Volumes I and 2. Derrick resides in Colorado and continues compiling unpublished works by Dr. John H. Watson.

Maurice Barkley lives with his wife Marie in a suburb of Rochester, New York. Retired from a career as a commercial artist and builder of tree houses, he is writing and busy reinforcing the stereotype of a pesky househusband. His other Sherlock Holmes stories can be found on Amazon. *https://www.amazon.com/author/mauricebarkleys*

Sir Arthur Conan Doyle (1859-1930) *Holmes Chronicler Emeritus.* If not for him, this anthology would not exist. Author, physician, patriot, sportsman, spiritualist, husband and father, and advocate for the oppressed. He is remembered and honored for the purposes of this collection by being the man who introduced Sherlock Holmes to the world. Through fifty-six Holmes short stories, four novels, and additional Apocryphal entries, Doyle revolutionized mystery stories and also greatly influenced and improved police forensic methods and techniques for the betterment of all. *Steel True Blade Straight.*

Steve Emecz's main field is technology, in which he has been working for about twenty years. Following multiple senior roles at Xerox, where he grew their European eCommerce from $6m to $200m, Steve joined platform provider Venda, and moved across to Powa in 2010. Today, Steve is CCO at collectAI in Hamburg, a German fintech company using Artificial Intelligence to help companies with their debt collection. Steve is a regular trade show speaker on the subject of eCommerce, and his tech career has taken him to more than fifty countries – so he's no stranger to planes and airports. He wrote two novels (one a bestseller) in the 1990's, and a screenplay in 2001. Shortly after, he set up MX Publishing, specialising in NLP books. In 2008, MX published its first Sherlock Holmes book, and MX has gone on to become the largest specialist Holmes publisher in the world. MX is a social enterprise and supports two main causes. The first is Happy Life, a children's rescue project in Nairobi, Kenya, where he and his wife, Sharon, spend every Christmas at the rescue centre in Kasarani. In 2014, they wrote a short book about the project, *The Happy Life Story.* The second is the Stepping Stones School, of which Steve is a patron. Stepping Stones is located at Undershaw, Sir Arthur Conan Doyle's former home.

Steven Ehrman is an American musician and author of the *Sherlock Holmes Uncovered* tales. These are traditional Sherlock Holmes stories with every effort to adhere to the canon. He is a lifelong admirer of Sir Arthur Conan Doyle and spent countless hours as a youth reading The Master's works.

Paul A. Freeman is the author of *Rumours of Ophir*, a novel which was taught in Zimbabwean high schools and has been translated into German. In addition to having two crime novels, a children's book, and an 18,000-word narrative poem commercially published, Paul is also the author over a hundred published short stories, articles, and poems. Paul currently works in Abu Dhabi, where he lives with his wife and three children

James R. "Jim" French became a morning Disc Jockey on KIRO (AM) in Seattle in 1959. He later founded *Imagination Theatre*, a syndicated program that broadcast to over one-hundred-and-twenty stations in the U.S. and Canada, and also on the XM Satellite Radio system all over North America. Actors in French's dramas included John Patrick Lowrie, Larry Albert, Patty Duke, Russell Johnson, Tom Smothers, Keenan Wynn, Roddy MacDowall, Ruta Lee, John Astin, Cynthia Lauren Tewes, and Richard Sanders. Mr. French stated, "To me, the characters of Sherlock Holmes and Doctor Watson always seemed to be figures Doyle created as a challenge to lesser writers. He gave us two interesting characters – different from each other in their histories, talents, and experience, but complimentary as a team – who have been applied to a variety of situations and plots far beyond the times and places in The Canon. In the hands of different writers, Holmes and Watson have lent their identities to different times, ages, and even genders. But I wanted to break no new ground. I feel Sir Arthur provided us with enough references to locations, landmarks, and the social conditions of his time, to give a pretty large canvas on which to paint our own images and actions to animate Holmes and Watson." Mr. French passed away at the age of eight-nine on December 20th, 2017, the day that his contribution to this book was being edited. He shall be missed.

Mark A. Gagen BSI is co-founder of Wessex Press, sponsor of the popular *From Gillette to Brett* conferences, and publisher of *The Sherlock Holmes Reference Library* and many other fine Sherlockian titles. A life-long Holmes enthusiast, he is a member of *The Baker Street Irregulars* and *The Illustrious Clients of Indianapolis*. A graphic artist by profession, his work is often seen on the covers of *The Baker Street Journal* and various BSI books.

Jayantika Ganguly BSI is the General Secretary and Editor of the *Sherlock Holmes Society of India*, a member of the *Sherlock Holmes Society of London*, and the *Czech Sherlock Holmes Society*. She is the author of *The Holmes Sutra* (MX 2014). She is a corporate lawyer working with one of the Big Six law firms.

Dick Gillman is an English writer and acrylic artist living in Brittany, France with his wife Alex, Truffle, their Black Labrador, and Jean-Claude, their Breton cat. During his retirement from teaching, he has written over twenty Sherlock Holmes short stories which are published as both e-books and paperbacks. His contribution to the superb MX Sherlock Holmes collection, published in October 2015, was entitled "The Man on Westminster Bridge" and had the privilege of being chosen as the anchor story in *The MX Book of New Sherlock Holmes Stories – Part II (1890-1895).*

Melissa Grigsby, Head Teacher of Stepping Stones School, is driven by a passion to open the doors to learners with complex and layered special needs that just make society feel two steps too far away. Based on the Surrey/Hampshire border in England, her time is spent between a great school at the prestigious home of Conan Doyle, and her two children, dogs, and horses, so there never a dull moment.

John Atkinson Grimshaw (1836-1893) was born in Leeds, England. His amazing paintings, usually featuring twilight or night scenes illuminated by gas-lamps or moonlight, are easily recognizable, and are often used on the covers of books about The Great Detective to set the mood, as shadowy figures move in the distance through misty mysterious settings and over rain-slicked streets.

Arthur Hall was born in Aston, Birmingham, UK, in 1944. He discovered his interest in writing during his schooldays, along with a love of fictional adventure and suspense. His first novel, *Sole Contact,* was an espionage story about an ultra-secret government department known as "Sector Three", and was followed, to date, by three sequels. Other works include four Sherlock Holmes novels, *The Demon of the Dusk, The One Hundred Percent Society, The Secret Assassin,* and *The Phantom Killer,* as well as a collection of short stories, and a modern detective novel. He lives in the West Midlands, United Kingdom.

Greg Hatcher has been writing for one outlet or another since 1992. He was a contributing editor at *WITH* magazine for over a decade, and during that time he was a three-time winner of the Higher Goals Award for children's writing; once for fiction and twice for non-fiction. After that he wrote a weekly column for ten years and change at *Comic Book Resources*, as one of the rotating features on the *Comics Should Be Good!*

blog. Currently he has a weekly column at *Atomic Junk Shop* (*www.atomicjunkshop.com*) He also teaches writing in the Young Authors classes offered as part of the Seattle YMCA's Afterschool Arts Program for students in the 6th through the 12th grade. A lifelong mystery fan, he has written Nero Wolfe pastiches for the Wolfe Pack *Gazette* and several Sherlock Holmes adventures for Airship 27's *Sherlock Holmes: Consulting Detective* series. He lives in Burien, Washington, with his wife Julie, their cat Magdalene, and ten thousand books and comics.

Mike Hogan writes mostly historical novels and short stories, many set in Victorian London and featuring Sherlock Holmes and Doctor Watson. He read the Conan Doyle stories at school with great enjoyment, but hadn't thought much about Sherlock Holmes until, having missed the Granada/Jeremy Brett TV series when it was originally shown in the eighties, he came across a box set of videos in a street market and was hooked on Holmes again. He started writing Sherlock Holmes pastiches several years ago, having great fun re-imagining situations for the Conan Doyle characters to act in. The relationship between Holmes and Watson fascinates him as one of the great literary friendships. (He's also a huge admirer of Patrick O'Brian's Aubrey-Maturin novels). Like Captain Aubrey and Doctor Maturin, Holmes and Watson are an odd couple, differing in almost every facet of their characters, but sharing a common sense of decency and a common humanity. Living with Sherlock Holmes can't have been easy, and Mike enjoys adding a stronger vein of "pawky humour" into the Conan Doyle mix, even letting Watson have the second-to-last word on occasions. His books include *Sherlock Holmes and the Scottish Question*; *The Gory Season – Sherlock Holmes, Jack the Ripper and the Thames Torso Murders* and the Sherlock Holmes & Young Winston 1887 Trilogy (*The Deadwood Stage*; *The Jubilee Plot*; and *The Giant Moles*), He has also written the following short story collections: *Sherlock Holmes: Murder at the Savoy and Other Stories*, *Sherlock Holmes: The Skull of Kohada Koheiji and Other Stories*, and *Sherlock Holmes: Murder on the Brighton Line and Other Stories*. *www.mikehoganbooks.com*

Roger Johnson BSI, ASH is a retired librarian, now working as a volunteer assistant at the Essex Police Museum. In his spare time, he is commissioning editor of *The Sherlock Holmes Journal*, an occasional lecturer, and a frequent contributor to The Writings About the Writings. His sole work of Holmesian pastiche was published in 1997 in Mike Ashley's anthology *The Mammoth Book of New Sherlock Holmes Adventures*, and he has the greatest respect for the many authors who have contributed new tales to the present mighty trilogy. Like his wife, Jean Upton, he is a member of both *The Baker Street Irregulars* and *The Adventuresses of Sherlock Holmes.*

Kelvin I. Jones is the author of six books about Sherlock Holmes and the definitive biography of Conan Doyle as a spiritualist, *Conan Doyle and The Spirits*. A member of *The Sherlock Holmes Society of London*, he has published numerous short occult and ghost stories in British anthologies over the last thirty years. His work has appeared on BBC Radio, and in 1984 he won the Mason Hall Literary Award for his poem cycle about the survivors of Hiroshima and Nagasaki, recently reprinted as "Omega". (Oakmagic Publications) A one-time teacher of creative writing at the University of East Anglia, he is also the author of four crime novels featuring his ex-met sleuth John Bottrell, who first appeared in *Stone Dead*. He has over fifty titles on Kindle, and is also the author of several novellas and short story collections featuring a Norwich based detective, DCI Ketch, an intrepid sleuth who invesitgates East Anglian murder cases. He also published a series of short stories about an Edwardian psychic detective, Dr. John

Carter (*Carter's Occult Casebook*). Ramsey Campbell, the British horror writer, and Francis King, the renowned novelist, have both compared his supernatural stories to those of M. R. James. He has also published children's fiction, namely *Odin's Eye*, and, in collaboration with his wife Debbie, *The Dark Entry*. Since 1995, he has been the proprietor of Oakmagic Publications, publishers of British folklore and of his fiction titles. (See *www.oakmagicpublications.co.uk*)He lives in Norfolk.

David Marcum plays The Game with deadly seriousness. He first discovered Sherlock Holmes in 1975, at the age of ten, when he received an abridged version of *The Adventures* during a trade. Since that time, David has collected literally thousands of traditional Holmes pastiches in the form of novels, short stories, radio and television episodes, movies and scripts, comics, fan-fiction, and unpublished manuscripts. He is the author of *The Papers of Sherlock Holmes Vol.'s I* and *II* (2011, 2013), *Sherlock Holmes and A Quantity of Debt* (2013, 2016), *Sherlock Holmes – Tangled Skeins* (2015, 2017), and *The Papers of Solar Pons* (2017). Additionally, he is the editor of the three-volume set *Sherlock Holmes in Montague Street* (2014, recasting Arthur Morrison's Martin Hewitt stories as early Holmes adventures,), the two-volume collection of Great Hiatus stories, *Holmes Away From Home* (2016), *Sherlock Holmes: Before Baker Street* (2017), *Imagination Theatre's Sherlock Holmes* (2017), a number of forthcoming volumes, and the ongoing collection, *The MX Book of New Sherlock Holmes Stories* (2015-), now at ten volumes, with two more in preparation as of this writing. He has contributed stories, essays, and scripts to *The Baker Street Journal, The Strand Magazine, The Watsonian, Beyond Watson, Sherlock Holmes Mystery Magazine, About Sixty, About Being a Sherlockian, The Solar Pons Gazette*, Imagination Theater, *The Proceedings of the Pondicherry Lodge*, and *The Gazette*, the journal of the Nero Wolfe *Wolfe Pack*. He began his adult work life as a Federal Investigator for an obscure U.S. Government agency, before the organization was eliminated. He returned to school for a second degree, and is now a licensed Civil Engineer, living in Tennessee with his wife and son. He is a member of *The Sherlock Holmes Society of London, The Nashville Scholars of the Three Pipe Problem* (The Engineer's Thumb"), *The Occupants of the Full House, The Diogenes Club of Washington, D.C.* (all Scions of *The Baker Street Irregulars*), *The Sherlock Holmes Society of India* (as a Patron), *The John H. Watson Society* ("Marker"), *The Praed Street Irregulars* ("The Obrisset Snuff Box"), *The Solar Pons Society of London*, and *The Diogenes Club West (East Tennessee Annex)*, a curious and unofficial Scion of one. Since the age of nineteen, he has worn a deerstalker as his regular-and-only hat from autumn to spring. In 2013, he and his deerstalker were finally able make his first trip-of-a-lifetime Holmes Pilgrimage to England, with return Pilgrimages in 2015 and 2016, where you may have spotted him. If you ever run into him and his deerstalker out and about, feel free to say hello!

New Yorker **Nicholas Meyer** is the author of three Sherlock Holmes novels, *The Seven-Per-Cent Solution* (forty weeks on the New York Times bestseller list), *The West End Horror*, and *The Canary Trainer*. His screen adaptation of *The Seven-Per-Cent Solution* was nominated for an Oscar. In addition, Meyer has written and/or directed *Star Treks II, IV*, and *VI*, as well as several other films and novels. He also directed *The Day After*, the most watched film for television ever broadcast. *The Day After* garnered one-hundred-million viewers in a single night and changed Ronald Reagan's mind about a winnable nuclear war. He lives in Los Angeles and is currently working on *Star Trek: Discovery*.

Will Murray is the author of over seventy novels, including forty *Destroyer* novels and seven posthumous *Doc Savage* collaborations with Lester Dent, under the name Kenneth

Robeson, for Bantam Books in the 1990's. Since 2011, he has written fourteen additional Doc Savage adventures for Altus Press, two of which co-starred The Shadow, as well as a solo Pat Savage novel. His 2015 Tarzan novel, *Return to Pal-Ul-Don*, was followed by *King Kong vs. Tarzan* in 2016. Murray has written short stories featuring such classic characters as Batman, Superman, Wonder Woman, Spider-Man, Ant-Man, the Hulk, Honey West, the Spider, the Avenger, the Green Hornet, the Phantom, and Cthulhu. A previous Murray Sherlock Holmes story appeared in Moonstone's *Sherlock Holmes: The Crossovers Casebook*, and another is forthcoming in *Sherlock Holmes and Doctor Was Not*, involving H. P. Lovecraft's Dr. Herbert West. Additionally, his "The Adventure of the Glassy Ghost" appeared in *The MX Book of New Sherlock Holmes Stories Part VIII – Eliminate the Impossible: 1892-1905.*

Sidney Paget (1860-1908), a few of whose illustrations are used within this anthology, was born in London, and like his two older brothers, became a famed illustrator and painter. He completed over three-hundred-and-fifty drawings for the Sherlock Holmes stories that were first published in *The Strand* magazine, defining Holmes's image forever after in the public mind.

Robert Perret is a writer, librarian, and devout Sherlockian living on the Palouse. His Sherlockian publications include "The Canaries of Clee Hills Mine" in *An Improbable Truth: The Paranormal Adventures of Sherlock Holmes*, "For King and Country" in *The Science of Deduction*, and "How Hope Learned the Trick" in *NonBinary Review*. He considers himself to be a pan-Sherlockian and a one-man Scion out on the lonely moors of Idaho. Robert has recently authored a yet-unpublished scholarly article tentatively entitled "A Study in Scholarship: The Case of the *Baker Street Journal*". More information is available at *www.robertperret.com*

Martin Rosenstock studied English, American, and German literature. In 2008, he received a Ph.D. from the University of California, Santa Barbara for looking into what happens when things go badly – as they do from time to time – for detectives in German-language literature. After job hopping around the colder latitudes of the U.S. for three years, he decided to return to warmer climes. In 2011, he took a job at Gulf University for Science and Technology in Kuwait, where he currently teaches. When not brooding over plot twists, he spends too much time and money traveling the Indian Ocean littoral. There is a novel somewhere there, he feels sure.

G. L. Schulze is a life-long resident of Michigan and a retired officer with the Michigan Department of Corrections. Gen enjoys gardening, walking, woodworking, wood burning, and beadwork, as well as reading and writing. She also enjoys spending time with her rescue dog, Java. She is the author of six books in her *Young Detectives' Mystery Series*, as well as her first Sherlock Holmes novel, *Gray Manor*. A second Holmes novel, *The Ring and The Box, A Sherlock Holmes Mystery of Ancient Egypt* is slated for release in early spring. For further information about Gen's books visit her Amazon link at *https://www.amazon.com/Gen-Schulze/e/B00KTH36LO*

Tim Symonds was born in London. He grew up in Somerset, Dorset, and Guernsey. After several years in East and Central Africa, he settled in California and graduated Phi Beta Kappa in Political Science from UCLA. He is a Fellow of the *Royal Geographical Society*. He writes his novels in the woods and hidden valleys surrounding his home in the High Weald of East Sussex. Dr. Watson knew the untamed region well. In "The Adventure of Black Peter", Watson wrote, "*the Weald was once part of that great forest*

400

which for so long held the Saxon invaders at bay." Tim's novels are published by MX Publishing. His latest is titled *Sherlock Holmes and the Nine Dragon Sigil.* Previous novels include *Sherlock Holmes and The Sword of Osman, Sherlock Holmes and the Mystery of Einstein's Daughter, Sherlock Holmes and the Dead Boer at Scotney Castle,* and *Sherlock Holmes and the Case of The Bulgarian Codex.*

Thaddeus Tuffentsamer is the author of the young adult series, *F.A.R.T.S. The Federal Agency for Reconnaissance and Tactical Services,* and the satirical self-help book, *Are You SURE About That? Observations and Life Lessons from a High Functioning Sociopath.* He resides in Goodyear, AZ, with his wife and youngest daughter. He has always been a fan of Sherlock Holmes, but his passion was reignited when his daughter took an interest in reading those wonderful adventures, for which they together now share a deep appreciation. He is not on social media – doesn't know how – but loves to connect personally with his readers by email at *thaddeustuffentsamer@gmail.com* His books can be found on Amazon.

Peter Coe Verbica grew up on a commercial cattle ranch in Northern California, where he learned the value of a strong work ethic. He works for the Wealth Management Group of a global investment bank, and is an Adjunct Professor in the Economics Department at SJSU. He is the author of numerous books, including *Left at the Gate and Other Poems, Hard-Won Cowboy Wisdom (Not Necessarily in Order of Importance), A Key to the Grove and Other Poems,* and *The Missing Tales of Sherlock Holmes (as Compiled by Peter Coe Verbica, JD).* Mr. Verbica obtained a JD from Santa Clara University School of Law, an MS from Massachusetts Institute of Technology, and a BA in English from Santa Clara University. He is the co-inventor on a number of patents, has served as a Managing Member of three venture capital firms, and the CFO of one of the portfolio companies. He is an unabashed advocate of cowboy culture and enjoys creative writing, hiking, and tennis. He is married with four daughters. For more information, or to contact the author, please go to *www.hardwoncowboywisdom.com.*

Daniel D. Victor, a Ph.D. in American literature, is a retired high school English teacher who taught in the Los Angeles Unified School District for forty-six years. His doctoral dissertation on little-known American author, David Graham Phillips, led to the creation of Victor's first Sherlock Holmes pastiche, *The Seventh Bullet,* in which Holmes investigates Phillips' actual murder. Victor's second novel, *A Study in Synchronicity,* is a two-stranded murder mystery, which features a Sherlock Holmes-like private eye. He currently writes the ongoing series *Sherlock Holmes and the American Literati.* Each novel introduces Holmes to a different American author who actually passed through London at the turn of the century. In *The Final Page of Baker Street,* Holmes meets Raymond Chandler; in *The Baron of Brede Place,* Stephen Crane; in *Seventeen Minutes to Baker Street,* Mark Twain; and *The Outrage at the Diogenes Club,* Jack London. Victor, who is also writing a novel about his early years as a teacher, lives with his wife in Los Angeles, California. They have two adult sons.

The following contributors appear
in the companion volume
The MX Book of New Sherlock Holmes Stories
Part IX – 2018 Annual (1879-1895)

Deanna Baran lives in a remote part of Texas where cowboys may still be seen in their natural habitat. A librarian and former museum curator, she writes in between cups of tea, playing *Go*, and trading postcards with people around the world. This is her latest venture into the foggy streets of gaslit London.

S.F. Bennett was born and raised in London, studying History at Queen Mary and Westfield College, and Journalism at City University at the Postgraduate level, before moving to Devon in 2013. The author lectures on Conan Doyle, Sherlock Holmes, and 19th century detective fiction, and has had articles on various aspects from The Canon published in *The Journal of the Sherlock Holmes Society of London* and *The Torr*, the journal of *The Poor Folk Upon The Moors*, the Sherlock Holmes Society of the South West of England. Her first published novel is *The Secret Diary of Mycroft Holmes: The Thoughts and Reminiscences of Sherlock Holmes's Elder Brother, 1880-1888* (2017).

Nick Cardillo has loved Sherlock Holmes ever since he was first introduced to the detective in *The Great Illustrated Classics* edition of *The Adventures of Sherlock Holmes* at the age of six. His devotion to the Baker Street detective duo has only increased over the years, and Nick is thrilled to be taking these proper steps into the Sherlock Holmes Community. His first published story, "The Adventure of the Traveling Corpse", appeared in *The MX Book of New Sherlock Holmes Stories – Part VI: 2017 Annual*, and his "The Haunting of Hamilton Gardens" was published in *PART VIII – Eliminate the Impossible: 1892-1905*. A devout fan of The Golden Age of Detective Fiction, Hammer Horror, and *Doctor Who*, Nick co-writes the Sherlockian blog, *Back on Baker Street*, which analyses over seventy years of Sherlock Holmes film and culture. He is a student at Susquehanna University.

Leslie Charteris was born in Singapore on May 12th, 1907. With his mother and brother, he moved to England in 1919 and attended Rossall School in Lancashire before moving on to Cambridge University to study law. His studies there came to a halt when a publisher accepted his first novel. His third one, entitled *Meet the Tiger*, was written when he was twenty years old and published in September 1928. It introduced the world to Simon Templar, *aka* The Saint. He continued to write about The Saint until 1983 when the last book, *Salvage for The Saint*, was published. The books, which have been translated into over thirty languages, number nearly a hundred and have sold over forty-million copies around the world. They've inspired, to date, fifteen feature films, three television series, ten radio series, and a comic strip that was written by Charteris and syndicated around the world for over a decade. He enjoyed travelling, but settled for long periods in Hollywood, Florida, and finally in Surrey, England. He was awarded the Cartier Diamond Dagger by the *Crime Writers' Association* in 1992, in recognition of a lifetime of achievement. He died the following year.

Ian Dickerson was just nine years old when he discovered The Saint. Shortly after that, he discovered Sherlock Holmes. The Saint won, for a while anyway. He struck up a friendship with The Saint's creator, Leslie Charteris and his family. With their permission, he spent six weeks studying the Leslie Charteris collection at Boston University and went on to write, direct, and produce documentaries on the making of *The Saint* and *Return of The Saint*, which have been released on DVD. He oversaw the recent reprints of almost fifty of the original Saint books in both the US and UK, and was a co-producer on the 2017 TV movie of *The Saint*. When he discovered that Charteris had written Sherlock Holmes stories as well – well, there was the excuse he needed to revisit The Canon. He's consequently written and edited three books on Holmes' radio adventures. For the sake of what little sanity he has, Ian has also written about a wide range of subjects, none of which come with a halo, including talking mashed potatoes, Lord Grade, and satellite links. Ian lives in Hampshire with his wife and two children. And an awful lot of books by Leslie Charteris. Not quite so many by Conan Doyle, though.

C.H. Dye first discovered Sherlock Holmes when she was eleven, in a collection that ended at the Reichenbach Falls. It was another six months before she discovered *The Hound of the Baskervilles*, and two weeks after that before a librarian handed her *The Return.* She has loved the stories ever since. She has written fan-fiction, and her first published pastiche, "The Tale of the Forty Thieves", was included in *The MX Book of New Sherlock Holmes Stories – Part I: 1881-1889.* Her story "A Christmas Goose" was in *The MX Book of New Sherlock Holmes Stories – Part V: Christmas Adventures*, and "The Mysterious Mourner" in *The MX Book of New Sherlock Holmes Stories – Part VIII – Eliminate the Impossible: 1892-1905*

Sonia Fetherston BSI is a member of the illustrious *Baker Street Irregulars.* For almost thirty years, she's been a frequent contributor to Sherlockian anthologies, including Calabash Press's acclaimed *Case Files* series, and Wildside Press's *About* series. Sonia's byline often appears in the pages of *The Baker Street Journal, The Journal* of the *Sherlock Holmes Society of London, Canadian Holmes*, and the Sydney Passengers' *Log.* Her work earned her the coveted Morley-Montgomery Award from the *Baker Street Irregulars*, and the Derek Murdoch Memorial Award from *The Bootmakers of Toronto.* Sonia is author of *Prince of the Realm: The Most Irregular James Bliss Austin* (BSI Press, 2014). She's at work on another biography for the BSI, this time about Julian Wolff.

David Friend lives in Wales, UK, where he divides his time between watching old detective films and thinking about old detective films. He's been scribbling out stories for twenty years and hopes, some day, to write something half-decent. Most of what he pens is set in a 1930's world of non-stop adventure with debonair sleuths, kick-ass damsels, criminal masterminds, and narrow escapes, and he wishes he could live there. He's currently working on a collection of Sherlock Holmes stories and a series based around *The Strange Investigators*, an eccentric team of private detectives out to solve the most peculiar and perplexing mysteries around. He thinks of it as P.G. Wodehouse crossed with Edgar Allen Poe, only not as good.

Stephen Gaspar is a writer of historical detective fiction. He has written two Sherlock Holmes books: *The Canadian Adventures of Sherlock Holmes* and *Cold-Hearted Murder.* Some of his detectives are a Roman Tribune, a medieval monk, and a Templar knight. He was born and lives in Windsor, Ontario, Canada.

Denis Green was born in London, England in April 1905. He grew up mostly in London's Savoy Theatre where his father, Richard Green, was a principal in many

403

Gilbert and Sullivan productions, A Flying Officer with RAF until 1924, he then spent four years managing a tea estate in North India before making his stage debut in *Hamlet* with Leslie Howard in 1928. He made his first visit to America in 1931 and established a respectable stage career before appearing in films – including minor roles in the first two Rathbone and Bruce Holmes films – and developing a career in front of and behind the microphone during the golden age of radio. Green and Leslie Charteris met in 1938 and struck up a lifelong friendship. Always busy, be it on stage, radio, film or television, Green passed away at the age of fifty in New York.

James Moffett is a Masters graduate in Professional Writing, with a specialisation in novel and non-fiction writing. He also has an extensive background in media studies. James began developing a passion for writing when contributing to his University's student magazine. His interest in the literary character of Sherlock Holmes was deep-rooted in his youth. He released his first publication of eight interconnected short stories titled *The Trials of Sherlock Holmes* in 2017, along with a contribution to *The MX Book of New Sherlock Holmes Stories - Part VII: Eliminate The Impossible: 1880-1891*, with a short story entitled "The Blank Photograph".

Mark Mower is a member of the *Crime Writers' Association, The Sherlock Holmes Society of London* and *The Solar Pons Society of London*. He writes true crime stories and fictional mysteries. His first two volumes of Holmes pastiches were entitled *A Farewell to Baker Street* and *Sherlock Holmes: The Baker Street Case-Files* (both with MX Publishing) and, to date, he has contributed chapters to six parts of the ongoing *The MX Book of New Sherlock Holmes Stories*. He has also had stories in two anthologies by Belanger Books: *Holmes Away From Home: Adventures from the Great Hiatus – Volume II – 1893-1894* (2016) and *Sherlock Holmes: Before Baker Street* (2017). More are bound to follow. Mark's non-fiction works include *Bloody British History: Norwich* (The History Press, 2014), *Suffolk Murders* (The History Press, 2011) and *Zeppelin Over Suffolk* (Pen & Sword Books, 2008).

Tracy J. Revels, a Sherlockian from the age of eleven, is a professor of history at Wofford College in Spartanburg, South Carolina. She is a member of *The Survivors of the Gloria Scott* and *The Studious Scarlets Society*, and is a past recipient of the Beacon Society Award. Almost every semester, she teaches a class that covers The Canon, either to college students or to senior citizens. She is also the author of three supernatural Sherlockian pastiches with MX (*Shadowfall, Shadowblood*, and *Shadowwraith*), and a regular contributor to her scion's newsletter. She also has some notoriety as an author of very silly skits: For proof, see "The Adventure of the Adversarial Adventuress" and "Occupy Baker Street" on YouTube. When not studying Sherlock Holmes, she can be found researching the history of her native state, and has written books on Florida in the Civil War and on the development of Florida's tourism industry.

Roger Riccard of Los Angeles, California, U.S.A., is a descendant of the Roses of Kilravock in Highland Scotland. He is the author of two previous Sherlock Holmes novels, *The Case of the Poisoned Lilly* and *The Case of the Twain Papers*, a series of short stories in two volumes, *Sherlock Holmes: Adventures for the Twelve Days of Christmas* and *Further Adventures for the Twelve Days of Christmas*, and the new series *A Sherlock Holmes Alphabet of Cases,* all of which are published by Baker Street Studios. He has another novel and a non-fiction Holmes reference work in various stages of completion. He became a Sherlock Holmes enthusiast as a teenager (many, many years ago), and, like all fans of The Great Detective, yearned for more stories after reading The

Canon over and over. It was the Granada Television performances of Jeremy Brett and Edward Hardwicke, and the encouragement of his wife, Rosilyn, that at last inspired him to write his own Holmes adventures, using the Granada actor portrayals as his guide. He has been called "The best pastiche writer since Val Andrews" by the *Sherlockian E-Times*.

Geri Schear is a novelist and short story writer. Her work has been published in literary journals in the U.S. and Ireland. Her first novel, *A Biased Judgement: The Diaries of Sherlock Holmes 1897* was released to critical acclaim in 2014. The sequel, *Sherlock Holmes and the Other Woman* was published in 2015, and *Return to Reichenbach* in 2016. She lives in Kells, Ireland.

Shane Simmons is a multi-award-winning screenwriter and graphic novelist whose work has appeared in international film festivals, museums, and lectures about design and structure. His best-known piece of fiction, *The Long and Unlearned Life of Roland Gethers*, has been discussed in multiple books and academic journals about sequential art, and his short stories have been printed in critically praised anthologies of history, crime, and horror. He lives in Montreal with his wife and too many cats. Follow him at *eyestrainproductions.com* and *@Shane_Eyestrain*

Robert V. Stapleton was born and brought up in Leeds, Yorkshire, England, and studied at Durham University. After working in various parts of the country as an Anglican parish priest, he is now retired and lives with his wife in North Yorkshire. As a member of his local writing group, he now has time to develop his other life as a writer of adventure stories. He has recently had a number of short stories published, and he is hoping to have a couple of completed novels published at some time in the future.

Amy Thomas is a member of the *Baker Street Babes* Podcast, and the author of *The Detective and The Woman* mystery novels featuring Sherlock Holmes and Irene Adler. She blogs at *girlmeetssherlock.wordpress.com*, and she writes and edits professionally from her home in Fort Myers, Florida.

Kevin Thornton lives in Fort McMurray, Alberta, Canada. It is a place chiefly known for being cold. How cold? The type of cold where Fahrenheit and Celsius meet at minus forty and say to each other, "We have to stop doing this." Kevin writes poetry and short stories that are published and read by dozens of people, and books that are not. Nevertheless, he has been a finalist in the *Canadian Crime Writers* awards six times, and was honoured with the Literature "Buffy" award in his locale up there in the north (where we might have mentioned it is cold). Kevin is or has been a member of the *Crime Writers Association*, the *Edmonton Poetry Festival*, the *International Thriller Writers*, the *Writers' Guild of Alberta*, the *Crime Writers of Canada*, and the *KEYS*, the Catholic Writers Guild founded by two chaps called Chesterton and Knox, albeit before his time. He studied at one of those universities that had two Nobel Laureates in Literature on the staff. It didn't seem to do much good. Kevin now works as a writer and editor, having been a contractor for the Canadian military, a member of the South African Air Force, and a worker of such peripatetic habits that he is now on his fourth continent and many-eth country.

Marcia Wilson is a freelance researcher and illustrator who likes to work in a style compatible for the color blind and visually impaired. She is Canon-centric, and her first MX offering, *You Buy Bones*, uses the point-of-view of Scotland Yard to show the unique talents of Dr. Watson. This continued with the publication of *Test of the Professionals: The Adventure of the Flying Blue Pidgeon* and *The Peaceful Night Poisonings.* She can be contacted at: *gravelgirty.deviantart.com*

The MX Book of New Sherlock Holmes Stories

Edited by David Marcum
(MX Publishing, 2015-   )

Part I: 1881-1889
Part II: 1890-1895
Part III: 1896-1929
Part IV: 2016 Annual
Part V: Christmas Adventures
Part VI: 2017 Annual
Part VII: Eliminate the Impossible – 1880-1891
Part VIII: Eliminate the Impossible – 1892-1905
Part IX: 2018 Annual (1879-1895)
Part X: 2018 Annual (1896-1916)

In Preparation
Part XI: Some Untold Cases
Part XII: 2019 Annual

. . . and more to come!

The MX Book of New Sherlock Holmes Stories

Edited by David Marcum

(MX Publishing, 2015-   )

"This is the finest volume of Sherlockian fiction I have
ever read, and I have read, literally, thousands."
– Philip K. Jones

"Beyond Impressive . . . This is a
splendid venture for a great cause!
– Roger Johnson, Editor, *The Sherlock Holmes Journal*,
The Sherlock Holmes Society of London

MX Publishing

MX Publishing is the world's largest specialist Sherlock Holmes publisher, with several hundred titles and authors creating the latest in Sherlock Holmes fiction and non-fiction.

From traditional short stories and novels to travel guides and quiz books, MX Publishing caters to all Holmes fans.

The collection includes leading titles such as *Benedict Cumberbatch In Transition* and *The Norwood Author*, which won the 2011 *Tony Howlett Award* (Sherlock Holmes Book of the Year).

MX Publishing also has one of the largest communities of Holmes fans on *Facebook*, with regular contributions from dozens of authors.

www.mxpublishing.co.uk (UK)
and
www.mxpublishing.com (USA)

Lightning Source UK Ltd.
Milton Keynes UK
UKHW01n0617130518
322473UK00001B/12/P